**ANNABELLE WAS STEPPING TOWARD
THE TABLE NEAREST THE ARCHWAY
THAT LED TO THE LODGE'S LOBBY
WHEN THE SIGHT OF
A SOLITARY MAN IN BLACK
FROZE HER IN PLACE**

Phineas was watching her, as though he'd been following her progress along the outer edge of the dining room . . . waiting for her to notice him. He held her gaze with the pale, penetrating green eyes that had often made her heart thud in her chest as she anticipated his judgment—his criticism and correction.

The blood rushed from Annabelle's head. She wasn't aware that she'd dropped the two big pitchers until she heard the noisy clatter of plastic hitting the hardwood floor and felt ice water filling her shoes.

What's Phineas doing here? How did he find me—and what does he want?

Light Shines on
PROMISE LODGE

Charlotte Hubbard

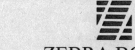

ZEBRA BOOKS
KENSINGTON PUBLISHING CORP.
www.kensingtonbooks.com

ZEBRA BOOKS are published by

Kensington Publishing Corp.
119 West 40th Street
New York, NY 10018

All Kensington titles, imprints, and distributed lines are available at special quantity discounts for bulk purchases for sales promotion, premiums, fund-raising, educational, or institutional use.

Special book excerpts or customized printings can also be created to fit specific needs. For details, write or phone the office of the Kensington Sales Manager: Attn.: Sales Department. Kensington Publishing Corp., 119 West 40th Street, New York, NY 10018. Phone: 1-800-221-2647.

Zebra and the Z logo Reg. U.S. Pat. & TM Off.
BOUQUET Reg. U.S. Pat. & TM Off.

First Printing: April 2020
ISBN-13: 978-1-4201-4511-3
ISBN-10: 1-4201-4511-8

ISBN-13: 978-1-4201-4514-4 (eBook)
ISBN-10: 1-4201-4514-2 (eBook)

10 9 8 7 6 5 4 3 2 1

Printed in the United States of America

For Neal, the light of my life these past 45 years—and the one who came up with the perfect twist in this tale!

ACKNOWLEDGMENTS

Many thanks to You, Lord, for leading me through the final book of this series!

Once again I'm deeply indebted to my editor, Alicia Condon, and to my agent Evan Marshall for helping me bring this series to a satisfying conclusion. Many thanks to both of you for helping me bring these Amish stories to readers—and thanks, as well, for the assurance that we'll be doing more books now that this series is complete!

Blessings on you, Vicki Harding, my research assistant in Jamesport, Missouri, for answering my questions so quickly—and for keeping your finger on the pulse of Amish life there. Blessings on you and your family, as well, Joe Burkholder, as you pursue a faith path that has been more rewarding but hasn't been easy.

Psalm 27:1 KJV

The Lord is my light and my salvation; whom shall I fear? The Lord is the strength of my life; of whom shall I be afraid?

Matthew 5:16 KJV

Let Your light so shine before men, that they may see Your good works, and glorify Your Father which is in heaven.

Chapter One

As Annabelle Beachey gazed at the happy couple standing before Bishop Monroe Burkholder to exchange their wedding vows, she fought tears. During the four months she'd spent in an apartment at Promise Lodge, she'd become good friends with the bride, Frances Lehman, and she'd acquired a lot of respect for the groom, Preacher Marlin Kurtz. The love light on their faces shone as a testament to the devotion that had grown between them during their summertime courtship—a brilliant example of how God worked out His purpose through the lives of those who kept His faith, even after they'd been widowed.

Annabelle sighed with the rightness of it all. The women around her dabbed at their eyes as Preacher Marlin repeated his vows in an endearingly confident voice, gazing at Frances as though she were the only woman in the world. Folks here were still in awe because Marlin had bought back all the furnishings Frances had consigned to an auction in May, thinking she had to sell everything to get by because her first husband hadn't left her with much.

My husband didn't leave me with much, either. He just left me.

Annabelle sat straighter on the pew bench, trying not to

let her troubles overshadow the day's joy. God had surely
guided her to come to Promise Lodge last May, where
the friends gathered in this room had taken her in—had
provided her an apartment and their unconditional encouragement after they'd heard that Phineas had abandoned
both her and the Old Order faith.

"I, Marlin, take you, Frances, to be my lawfully wedded
wife," the handsome preacher repeated after Bishop
Monroe.

Annabelle pressed her lips together to keep them from
trembling. She and Phineas had taken the same vows more
than twenty years ago. It had wounded her deeply when
her husband had declared—without any warning or apparent remorse—that he'd grown tired of the constraints of
marriage and the Amish faith. It seemed Phineas had intended to leave without even telling her—except she'd
caught him looking for her egg money in the pantry.

She had no idea where he'd gone. And because Amish
couples weren't allowed to divorce, her only chance at
finding another husband would come after Phineas passed
away. How would she even know when that happened?
And meanwhile, how was she supposed to get by? Living
as her brother-in-law's dependent, beholden to him for
every morsel she ate, hadn't been a desirable option, so
she'd taken a huge chance and found her way from Pennsylvania to Promise Lodge. She'd read in *The Budget* about
this progressive Plain settlement in Missouri, where single
women could live in comfortable apartments and make
a fresh start among families who also sought brighter
futures.

Best decision you ever made, too, Annabelle reminded
herself. She'd found her niche here, sewing clothes for
Frances's widowed brother-in-law and three young men
who hadn't yet married. Living among Plain women who

managed a cheese factory, a dairy, a produce stand, and a pie business had given her the incentive to figure out how to support herself, and she planned to expand her sewing business by advertising it in town.

Once this painfully romantic wedding is behind you, you can get on with the contentment and purpose you've settled into here.

Annabelle put on a smile, determined not to succumb to her personal problems while everyone around her was sharing the joy that Marlin and Frances exuded.

"Friends," Bishop Monroe proclaimed with a wide smile, "it's my honor and privilege to present Mr. and Mrs. Marlin Kurtz."

As applause filled the lodge's big meeting room, Annabelle rose with the women around her. The best cure for her blues was making herself useful, helping Beulah and Ruby Kuhn set out the wedding feast they'd prepared. The *maidel* Mennonite sisters were the queens of the kitchen when it came to cooking for large gatherings—and as Annabelle passed through the dining room, she inhaled deeply to soothe her frazzled soul.

"Your ham and brisket smell so *gut* it was all I could do to stay seated during the wedding," she teased as she entered the kitchen. "I was trying to think up an excuse for slipping back here to sample some of it—to be sure it was fit for our guests, of course."

Ruby and Beulah laughed as they headed toward the ovens. Their bright floral-print dresses fluttered with their quick, efficient movements as Beulah slipped her hands into mitts while Ruby lowered the oven doors. The hair tucked up under their small, round Mennonite *kapps* was silvery, but nobody could call them old.

"I was pleased that Marlin asked for ham," Beulah remarked, deftly lifting the blue graniteware roasters onto the nearest butcher-block countertops. "It's a tasty way to feed a lot of folks with a minimum of fuss—"

"And the pineapple rings and maraschino cherries make it look pretty from the get-go," Ruby put in. "Chicken and stuffing might be the traditional wedding dish, but it looks awfully bland. And who says you have to have that for your second wedding just because you served it the first time?"

"Tickles me pink that Frances and Marlin have finally tied the knot—even if Frances cut the usual mourning period a little short," Beulah said. "Seems to me that pining on and on for Floyd might've been a slap in the face to God anyway, if we believe Floyd has gone to his reward with Jesus. We should be joyful about that, even as we acknowledge that Frances misses him."

Annabelle considered this new slant on mourning as she sliced the ham and placed it into a metal steam table pan. Did she have it all wrong, feeling sorry for herself because Phineas had abandoned her? After all, she'd done nothing to provoke his departure, so surely God didn't hold her accountable for her husband's misdeeds. Maybe He'd offered her a chance at a whole new life when Phineas had gone his own way, even if her options for remarriage were severely limited.

God's ways are not our ways, and they're often mysterious to us, she reminded herself. *I've felt humiliated and depressed about being abandoned, but maybe I should look at it from another angle. None of these other women have allowed their troubles to get them down.*

Annabelle felt as though a heavy cloak of sadness was being lifted from her shoulders. As she sliced a second large ham, a genuine smile lit up her face. She had friends back in Bird-in-Hand who would secretly love the freedom of living without the overbearing men they'd married.

Freedom. Mattie, Christine, and Rosetta Bender, the original founders of Promise Lodge, had pooled their resources to buy an abandoned church camp so they'd be free from an oppressive bishop—and they'd been able to do that because they were widowed or single at the time. All three of them had gotten married this past year, to wonderful men who allowed them to make their own choices, so maybe there'd be another chance for Annabelle to find that same sort of happiness someday. At Promise Lodge, the bright blue sky was the limit.

"It's *gut* to see that smile on your face, Annabelle," Ruby said softly. She took up a sharp knife and began carving a beef brisket into thin slices as several other women came in to help them set out the meal. "At one point during the wedding, I was wondering if you'd bitten into a sour pickle—but then, I suppose weddings can heap a lot of difficult memories on some folks. Not that I'm prying, understand."

Annabelle placed another stack of ham slices in the metal pan. "You've pegged it right, Ruby. But it's occurred to me that nobody else is making me feel down and out about my situation. My own thoughts are to blame, and I've decided to give thanks for the life I have now. God is *gut*."

"All the time," Beulah and Ruby chorused.

Ruby smiled wistfully. "My sister and I act as though we have no regrets about remaining *maidels*, but deep down, every young girl has her dreams of a happily ever after, ain't so?"

"*Jah*, when I think about the chances I've missed to hound a husband to distraction, I feel sort of sad," Beulah teased. "But God knew what He was doing, steering away the fellows I would've made miserable with my smart mouth and demanding ways. Not many men would've tolerated Ruby's and my independent streaks. Things are better all around because we stuck together and made our own way."

"And we did our brother, Delbert, and his family a favor by coming here, too," Ruby put in. "He felt he was doing his duty, letting us live in his crowded house with his wife and her *mamm* and their eight kids—"

"And only one bathroom," Beulah interjected.

"—but our whole family's better off because Beulah and I left the nest," Ruby finished. "And now that we're not expected to watch those kids all the time, we've found a life with a purpose that truly suits us. Maybe to most folks, that sounds selfish, but that's their opinion—and we've held on to ours."

Annabelle had done some mental math as she sliced the last of the ham. "Thirteen people and one bathroom," she murmured. "Your apartments upstairs must feel like paradise by comparison. But don't you miss your family? And the kids?"

Beulah smiled, stacking the empty roasting pans to get them out of the way. "They weren't our kids," she pointed out. "Ruby and I wondered if Delbert's wife would've been happier without so many of them—but that's a prickly subject we *maidels* knew better than to mention."

"And it was none of our beeswax anyway," Ruby added with a laugh.

Annabelle pondered this while she arranged the pineapple rings and cherries over the ham slices. The Lord hadn't blessed her and Phineas with children, so she knew about keeping her opinions to herself concerning other couples' parenting. God had His reasons for leaving them childless . . . and maybe He'd foreseen the day when Phineas would take off. Maybe He'd been watching out for her all along, not burdening her with dependent mouths to feed as He prepared her for a time when she'd need to make her own way.

When she carried the pan of ham to the steam table, Frances and Marlin were entering the lodge's big dining room ahead of their guests. "Annabelle, that looks so pretty!" Frances exclaimed. "It's a party in a pan!"

"*Denki* for the effort you ladies have put into making our dinner so special," Preacher Marlin said. "I've eaten a lot of wedding meals here of late, but now that it's our big day, the food looks even more glorious than usual!"

"We're all happy to be a part of your celebration," Annabelle said. And she meant it. She *was* happy, now that she'd reconsidered her situation.

As the dining room filled with wedding guests, Annabelle looked around. Folks who lived at Promise Lodge, as well as family and friends of the Kurtzes from Iowa and some far-flung relatives of the Lehmans, ambled between long tables that were draped in white tablecloths. Christine Burkholder and her daughters were filling water glasses while Mattie Troyer and Rosetta Wickey were at the dessert table, cutting slices of pie and arranging cookies on platters.

Frances's daughter Gloria and Marlin's daughter-in-law, Minerva, wheeled out a metal cart loaded with steaming pans of brisket, mashed potatoes, and green bean casserole. Bishop Monroe, who towered above most of the other folks, brought up the rear of the crowd, coming into the dining room along with Preachers Amos Troyer and Eli Peterscheim. His smile was warm as he raised his hands.

"Let's give thanks for the food," he called out over the crowd's chatter. "Then the party can really get started!"

Annabelle bowed her head along with everyone else.

In the hush of the large room, folks stood reverently as Bishop Monroe led them in prayer.

"Gracious God, we thank You for every *gut* and perfect gift You give us, every day of our lives," he said in his rich baritone voice. "Bless this food to our use, bless the hands that prepared it, and bless us all to Your purpose. Amen."

As folks found places at the long tables, Beulah addressed the wedding party, who were seated at the raised *eck* table in the corner of the room. "Frances and Marlin, we're ready for you to fill your plates and enjoy your special day," she called out. "Congratulations from every one of us!"

People applauded briefly as Marlin grasped Frances's hand and started toward the buffet table. His teenage children, Fannie and Lowell, followed them while Frances's younger daughter, Mary Kate, and her son-in-law, Roman, fell into place behind them. Baby David squawked excitedly in Roman's arm, as though he thought all the fuss was being made for him. Marlin's son, Harley, waited while Minerva and Gloria came from the kitchen to join the others in the line.

Annabelle smiled at the blended family that had been formed by Frances and Marlin's union. Harley and Gloria had objected long and loudly to their parents' courtship, yet they'd come to an understanding about his *dat* and her *mamm* needing the love and companionship a second marriage would bring them.

Annabelle returned Gloria's little wave, pleased that this young woman had matured so much over the summer. Gloria had once been flighty and boy crazy, but Rosetta had hired her to manage the upstairs apartments and the ten cabins that sat behind the lodge. Gloria had also started writing the community's weekly article for *The Budget*, thereby accepting a lot of responsibility and gaining people's respect. At twenty-three, she was a shining example of how a life could be transformed by the encouragement of a fine role model like Rosetta.

It's all about finding a worthwhile purpose, Annabelle mused as she returned to the kitchen. The Kuhn sisters were pulling more pans of hot food from the oven, to be ready when the first pans ran out.

"Wonder what Daisy's barking about?" Ruby asked as she removed the foil from a pan of green bean casserole. "She must've left Harley's sheep to see about the excitement here at the lodge—"

"*Jah*, she's been on Noah's porch across the road this morning, watching for wedding guests to herd. Border collies are like that," Beulah remarked as she covered the green bean casserole with French fried onions. She turned to Annabelle. "Go fill a plate now—before the guests gobble up all the food," she teased. "If we take turns eating, we'll have helpers to replenish the food all during the meal."

Spotting some large plastic pitchers of ice water, Annabelle reached for them. "I'll eat as soon as I refill the pitchers on the tables," she said. "It's a warm day for the sixth of October, and folks are thirsty."

With a pitcher in each hand, she made her way into the crowded dining room. The tables were close together to accommodate the large crowd, so Annabelle walked along the tables' ends and had someone pass her the pitchers that needed refilling. She was stepping toward the table nearest the archway that led to the lodge's lobby when the sight of a solitary man in black froze her in place.

Phineas was watching her, as though he'd been following her progress along the outer edge of the dining room . . . waiting for her to notice him. He held her gaze with the pale, penetrating green eyes that had often made her heart thud in her chest as she anticipated his judgment—his criticism and correction.

The blood rushed from Annabelle's head. She wasn't aware that she'd dropped the two big pitchers until she heard the noisy clatter of plastic hitting the hardwood floor and felt ice water filling her shoes.

What's Phineas doing here? How did he find me—and what does he want?

Chapter Two

As Phineas stepped toward her, Annabelle lost all track of the crowd's presence. She was too stunned by her runaway husband's unexpected reappearance to be cognizant of anything other than his questioning gaze and the voice that could always make her feel guilty, even when she wasn't.

"I came back for you, Annabelle, and you weren't home," he said softly.

Annabelle blinked. "You must've noticed that your brother's taken over the farm," she blurted. "He constantly reminded me that I was his *duty*—a burden you'd left him to bear. So I packed up and left."

Phineas frowned, but then he flashed his most charming smile. "Let's forget about Eldon," he said with a shrug. "I've reestablished my business in Ohio, so we can take up where we left off, Annabelle. Just you and me, free to live a better life without the church telling us what we can't do."

Red flags shot up like fiery antennae, reminding Annabelle of Phineas's way of glossing over mistakes. It suddenly seemed ironic that a man who made his living remodeling and restoring houses had torn their home apart several months ago without any apparent remorse.

"I have no interest in living English," she stated. She took a deep breath to fortify herself. "My salvation is in the Lord—and in the Old Order, which has stood by me after you left me without two nickels to rub together. I've reestablished myself, too, Phineas, and I'm staying right here."

Where had this show of backbone come from? Annabelle surprised herself, so quickly defying the man she'd obeyed for more than twenty years. Her husband's expression told her that he, too, was shocked by her refusal to do his bidding.

"Annabelle, are you all right?" Ruby asked in a concerned voice.

"When we heard the pitchers hit the floor, we got worried." Beulah placed a warm hand on Annabelle's shoulder, bringing her out of her daze. "Do you know this man, Annabelle? Or is he asking about coming here to live at Promise Lodge?"

Annabelle felt extremely grateful to the Kuhn sisters for showing up with towels and true concern as she ran out of things to say to her absentee husband. She broke the gaze with which he'd been holding her captive, aware that Ruby was mopping the water from the floor around her feet while Beulah remained beside her, lending support.

"This is Phineas," Annabelle murmured, thankful that the guests around them were resuming their conversations. "He says he's come back for me."

The Kuhns' raised eyebrows and wary expressions said what Annabelle hadn't yet been able to put into words. Phineas would surely realize that she'd painted a dark, unflattering picture of him—but before he could protest, Bishop Monroe strode over to join them.

"Hello there," he said as he extended his hand to Phineas.

"Welcome to Promise Lodge and the wedding dinner that's in progress. I'm Bishop Monroe Burkholder—"

"And I'm Annabelle's husband, Phineas Beachey," he replied. As he shook the bishop's hand, he sounded pleased to meet a man who would surely restore order and support his rightful role in Annabelle's life. "Imagine my surprise when I returned to our home in Pennsylvania to find that my wife had left—"

"But you've found her now," Bishop Monroe interrupted smoothly, "and you both have a lot of talking to do. How about if you fill a plate and we'll find you a place to sit, Phineas? Plenty of time for you and Annabelle to discuss your differences after our wedding guests have gone home."

Gratitude welled up inside Annabelle, for who would dare defy the burly, positive-minded bishop? Even though Phineas no longer followed the Old Order's ways, he kept the rest of his rant to himself—perhaps because Monroe was head and shoulders taller than he was.

"Thank you, Monroe," Phineas said as he released the bishop's hand. "I appreciate your hospitality—and we *will* talk later," he added with a purposeful look at Annabelle.

"*Jah*, we will," she agreed. "You go right ahead and eat while I see to things in the kitchen. That much hasn't changed, anyway."

Aware of the crowd's curious glances, Annabelle grabbed the wet towels from the floor and followed Ruby around the outer edge of the dining room. Beulah came right behind her with the empty pitchers. By the time they'd reached the kitchen, Christine and Mattie had joined them, along with Rosetta and a few of the other women. Annabelle appreciated their support, but before she answered the questions on their faces, she sat down on a chair to remove her saturated black shoes.

"Ladies," Beulah said in a low voice, "the fellow in the doorway was Phineas Beachey, Annabelle's runaway husband. That must be who the dog was barking at."

"What does he want?" Mattie demanded suspiciously.

Annabelle shook her head. "Truth be told, I was so startled to see him that the room started to spin—and then I dropped those pitchers," she replied breathlessly. "Somehow he's found me. Says he's reestablished his remodeling business in Ohio, and he figures we'll take up where we left off before he abandoned me."

"And what do *you* want, Annabelle?" Ruby put in quickly. "It's not our place to pry into your personal business—"

"But we won't let Phineas waltz in here and expect you to dance to his tune if you don't want to," Beulah added with a decisive nod. "Not after the way he left you *and* the Old Order."

"*Jah*, forsaking his vows to the church is the one unforgivable sin, the way most bishops see it," Christine remarked. "He's got some consequences to face. Lots of Amish districts believe he's forfeited any chance for reconciliation, let alone salvation."

After she'd removed her wet, black stockings, Annabelle shook her head. "From what I could tell, he doesn't give two hoots about what the Amish church believes anymore. He was upset because I wasn't at home where he'd left me—and he seems to think I'll go blithely along with whatever he wants, and that I'll leave the church, too."

The kitchen rang with a stunned silence as the ladies surrounding her considered the seriousness of what she'd said. Annabelle gazed at each of their faces, grateful for the friendship and support she saw. "No matter what happens, I want you all to know how much I appreciate the way you've stood by me from the moment I showed up at

Promise Lodge," she murmured. "It's an honor to call you my friends."

"And your friends intend to stick with you," Rosetta insisted. She squeezed Annabelle's shoulder. "I suspect Phineas will be here for a while as you iron out this difficult situation. I'll ask Gloria to speak with him about renting one of the cabins—"

"Unless you'd rather tell him to find a place in Forest Grove or Cloverdale," Ruby put in. "Maybe we don't want him around, considering what you've told us about him."

Annabelle blinked at the rancor in Ruby's voice. Had she made Phineas out to be a total villain these past few months? Or was her *maidel* friend merely trying to make her feel better? "Maybe Phineas should stay in a cabin, so we don't keep Monroe and the preachers waiting on his comings and goings while we iron this out," she said with a sigh. "I don't even know if he hired a driver or drove himself all the way out here in a buggy. It was a *short* conversation, partly because I was too stunned to hold up my end of it."

"We're blessed to have levelheaded leaders in our congregation," Christine said, "and those four men will determine where Phineas stands, as far as the Old Order is concerned. But don't forget how far you've come, Annabelle. It would be a shame to give up your sewing business—not to mention the independence you've found here."

"That'll be a sticking point for Phineas," she murmured. "He's already appalled at the way I've answered his questions—rather than tucking my tail between my legs and lowering my eyes."

"You'll figure it out, dear," Mattie assured her gently.

"*Jah*, all things work to the *gut* for those who love the

Lord," Beulah said with a nod. "Meanwhile, I suspect we need to check the buffet table."

"Why don't you fix a plate and let the rest of us handle the dinner details?" Ruby suggested kindly. "I can understand why you wouldn't want to be out there with Phineas watching your every move."

After her friends headed back to the dining room, Annabelle sighed loudly. Everywhere she looked, there were pans of food covered with foil, along with a stack of everyday plates so the helpers could eat in the kitchen because the dining room was full. The aromas of ham, brisket, and fresh-perked coffee lingered around the worktable where she sat. She'd really been looking forward to a soul-satisfying dinner followed by a piece of pie and a slice of the beautiful wedding cake Ruby had baked and decorated.

So much food, so little appetite. Just when you put your loneliness and disappointment behind you, the man who caused it shows up.

Annabelle shoved her soggy shoes under the worktable. With a last look at all the glorious food around her, she padded barefoot over to the sink. She couldn't just sit and stew in her own juice while her friends kept working to make the meal a seamless success for Frances and Marlin.

As she ran hot water and squeezed liquid dish soap into it, Annabelle realized that her dreams were a lot like the bubbles that rose from the sink: shiny and colored with hope so transparent and fragile that the least little bump could pop them.

"I have to do better. I have to stand up for myself," she whispered as she began putting dirty utensils and dishes into the water. It would take more than dreams and hope to convince Phineas that the new life she'd made for herself was better than abandoning Old Order ways, which had guided her all her life. He was still her husband, but in the church's eyes he'd committed a serious sin.

Only God knew how this situation would settle out. Annabelle had to trust that the religious leaders of Promise Lodge would listen to His guidance—and convince Phineas to do the same.

Chapter Three

Gloria stood at the dessert table, listening carefully to Rosetta's suggestions as she mentally prepared herself to meet Phineas Beachey. She gripped her clipboard, which held a copy of the Promise Lodge rental agreement, eager to do her job correctly—yet wary of dealing with the man who'd abandoned Annabelle and their faith.

She'd never met anyone who'd left the Old Order. While he was alive, her father had preached many a sermon about the perils—the dire, eternal consequences—that awaited folks who broke their baptismal vows.

"If you approach him now, while he's sitting with Bishop Monroe and Preacher Amos, it'll be easier," Rosetta pointed out with an encouraging smile. "And if you want me to go with you, I will. We're assuming he'll be a tough customer, but maybe that's not the way of it at all. Maybe he's come to make amends, so we should give him the benefit of the doubt—and truth be told, his business with Annabelle isn't *our* business."

Gloria bit back a smile. The women in the kitchen wanted to *make* it their business to find out about Phineas, and they were buzzing about what would come of his presence here. "*Jah*, you're right," she said, stealing a glance at the man in question. "Mr. Beachey needs lodging, and we can provide it. It's a basic transaction—just like you rented a cabin to Cyrus and Jonathan Helmuth when they came here to work at their cousins' landscaping business."

"That's the best way to look at it." Rosetta beamed at her. "See there? I knew you were the right person to hire as my lodge manager. You'll do just fine with Phineas—but I'll come with you if you want me to," she repeated.

"I'm on it," Gloria said, standing taller. "With Monroe and Amos and all these other folks around, what can he do—except say that he'll either rent a cabin or that he'll head into town to find a place to stay?"

Smiling resolutely, Gloria walked toward the table where Phineas was finishing his apple pie. He was a striking man with graying hair and a neatly trimmed beard that gave him a distinguished air—until he looked up at her with his pale green eyes. Gloria stopped a few feet from the table, intimidated by the sinister aura his black English clothing and unnerving gaze created. She was relieved when Monroe and Amos caught sight of her.

"Gloria, you surely must be a mind reader," Bishop Monroe said, gesturing at the man across from him. "This is Phineas Beachey, and he's going to be here at Promise Lodge for a while. Phineas, this is Gloria Lehman. She manages the apartments and cabins we've been telling you about."

Grateful that the bishop had made the introductions, Gloria nodded at Phineas. "Pleased to meet you," she said as she set her clipboard on the table beside him. "If you'd like to look at our cabins, we can go anytime you're ready. The wedding guests who've been staying in them have given their permission for us to step inside so you can choose the one you like best—unless you'd rather find a room in Forest Grove."

Phineas skimmed the rental agreement, frowning slightly.

"I've already sent my driver back to Ohio, figuring I could stay here," he murmured. When he focused on Gloria again, he assessed her for a long moment.

She braced herself. Was Phineas about to criticize her or the rental agreement? His green-eyed gaze felt predatory, as though he was accustomed to staring folks down until they submitted.

"Are these wedding guests paying to stay?" he challenged, gesturing at the people who sat at nearby tables. "This is the first place I've ever been where hospitality wasn't offered as a common courtesy—"

"We're pleased to offer lodging when folks come— whether or not we were expecting them," Preacher Amos put in purposefully. "For the wedding, we're not charging the newlyweds' family and friends—"

"But we ask folks who're staying awhile to pay a minimal rent," Bishop Monroe continued firmly. "Otherwise, the ladies and the two young men who currently live in our apartments and a cabin would be covering the cost of your food—which adds up, if you stay for any length of time."

Phineas's eyes narrowed. "How does Annabelle pay any rent?" he asked in a low voice. "She's accused me of leaving her destitute, when in fact she had an entire farm at her disposal in Lancaster County. Ever since I arrived, the expressions on your faces have told me she's painted a very dark portrait of me, and of our relationship."

Gloria couldn't deny that Annabelle's descriptions of her husband had been less than flattering. She didn't feel it was a good idea to mention the Coffee Can Fund, started by the Kuhns and other women with successful businesses to help ladies who couldn't afford to pay rent right away.

"Annabelle does a lot of sewing for folks hereabouts," Preacher Amos replied smoothly. "She and the other lodge residents all support themselves with their businesses, just as our two young men work at the Helmuth Nursery you saw on the state highway. At Promise Lodge, we believe in carrying our weight instead of expecting our neighbors to cover our expenses—and if you're here to patch things up with Annabelle, you'll be a part of the Promise Lodge community for a while, ain't so?"

"And who knows?" Bishop Monroe asked before Phineas could respond. "You might come to enjoy our settlement so much that you decide to stay. All of us here came for a visit and liked what we found, so we relocated."

"Let's not make any rash assumptions," Phineas said bluntly. He looked around the dining room, where the women were picking up the dirty dishes as the guests chatted at their tables or visited with the wedding party on the *eck*. "Why do I have to stay in one of those dilapidated cabins out back? The lodge looks like a much nicer place."

"The apartments upstairs are for ladies only," Gloria explained. Why was Phineas so determined to be disagreeable? And how could he judge the condition of their ten cozy cabins before he'd even looked inside them?

"When the gal who owns the lodge wanted to rent out rooms, the bishop at that time decided that men couldn't live upstairs with women—for obvious reasons," Preacher Amos continued. "We're sorry if you feel these arrangements are inhospitable, Phineas. It's not our intention to put you off."

"All of the families who've come here stayed in the cabins while their homes were being built," Bishop Monroe pointed out. "We were quite comfortable—and we paid for our meals, too—so it's not as though you'd be doing anything we haven't done ourselves."

Phineas glanced at the clipboard again and rose from his chair. "All right, young lady, let's get on with it. Maybe

I'll be in a better mood after I've rested from the long drive out here to track down my wife."

Gloria's heart faltered, until Bishop Monroe and Preacher Amos stood up to go with them. Amos gestured for Phineas to precede him toward the front door, striking up a conversation about where in Ohio he'd come from. As the bishop fell in beside Gloria, he winked.

"You're doing just fine, Gloria," he murmured beneath the sound of other folks' voices.

"*Are* we being rude and inhospitable?" she whispered as they walked several paces behind Amos and Phineas. "Maybe I should've waited until tomorrow to mention the part about paying rent. Maybe he's only staying a couple of days—"

"Phineas impresses me as a man who feels entitled to special treatment, and who doesn't like young women being in charge," the bishop put in quickly. "I hope he's truly here to reconcile with Annabelle rather than to make her see things his way. The rent we're asking is peanuts, compared to the debt he owes for breaking the vows he made to God and to his wife."

Gloria nodded, stepping out onto the porch after Bishop Monroe held the door for her. "Some of the women are saying he's committed the one unforgivable sin," she said softly. "Is that true, Bishop?"

Monroe sighed as he walked alongside her. "In more conservative Amish settlements, folks wouldn't even be speaking to Phineas for what he's done," he replied. "But he's come a long way to visit with Annabelle, so I prefer to watch and wait—to watch the way he treats his wife, and to wait on the advice I get from God and our three preachers."

Gloria was grateful that such a wise, patient man had

taken over as bishop after her *dat* had died several months earlier. Ahead of them, Preacher Amos told Daisy to be quiet and lie down under a tree so she wouldn't pester them. The black-and-white dog did as she was told, but she watched Phineas warily.

When Amos held the door of the cabin nearest the lodge, Phineas stepped inside. He emerged quickly and was entering the second cabin before Gloria and the bishop joined them. Phineas's expression was impossible to read when he stepped outside again.

"The fourth cabin's a bit bigger, and it's available," Gloria remarked, "but number three is occupied by those brothers who work at the nursery."

Phineas gave her a purposeful look. "Single, are they?" he asked. "I can't understand why an attractive girl like yourself hasn't latched on to one of them."

Gloria's cheeks burned as she held the clipboard to her chest like a shield. Why had his statement begun as an apparent compliment, only to smack her in the face by the time he'd completed it? She wasn't about to admit that the two young men she'd fallen for had chosen other girls—and the longer he looked at her, the less inclined Gloria felt to talk to Phineas at all.

No wonder Daisy barked at this guy. Dogs know who's trustworthy and who's not.

"Gloria's a sensible young lady, waiting for the right man to come along," Preacher Amos replied. "We might as well warn you that the women here are more independent—*progressive*—than you're probably accustomed to, Phineas. It takes some getting used to, but we believe we're following God's will by allowing our ladies to think for themselves."

"Really." Phineas's eyebrows rose in disapproval. "I

suppose I should thank you for tipping me off about the *attitude* I'll be dealing with when I speak to Annabelle. I can't think you've done me any favors, however."

Somehow Gloria kept her opinions to herself as Phineas quickly looked at the remaining cabins and chose the tenth one, farthest from the lodge. After he scribbled his name on the rental agreement, he pulled a money clip from his trousers pocket and peeled away four bills.

"This should keep me in your good graces for a while," he muttered. "Since I can't claim the cabin until the wedding guests leave, I'm going to walk around the property for a while. I need a lot of fresh air to prepare myself for what lies ahead."

Phineas strode off abruptly, leaving Gloria, the bishop, and the preacher to stare after him.

"Odd duck," Amos murmured. "Bears out the old adage about how opposites attract, I'd say."

"*Jah*, I can't imagine Annabelle putting up with Phineas's surliness," Bishop Monroe said with a shake of his head. "But then, in a lot of Amish homes the woman doesn't have any say about it."

Gloria was staring at the money he'd given her. She'd never handled hundred-dollar bills. "He must be doing pretty well these days, considering that he was searching the pantry for her egg money before he left Annabelle," she whispered. "This cash covers two months' rent, and he just whipped it out of his pocket as though it was no big deal."

Preacher Amos grunted. "Money talks. But it doesn't necessarily tell you the truth about the man who flashes it," he observed. "It's best if we allow this situation with Annabelle to play out without judging either one of them. God's the only one who has the right to do that, after all."

"At least he paid ahead," Bishop Monroe said. "If he ducks out on Annabelle again, he hasn't left you short." He followed Phineas's progress up the road that passed everyone's homes before he smiled at her again. "Shall we return to the party? Must be about time for Marlin and Frances to cut their cake."

As Gloria folded the bills into her apron pocket, she wasn't sure what to think. Was Phineas planning to stay until the first week of December? Or was he subtly wielding his power, expecting his money to override any objections the bishop and the preachers might make about the way he'd abandoned his wife and their faith?

Cyrus Helmuth sat taller as Gloria entered the dining room behind Bishop Monroe, holding her clipboard. She looked especially fetching in a dress of deep red orange that set off her olive complexion and the dark brown hair tucked under her *kapp*.

"You know," he remarked to his brother Jonathan, who sat beside him at the table, "I think Gloria might be coming around. Now that she's our scribe for *The Budget*, along with managing Rosetta's rentals, she doesn't seem like such an airhead anymore."

Jonathan's eyebrows rose as he, too, watched Gloria enter the kitchen. "Spoken like a man in *love*," he teased. "Since when are you sweet on Miss Lehman?"

"Lay off that talk, man!" Cyrus replied as he playfully punched Jonathan's arm. "I'm just saying that Gloria's changed. Remember how she used to follow Allen around like a lovesick puppy, spying on him and baking those brickbat brownies for him?"

"Why would you care, unless you're *interested*?" his

brother challenged. "It's one thing to take our instruction for joining the church with Allen so he's not the only one in the class, but it's another thing altogether if you're eyeballing Gloria. Maybe today's wedding and Allen's engagement to Phoebe are getting you in the mood, eh?"

Jonathan's remark caught Cyrus by surprise. The two of them had been working six days a week all spring and summer to help their older cousins, Simon and Sam Helmuth, establish their landscaping nursery, so they hadn't had a lot of time for dating. He'd flirted with Maria Zehr, who'd briefly operated a bakery at Promise Lodge before she'd moved back to Cloverdale, but other than that, the only available girls had been Gloria Lehman and Phoebe and Laura Hershberger.

And now that Phoebe's hitching up with Allen, only two are left—unless you broaden your horizons and start scouting around Forest Grove . . . or Cloverdale, where Maria is.

"I rest my case. If you have no response, you're susceptible to wedding fever," Jonathan remarked lightly. "Better stay away from that cake Frances and Marlin are cutting, or you'll catch it *bad*."

Cyrus turned for a better view of the *eck*, where the middle-aged newlyweds stood together holding a cake knife. As they made the first cut, folks in the dining room clapped and cheered them on. Gloria's *mamm* was blushing like a young woman, and Preacher Marlin—who had his own married children—appeared absolutely ecstatic. They'd both lost their original longtime spouses, yet they seemed as head over heels as a couple just starting out.

"Maybe you'd better have my piece of cake as well as your own," Cyrus challenged his brother. "Here you are at twenty-four—*much* older than I am—and you've got no prospects at all. What's your problem?"

"Puh! I could have women swarming around me like bees if I—"

"So why don't you?" Cyrus shot back. "You've had the same opportunities I've had."

"Are you calling me out? Saying I couldn't latch on to any girl I wanted?" Jonathan said in a deceptively calm voice.

Something about the tilt of his brother's eyebrows and the light in his brown eyes sent a surge of adrenaline through Cyrus's system. When they'd been growing up in Ohio, they'd attended a one-room schoolhouse and their church district's Singings with the same neighborhood girls. It was a matter of personal pride that he'd bested Jonathan at baseball, volleyball, and anything involving physical prowess even though he was four years younger and four inches shorter than his more studious, laid-back brother.

Coming from a large family with four other sons, they'd jumped at the opportunity to move to Missouri with Simon and Sam, who'd offered them steady work and a way to see a different part of the country—not to mention a chance to meet young women who weren't distantly related to them. Was it the ticking of his biological clock goading him, or was he rising to Jonathan's challenge?

"So prove it," Cyrus heard himself say beneath the happy chatter that filled the dining room. "If you're not engaged by Thanksgiving, you owe me five hundred bucks!"

Jonathan let out a short laugh. "Where am I supposed to come up with that kind of cash? And what about you? Money burns a hole in your pocket."

Cyrus shrugged, suddenly tingling with his brazen

idea. "You don't fool me for a minute, big brother—you're cheap and you never spend any money, so you've got to have a bunch of it stashed away. And if you've got a woman by then, you won't have to worry about paying me off, ain't so?"

"And you think I'm going to let you sit idly by while I'm out busting my butt for the next month and a half?" Jonathan demanded in a voice that throbbed with Cyrus's challenge. "Same goes for you, kid. If you're not engaged by Thanksgiving, you'll be paying *me* that five hundred bucks!"

"You're on!" Cyrus blurted, pumping the hand Jonathan offered. They sat almost nose to nose, silently daring each other to back down—but Cyrus refused to look away first. "Hey, if we're soon to take our vows and join the church, we might as well have some fun along the way, *jah*?"

"*Jah*, it'll be *great* fun watching you scramble to get a girl when I've got all the best ones throwing themselves at *me*!"

"Like that'll ever happen," Cyrus fired back.

"We'll see about that, won't we?" Jonathan challenged him. "And because you're younger and full of hotshot ideas today, you can bring me back a piece of that cake when you go to fetch your own."

"Already playing the age card," Cyrus teased as he rose from his chair. "We'll see what your excuse is come Thanksgiving, when I've got a woman by my side and you don't."

He joined the line of guests going toward the *eck*, where Mary Kate and Minerva were now cutting the cake and plating it. When Gloria joined them to hand filled plates to the folks in the line, Cyrus was once again struck by her poise. Her movements were graceful and fluid, and she beamed at each person as she handed him or her a slice of cake.

She's really a looker, he suddenly realized. He'd been at Promise Lodge slightly more than eight months, yet he'd never noticed what potential Gloria Lehman had. Because she'd been pursuing Allen Troyer so ardently—and making a fool of herself in the process—her big brown eyes and long lashes had gotten right past him. As he stepped up to the table to receive his cake from her, however, Cyrus felt a tickle of excitement along his spine.

"There you go, Cyrus," she said, smiling sweetly. Her fingertips brushed his as she handed him a plate.

"Say, could we—could we maybe take a boat ride on the lake this evening?" Her touch had muddled him, so his thoughts were awkwardly somersaulting forward. "Or if you'd rather do something else—"

"I *love* being on the water," Gloria interrupted softly. "What time?"

Cyrus suddenly felt about fourteen, and he could only hope his brain was connected to his mouth so he sounded coherent. If he recalled correctly, Gloria was three years older than he was, so he had to rise to her level—and stay there. "How about six? After all the wedding activities are over?"

"I'll meet you at the dock." Her smile appeared a little dazed, as though his invitation had caught her off-guard. Then she noticed how many people were behind him, awaiting their cake. "See you later, Cyrus!"

"*Jah*," he murmured. "Later."

He was taking his place at the table beside Jonathan when it occurred to him that he hadn't gotten his brother any cake. Cyrus stuck a big forkful of the traditional white-on-white confection in his mouth, making Jonathan speak first.

"Forget something?" his brother asked, tapping the edge of Cyrus's plate.

Cyrus nailed him with a triumphant gaze. "It's every man for himself now, so get your own cake," he said with a chuckle. "I have a date with Gloria this evening."

Chapter Four

Phoebe Hershberger sighed with delight as she stood in the unfinished front room of what would soon be the home she shared with her beloved, Allen Troyer. She'd splattered paint on her oldest dress and the kerchief covering her hair, but she didn't mind.

"It's a dream come true," she murmured as she recoated her roller with paint. "You and your *dat* and the other men have outdone yourselves building this place! And look at the shade we'll have on sunny summer evenings—every day for the rest of our lives."

Allen glanced up from the baseboard he'd been painting. "You chose a *gut* spot for your house, Phoebe," he said with a grin. "I'm just lucky you want me to share it with you."

"And I feel like the Queen of Everything, looking out over the lot you chose next to mine, right alongside the lake," she replied. "Thanks to our generous parents, we have the prettiest plots in Promise Lodge, if you ask me."

As she covered the upper section of the wall with butter-yellow paint Phoebe laughed, something she did often these days. In a few short weeks, Allen would be baptized into the church and then they would marry, after a summer courtship during which they'd helped build the house that overlooked Rainbow Lake. When she'd covered the wall with paint, she came down from her ladder to stand in front of the big picture window. Every time she gazed out, she was amazed at the array of wildflowers and trees in the yard—not to mention the view she had of the large plots where Mattie Troyer raised vegetables for her roadside stand, and beyond that, the lodge and the Helmuths' nursery.

"The leaves are starting to turn," she remarked softly. "We'll soon have a yard full of yellow, red, and orange leaves from all these maple trees."

"And since we don't have any grass seeded yet, we'll just let those leaves stay where they land," Allen said. "With the orders I've taken to build more tiny homes before winter, I won't have much time for raking anyway."

"I don't anticipate a decline in the number of pies Irene and I bake, either," Phoebe remarked. "So we can sit on the porch of an evening and take in the fall foliage—and watch the folks who come and go. Hmmm," she added as she watched a lithe figure cross Allen's grassy lot down the hill. "Why do you suppose Gloria's heading for the dock on the far side of the lake?"

Allen set down his paintbrush before he joined her at the window. "I haven't the foggiest. I'm just glad she finally got the message and stopped pestering me about—aha!" he said, pointing toward the line of cabins behind the lodge. "That's Cyrus, ain't so? Do you suppose the two of them are an item now?"

Phoebe eased against him as he slipped his arm around her. "I have no idea. I didn't see any sign of that at the wedding or the meal today—but there were a lot of people there, and I was busy."

"After all the times Gloria's spied on us, it's sort of fun to be watching *her*," Allen said with a chuckle. "I had no clue that Cyrus was interested in her."

"Maybe it was her idea," Phoebe suggested. "Maybe Gloria talked him into meeting her at the lake, and he had no graceful way out—although she hasn't seemed as boy crazy since Rosetta hired her to manage the apartments and cabins."

"Time will tell. She's a hard one to steer clear of when she's got it in her head that—oh, Cyrus is untying the rowboat," Allen murmured. "He looks like a man on a mission."

Phoebe leaned forward, intent on watching the pair across the lake. The days were already growing shorter and daylight was fading, so it was hard to distinguish Gloria's and Cyrus's facial features. "Shouldn't he leave the boat tied until both of them are sitting in it? So it won't shift from side to side that way?"

"*Jah*, that's the safest way to do it," Allen agreed. "Cyrus might be showing off a little—"

"Gloria's not looking any too confident, stepping down the ladder to grab his hand before—they've overturned!" Phoebe cried. "What if they can't swim?"

"I'm going down there," Allen said as he raced toward the front door.

Phoebe ran right behind him. When she saw that Allen was heading down the hillside, which was covered with underbrush, she chose the dirt roadway as a safer place to run in her bare feet. It was a relief to see two figures thrashing in the water below, safely away from the overturned rowboat, and to hear Gloria's cries. By the time Phoebe was down the hill, Allen was running around the lake to help the pair in the water—and Cyrus was swimming toward the shore with Gloria in the crook of his arm.

"Are you all right?" Phoebe asked breathlessly as she reached her fiancé and their two friends. Allen was crouching low with his hand extended to help Cyrus out of the water—but Cyrus boosted Gloria toward the lake's edge so Allen could help her instead. As she came up onto shore, Phoebe grabbed the poor girl's hand.

"Oh!" Gloria sputtered. "This was *not* what I had in mind when—"

"I'm really sorry, Gloria!" Cyrus protested as he nimbly hopped onto the bank. "I thought you had your balance—"

"My foot slipped before I could—" Gloria scrambled to her feet, appearing ready to burst into tears. Her dark red-orange dress and white apron, which were smeared with mud, clung wetly to her body. Her waterlogged bun was tumbling loose around her shoulders—and her *kapp* was bobbing slowly away from them in the water, its two strings curling and uncurling with the waves she and Cyrus had created in the lake.

"How about if I jump in again and push that boat toward the dock, and you grab hold of it?" Cyrus suggested to Allen. "Between the two of us, we can flip it right-side up."

Phoebe slipped her arm around Gloria's shaking shoulders. "Shall we get you back to your apartment and into some dry clothes?" she asked softly. "Lots of the wedding guests have left—and from the looks of the lights in the lodge, our neighbors are still in the dining room. Maybe we can slip into the mudroom and up the back stairs without anybody seeing you."

Gloria sniffed miserably. "*Jah*, let's go," she mumbled as they started walking. "It'll be a while before I can face Cyrus again—or talk to him without bawling like a baby."

"Well, you got a shock when you fell into the lake," Phoebe pointed out as they walked across the grass. "Anybody would be upset."

Gloria released a shuddery breath. "I feel so stupid," she whimpered. "I was all excited about—I was so surprised when Cyrus asked me to meet him out here for a boat ride, and now this!"

Despite the way Gloria had spied on her and Allen earlier in the summer—and had even tattled on them in church for kissing in Allen's tiny home—Phoebe felt sorry for the drenched young woman. Allen, Cyrus, and Jonathan had constantly made fun of Gloria and the awful brownies she'd baked while trying to attract their favor. She hoped that Cyrus had sincerely wanted to spend time with Gloria, rather than playing a cruel joke on her to embarrass her further.

"Let's give him another chance," Phoebe said gently. "Sometimes Cyrus gets gung-ho about an idea and he doesn't realize that other folks aren't as quick or as strong as he is."

"*Jah*, he's a really *gut* swimmer. From my apartment window, I've seen him dive off the dock wearing nothing but English swimming trunks," Gloria admitted with a hint of a smile. "He waits until nearly dark, when he thinks nobody's watching."

Phoebe laughed softly. "So even though you fell in, and you feel really stupid about it, you probably weren't in any real danger?" she asked. "I mean—at least the boat didn't hit you on the head when it capsized."

"Well, maybe after I change into some dry clothes and settle down, I can think about how it felt to have his arm around me," Gloria murmured. "Strong as he is, Cyrus was swimming toward the shore and tugging me along as though I didn't weigh a thing."

"Not a bad way to look at it," Phoebe remarked as they approached the back of Roman and Mary Kate's house. From this point, the lodge was a straight shot across the road and between Mattie's produce plots.

When they reached the front yard, Gloria looked to the right and the left. "I can make it from here," she said. "If I stay behind that big patch of Mattie's Indian corn, the stalks will hide me until I'm just a few yards from the lodge's back door. *Denki*, Phoebe," she added, clasping her hand. "You're a *gut* friend to look after me."

Phoebe squeezed her fingers. "I'm glad nobody was hurt. See you later, Gloria."

She watched as the slender young woman jogged across the road, clutching her wet hair to keep it from unwinding further. Luckily, Mattie had left the stalks intact after picking her sweet corn—before long she would cut them so she could sell them as dried autumn decorations. When Gloria disappeared around the far edge of the produce plot, Phoebe strode along the new dirt road that wound its way up the hill toward the almost-finished house where she and Allen had been painting.

She'd lit a lamp in the kitchen and was wrapping their paint rollers in aluminum foil when she heard the front door open and close. When Allen appeared in the entry to the kitchen, Phoebe smiled at him.

"What was Cyrus's version of the story?" she asked. "Gloria was pleasantly surprised that he'd asked her to meet him at the lake, as though this was their first outing."

Allen joined her at the counter and ran water into a plastic pail to clean his paintbrushes. "I think he intended to take Gloria for a nice, quiet ride around the lake—but when she fell in, he didn't mind playing the hero, either," he said with a shake of his head. "Said something about pulling her up against him as he swam to shore with her. You know how it is with us guys, looking for any opportunity for a little *togetherness*."

"*Jah*, I do know," Phoebe replied softly.

When Allen slung his arm around her shoulders to pull her close for a kiss, she dreamed that their marriage would always be this affectionate. This perfect.

Jonathan stashed his binoculars inside the cabin door and sat on the small front stoop with a hunting magazine, thinking of what to say when Cyrus returned. He couldn't let his brother know that he'd witnessed the entire five-minute fiasco of his date with Gloria—but he couldn't pass up the chance to razz him, either. Jonathan envied his younger, more athletic sibling because he'd always had such an easy time of impressing females of any age. Alongside Cyrus, Jonathan felt clumsy and slow. He was much better at keeping the books for the nursery than he was at keeping company with girls.

He had no idea how to convince anyone to go out with him, much less agree to marry him in the next month and a half. He'd squirreled away a couple hundred bucks in the bank in Forest Grove, so maybe it would be easier to hand the money over when Cyrus got engaged than to worry about—

Hey, it's not a done deal. Cyrus could blow it. And maybe it's time you put yourself out there. Do you really want to spend the rest of your life alone?

Jonathan stifled a laugh as his kid brother crossed the grass. With his shirt and pants clinging to him and his dark hair plastered wetly to his head, Cyrus didn't look like such a hotshot. "What happened to *you*?" he called out nonchalantly. "Did you make a smart remark and Gloria pushed you in?"

Cyrus laughed. "For somebody who said she *loves* to be on the water, Gloria wasn't so good at getting into the boat," he replied as he sat down beside Jonathan. "When she turned us over, I made *gut* on a bad situation, however. Got her to shore with my best lifesaving technique—got up close and personal with her, if you know what I mean."

Jonathan sighed inwardly. The only females he'd come into close bodily contact with were old enough to be his mother. "So does this mean you'll be taking her out again? Or did the whole ordeal scare her off?"

"Gloria?" Cyrus joked. "Have you ever known her to be put off by any type of attention a guy paid her? She was embarrassed about getting soaked, but she'll come around." He grabbed the cover of Jonathan's magazine, shaking his head. "So you're studying up on hunting strategies—when it's too dark to read? At this rate, you won't get a girl *or* a deer this season."

"We'll see about that," Jonathan countered. "I can recall times when I put meat in the freezer and you missed your shots because the deer heard you rustling around."

"Puh." Cyrus pushed his wet hair back from his face, one eyebrow rising. "You're not backing out of our bet, are you? You've let a perfect evening go by, sitting at home like a *maidel* instead of—"

"Some girls prefer the strong, silent type," Jonathan put in. "I'm making my plans, figuring out the best way to approach the woman of my dreams."

"And who would *that* be?"

"Why would I tell *you*?" he fired back. "With five hundred bucks riding on this deal, you're probably desperate enough to talk trash to her before I even ask her out."

"That's a lame excuse and you know it—wetter and soggier than these clothes I'm going to get out of," Cyrus said as he stood up. "*Gut* luck with your plans, 'cause you're gonna need it. Gloria and I are tight, man. You don't stand a chance."

As the door closed behind his brother, Jonathan sagged against the side of the cabin. As always, his little brother had seen right through him. He didn't have a plan, and he had no idea about whom to approach for a date. He didn't know any girls in Forest Grove, and although he'd joked around with Maria Zehr when she'd lived at Promise Lodge, she'd paid more attention to Allen and Cyrus than to him. Laura Hershberger was cute, but at seventeen, she was way too young—and now that her *mamm* had married the bishop, any guy who asked her out would have to toe a higher mark.

He thought about the girls he'd waited on at the nursery, but most of them were English—and he'd soon be joining the Old Order. What with Bishop Monroe and three preachers leading the sessions about their religion and the responsibilities of church membership, there was no backing out at this point, especially on the off chance that he could attract a young woman from the outside world.

Jonathan sighed as darkness fell, filled with the calls of cicadas and the frogs at the lake. Summer was over, fall would speed by with work at the nursery—and then Thanksgiving would be upon him. Winter would bring him more time to socialize, but by then his kid brother would have one hand on his fiancée's shoulder and the other hand out for the money they'd wagered.

Shake a leg. There's got to be somebody out there, and some way to convince her you deserve her time . . . her heart.

Chapter Five

On Saturday morning, Annabelle took special care to be sure her dark blue dress, black apron, and heart-shaped *kapp* looked their best before she went downstairs to breakfast—or was she stalling, nervous about facing Phineas? Even though she could remain surrounded by her supportive friends whenever he was present, she hadn't slept well. She felt uneasy about the tactics her husband might use to persuade her to leave Promise Lodge, because he'd always had a power about him, a presence that commanded respect and submission . . . and after the past months of not answering to him, Annabelle wasn't sure she wanted to start up again.

But Phineas was her husband. No matter what he'd done, she'd made a vow to be his wife until death parted them.

Annabelle slowly went down the back stairway to the kitchen, trying to compose her thoughts and her nerves. Aromas of percolating coffee, cinnamon rolls, and bacon ordinarily made her excited about starting the day, yet she hesitated. Maybe a cup of that coffee and the company of the Kuhn sisters would prepare her for meeting with Phineas, whenever he chose to make his appearance—

But he was already in the kitchen. Waiting for her to descend the last few stairs.

Annabelle gripped the handrail. The last thing she wanted was to stumble, to lose the shred of composure she'd mustered as she'd left the safety of her apartment. As always, Phineas expected her to speak first.

"*Gut—gut* morning," she stammered. Why was he in the kitchen? Had he barged in on Beulah and Ruby, not caring that he'd interrupted their morning routine?

After Beulah had pulled a pan of puffy, perfect cinnamon rolls from the oven, she glanced apologetically at Annabelle, confirming her suspicion. "*Gut* morning, Annabelle," she said with forced cheerfulness. "Seems our guest was up before the chickens—"

"*Jah*, he was already here when we came downstairs," Ruby put in as she turned the bacon in the skillet. "Says his body clock is still on eastern time, so he's ready for breakfast."

Annabelle fought a frown. Did Phineas figure these women would step to his beat just because he was a male guest? How rude of him! And what was he doing in the kitchen so early, in the lodge where only women were living?

Was he rifling through the pantry, looking for whatever cash might be stashed there?

The thought made Annabelle bristle. She stood taller on the bottom step, determined not to knuckle under to his arrogance—or to those light green eyes that had seemed so exotic, so bewitching, when she'd been a young woman in love. "So who's been cooking for you since you left home?" she asked quietly.

Phineas's eyebrows rose, but before he could reprimand her for such an impertinent question, Annabelle continued.

"Here at Promise Lodge, we serve our meals when everyone gets to the table—and that includes Gloria, along with Cyrus and Jonathan Helmuth," she explained. "Now, if you'll please move out of my way, I'll help Ruby and Beulah."

After making her wait a few moments longer than necessary, Phineas stepped aside. "I was eager to see you, hoping we could talk before anyone else was around," he murmured. "Can you fault me for the fact that I've missed you, Annabelle?"

She blinked. Just like that, his face had softened with an endearing smile, and his voice thrummed with affection. His English haircut and clothing—a sage-green shirt and brown pleated trousers—complemented his lithe, lean body, and for a moment Annabelle was taken in by how handsome he looked.

But he's been living English. And he has a lot of explaining to do. You'd better not say you've missed him, as well, because you'd be lying.

"I try not to find fault with anybody this early in the morning," Annabelle replied as she went to the cupboard. "It gets the day off to an unfortunate start."

Feeling the weight of his gaze on her back, she took down seven plates and prayed she'd make it to the table without dropping them. Annabelle wasn't surprised when Phineas followed her into the dining room, but she remained focused on placing each plate in front of a chair. She was relieved when Ruby bustled in moments later with their silverware. The sounds of the front door and voices in the lobby were music to her nervous ears.

"Hope you ladies have cooked up a lot of that bacon I smell," Cyrus called out as he came in with his brother. "I'm so hungry, I could eat the whole hog by myself!"

"That's because he had the shortest date in history last night, and he and Gloria ended up in the lake," Jonathan teased. He paused to assess the scene, smiling politely. "*Gut* morning, Phineas. Nice to have you joining us for breakfast."

"*Jah*, welcome to Promise Lodge," Cyrus put in as he stepped forward with his hand extended. "Saw you come in yesterday, but we didn't get introduced. I'm Cyrus Helmuth and I claim this guy beside me—Jonathan—as my older brother."

The tension in the room eased a bit as Phineas shook the young men's hands and made conversation about their work at the nursery. When Annabelle returned to the kitchen, Beulah had finished drizzling thick white frosting over the pan of cinnamon rolls. She was talking softly with Gloria, who'd just come downstairs.

"Fair warning—because the menfolk are talking about you out there," Beulah remarked to the young woman as she nodded toward the dining room. Her face creased with a smile. "Did you really spend time with Cyrus last night? I think that's a wonderful-*gut*—"

"Let's just say we got off to an *awkward* start," Gloria said with a shake of her head. She listened attentively to the men's conversation as she drew a bread knife beneath the rows of warm cinnamon rolls. "It's much more interesting to wonder why our new guest was roaming the grounds at all hours last night. What with the full moon, I had no trouble seeing Phineas walk over to Christine's barn, and then to Phoebe and Irene's pie shop before he stepped into your cheese factory."

Annabelle's eyes widened—but not nearly as far as Beulah's and Ruby's did. "What's he up to?" she whispered. "Do you suppose we should tell Bishop Monroe about this? Phineas has no business snooping around, just because we don't lock any doors. It's not only impolite, it's *wrong*!"

Ruby thought about her response as she began to arrange the fresh rolls on a big platter. "Maybe he's only curious. As long as we don't find anything missing, there's not much we can say—"

"But I'm glad you mentioned it, Gloria," Beulah cut in with a nod. "If we hear that folks suspect an intruder's been in their homes and shops, we'll know who it is."

Annabelle pressed her lips together as she grasped the big glass pan that held a ham and hash-brown casserole. Had Phineas become a thief? If his reestablished remodeling business was doing as well as he'd implied earlier, why would he need to steal from the folks who'd welcomed him to this community?

She didn't like the way her suspicions were rising like yeast rolls in a pan, warmed by the heat of her friends' speculation and her own doubts about the man her husband might have become. Annabelle remained quiet as she and the other ladies set out the bacon, cinnamon rolls, casserole, and a bowl of canned peach halves before taking their places at the table. As always, the women sat on one side and the men faced them. When they bowed their heads for a short, silent prayer, she sensed Phineas was watching her rather than saying grace. Annabelle closed her eyes tightly.

Lord, we need Your help keeping this situation in perspective, she prayed fervently. *Help me to separate the truth about Phineas and his reason for being here from the way my suspicious imagination tends to run amok.*

As she passed the platter of cinnamon rolls to Gloria, Annabelle couldn't miss the pink spots in the girl's cheeks—because Cyrus was gazing intently at her from across the table. Her heart lightened. Watching a romance blossom between these two young adults would provide a welcome diversion from the issues she and Phineas would be dealing with over the next few days—starting as soon as breakfast was over, most likely.

Annabelle sighed at the thought of the tactics her husband might use to lure her away from the friends and the comfortable life she'd found at Promise Lodge. As the rest of the food was passed and Jonathan and Cyrus focused on their breakfast, an uneasy silence settled over the table. At the sound of the front door opening, however, everyone looked toward the lobby.

Bishop Monroe stopped in the dining room doorway, removing his black straw hat. "*Gut* morning, folks!" he said. "Quiet as it was, I didn't want to interrupt your prayer."

"Come in, Bishop, and have a seat!" Beulah called out.

"I'll bring you a plate and you can join us!" Ruby put in as she rose from her chair. "We're just starting to eat."

Was it her imagination, or did Bishop Monroe quickly assess the tense situation and flash her a wink? Annabelle was grateful for his timely appearance.

"Christine's already fed me," he remarked as he pulled out the empty chair next to Phineas, "but who am I to refuse a warm cinnamon roll? We fellows figure to finish shingling the roof on Allen and Phoebe's new house this morning, so I'll burn it off, right?" he teased.

Monroe offered his hand to Phineas. "You can join us if you'd like, seeing's how you're a man of the trade."

Phineas returned the bishop's grip. "I'm impressed with the homes you've built here," he said, "and the view from the one you're working on is probably the best of any at

Promise Lodge. But I have business to attend to this morning, with Annabelle."

"I can understand your priorities," Monroe put in smoothly. He accepted the plate Ruby brought him, and then he took his time choosing a cinnamon roll from the platter. "We at Promise Lodge also have priorities, Phineas, and one of them is to provide our residents with a place to live in a community that adheres to the tenets of our Plain faith. If I understand correctly, you've chosen to leave the Old Order, and you're here to convince your wife to forsake her baptismal vow, as well. Do I have that right?"

The dining room rang with absolute silence. Annabelle wondered if everyone else at the table could hear the rapid pounding of her heart as she waited for Phineas to respond.

"That's correct," he muttered. "Although I don't see that it's any of your business, what I discuss with my wife."

"Ah, but it is," Monroe said without missing a beat. He paused with his cinnamon roll partially unwound, holding Phineas's gaze with his deep green eyes . . . eyes that didn't threaten, but didn't back down, either. "Any time someone intends to lead one of my members away from the salvation of our Lord, it's my job—my highest calling—to intervene. If Annabelle were choosing of her own accord to go back on the promise she made to God, that would be a different matter—but I would still do everything in my power to talk her out of it."

"I have no intention of leaving the Old Order," Annabelle stated softly. Bishop Monroe's stalwart support had given her the strength to speak up, but even so, she clasped her hands in her lap so no one could see them trembling. "If Phineas wants me back, he'll have to return to Amish ways—if he hasn't already burned his bridges by jumping the fence."

Phineas smacked his fork on the table, leaning forward. "You're still my wife, Annabelle, and we're together forever," he whispered tersely. "I *love* you, and I'm trying to provide you a better life by—"

"*Gut* morning to you, folks! Can someone here direct me to Monroe Burkholder, the bishop of this beautiful community?"

Annabelle gasped, startled by the sonorous male voice that had interrupted her husband's tirade. She'd been so intent on Phineas and Monroe's exchange that she hadn't heard the front door open, but there was no missing the man who stood in the dining room doorway. He was as burly as Bishop Monroe but not quite as tall, and he exuded an air of confident competence as he removed his broad-brimmed black hat. Had he been listening to their conversation for a while, or had he walked in unaware of the unfolding drama?

"I'm Monroe Burkholder," the bishop said as he rose from his place at the table. "You're in time to join us for some breakfast if you'd like—"

"And I'd be pleased to accept your invitation!" the stranger said as he approached them. "I've been driving for several days to reach Promise, Missouri, and it's *gut* to finally arrive. I'm Bishop Clayton King from Paradise, in Lancaster County, Pennsylvania, and I'm here on behalf of the Council of Bishops."

Annabelle blinked. Why would a bishop come such a long way in a horse-drawn buggy rather than hiring an English driver, as she had? But more to the point, why was he here? Paradise was a mere hop, skip, and a jump from where she and Phineas had lived in Bird-in-Hand—less than a five-mile drive—so for a fleeting moment, she wondered if he'd come to summon the two of them back home.

The tightening of her husband's jaw suggested that he was wary about this bishop's arrival, too. But as Bishop Clayton chose the empty chair on Monroe's other side—which happened to be at the head of the table—everyone forgot the tension that had been building like thunderheads before the newcomer had arrived.

"What can I do for you?" Monroe asked as he shifted the platters and casserole pan so their guest could fill the plate Ruby was setting before him. "You've come a long way to find me when you might've called or written a letter instead."

Bishop Clayton inhaled deeply as he spooned a large amount of the steaming ham and hash-brown casserole onto his plate. He was a handsome fellow. His ebony hair, streaked with silver at his temples, feathered back from a full, boyish face framed by a well-trimmed black beard. Annabelle tried not to be obvious about staring at him, wondering if she'd ever seen him back home—until Clayton glanced up and locked his gaze with hers.

His chocolate-brown eyes made her quiver. Annabelle's cheeks went hot and she quickly looked down at her plate, hoping no one had noticed her reaction to the newcomer, whom she was certain she'd never met. She would've *remembered* such a striking, magnetic man had she ever seen him around Lancaster County.

"My purpose at Promise Lodge is best carried out in person," Bishop Clayton said as he chose the largest remaining cinnamon roll on the platter. "At a recent meeting of the council, your community was a topic of much conversation. After careful study of your weekly columns in *The Budget*, dating back to last year when Rosetta Bender submitted the very first one describing how she and her sisters founded your community by acquiring a former church camp, we've been extremely concerned about the *progressive* path you've followed—a path we fear is leading you *away* from God's purpose rather than toward His everlasting salvation," he added in a sonorous voice that filled the dining room.

Monroe stared at King, his cinnamon roll forgotten in his hand, as though he was waiting for the man beside him to drop the other shoe.

Bishop Clayton's dark brows rose expressively when he met Monroe's gaze. "We have a lot to talk about, don't we?"

Chapter Six

Gloria stopped running water into the sink when Beulah beckoned her and Ruby and Annabelle into the mudroom, away from the dining room door. Cleaning up after breakfast had been their reason for leaving the table—not to mention the escalating tension Bishop Clayton was creating.

"Gloria, you'd better alert Rosetta and her sisters about this visitor who seems determined to undermine everything they've accomplished at Promise Lodge," Beulah whispered. "I don't dare call them on the phone, for fear the men will hear me."

"*Jah*, and see if Preacher Amos and Preacher Eli can come over here to help Monroe," Ruby suggested, glancing over her shoulder toward the dining room. "I hate to bother Marlin the morning after his wedding—"

"But he'd want to know what's going on," Beulah insisted. "Just do your best to let folks know what's happening."

Annabelle sighed. "Bad enough that Phineas got our suspicions up first thing this morning," she muttered. "Now this new fellow's saying we're on the path to perdition. If he's a bishop from Paradise, you'd think I would've run across his name in all my years of living right down the road."

"Scoot along now, sweetie," Beulah urged as she

opened the back door for Gloria. "We'll keep busy in the kitchen, so the men don't get suspicious about how quiet we are."

Gloria slipped outside, her thoughts racing. Parked in the grass near the lodge, Bishop Clayton's black buggy glimmered in the sun—and so did his sleek bay Thoroughbred with the black mane and tail.

For a horse and rig that have traveled all the way from Pennsylvania, they sure don't look dusty from the road, Gloria thought, but she had more important matters to concentrate on. Rather than running to the Wickey place on the hill—because the men might spot her through the dining room window—she headed toward Bishop Monroe's house to speak with Christine. The sisters could notify each other without Bishop Clayton being the wiser.

As she reached the road, she spotted the man she most needed to see. "Amos!" she called after him as he crossed his back lawn. "Amos, wait up!"

The preacher turned, smiling at her as he adjusted his tool belt. "*Gut* morning, Gloria! You're starting the day at a run, it seems."

"We've got a stranger at the lodge, and you need to meet him," she explained as she jogged up to him. "His name's Clayton King, and he's a bishop from out east who's come to tell us we're way too progressive. He's at the lodge with Bishop Monroe and Phineas, saying that Rosetta's columns in *The Budget* have prompted his visit—"

"Easy now," Amos said, gently grasping her shoulder. "Where's he from again?"

Gloria sucked in some cool morning air to settle herself. "Lancaster County—says the Council of Bishops has sent him here—"

His forehead puckered. "Sounds a bit odd—but I'll

catch Eli before he climbs up to the roof at Allen's house," he said. "We'll head on over to see what's cooking."

"I'm on my way to warn Christine and her sisters," Gloria said. "We suspect this guy intends to read us the riot act about how the women here have their say about things."

Amos laughed. "*Denki* for letting me know what to expect—especially since I was the first man who let the Bender sisters have their way about settling this place."

Gloria set off again. The next place up the road had been her home before she'd moved to her lodge apartment, but Gloria didn't want to barge in on her *mamm* and Marlin. At the curve sat her Uncle Lester's place, but he was installing windows in a community west of Forest Grove this morning, so she kept going. As she jogged farther up the road, Bishop Monroe's red barns and pastures came into view. His Clydesdales were peacefully grazing in the lush green grass, and Daisy was observing them from beneath a tree.

As Gloria approached the Burkholders' tall white house, she saw a figure in blue wielding a hoe. "Christine!" she called, making a beeline for the garden.

The woman turned, shielding her eyes from the sun with her hand. "Gloria! What's so urgent that you've run all the way over here?"

Gloria slowed as she approached the patch scattered with pumpkins and squash, where Christine was hoeing the weeds between the vines. Her heart was thudding rapidly. "We—we thought you ought to know—about the bishop who showed up this morning," she said between gasps. "He's come from out east to—to make us mend our progressive ways!"

Christine gripped her hoe handle. "Take a minute to catch your breath, sweetie. You're not making any sense."

Gloria inhaled more air and released it. "His name's

Clayton King," she continued when she could speak again. "He's from the Council of Bishops—and they've read Rosetta's columns in *The Budget*—and they think we're headed to hell in a hand basket."

Christine's eyes widened. "Is that so?" she asked with a little laugh.

"He was discussing it with Monroe when I left the lodge," Gloria continued. "Beulah thought you and your sisters would want to be forewarned."

"Let's get you some lemonade," Christine suggested, slinging her arm around Gloria's shoulders. "I'll give Rosetta a call—"

"Amos and Eli are on their way over to give Monroe some support," Gloria put in as they started toward the back door.

Christine's eyebrow rose. "You don't think Monroe can handle this fellow on his own?"

Gloria considered her answer for a moment. "There's something about Bishop Clayton that you just don't argue with," she replied. "Monroe was already in the thick of things with Phineas when Clayton walked in, so the tension was cranked up pretty tight by the time I left."

"Ah. Sounds like my husband's got more on his plate than a second breakfast. But we'll handle it." Christine held open the door and gestured for Gloria to enter the kitchen. "Help yourself to the lemonade in the fridge, and there's a cookie plate on the counter. Rosetta's phone's in her kitchen, so chances are *gut* she'll pick up right away."

Gloria nodded, watching Christine cross the yard toward the white phone shanty at the road. When Rosetta had married a Mennonite, she'd come into several conveniences—such as a phone inside her house and electrical appliances—but she kept in close contact with her sisters. Rosetta still owned the lodge building and the cabins behind it, and as Gloria poured a glass of cold lemonade she realized that all of these details would soon come to Bishop Clayton's attention.

No doubt their guest would give Monroe quite a dressing-down for allowing Rosetta to marry a man who wasn't Amish—which was the most controversial decision their bishop had made since he'd arrived.

As Gloria bit into a soft, fresh chocolate chip cookie, she realized that her *dat*, the previous bishop, would *never* have condoned such a union. Even though he'd liked Rosetta a lot, Bishop Floyd would've shunned her if she'd gone through with her wedding to Truman Wickey. He was a bishop who'd upheld the same Old Order faith his forebears had held dear, without making allowances for more modern times.

But a lot of things have changed since Dat passed.

A wave of sadness washed over Gloria at the memory of her deceased father. She sighed and took another cookie from the plate. How did Dat feel about Mamm getting remarried—and about the new position Gloria held as the manager of the lodge apartments—as he looked down on them from heaven?

Gloria smiled. Without thinking about it, she'd chosen a sweet, spicy oatmeal cookie with a drizzle of icing—Dat's favorite treat. It seemed like a sign that he surely must be with her in spirit.

Maybe you could lend us a hand here, Dat. You always said we could ask for assistance from God and the cloud of witnesses who surround us in this life. All of a sudden, we seem to have more than our share of complications because two men have shown up out of the blue.

And while you're at it, Gloria added as she savored another bite of the cookie, *give me some advice about*

Cyrus. He's been here several months, yet he's just now figuring out that I exist. What's going on with that?

By the time Christine emerged from the phone shanty, Gloria felt greatly refreshed. Dat had been right. Maybe if she spent more time in prayer, she'd be more focused and less vulnerable to the ups and downs of daily life. "You reached Rosetta, *jah*?" she called out.

Christine nodded. "Matter of fact, Mattie was helping her sort through the quilts Truman's *mamm* has stashed away over the years," she replied. "But she said that could wait. If Bishop Clayton gets high-toned about the way we run things, Rosetta thought we'd be too hot and bothered to need blankets, anyway!"

Gloria laughed out loud. Rosetta's humorous remark sounded typical of her positive outlook.

"We sisters are going to meet at Mattie's produce stand and make our entrance together," Christine went on. "It's better if our visitor knows whom he's dealing with straightaway. By that time, Amos and Eli will have arrived, as well. Shall we head down the hill?"

Gloria nodded and fell into step with her. "*Denki* for the lemonade and cookies," she said. "When I got downstairs this morning and saw that Phineas was already watching Annabelle like a hawk—and then Clayton King showed up—I didn't eat much breakfast."

"Men can have that effect on our appetites," Christine remarked as they walked down the road. "All teasing aside, however, we'll need to listen carefully to this King fellow. If we've attracted the attention of the bishops out east, we might be in for more criticism and more high-level guests in the future. A lot of church leaders won't want their congregations—especially their women—getting any wild ideas about the way we've worked things to our advantage here."

Gloria considered these ideas as they passed Uncle Lester's house. "Can Bishop Clayton make us change the way we do things?"

Christine shrugged. "It's best to leave those details to Monroe and the preachers," she replied. "They'll know how to deal with bishops who worship a God who hasn't changed one iota since time out of mind—since before the Bible was written."

Gloria recalled her *dat* preaching about how God never changed, but she'd been daydreaming during most of the long sermons she'd heard over her lifetime. "So if God never changes, why are we so sure we're doing the right things by allowing women more freedom?"

Christine smiled. "After much prayer and listening to God's response, Monroe—and even Amos, who's a hard nut to crack—believe that because Jesus respected women and treated them as equals, we can do the same here at Promise Lodge," she explained. "God never changes, but our perceptions of Him have evolved more than most other Old Order communities feel comfortable with. It'll be interesting to hear what Bishop Clayton has to say about that—but it won't be easy to listen to his criticism."

As they passed Mattie and Amos's place, Gloria sighed. She was already tired of the havoc Phineas was creating for poor Annabelle, and she didn't relish the thought of another newcomer trying to change everyone's lives. "See you later," she said as the little white bakery building came into sight. "I'll tell Phoebe and Irene what's happening before they take their pies to town."

Nodding, Christine strode toward the entrance to the Promise Lodge property, where Mattie's produce stand sat.

Gloria opened the door to Promise Lodge Pies and peered inside. Aromas of fruit and sugar and spices filled the air. The tables across the small front room were covered with cooling pies. Behind the back counter, Phoebe and her partner, Irene Wickey, chatted happily as they fitted top crusts onto the pies they'd soon put into the oven. "You ladies have been busy this morning!" Gloria called out as she stepped inside.

When her friends looked up, both of them slender blondes wearing kerchiefs and flour-dusted aprons, they looked enough alike to be mother and daughter. Irene waved her wooden spoon. "Now that it's fall, we get up before daylight—but our Saturday's work is almost done," she added. "We're baking a few extra pies from our left-over dough and filling so those ingredients won't spend the weekend in the fridge."

Gloria inhaled deeply, identifying the deep sweetness of the pecan pies on the table as well as the tang of the goose-berry pie Phoebe was putting together. "I don't know how you do it," she murmured wistfully. "I've *never* baked a picture-perfect pie—let alone one that's fit to eat—yet you ladies bake dozens of them in a day."

Irene smiled kindly at her. "You're welcome to watch us anytime, honey."

"Maybe we could choose one kind of pie you'd like to bake and help you until you can make that recipe with your eyes closed," Phoebe suggested.

"Truth be told, when Truman was a boy, I wasn't much of a pie maker," Irene admitted in a nostalgic tone. "But he and his *dat* were *gut* sports and they ate my mistakes. I've had years of practice now—"

"And we know that even if a pie gets a little too brown around the edges, or the filling doesn't set up just right," Phoebe put in, "folks still think it's a treat—partly because they didn't make it themselves."

Gloria nodded, even though she doubted pie baking would ever be easy for her. "Say—was everything in *gut* order when you came in this morning?" she asked, glancing around the bakery. "I saw Phineas prowling the grounds last night, and he came in here."

Phoebe's and Irene's eyes widened. "I—I didn't notice that anything had been bothered," Irene replied.

"Nothing's missing, if that's what you mean," Phoebe added warily. "Why do you suppose he came in?"

Gloria shrugged. "He went into Christine's barn with her cows, too—and he checked out the Kuhns' cheese factory," she said. "Maybe he wasn't able to sleep and his curiosity was getting the best of him—but Annabelle was plenty irritated when she heard he'd been snooping. Phineas was in the kitchen this morning before Ruby and Beulah got downstairs to start breakfast, too."

Irene's brow furrowed. "I suppose it's best that we know he's inclined to wander around," she remarked doubtfully. "Anybody could come in the lodge late at night and the five of us gals living upstairs would probably never know it. Those walls are sturdy. We don't even hear one another when we're in our apartments getting ready for bed."

"If you suspect Phineas is going where he's not supposed to—like upstairs—you should tell Monroe and the preachers about it," Phoebe said firmly.

Gloria sighed. "I should probably ask Rosetta how to keep that from happening, too. We may have to install dead bolts on the doors—but even locks won't keep, um, *challenging* folks from visiting Promise Lodge."

Recalling the purpose of her visit, Gloria continued. "At breakfast, as Phineas insisted he was taking Annabelle away from the Old Order, a Bishop Clayton King came in," she recounted. "He said he was from the Council of Bishops in Lancaster County, and that he was here to set Promise Lodge back on the straight and narrow. He thinks we've gotten too progressive for our own *gut*."

"Why would he think that, if he just showed up this morning?" Irene asked with a puzzled frown.

"He and those other bishops out east have been reading our posts in *The Budget*," Gloria replied. She was already tiring of Clayton King's mission, and she hadn't even gotten fully acquainted with him. "Beulah asked me to let folks know about it—especially the women running businesses, and Rosetta. When I left, King was doing the talking and Bishop Monroe couldn't get a word in edgewise."

Phoebe and Irene crimped the edges of their piecrusts, cogitating over the information Gloria had just given them. Once again she envied their expertise, their effortless way of creating perfection in a pie pan. When Phoebe had slipped the final three pies into the oven, they gave Gloria their attention again.

"I suppose the first thing this fellow's going to jump on is the fact that Rosetta married my Truman, and that all of you Amish are fine with it," Irene said softly.

"He'll have something to say about us allowing single gals to rent lodge apartments and support themselves, too," Phoebe put in with a shake of her head. "We've gotten so accustomed to Bishop Monroe's more liberal way of doing things, we'll be in for a real shock if this Bishop Clayton starts flinging our *sins* in our faces. Like our bishop back in Coldstream used to do."

"Bishop Clayton won't like it one bit that our three women founders sold their farms to move away from that bishop," Irene pointed out. "He'll interpret that as the ultimate show of disrespect for the leader God chose to be in charge of them."

While Phoebe stacked their dirty bowls and utensils, Irene began to sweep around the worktable. "Once we get our pies labeled and packed into the van, we'll let you take the three extra ones back to the lodge with you, Gloria," she said. "Sounds like things there could use a little sweetening up."

"That's a fine idea," Gloria agreed. "I suspect that by the time word gets around, most everyone will be going to the lodge to meet this fellow. It could turn into a Saturday night potluck in the blink of an eye."

"So maybe it was God who whispered in our ears about making those extra pies this morning," Phoebe said lightly—although she sounded perfectly sincere. "Maybe He already knew we could make a contribution, and we've been carrying out His will without even realizing it." Her expression grew pensive, even as her blue eyes twinkled. "Because really, who's to say we *weren't* doing His will? Seems to me that topic's open to a lot of interpretations, on a lot of levels."

"I think you just hit a big nail smack on the head, Phoebe," Irene said. "We might need to remind ourselves—and maybe this King fellow—that the leaders of Promise Lodge have been following what they believe is God's will all along. But then, I'm a Mennonite, so I should keep my mouth shut, ain't so?"

"You're one of us, Irene, and your opinion counts!" Gloria said emphatically. "Truth be told, you two have made me feel better about this whole situation."

When she glanced out the window, Gloria saw Bishop Monroe and the preachers—including newlywed Marlin—coming down the lodge steps with Clayton King. Uncle Lester had returned from work, and he appeared pleased to be included in a group of such fine men. Gloria's heart welled up with hope.

"You know, we have three fine preachers and a bishop whose hearts are in the right place—and it's clear that God has blessed us all since we moved here from our previous homes," Gloria remarked proudly. "How can Bishop Clayton prevail? When he finds out how things work here, he'll either go back to Lancaster County with a different tale to tell that council, or he'll want to come and live at Promise Lodge himself!"

"I hope you're right, dearie," Irene murmured. "We'll leave your pies on the worktable and pray for the best."

Chapter Seven

The tension eased from Annabelle's shoulders after the menfolk offered to show Bishop Clayton around Promise Lodge—but when she looked through the kitchen window, she saw that Phineas wasn't among them. Daisy was running toward the group, however, barking and eyeing their newest guest, as well as the strange buggy and the fine horse in the lodge's side yard.

"Go on now, Daisy," Bishop Monroe said, waving her off. "Nothing here for you to get so excited about, girl."

Daisy senses more than we do about Clayton King— just as she barked when Phineas first showed up, Annabelle mused. *With any luck, Phineas has returned to his cabin . . . but most likely, he's waiting in the dining room. He won't let me off so easily.*

Annabelle decided to remain in the kitchen, surrounded by the other women, for as long as she could get by with it.

"I think we made some points with Bishop Clayton, suggesting we have a picnic for everyone tomorrow," Mattie was saying. "It's not a church Sunday, so he won't be preaching any sermons about our wayward tendencies—"

"I bet he'll make the most of being the guest of honor, though," Christine pointed out. "He's certainly got a way with words—but tomorrow my Laura turns eighteen, and I don't want her special day to be eclipsed by a big-wig bishop."

"You're absolutely right!" Ruby said as she headed toward the pantry. "How about if Beulah and I make some pretty sheet cakes, and maybe somebody could bring homemade ice cream to go with them?"

"What a *gut* idea! We won't have many more occasions for homemade ice cream this season," Frances Lehman put in. "I'll make chocolate—and I bet my new son, Lowell, will be happy to crank the ice-cream freezer if he gets to be the tester!"

"I'll bring vanilla, along with some toppings," Rosetta offered. "Truman loves homemade ice cream, and we've found several jars of flavored syrup on Irene's pantry shelves that need to be used up."

Annabelle opened the deep freeze in the mudroom and took out two big packets wrapped in white butcher paper. "Here's the shaved ham we bought on sale last week. I could stir up a big batch of barbeque sauce to simmer it in and make some buns for sandwiches."

"Perfect picnic food," Beulah said. "We can keep it warm in the steam table."

"I'll bring a big relish tray and a platter of deviled eggs," Mattie put in. "I'm glad we've gotten this picnic—and Laura's birthday—off to a *gut* start. The way to a man's heart has always been through his stomach, and I can't think Bishop Clayton's any different. Especially because I've heard no mention of a wife or family."

"We'll ask him about that tomorrow," said Christine. "We should be ready with all sorts of topics, in case the conversation focuses on our tendency to be too independent!"

Annabelle laughed along with the other gals, hoping that

Phineas was listening. He needed to see that the women of Promise Lodge refused to be any man's doormat. Everyone turned when Gloria stepped into the mudroom with a double pie carrier in one hand and a dome-covered gooseberry pie in the other.

"Looks like you visited Promise Lodge Pies at the right time!" Beulah crowed. "We're planning a picnic for everybody tomorrow at noon, to welcome Bishop Clayton."

"Might not hurt to take one of these over to Lester's place," Frances suggested as she helped her daughter set the pies on the counter. "Lester stopped in, and he's offered Bishop Clayton a room at his house. I told them I'd go over this evening with their supper."

"It's a *gut* thing we cleaned his place last week." Gloria glanced eagerly around the group. "What's Bishop Clayton like? What did he say when you ladies all showed up *out of the blue*?"

Mattie laughed. "It took some of the wind out of his sails when he learned that we founding sisters all got married this year, like the faithful Amish women we are—and that two of us married church leaders. We didn't mention the part about Rosetta hitching up with a Mennonite."

"*Jah*, he seemed to be on his *gut* behavior, just taking in names and faces for now," Ruby remarked. "But if he's followed all of your columns in *The Budget* since the founding of Promise Lodge, he's sure to mention that part someday."

"And our ongoing conversation with him should be a two-way street," Rosetta said firmly. "It would be interesting—helpful to our cause—to know about the district Bishop Clayton serves, and maybe find out what folks think of him, ain't so? Surely some of us here have far-flung cousins or friends from out east—"

Annabelle held up her hand, nodding and then pointing purposefully toward the dining room. The faces around her lit up with the realization that Phineas might be able to hear their conversation. Snatching the lined tablet and pen they used for their ongoing shopping list, Annabelle scribbled, "I'll write some letters to friends. Our farm was just a few miles from Paradise, where B. C. is from."

As the note made its way around the circle of women, they nodded and smiled at Annabelle. She felt good being able to help these women—and it would be wonderful to hear from her friends back home as she satisfied her own curiosity about Clayton King.

Rosetta had brought along a sack of her goats' milk soaps to restock her display in the lobby, so—winking at the ladies—she headed through the dining room with it. "Phineas!" she exclaimed, as though she was surprised to see him. "I thought you might've gone off with the other men and Bishop Clayton."

Annabelle smiled as she listened for her husband's response.

"I've nothing to say to King," he said tersely. "I've got plenty to talk to Annabelle about, however, yet it seems I'm always *waiting* for her. Have you women finished your picnic planning?"

"We have," Rosetta replied cheerfully, "and we hope you'll join us for the festivities tomorrow. It'll be a fine time for you to meet folks, and to share a wonderful-*gut* meal with us. Here—you might enjoy a bar of this orange and cornmeal soap," she added. "Most men find it cleans the grime from their hands without making them smell too girly."

Annabelle nearly laughed out loud at the thought of Phineas washing with scented soap, yet she appreciated Rosetta's efforts to soften him up.

"I suppose you expect me to pay for this?" Phineas shot back.

"Oh no," Rosetta assured him without missing a beat. "I sell it to lots of customers hereabouts, but I'm happy for my friends and our guests to have as much of it as they want. My goats and I enjoy being useful, you see."

Once again Annabelle felt embarrassed by her husband's testiness—the chip he'd been carrying on his shoulder since he'd arrived. It was such a blessing that Rosetta and her sisters kept a positive attitude no matter what was going on around them. But all too soon they were on their way back to their homes. As though Ruby and Beulah sensed that Annabelle needed their company, they stayed in the kitchen to bake Laura's birthday cakes. Annabelle was happy to help them.

She wasn't surprised when Phineas appeared in the doorway, one eyebrow raised as he looked at her. "Is it finally my turn?"

Annabelle knew better than to keep her husband waiting any longer, so she set aside the two cake pans she'd sprayed. "Let's take a walk," she suggested, figuring to keep Phineas out where other people would see them. "It's a beautiful day."

"Is it?" he demanded. "I've spent the entire morning hanging around in the dining room, waiting for *you*. It's obvious your priorities have changed since—"

"Your priorities—and your attitude—could use a change, too, mister!" Annabelle blurted. "For a man who's come to lure me away, you're being awfully cranky. Any reasonable woman would've stopped listening to you long ago."

Annabelle's blood stilled in her veins. Why had she sassed Phineas? He would only be angrier with her—

But every word is true! He should know that honey

attracts better than vinegar, when it comes to turning a woman's head . . . and reclaiming her heart.

"I totally agree," Beulah remarked as she continued measuring ingredients for the cakes. "Folks here make a point of being pleasant and polite, Phineas, so you're coming across like a big dill pickle, by comparison. Just saying."

Annabelle held her breath, awaiting her husband's comeback. He remained silent, however, before beckoning her with his hand. "Let's take that walk, Annabelle. We have much to discuss."

Why did she feel like a lamb being led to slaughter as she followed Phineas through the dining room? Annabelle allowed him to open the front door, and as she stepped out onto the lodge's big front porch she inhaled deeply to steady her nerves.

Help me out, Lord. Phineas seems to be provoking my mouthy side this morning, and that's not a gut way to behave right now.

Annabelle paused on the top of the stairs, gazing out over the lush green grass and the maple trees, which were now tinted with orange and gold. Beyond Mattie's partially cleared produce plots, Christine's black-and-white Holsteins grazed in the pasture. The surface of Rainbow Lake resembled a mirror, utterly smooth as it reflected a few fluffy white clouds and the blue sky. Up the hill, Allen Troyer and Phoebe Hershberger's future home sat nestled among more trees that were taking on their autumn colors.

"It's a pretty tract of land these people have settled," Phineas remarked as he came up beside her. "How long have they been here?"

"About a year and a half," Annabelle replied. Even though he spoke as though she wasn't among the residents, she was relieved to hear sincere admiration in his voice.

She remained wary of where this line of conversation might lead, however.

"They've made a lot of progress, building so many homes and getting so many businesses up and running," her husband continued. "And they seem to be prospering without a lot of help from nearby Mennonites or English, which is unusual."

"Well, I understand that before he married Rosetta, Truman Wickey cleared a lot of the land, dug holes for the foundations, and laid out the main road with his heavy equipment—he's a Mennonite landscaping contractor," she added. "But otherwise, *jah*, these folks have established Promise Lodge in an incredibly short time. They're *gut* people. My kind of people."

Phineas shifted closer, until his shirtsleeve brushed her arm. "I agree with that—although I have to wonder about Clayton King coming here from Paradise to sniff around. He must've taken over as the new bishop for one of the Lancaster church districts since we've been gone, because I've never heard of him."

Annabelle's pulse settled into a more regular, calm beat. It was a relief to be having a normal conversation—about someone other than herself. "Me neither."

"And it's *interesting* that King has already wormed his way into Lester Lehman's home rather than settling for a cabin," Phineas remarked a bit more sharply. He clasped his hands behind him, gazing at her. "It's also quite obvious that he's got eyes for *you*, Annabelle. Be very careful."

Be very careful. What was that supposed to mean? Annabelle detected a note of envy in her husband's observations—and a warning. She turned her face, although Phineas had probably already noticed her pink cheeks. "Why would a bishop from out east have any reason to notice me?" she asked softly. "I've done nothing to attract his—"

"He's an unattached man away from the prying eyes of his district," Phineas interrupted. "And you're an attractive woman who appears to be at loose ends, as well. Men can sense these things, and King's the type to use his position—his charisma—to his advantage. Don't fall for it."

Annabelle's eyes widened. Phineas had called her *attractive*. And Bishop Clayton did indeed possess an allure—an unwavering confidence—along with a voice and a smile that any woman with eyes and ears would notice. But why had Phineas zeroed in on these qualities? Why did he think she would respond to the visiting bishop's attention?

Because you already have. Your face is an open book and your heart is hungry.

Annabelle started down the stairs, eager to keep moving. "So you don't think Bishop Clayton's married?" she asked, hoping to redirect her husband's line of thought.

"King seems smooth to the point of being slick," Phineas replied as he started down the steps alongside her. "I've learned a few things by living English. King's not telling everything he knows—and Monroe Burkholder's too upstanding a man to realize that."

Annabelle sucked in her breath. "What do you mean? Why would anyone come here to take advantage of Bishop Monroe—or any of us?"

Phineas wrapped his hand around hers as they crossed the lawn. "I don't know. But it'll make my stay here even more interesting while I win you back, Annabelle."

She blinked. As they approached Lester Lehman's place, where Bishop Clayton stood chatting with Monroe and the other men, she got an odd feeling as Phineas smiled broadly and waved to them.

He's parading me in front of them. Phineas is claiming me with the clasp of his hand, so all those men will see that I belong to him.

She could recall a time when she would've been giddy over such a display of Phineas's affection, yet a worm of uneasiness squirmed in her soul. Her husband was speaking more gently now, seeming to enjoy her company, yet Annabelle felt like a prize to be won in some sort of competition.

And from Lester's porch, the intensity of Bishop Clayton's gaze told her that the game was on.

Chapter Eight

On Sunday, Cyrus looked around the crowd gathered outside the lodge, searching for Gloria before the picnic got underway—because he suspected that once Clayton King accepted Bishop Monroe's invitation to say a few words, they were in for a sermon. King impressed him as the sort who would preach at every possible opportunity.

And why was he here, anyway?

Cyrus forgot all about the visiting bishop, however, when he spotted Gloria coming down the steps with a double pie carrier in her hand. The dark brown hair tucked beneath her *kapp* glimmered richly in the sunlight, matching her sparkling brown eyes, and in her cape dress of deep lavender she was too cute to ignore. He quickly made his way over to the dessert table.

"I don't suppose you made those pies?" he teased when he came up beside her. Then he kicked himself. *Why would Gloria want to be reminded that she isn't much of a cook, dummy?*

Gloria, however, seemed delighted to see him. "I don't suppose I did," she replied lightly, "but these pies from Phoebe and Irene's bakery will be the best desserts here, ain't so?"

"Can't argue with that," Cyrus agreed as she removed

the lids from the metal carrier. "I'm a big fan of cherry pie—and that rhubarb pie won't last long, either, once folks realize it's here. Always a *gut* idea to visit the dessert table first, before you fill your plate with the real meal, to be sure you get the goodies you really want."

Gloria's smile told him her mind was following his flirtatious train of thought. "And what goodies do you really want, Cyrus?" she whispered.

His pulse shot off like a racehorse leaving the starting gate. She'd beaten him to the punch! She'd obviously gotten past the humiliation of falling into the lake, so Cyrus answered her question without a lick of hesitation.

"Time alone with you, Gloria," he replied, standing so close that he caught the clean scent of her. "And a kiss. Hopefully more than one, *jah*?"

Gloria's eyes lit up as she sliced the pies. "That could probably be arranged. Where shall we go? And when?"

Cyrus had daydreamed about this moment so many times, his suggestion popped right out of his mouth. "After we eat, I'll take my dirty dishes to the washtub—"

"And I'll go inside to use the bathroom," she put in. "Instead of coming back out here, I'll head out through the mudroom to meet you—"

"Behind Allen and Phoebe's new place," Cyrus suggested. "This being Sunday, nobody'll be up there working, so—"

"We'll have those shady woods all to ourselves," Gloria finished with a smile.

Cyrus's heart was pounding so hard that he didn't have a clue what was going on around them—until Bishop Monroe raised his hand to get everyone's attention.

"Folks, our guest of honor, Bishop Clayton King, wants to answer some of the questions you've been asking," he announced. "I told him we could spare him a few minutes before we eat, and he promised to keep it short—much shorter than a Sunday sermon!"

Everyone laughed as King positioned himself on the top step. Cyrus sighed. Long tables in the shade were covered with food, and some folks had already taken seats at other tables—or were sitting in lawn chairs in the yard—so it seemed like the perfect time for loading their plates. But he politely focused on the visiting bishop, pleased that Gloria remained beside him.

Wearing a brilliant white Sunday-best shirt, his broad-brimmed black hat, and well-cut black pants, Bishop Clayton outshone the other men, who'd come dressed for a picnic in their colored shirts and everyday pants. King wore his silver-spangled dark hair and beard shorter than most of the local fellows did, too, which made him appear a cut above them—even though the Old Order Amish were all about conforming so that no one stood out in a crowd.

"My friends, I've come to help you see the light," King began in a voice that resonated richly. "Jesus said, 'I am the light of the world,' and the book of Matthew, chapter five, tells us to 'Let Your light so shine before men, that they may see Your good works, and glorify Your Father which is in heaven.'" He paused to look a few folks in the eye. "But as the Council of Bishops sees it, Promise Lodge has hidden its light beneath a proverbial bushel basket woven from progressive ideas that are leading you *away* from God's favor and salvation."

Cyrus sighed inwardly. He'd once sat through part of a revival meeting in a park, where the English preacher had spoken at great length in this same vein—and the facial expressions around him confirmed that King had planted the first seeds of doubt in a few people's minds. Cyrus was tempted to slip away, hoping Gloria would follow, except she tucked her hand into the crook of his arm.

Cyrus lost all power to think about anything except the nearness of the lovely young woman beside him, so he stood stock-still, pretending to listen.

"Those of us on the council eagerly follow the news of newly formed Amish communities as reported in *The Budget*," King continued. "Although we're impressed with the progress Promise Lodge has made in a very short time, we're *quite* concerned about the worldly, English influence that has slithered into your Old Order faith, much as the serpent beguiled Eve in the Garden."

Folks were shifting uneasily, remaining absolutely silent as King went on. He spoke earnestly, leaning into his words like a father trying to save the souls of his children . . . casting a spell like an invisible web of righteousness that wouldn't allow them to fall into the everlasting fires of hell.

"Promise Lodge appears to be very prosperous," Bishop Clayton said in a near-whisper, "and I—the council—would hate to see you lose everything you've come to love here. But we fear you've turned a deaf ear to the teachings of our Lord, adopting your own worldly path rather than remaining within the confines of the *Ordnung*, which forbids members to marry outside the Old Order and expects women to stay home and submit to their menfolk."

When murmurings rose from the crowd, King pressed his palms together in an attitude of prayer, further beseeching the crowd to heed his warning. "This picnic isn't the time or place for me to further explore the consequences of such wayward tendencies, friends, but I ask you all to pray fervently over this message I've brought you. We'll speak more on these topics in the days to come, and it's my hope—yea, my highest mission—to lead you back into God's unchanging, everlasting light."

Cyrus blinked. The angle of the noonday sun suddenly bathed Clayton King in the brilliance of a halo so bright that Cyrus had to glance away—and that's when he noticed the fear in Gloria's dark eyes. As she gazed at the bishop on the porch, mesmerized, she appeared very doubtful about the future of the community she'd come to love.

"Come on, honey-girl, let's go for a walk," he whispered. Other folks were starting to move around and speak in low voices, so Cyrus steered Gloria toward the back of the lodge. "We can eat later, after we digest what we just heard."

When they were out of sight, Gloria turned to Cyrus, her forehead puckered with a frown. "Do you think he'll make us shut down the apartments?" she whispered. "Does this mean that the Kuhn sisters and Irene will have to go back to living with their menfolk—and that Mattie and Christine can no longer run the produce stand and the dairy?"

Cyrus's eyes widened. In mere moments, Clayton King had convinced this young woman that Promise Lodge was doomed. Gloria might be innocent of the ways of the world, but she didn't deserve to be brainwashed by a bishop who obviously loved playing to a crowd.

"Let's not jump to conclusions, sweetie," he said, gently grasping her shoulder. "The folks who founded Promise Lodge haven't come so far by forgetting about God, as King was suggesting."

"But nobody said anything!" Gloria protested. "Why didn't Bishop Monroe or—or Preacher Amos—stand up to Bishop Clayton and explain how we do things here?"

"They will," Cyrus assured her. "They were being polite, letting King have his say while everyone could listen to him at the same time. I can't see Mattie, Christine, or Rosetta—or even Irene—giving up their successful businesses to stay home and be *haus fraus*. Can you?"

Gloria blinked, considering what he'd said. "Not really,"

she admitted with a smile. "And their husbands will surely set Bishop Clayton straight about why they allow their wives to run businesses—"

"And let's not forget that those gals originally went into business to support themselves," he pointed out. "Truth be told, every one of them is at home a *gut* bit of the time. And it isn't as though they have kids to look after."

Gloria let out the breath she'd been holding. "*Jah*, there's that."

"Don't let King's speech upset you, Gloria. He's a smooth talker, big on quoting the Bible to drive his points home, but he's no match for Bishop Monroe and the other folks who've made new lives for themselves here." Cyrus smiled at her, pleased at the way she'd gravitated close enough to him that he could encircle her with his arms.

Gloria's smile came out like the sunshine after rain. "You're right, Cyrus," she murmured as she looked at him adoringly. "He's probably all bark and no bite."

"And I'm all kiss," he whispered. "What do you say, pretty girl? We're all alone and—"

When she stood on tiptoe, her eyes closed tightly, Cyrus reveled in the warm sweetness of her lips. Gloria relaxed in his arms as the kiss deepened, and it was several long, lovely seconds before she eased away.

"That was perfect," she whispered. Her brown eyes were as wide as saucers and they reminded him of hot coffee—or maple syrup, dark and sweet.

"It was," he agreed breathlessly. "But maybe we should get back—"

"Before folks wonder where we went," Gloria said as she slipped out of his embrace. "My *mamm*—and Preacher Marlin—would think we were misbehaving in a big way if they knew we were kissing right after Bishop Clayton warned us about our wayward tendencies."

Cyrus gestured for Gloria to precede him as they rejoined the gathering on the front lawn—because if she lingered one second longer, he'd be kissing her again. She returned to the dessert table to help Laura put slices of pie on plates, her cheeks tinted a delicate shade of pink. When he saw Jonathan in line at the long buffet table, ready to fill his plate, Cyrus flashed him a triumphant thumbs-up.

"Score another point for *me*," he teased when he reached his brother. "First kiss—first base. And you are miles behind!"

"Puh!" Jonathan shot back. "I'm a man with a plan, and you're full of yourself. It's Laura's birthday, and I'm going to be the best present she's ever received."

"Laura, eh? Settling for the last apple on the tree, figuring she's as desperate to be picked as you are?" Cyrus challenged as he took a paper plate from the stack.

Jonathan stabbed thin slices of ham bathed in barbeque sauce and arranged them on his open bun. "How can you say that? Laura's a delightful girl—"

"And she's what—eighteen? You're hoping she'll be impressed that an older man's asking her out?" Cyrus shrugged playfully. Laura *was* a delightful girl—and cute—but razzing his brother was part of the game. "Well, *gut* luck to you, guy. You're gonna need it, if you're not ready to cough up five hundred bucks."

Jonathan barely tasted his food as he racked his brain for the perfect opening line—the invitation that Laura would find irresistible. He was hoping to find a time and place that would be private, or at least away from his younger brother's watchful eye, because if Cyrus observed them, Jonathan knew he'd be teased forever about what he had—or hadn't—done to convince Laura to go out with him.

Why does this feel so difficult? Laura's a nice person—much nicer than Cyrus—and if she's not interested, she'll at least let you down easy.

Jonathan swallowed hard to get his bite of ham sandwich down. If Laura wasn't interested, he was back to square one—back to nowhere. He was making this invitation much harder than it needed to be, but there was no denying that his brother was more experienced and more suave when it came to getting girls to notice him. Would Laura think he was a total nerd? Hopelessly clueless?

When Jonathan saw Beulah and Ruby coming down the porch steps, each of them carrying a large sheet cake, he sat up straighter. Across the crowd, Laura's face lit up with surprise when she surmised that the cakes were for her.

Look at her, man—she's gorgeous. What would it feel like to have those baby blues focused on you as though you were the only guy in the world?

When Cyrus rose to refill his plate, gesticulating toward the Kuhn sisters as they lit the candles on one of the cakes, Jonathan got a sudden idea. What was a birthday without presents? What could he give Laura that would tell her he was sincerely interested in her—and not just going along with a bet he knew better than to mention?

A few moments later, Jonathan was loping across the lawn as though he was headed to his cabin, except he kept going. He heard Christine announcing to everyone that they were all invited to celebrate Laura's eighteenth birthday, and then the air was filled with voices singing "Happy Birthday"—

And as Jonathan entered the back door of the greenhouse where his cousins, Sam and Simon, sold all manner of pumpkins, mums, and ornamental gourds, he spotted exactly what he wanted to give Laura. The ceramic planter was painted in bright colors—depicting a smiling yellow scarecrow in a red hat and blue overalls, holding a big green basket—and it held an orange mum that was blooming profusely. The overall effect was cheerful, like Laura, and Jonathan could already imagine her beaming at him as he gave it to her. He lifted the planter from the table and left a twenty-dollar bill in its place, so no one would think the item had been stolen.

As he closed the greenhouse door behind him, Jonathan's heartbeat settled into a happy thrum. He was on the right track—he just knew it.

When he was making his way back to the picnic, however, he realized that everyone—including Cyrus—would see what he was doing . . . and if Laura happened to reject him in front of all those people, Jonathan sensed he'd never ask another woman for a date.

He detoured behind the ten cabins and placed the mum on the small concrete slab at the back door of the one he shared with his brother. Then he moseyed back toward the crowd, where folks were lining up to fetch a piece of Laura's birthday cake and congratulate her. Somehow he found himself at the end of the queue of well-wishers—and Cyrus was nowhere in sight—

And then he was face to face with Laura, holding out his empty plate.

"Chocolate or lemon?" she asked with a bright smile. "And we have homemade ice cream to go with it, too!"

Jonathan felt tongue-tied, yet he heard himself say, "What if I have a piece of each, with a scoop of that vanilla ice cream? And—and what if you fix your plate and join me, Laura?"

Her mouth dropped open. She looked downright dazzled

by his invitation. "*Jah*, I'd like that," she murmured as she placed two large squares of cake on his plate. "Where shall we go?"

"How about if I set out a couple of chairs behind my cabin? It's shady there—and if Bishop Clayton feels another sermon coming on, we won't have to listen."

Where had that come from? It wasn't his way to make light of church leaders—but Laura's mouth was an O and her eyes were twinkling. "I'll be there as soon as I scoop us up some extra ice cream!" she replied. "I wouldn't be a bit surprised if he started in on us again while everyone's eating their cake."

Somehow Jonathan's feet carried him away from the crowd, because his mind was too awash in wonder to guide him anywhere. Laura had said *yes*, just like that! She seemed delighted to have an excuse to get away from the picnic.

When he reached the cabin, he quickly carried out the two chairs from the small table where he and Cyrus sometimes ate—and then he hauled out the table, too. Jonathan had just set the scarecrow planter in the center of the table when Laura appeared from around the side of his cabin. She had the mischievous look of one who was skipping a church service. And she was giggling!

"How did you know?" she teased as she slipped into one of the chairs. She set down her plate, as well as a bowl that held several scoops of chocolate and vanilla ice cream. "Bishop Clayton was starting up the porch stairs as I was scooping our ice cream! We escaped just in time!"

Now that Jonathan had performed the minor miracle of convincing Laura to join him, he had a shy moment when his mind couldn't form words. He was aware of gazing at her with what was probably a goofy grin on his face, yet she didn't seem to think he was acting weird.

"What a wonderful birthday surprise!" Laura said, patting the chair beside her. "First the Kuhn sisters bringing out two big cakes—and everyone singing to me!—and now I'm here with you for our own private party. There must be something magical about turning eighteen if so many fine, fun things are happening."

There must be something magical about turning eighteen . . .

As he sat down, Jonathan watched her lips move. He was held spellbound by the sight of Laura lifting a big spoonful of ice cream to her mouth before he reminded himself to hold up his end of the conversation. "Eighteen," he repeated softly. "It's a big milestone. By then you've been out of school awhile and you've had time to figure out what to do with the rest of your life—"

"Oh, I haven't settled on any one option," Laura put in with a decisive nod. "I enjoy baking and selling my goodies at Mattie's produce stand, because you meet interesting people there. But if another opportunity comes along, I'm on it! Phoebe and the other ladies here are my inspiration because most of them—like my *mamm*—started entirely new lives and businesses when they were forty—or older!"

Jonathan cut a forkful of cake, relieved that Laura was a talker. She'd made an interesting observation, too, rather than nattering about every inconsequential thing that came to mind. "I've been impressed by *all* of the residents of Promise Lodge since I arrived last winter," he remarked. "You think outside the box instead of assuming that things have to be done the same old way. Bishop Monroe's a fine example, training and selling his Clydesdales to folks who show them rather than farm with them."

"Oh, but those horses are beautiful, and so *huge*," Laura

said breathlessly. "And it's wonderful, the way Bishop Monroe has hired Lowell Kurtz and Lavern Peterscheim to help him, too. By the time they've finished school, those boys will be ready for new careers instead of automatically going into their *dat*s' barrel-making and blacksmithing trades."

Jonathan nodded. "Truth be told, Sam and Simon's nursery business is already much busier and more profitable than the store we left behind in Ohio," he said. "Cyrus and I were lucky they asked us to come along, because our futures would've been limited back home, where their older brothers were in charge of the business."

Laura's blue eyes sparkled as she focused on her bite of ice cream. "You're meeting some new girls, too," she said softly. "When families intermarry and swim in the same gene pool for too many generations, you run into problems when the kids come along."

Jonathan swallowed hard. The idea of marrying and making babies had always seemed intimidating—a dream he could never attain—yet Laura was discussing it matter-of-factly without overtly hinting that he should marry her.

Or was she flirting with him, and he wasn't savvy enough to realize it?

When Laura looked at him, Jonathan's world stood still . . . until a little tickle of happiness deep down in his soul gave him the nerve to hold her gaze for what seemed like forever.

Laura smiled and relaxed in her chair. "I'm really glad you asked me over, Jonathan," she murmured. "Before, you've always been with Allen and Cyrus, and I never really got a chance to know you for *you*—because those guys are always horsing around or ganging up on Gloria." She let out a contented sigh. "It's so quiet and nice here. And look at this! You've even put a centerpiece on the table. Most guys wouldn't have a clue about doing that."

"I—that's for you!" Jonathan blurted. His nerves came back in full force, because he really wanted her to like his gift. "It's colorful and cheerful—like you!—so it's your birthday present, Laura. I—I'm glad you noticed it."

Her smile was nothing short of glorious. "Wow," she murmured as she picked up the planter. She turned it this way and that, smiling at the ceramic scarecrow and the mum's bright orange flowers. "What a wonderful-*gut* gift. I can plant the mum to bloom again next year, and even if it doesn't make it—because I don't have much of a green thumb—I'll still have the planter you gave me. *Denki*, Jonathan."

"You're welcome," he whispered. He was too awestruck to say anything more.

After a moment, Laura teasingly tapped his plate with her spoon. "You've got a puddle of ice cream. The only way to keep it from running over is to slurp it straight from the plate, ain't so?"

"Or to soak it up with my other piece of cake," he said as he pressed the remaining cake into the melted ice cream with his fork. "Slurping from my plate would lead to disaster, for sure and for certain."

"Oh, but there's a technique to it—see?"

Before Jonathan could blink, Laura tipped her plate so the liquid ran neatly between her lips without spilling a single drop. She'd obviously practiced this move—but her expertise was soon lost on him. All he could see was her lovely neck stretching toward the plate . . . her lips moving on the rim . . . her throat muscles contracting each time she swallowed. All the while, she was trying not to giggle and make a mess.

"Now you try it!" she urged him when she'd lowered

her plate. "A guy with steady, strong hands like yours won't have any problem at all."

She'd noticed his hands? Immediately they began to tremble—one more reason Jonathan didn't dare drain his plate the way Laura had. She was gazing at him with such sparkling eyes, however, that he didn't want to disappoint her—didn't want to lose the lightness of the moment— so he grabbed the bowl that held the remaining scoops of ice cream.

With his fork, he deftly kept the blobs of melting choco- late and vanilla in the bowl as he lifted it to his lips. It was all he could do to concentrate on sipping the sweet, thick liquid as Laura followed his every move. Many times he and Cyrus had drained their cereal bowls this way, so he made short work of the melted ice cream before returning the bowl to the table.

"How'd I do?" he asked, glancing down at his shirt. He was relieved that he hadn't spilled anything, because Cyrus would never let him hear the end of it.

Laura laughed. "*Anybody* can drink from a bowl, but I'll let you off easy this time," she teased. "It's my birthday, so I can play nice. And since I'm eighteen now, you can kiss me, *jah*?"

Jonathan's mouth dropped open, yet the color rising in Laura's cheeks told him she was as surprised by her flirta- tious suggestion as he was. It seemed reassuring that such a levelheaded girl could blurt out words before thinking about them—the way he sometimes did. And if she wanted him to kiss her . . . had she been thinking about such a kiss before their impromptu private party?

Jonathan watched his hand as it gently cupped Laura's soft cheek, as though he had no control over it. Laura eased toward him, appearing jittery yet determined to make the most of this moment. It was up to him as the man, the older one, to lead the way into whatever a kiss might bring, wasn't it?

When his lips met hers, magic happened. They didn't kiss for nearly long enough, but when her sigh mingled with his, Jonathan eased away before he could mess things up—or overthink a simple gesture of affection that most guys his age took for granted.

Laura's cheeks were bright pink. "I—I hope you don't think I was too—"

"I can't think," he whispered.

"Nobody's ever kissed me, but I thought since it was my birthday—"

"Nobody's ever kissed me, either."

Jonathan froze. Why had he admitted such incriminating information? He was twenty-four, and he'd been to Singings and the other group social activities that all Amish kids participated in, but now he felt so exposed he might as well be sitting beside Laura without any clothes on.

He looked away, waiting for her to question him. Or mock him. After sharing such a brief, lovely moment, he'd surely messed up any chance of ever spending time with Laura again—

"We all have to start somewhere, with somebody," she murmured. "I'm glad I got to start with you, Jonathan."

His heart got softer than the ice cream left in the bowl. When he looked at Laura again, she seemed younger and more fragile—more vulnerable—than when she'd first joined him. And he loved her for it.

"Me too," he whispered as he took her hand.

Chapter Nine

Annabelle inhaled deeply as she pulled two pans of date-raisin spice bars from the oven. The entire lodge smelled like cinnamon and ground cloves—and she didn't even mind that the other ladies weren't around to taste the bars when they'd cooled. The Kuhns and Gloria had gone to Forest Grove with Irene and Phoebe when they delivered their pies, so Annabelle was savoring some quiet time in the kitchen. She'd put a pork roast into the oven and would soon add some potatoes and carrots, so supper would be ready when her friends got home.

Phineas was helping the men shingle the roof of Allen and Phoebe's house, so he wasn't demanding anything of her, either. She hadn't known such contentment since she'd spent time cooking in her own kitchen back home, before he'd abandoned her—and complicated her life beyond imagining.

As Annabelle spread a layer of powdered sugar frosting on the warm bars, she considered what to bake next—maybe biscuits or corn bread muffins, or a coffee cake. Tomorrow was Saturday, and the women would be preparing food to serve at the common meal after church on

Sunday. It would be a favor to Beulah and Ruby if they didn't have to fuss with everyone's breakfast, as well.

As she ran hot water into the sink, a sound in the mudroom made her turn. Annabelle's heart stilled warily. Bishop Clayton was stepping through the back door—and the way he held Annabelle's gaze told her it was no coincidence that he'd chosen this particular time to visit. She wished Daisy had barked a warning, but the dog was probably in the Kurtzes' pasture with Harley's sheep.

"Hello there, Bishop," Annabelle called out, hoping she sounded more confident than she felt. "If you're looking for lunch—or the Kuhns who cooked it—you're late."

"*Denki*, but the neighbors are keeping Lester's place stocked for us," he replied as he entered the kitchen. "I feasted on lasagna this noon, so food's the least of my concerns. It's *you* I've been worried about, Annabelle. You, and the tenuous situation you're in, no thanks to your truculent husband."

Annabelle had always resented folks who used fancy words, but she wasn't about to ask what *tenuous* and *truculent* meant—especially when he was referring to Phineas. Clayton King could talk in word circles, but he'd eventually come to his point. So she would wait him out.

"Worried?" she asked, turning back to her dishwater. "Doesn't the Bible tell us not to worry, because—as He does for the lilies of the field and the birds of the air—our Lord will provide for all our needs?"

Clayton glanced at the pans of frosted bars, his lips twitching with a smile. "You're a wise woman, Mrs. Beachey," he replied. "Which makes it all the more troublesome that Phineas has committed the unforgivable sin, putting you in limbo—because you can't leave him, and he can't be readmitted to the Old Order. He knowingly strayed from the path to salvation by forsaking his vow to the church, and now you're paying the price for his mistake, as well. I'm sorry, dear Annabelle," he added in a whisper.

Her heart thudded faster. Bishop Clayton was allowing no possibility at all for Phineas to reconcile with her or the church—to him, it was a black and white situation. Although most bishops would see her situation this way, Annabelle was grateful that Bishop Monroe had allowed for some gray area, some wiggle room, when he'd talked with her and Phineas these past few days.

This wasn't the time to challenge Bishop Clayton or to pit his opinion against Monroe's, however. He'd called her *dear Annabelle*, implying affection for her . . . perhaps in direct response to the way Phineas had clasped her hand a few days ago. It wasn't a game she wanted to play, but she saw no way out of it.

Annabelle was searching for a way to steer the conversation in a different direction when Clayton came to stand beside her. Once again she realized how tall and fit he was, how his suspenders skimmed a firm torso, and how his dark eyes burned with an inner fire. He held her gaze as he rolled the sleeves of his crisp white shirt to his elbows . . . which gave her the odd sensation that he was baring himself in a most intimate way, even though he remained fully clothed.

She blinked. He was taking the tea towel from the stove handle, as though he intended to dry the dishes—so she began to wash them. What else was she to do? The bishop seemed quite aware that they were alone in the lodge, and he wasn't giving her a chance to avoid the difficult topic he'd introduced.

"You don't have to help, you know," she said.

Clayton dried the hand-cranked beater and the bowl she'd washed. "Won't hurt me to engage in some kitchen duty while we talk," he remarked lightly. "I imagine you've missed your kids—especially your daughters and their help—since you left your home in Ohio."

Annabelle blinked. Had Phineas only told him they'd lived in Ohio, rather than down the road from him in Lancaster County? Had her husband also told Clayton they had daughters? She wasn't good at lying on the spur of the moment—

Something told her Clayton was fishing, and that she'd better play it straight so she didn't get caught. For one thing, she didn't like having to explain or apologize for her childless life. "God didn't bless Phineas and me with children," she murmured. "I've accepted His will about that matter and made the most of the life He's given me."

"It's a shame your husband didn't see fit to do the same," the bishop said without missing a beat. Then he smiled gently at her. "I didn't intend to ruffle your feathers, Annabelle. I just wanted you to know that you can confide in me. I'm sure you've been . . . unsettled by your husband's reappearance. And your quandary."

She focused on the pan she was scrubbing, wishing for a way to end this uncomfortable conversation.

"If you need to relocate," Clayton continued, "I'd be happy to help you establish yourself in a community that would welcome you and support you. Phineas must finally come to realize that he can't remain with you and that you won't live English with him. You *don't* intend to jump the fence, do you?"

"Of course not!" Annabelle blurted. She gripped the rim of the sink, hoping to maintain her hold on reality as Clayton made such an alarming offer. Somehow she found the strength to look him in the eye, aware that he was standing much too close to her. "I intend to stay right here at Promise Lodge, where I've already reestablished myself," she stated.

Her mind went blank. Annabelle reached into the dishwater for the silverware on the bottom of the sink, desperate for a safe topic of conversation. "What's your line of work, Bishop Clayton?" she asked. "I'm surprised you can be away from your shop so long—"

"I own a warehouse that supplies barrels of bulk groceries to Plain stores all over the Midwest," he replied as he dried more utensils. "We ship everything from noodles to baking mixes to popcorn and candies—which get bagged and labeled for sale by those stores' employees. My partner's running the business in my absence."

"Ah. You supply places like the bulk store in Forest Grove, where Irene and Phoebe sell their pies," Annabelle remarked. She hoped she hadn't brought up another point of contention with him, considering that he didn't like women to own businesses.

"That's right, and there's a similar store in Cloverdale and another one over in Morning Star. It's hard to find an Amish or Mennonite settlement that doesn't have such a business," Clayton remarked. He held Annabelle's gaze again, as though he knew how uncomfortable it made her. "I've spent some of my time here visiting those stores to see firsthand how they're doing."

Annabelle thrust her hands back into the dishwater so Clayton couldn't see how badly they were trembling. Folks had noticed his buggy coming and going, and he'd given her a plausible answer, yet she still didn't like the direction their conversation was taking. What could she say to convince him to leave her alone?

As though he could read her anxious thoughts, the bishop leaned his elbows on the rim of the sink to bring his eyes to the same level as hers. He had shifted subtly, until his arm was pressed firmly against her. "The business earns me a very comfortable living, Annabelle," he murmured.

"Again, if you'd care to relocate, I'd see that you were well taken care of."

Alarm bells jangled in Annabelle's mind. "Why have you come here today?" she demanded loudly. "And why have you come to Promise Lodge?"

As soon as those questions left her mouth, Annabelle knew she'd overstepped. But she was asking what all her friends wanted to know, wasn't she? Clayton had been tiptoeing around a lot of issues since he'd arrived, and folks were wondering why. He was a great one for asking them a lot of pressing questions, but not very forthcoming when it came to answering any.

Bishop Clayton's face softened as he focused on the spoons he was drying. "As I've said all along, it's my mission to shine light on your church members and the decisions they've been making," he replied. "I intend to preach on that topic, come Sunday. But right now, I'm enjoying the company of a woman I find . . . attractive. I lost my dear wife a few years ago, and life's a lonely place for a man without a mate."

Her pulse pounded so hard she feared Clayton might hear it, yet Annabelle dared to hold him to the same fire that he'd lit under her fragile soul. "And what about your kids? They surely need your support and presence now that they've lost their *mamm*—"

"They've married and left the district with their husbands," Clayton said with a shrug. He held her gaze with bottomless brown eyes that were mere inches away from hers. "The Council of Bishops sent me as their emissary because I didn't have a family who needed my presence. We had no idea I might run across a woman who . . . reminds me that I'm a man," he whispered.

"I've done no such thing!" Annabelle declared as she

stepped away from him. "You'd best be on your way, Bishop. The Kuhn sisters will be home any time now, and if they find you here alone with me—"

Clayton took his time hanging the dish towel on the stove handle. "God moves in mysterious ways," he quoted softly, "and so do I. When you change your mind, Annabelle, I'll be the first to know."

When the bishop slipped out through the mudroom door, Annabelle didn't know whether to laugh or cry—or swear. The nerve of that man, thinking he could cozy up to her and cast such *lines*, as though she were a fish that would snap at any sort of live, male bait! Insinuating that he would whisk her off in his buggy to reestablish her, because he was lonely and—and—

I'm enjoying the company of a woman I find attractive . . . a woman who reminds me that I'm a man.

Annabelle grabbed the newspaper from the worktable and fanned herself frantically. Clayton King was too smooth, too presumptuous by half—

But didn't it feel nice, hearing a handsome man say those things about you—and say them to your face?

She felt frightfully *ferhoodled*. In her conscience, she believed Clayton had overstepped the boundaries of propriety expected of an Old Order bishop—especially because she was a married woman in no position to go along with his suggestions. Yet her body and her betrayed heart had responded to him and his alluring words.

Annabelle didn't allow herself to look out the window, for fear Clayton would see her. Instead she went to the phone, grateful that the church leaders had allowed Rosetta to keep it indoors.

From memory she dialed the number of the neighbors who lived catty-corner behind their Lancaster County home—and who happened to be a preacher and his wife. Edna Schlabaugh wasn't an especially close friend, but Annabelle could get the answers she needed quicker than if she waited for responses to the letters she'd written to two other gals back home.

After the message machine in the Schlabaughs' phone shanty beeped, she said, "Edna, it's Annabelle Beachey, calling from Promise, Missouri. When you get a moment, could you call me? There's a bishop named Clayton King who's shown up here, saying he's from Paradise and that he operates a bulk grocery warehouse. I hope you can fill me in on him—and on all the news from around the neighborhood, too," she added.

After she gave the lodge's phone number and hung up, Annabelle felt a little stab of homesickness. Leaving the folks she'd known for so long had taken more of an emotional toll than she cared to admit—and all because Phineas had betrayed her and their faith, as well. Maybe that's why she was vulnerable to Bishop Clayton's persuasion.

But God led you to Promise Lodge, she reminded herself as she scrubbed potatoes and carrots for the evening meal she would share with her newfound friends. *You know His voice to be a true beacon, so maybe you should keep listening to Him rather than believing anything Clayton— or Phineas—tries to tell you.*

Monroe found great camaraderie working among his friends, and this sunny afternoon was the perfect time to put the roof on Allen and Phoebe's home—especially because Phineas had joined him and Amos and Marlin. As a remodeler, Beachey was running the heavy-duty nail gun without having to think about it—which meant he could talk and work at the same time. Monroe didn't want to let such an opportunity pass them by. Without any women—or Clayton King—within earshot, they could speak more freely.

"Maybe you're tired of this topic, Phineas," Monroe began as they worked side by side, "but do you have any inclination to return to the Amish church? I won't preach hellfire and damnation if you say no. I'd just like to know your feelings."

Beachey fired off another row of nails. "I suppose you're asking this on Annabelle's behalf—"

"Nope, this is a man-to-man thing," Monroe assured him. "Annabelle seems quite capable of speaking for herself."

"And in her defense," Amos said before he dropped another package of shingles with a *whump*, "she hasn't asked for our support or protection now that you've shown up."

"Why would she need protection?" Phineas shot back. "Has she told you such horrible things about me that you believe I'll abduct her or abuse her?"

"Nope," Marlin replied quickly from a couple yards away. "But when she said you'd abandoned her and the Old Order, we felt responsible for her well-being because left alone, on her own, she faces a very limited future. Surely you understood that when you took off."

"And surely you didn't think she'd want to join you in your English life," Amos put in. His voice was calm and conversational, yet he brooked no argument.

After a moment's consideration, Phineas set aside the nail gun and sat down on the shingled section of roof they'd just completed. Beneath the hum of the compressor on the ground below them, he began to speak.

"I felt trapped," he explained with a shake of his head. "The bishops out our way are much more conservative than you fellows. They were riding my butt about being away on a job when community projects like barn raisings— or putting on roofs, like this one—needed doing. They expected me to forego paying projects to work for them," he explained in a harsh tone. "They were even implying that if I didn't stop taking jobs on English projects to be at their beck and call, I was putting my personal salvation in jeopardy."

Phineas exhaled sharply, as though he was reliving the situation he'd described. "I didn't feel the need to keep supporting a district—a bishop—who chastised me for being a fully employed, responsible citizen who provided his wife a *gut* home and paid his bills and contributed more to the church than he was expected to. So I left."

Monroe's eyebrows rose. "I can see why you'd resent your bishop's attitude," he remarked, trimming the excess edge of a shingle with a quick cut of his knife. He stopped there, hoping Phineas would continue of his own accord.

"I guess I didn't think about the consequences for Annabelle," he admitted softly. "I figured she'd stick with me, no matter what. She'd also expressed complaints about some of the bishop's ideas—to me, but not to him, of course—so I left. Reestablished my business by working for an English outfit in Ohio that valued my remodeling expertise and my Amish work ethic."

Phineas paused, perplexed. "Can you understand why I was hurt and shocked when I went back for Annabelle and discovered she'd moved away without telling my brother where she'd gone?"

Amos cleared his throat, taking up where Monroe's questions had left off. "She told us you left without any warning—and that when your brother took over your farm, she didn't feel she could stay there. Any truth to that?"

Phineas glanced away. "My brother's got all the charm

of coarse sandpaper sometimes," he replied. "Then again, why would he assume that Annabelle could keep the farm running by herself? It had been the Beachey homeplace for generations, so he figured he had a right to it."

"So how'd you know to come to Promise Lodge for Annabelle?" Marlin asked after a moment. "Lancaster County's a long way from Missouri."

"You've got that right!" Phineas shot back with a laugh. Then he sobered. "It was sheer coincidence—or maybe the hand of God was guiding my eyes to the column in *The Budget*, where your scribe had reported Annabelle's arrival and said she was living with other gals in the lodge apartments."

"That column could've been referring to any one of probably two dozen Amish gals named Annabelle Beachey," Monroe pointed out.

"I hired a driver and took my chances," Phineas said. "Maybe that was the hand of God leading me, too, ain't so?"

Monroe considered what he'd heard and pressed a bit harder. "So you haven't given up on God," he observed as he took a seat on the roof beside Phineas. "You really gave up on your bishop."

"Which was the same exact reason the Bender sisters and I left Coldstream, up the road a ways, to purchase this place," Amos stated. He took a seat on the other side of Monroe to continue the conversation.

"We felt the bishop, Obadiah Chupp, was being unreasonably intrusive by insisting that those three sisters get married—or sell their farms to local men for much less than their market value," Amos recounted. "Chupp thought that because they were women they wouldn't know any better, or that they'd submit to his ruling because he was the bishop. But he was wrong about that. And he was way out of line, as I saw it—even though I was a preacher for the district."

Marlin, too, laid aside his tools and took a seat on the roof beside them. "So what are the chances that you'd rejoin the Old Order, say, if you felt comfortable here amongst us?" he asked gently. "Every one of us came to Promise Lodge to get away from something that wasn't working—or that didn't feel right to us, considering what God was whispering in our ears."

For several moments only the low drone of the compressor filled the air. Phineas kept his face expressionless as he considered Marlin's important question, gazing out over the panorama of the Promise Lodge property from high on this hill and this rooftop. Nobody could deny the beauty of the lush pastures, the turning trees, and all the new homes that had gone up in a very short time. To their left, Rainbow Lake shimmered in the sunlight. A fish jumped from the water and splashed down.

Phineas cleared his throat. "I was under the impression that my leaving couldn't be forgiven—that once I forsook the Amish faith, there was no coming back."

"But we're wondering if you really left the faith," Monroe pointed out. "Maybe that's a matter of interpretation."

"We'd be pleased to have you here, Phineas," Marlin put in quickly, "and we already know how happy Annabelle is, living amongst us."

"For the sake of maintaining the Old Order ways, we'd ask you to make a confession, so the congregation can vote about reinstating you," Amos said as though he was thinking aloud. "But I don't believe anyone here would vote against—"

"What about that guy right there?" Phineas stiffened, pointing toward the lodge.

Monroe and the two preachers fell silent. Clayton King

had come out the back door and was looking around as though he hoped no one had seen him. "What about King?" he asked softly. "He has issues with our liberal ways, but that doesn't affect your wanting to live here or to be reinstated—"

"Oh, King has *plenty* to say about me already being damned for eternity," Phineas insisted bitterly. "And *I* have an issue with him sneaking out of the lodge, because the other ladies are in town—so he was in there with Annabelle, alone. I don't trust that snake any farther than I could throw him."

Monroe was about to say something to soften Phineas's acidic remarks, but just then King spotted the four of them on the roof. He spread his feet and clasped his hands behind his back, gazing directly at Phineas, smiling like the cat that ate the canary. By the time King started toward the road and Lester's place, Phineas's fists were knots and his grimace was downright frightening.

"Easy now," Monroe murmured as he grasped Phineas's taut shoulder. "I'm not sure why, but King's trying to get your goat—"

"And it's working," Amos put in. "Anger and confrontation won't solve anything, you know. Maybe things aren't the way they appear—"

"Even so, Phineas," Marlin joined in, "three of our four church leaders have witnessed what's just happened, so we'll keep closer track of him—as long as you turn the other cheek and don't provoke Clayton any further."

Phineas scowled. "You expect me to sit idly by while he and Annabelle carry on—"

"Let's don't assume Annabelle is carrying on," Monroe said firmly. "Sure, in your shoes I'd feel hot under the collar, but don't lash out at her or accuse her of anything.

Get the facts, Phineas. If you get crosswise with her again, she might not want to reconcile with you."

"But she's my wife!" he blurted. "If I want to come back—and if you folks reinstate me into the faith—she has to take me!"

Amos cleared his throat. "It's one of our cardinal rules that men aren't allowed to mistreat, abuse, or harass their wives," he stated in a no-nonsense tone. "You might as well understand that right here and now, Phineas, because if the women get wind of you treating Annabelle badly, they won't tolerate it—and they'll tell us about it. Call us too progressive, but we consider husbands and wives as equals here."

After a moment, Phineas exhaled loudly. "I have a lot to think about," he said as he stood up. "Excuse me."

"*Denki* for your help today," Marlin called after him. "We're glad you're here."

Monroe and the two preachers watched as Phineas descended the slope of the roof with the agility of a cat before he clambered down the ladder at the side of the house. He was happy to hear a buggy coming, and to see the Kuhn sisters in the front seat of it as Phineas crossed the road on his way to the lodge.

"We haven't heard the last of this," Monroe murmured.

"It's best if we let the ladies take it from here," Marlin remarked. "They'll put Phineas in his place, and they'll stand by Annabelle in a heartbeat."

Monroe agreed. He was sorry that they were anticipating a problem—whether it was Phineas or Clayton who was causing it.

"Something tells me this'll be seed for King's sermon tomorrow," Amos said with a short laugh. "It could make for an exciting Sunday."

Chapter Ten

From his seat on the preachers' bench Sunday morning, Monroe surveyed the faces of his friends as Preacher Marlin brought the first sermon to a close. Folks were nodding in staunch agreement with their newest minister's assurances about God's promise, "I am with you always," as he retold the stories of Moses, King David—and even King Solomon, from whom God took most of the vast kingdom He'd entrusted to David.

"Because Solomon's hundreds of foreign wives had turned his heart away from God to worship their gods," Marlin said in a rising voice, "God punished King Solomon by relieving him of most of his kingdom. But God promised that if Solomon sought Him, He could still be found."

People were nodding, taking comfort and assurance from a man they'd come to love and trust. Monroe suspected that when Bishop Clayton preached the second sermon, the atmosphere in the lodge's meeting room would change dramatically. As they'd entered for the service, many folks had been whispering tensely, wondering if this would be the morning when King made his big pronouncement about Promise Lodge.

Monroe tried not to anticipate negativity, but he stole a glance at King, who sat at the opposite end of the preachers' bench on the other side of Amos. The visiting bishop's brow was furrowed—and he was silently counting on his fingers, as though keeping track of points he wished to make when it was his turn to preach. Then King hefted the big King James Bible onto his lap and flipped through it, shaking his head, as Marlin was speaking.

Monroe frowned. Not only was it rude to riffle through the Scriptures during another preacher's sermon, but the insistent whispering of the Bible's thin pages distracted folks in the congregation.

"Even in our most difficult times, even when we have failed to keep God's commandments or to follow His will for us," Marlin summarized in a resonant voice, "He does not abandon us if we follow Him and seek Him out. Even in the darkest hour of the cross, when Jesus asked why His Father *had* forsaken Him, God displayed His sorrow by shrouding the world with darkness at noon. And then He kept His promise yet again by raising Christ from the dead to reign with Him in heaven forever. Thanks be to this mighty God who has conquered sin and death and who loves us in spite of the many ways we turn away from Him."

"Amen," one of the men in the meeting room murmured as Marlin returned to the preachers' bench. Monroe, Amos, and Eli nodded to Marlin as he sat down, but Bishop Clayton sat clutching the Bible to his chest, staring at a spot on the floor as though the answers to the world's most pressing questions were written there.

After the first sermon, folks knelt on the floor for prayer. Monroe sighed as he bowed his head, sensing the tension in the room.

Lord, not my will but Thine. We could sure use Your help this morning as we take in whatever Your servant, Clayton King, might say to us.

Dark clouds had hovered in the sky all morning, so Monroe wasn't surprised when fat splats of rain began to hit the windows.

As the members rose from their knees to sit on the pew benches again, Bishop Clayton stood up to begin the second, longer sermon. Rather than waiting for Marlin, as the deacon, to read the day's scriptural passage, however, King held up the large, thick volume as though folks had never seen it before.

"Sorry to say this, my friends," he began in a voice that filled the room, "but this morning's first sermon played fast and loose with the Scriptures, to the point that we'd be here the rest of the day if I corrected all the fine points of Old Testament history about who actually said what to whom."

King paused to look closely at the congregation. "But that brings me to the message I was going to deliver anyway—because *fast and loose* also describes how the Promise Lodge community adheres to the basic, bedrock teachings of the Old Order."

Monroe winced. Beside him, Marlin's face was taking on color; his eyes widened when King's remark about his sermon sank in.

"I've been here long enough to see for myself how you folks do things," King continued with a heavy sigh. "And unfortunately, I can confirm the suspicions of the Council of Bishops that sent me here. You're headed down the path to spiritual destruction, following Satan's own lead."

To Monroe, the communal intake of breath was the sound of everyone's joy being sucked from the room. Clayton cut an imposing figure in his black suit, with his dark hair and beard trimmed shorter than most men at Promise Lodge wore them. He could've been a modern-day prophet as he continued. Even though King lowered his voice, the congregation resembled a roomful of school kids who'd shrunk down at their desks after the teacher had reprimanded them.

"I really hoped I wouldn't have to lay down the law," King began apologetically. He gazed at the members as though he truly regretted the sermon he felt compelled to preach. "But we Amish uphold our ancient ways because they lead us ever closer to God's salvation. However, when Mattie Schwartz, Christine Hershberger, and Rosetta Bender sold their farms and bought this campground property rather than reconciling with their bishop in Coldstream—*defying* him rather than following his leadership—they started a trickle of misbehavior that has swelled into a flood of negligence and disregard for the tenets of proper Amish life."

Monroe felt the pain on the faces of his wife and her sisters, as well as the scowl on Amos's weathered face. He was surprised that none of them stood up to defend the purchase of this land, except that they respected whoever was preaching because God had chosen him as a leader of the church. Thunder rumbled in the distance and the rain became a steady downpour.

"I find it especially unfortunate that Rosetta has led other Plain women astray by offering them apartments." Clayton turned toward the women's side, shaking his head. "You ladies seem so *proud* of your independent attitude, but to God it's a slap in the face. Our Lord desires your humility, so He decreed that the men of your families were to provide for you."

King cleared his throat before he continued. "Although it's encouraging that you three sisters have married and obeyed God's will to that extent, you continue to operate businesses as though your income is needed to keep your households afloat. From what I've observed, *no one* at Promise Lodge lacks for anything!" he added emphatically. "We'll discuss that further after I list the points you need to address immediately—preferably on your knees, as you beg God's forgiveness."

Monroe sensed that King's pause was more for dramatic effect—to make folks even more nervous—than to allow him to catch his breath or gather his thoughts. As a speaker, he was polished and confident. Tucking the big Bible beneath his arm, he turned to catch Amos's eye before he spoke again.

"I would be remiss if I didn't sketch your preacher, Amos Troyer, into this picture," Bishop Clayton said as he again faced the congregation. "God chose him many years ago to be a leader of the church, yet he was instrumental in allowing the Bender sisters to carry through on their outrageous plan to purchase this property. And he's gone along with their new rule, about Promise Lodge being a community where men are not allowed to chastise their wives—or to correct their faulty thinking about who God chose to be the head of Amish households.

"Never mind about the humility and submission the Bible teaches!" King added dramatically. "So from there, with a preacher in the lead, this community was headed down the slippery slope before anyone else even took up residence here."

Amos was gripping his knees as the color rose up from under his white shirt collar. Monroe felt compelled to stop Bishop Clayton's diatribe by standing up to defend the folks King had declared defiant and outside God's intentions—except King turned to focus on *him.*

Monroe's mouth went dry. He should've known his perceived sins would be hung out alongside his friends'.

"The most heinous infraction of Old Order ways I've

witnessed, however, is the fact that your bishop, Monroe Burkholder, not only condoned the marriage of an Amish woman to a Mennonite man, but he conducted the wedding service!" Bishop Clayton announced above the next rumble of thunder. He came across as a father pointing out the faults of his favorite, beloved child, but even so, Monroe felt a slow burn in his chest.

He swallowed his retort, however. *Many* Old Order bishops would chastise him for allowing an Amish woman and a Mennonite man to intermarry.

"And on the subject of your bishop, I was astounded— and greatly saddened—by the huge, beautiful horses I've seen grazing his lush pastureland," Bishop Clayton went on. "This brings me back to the subject of the prosperity I've seen at Promise Lodge. Those Clydesdales are the ultimate example of how you've misunderstood the rules of the *Ordnung*, because they're raised and trained for wealthy clients who show them as an expensive hobby rather than for any practical purpose that pleases God. They are the antithesis of the humility and simplicity God wants His people to exhibit as they pursue their livelihoods."

Monroe fought the urge to refute King's accusations . . . because he'd made a valid point: training expensive show horses wasn't a typical Amish endeavor because it catered to a wealthy English clientele rather than providing Plain neighbors with dependable farm or buggy horses.

When he'd taken over the Clydesdale business from the uncle who'd raised him, however, Monroe believed that God had gifted him with the skills and the physical strength he needed for a *reason*. He'd known from his boyhood that his uncle and God were equipping him for this elite livelihood, so although Monroe understood some folks' objections to it, he never apologized for continuing his work—or for making really good money at it.

It hurt Monroe to see the pained expressions on his congregation's faces, however. A few of the men were silently pleading with him to stand up to the visiting bishop who'd trampled on all the principles and progress they held most dear.

But Monroe kept his seat. Bishop Clayton wasn't finished, and interrupting—or arguing with—a church leader chosen by God was unacceptable behavior for him, just as it was for any other bishop.

"It's no small issue that Promise Lodge is a wealthy community, apparently laying up its treasure here on earth rather than in heaven," King put in ominously. "I admonish you all to remember the story in Matthew nineteen, where a rich young ruler asked Jesus how he could attain eternal life. That fellow left feeling quite disheartened when Christ told him to sell all he owned, give the money to the poor, and follow Him."

Bishop Clayton paused to meet several members' eyes. "Will your prosperity damn you in the end?" he demanded. "'It's easier for a camel to walk through the eye of a needle than for a rich man to enter heaven.'"

The meeting room got very quiet. Guilt prickled like a burr that had lodged between Monroe's shirt and his skin, and the faces around him reflected similar discomfort. No one at Promise Lodge had set out to acquire wealth, and not a soul among them could be classified as greedy, but every family in the room was doing well financially. And thanks to Floyd and Lester Lehman, they all lived in new homes with aluminum siding and windows.

Was it the outward appearance—the newness of their buildings—that gave King the impression of their prosperity? Surely he hadn't researched the residents' incomes, or their bank account balances. . . .

"Now that I've made my points to you folks, I'll report

my findings to the council," Bishop Clayton continued. "Those men will consider these matters, and in due time recommend remedies to restore your community to rightness with God. Are there any questions?"

Monroe's mouth dropped open. Had King just invited folks to air their grievances—to engage with him during the *sermon*? It was unheard of to turn the church service into a congregational meeting! The time for such a discussion would be during a members' meeting following the final hymn. Yet Truman Wickey stood up.

"With all due respect, Bishop Clayton," he began stridently, "do you think we didn't pray about these matters before we proceeded with them? Do you believe we would've founded Promise Lodge the way we did without first asking God's guidance—and then following what He told us to do?"

"*Jah*, you've got us all wrong!" Mattie Troyer muttered. "We believe we're carrying out God's will just as fervently as you're telling us we've started down the path to perdition."

"Things are different here in Missouri," Preacher Eli pointed out. "And historically, Amish folks have often broken away from a church district that no longer served their needs. That's a *gut* thing! It allows for geographical expansion, and for young men to relocate so they can afford their own land—and for differences of opinion—while keeping us all under the Old Order umbrella."

Another clap of thunder punctuated Eli's remark. Everyone looked toward the windows when the rain beat more loudly against them. King stood with his hands clasped behind him, as though he'd expected such an outpouring from Promise Lodge residents. He seemed unmoved by what he'd heard, though.

Bishop Clayton smiled slowly, aware of his power to hold his audience captive as he leaned toward Truman. "And your name would be—?"

"I'm Truman Wickey," he replied, "and the decision to allow my marriage to Rosetta came only after a *great* deal of prayer and—"

"Of course you'd say that," King interrupted smoothly. "You got what you wanted, so it's easy to believe that you and your friends have been doing God's will. The bishops in the council see it differently, however."

Monroe blinked. Although King had invited their input, he didn't intend to change his mind no matter what any of them said. His condescending tone silenced the congregation's whispering, and it compelled Monroe to stand and speak up.

"What do you propose we do about these issues you've raised, Bishop Clayton?" he asked loudly. "What do you think the council will expect us to change?"

King pivoted to face Monroe. "That's not for me to say. When the council responds to my report, I'll let you know."

Monroe struggled to keep a scowl off his face. He'd had all he could handle of King's attitude, his prophecy of doom. "So be it," he muttered. "Let's bring this service of *worship* to a proper close, shall we?"

Chapter Eleven

"What do you suppose that bunch of bishops back east is going to say about us?" Gloria asked softly. She and Laura had taken seats at the end of a table across from Cyrus and Jonathan, but their conversation felt stifled. The dining room was unusually quiet during the common meal.

Cyrus shrugged. "I'm sure we'll find out," he replied as he picked up his ham sandwich.

"And what're folks supposed to say to Bishop Clayton while we wait for his answers?" Laura murmured with a shake of her head. "He might be here awhile—"

"*Jah*, he doesn't seem any too eager to leave," Jonathan remarked. He glanced around to be sure Bishop Clayton wasn't within earshot. "But then, why would he? He's got a free place to stay with Lester, his meals are being provided, and the ladies are doing his laundry. Sounds like a pretty sweet deal."

"That doesn't mean *we* have to stick around," Cyrus said with the hint of a grin. "How about if we eat fast and get out of here—take our dessert with us? It's a shame to spend our afternoon surrounded by gloom and doom when we could go find some fun."

Gloria's eyes widened with the sense of adventure

behind Cyrus's suggestion. "There's a pan of Ruby's cinnamon bars in the pantry—"

"And what if we went to the ice-cream parlor in Forest Grove to eat them?" Laura chimed in softly. "It's open on Sunday afternoons—and it could be a double date!"

"I'm outta here!" Cyrus slapped his hand against the table. "Jonathan and I will go hitch up the buggy, and we'll meet you girls at the back door in five minutes."

"You're on!" Gloria said in a giddy whisper. She understood why the adults around them were feeling somber, but the opportunity to head into town with Cyrus and Jonathan was too good to pass up. Folks might gossip about where the four of them were going, but why should they care? Wasn't it only natural for young people to pair up and get away from the older folks on a Sunday afternoon?

A few moments later Cyrus headed for the lodge's front door with Jonathan close behind him. Gloria flashed Laura a conspiratorial smile as she got up and exited through the kitchen. By the time she'd taken the foil-covered pan of cinnamon bars from the pantry, Laura was joining her. They waited until they got outside to burst out laughing.

"What'll Ruby say when she sees her bars are gone?" Laura asked. "She and Beulah and Irene will be home from Cloverdale pretty soon, and they'll probably want some with their dinner."

"We'll tell them later that these bars went toward a *gut* cause," Gloria replied. "And they'll probably be glad they went to their Mennonite service today instead of hanging around here to hear the bad news."

"*Jah*, to them, I don't guess it matters much what Bishop Clayton says—unless he tells Rosetta she can't rent apartments to them any longer," Laura remarked. "Do you think that'll happen?"

Gloria sighed. "I sure hope not, because I'll lose my job.

But here come the guys," she said, pointing toward the approaching horse-drawn buggy. "No sense in worrying about what Bishop King or that council will do, when we can be out enjoying happier company this afternoon."

"*Jah*, the common meal was more like a funeral lunch. I feel bad for Bishop Monroe," Laura murmured. "He's a *gut* man and I can't believe he—or the rest of us here—have done anything so terribly wrong that God's going to condemn us forever."

When Cyrus pulled the black buggy up alongside the corner of the lodge, Jonathan hopped out of the front seat and opened the back door so Laura could scramble in ahead of him. Gloria quickly took her place beside Cyrus in the front.

"Here we go!" Cyrus said, urging the horse forward. "Making our escape!"

"*Jah*, let's make it a *gut* one, considering we're all set to join the Old Order in two weeks," Jonathan remarked. "There won't be any escaping that day, because everyone will be congratulating us—praising God that we've seen the light and joined the church."

Gloria's heart danced as she set the pan of bars on the floor. The windshield wipers swished rhythmically and the gravel crunched beneath their wheels. When she glanced toward the backseat, she was surprised to see that Jonathan had his arm around Laura's shoulders as though they were already a cozy couple.

How have they been seeing each other without my knowing?

Gloria forgot about the pair in the back, however, when Cyrus wrapped his large, warm hand around hers. She felt like a queen. It was a treat to see the Helmuth brothers dressed in their black Sunday trousers, vests, and straw hats with their crisp white shirts, because they usually came to the lodge for their meals in the worn broadfall pants and faded shirts they wore while working at the nursery. Both young men were handsome—but Cyrus was cuter.

He squeezed her hand. "Maybe we could sample those cinnamon bars on the way to town," he suggested. "We should probably bring Ruby something back with us, since we made off with her dessert."

"That would be generous of us, *jah*," Jonathan agreed. "She and her sister feed us well three times a day, and they never run short where the goodies are concerned."

Gloria removed the foil from the pan, loosened two of the dark, sugar-topped bars, and then passed the pan over her shoulder to Laura. Rather than handing a bar to Cyrus, she waved it playfully in front of his face. "Here comes the airplane," she teased in a singsong voice. "Open up so it can land in your mouth, baby boy."

Cyrus's lips closed over her fingers. The bars were cut into small squares and he took the entire cookie into his mouth, holding Gloria's gaze. "*Denki*, baby," he mumbled with his mouth full. "Sooo *gut*, you are. Sweet and spicy, like this cookie."

Gloria's heart thumped faster. The touch of his mouth against her skin and his unexpected endearments—in front of Laura and Jonathan—surprised her. "You're the spicy one," she murmured. "Like hot chili peppers when you kiss me."

"Watch out, now! You're setting the buggy on fire," Laura teased.

"*Jah*, shall we stop and get you a room?" Jonathan joined in.

Laughter filled the rig, and Gloria glowed with the rightness of it all—the way the four of them were having fun together, and the way her life was finally working out as she'd dreamed it would. She'd fallen hard for Roman Schwartz before he'd married her sister and she'd been in a one-sided love with Allen Troyer before Phoebe had claimed him, but those two fellows had apparently been practice runs for the real thing. This time, Cyrus had done the chasing and Gloria was delighted to be caught up in his flirtation . . . daring to hope that a lasting relationship would come of it.

A short time later they entered Herrick's Ice Cream Parlor, which featured an old-time soda fountain counter with rotating stools and a freezer case displaying more than twenty flavors of ice cream. Members of the Herrick family were making banana splits and mixing malts behind the counter. The place was filled with chatting customers who sat with cones and bowls of ice cream. Cyrus gestured toward an empty booth on the wall, allowing Gloria and Laura to sit down first.

"Now comes the hard part—deciding what flavors we want," Jonathan said.

Laura shrugged. "You can't go wrong. All of their ice cream is fabulous—so maybe we should order scoops of different flavors in a big bowl and share them."

"You're on!" Cyrus said. "We'll be back in a few."

After the guys had left the table to make their ice-cream choices, Gloria leaned toward Laura. "Is this fun, or what?" she whispered.

Laura beamed at her. "Who knew that we'd both be dating the Helmuth brothers?" she asked giddily. "My eighteenth birthday must've been magic, because Jonathan and I have spent time together twice this week."

"*Jah*, I never saw this coming with Cyrus, either," Gloria put in. "Just when I thought I was doomed to be a *maidel* all my life, he asked me out. I don't know *why*—but I'm not asking any questions!"

"Here they come," Laura whispered before flashing the brothers a big blue-eyed smile. "Oh my, would you look what they've brought us! We'll be here all day eating so much ice cream."

Cyrus laughed as he slid a big glass bowl piled with scoops of ice cream toward the center of their table. "What else do we have to do today—and why would we want to hurry back home?" he asked as he slid into the booth.

"Not sure how many scoops we got," Jonathan admitted as he positioned himself next to Laura and passed around spoons. "We told our server to give us their most popular flavors, and she couldn't have gotten another scoop into this bowl."

Laura put the pan of cinnamon bars beside the ice cream. "You can talk, or you can eat this ice cream before it turns to soup," she teased as she stuck a spoon into a scoop of dark chocolate.

Gloria spotted a scoop of butterscotch ripple and went for it just as Cyrus had the same idea. He laughed when their spoons collided—and then held a big spoonful of the ice cream in front of her mouth.

"You first," he murmured, his dark eyes glimmering. "It's all about you, Gloria. I'm just happy you let me hang around with you."

The couple across the table—indeed, the entire ice-cream parlor—vanished in a slow-spinning mist spun of fairy tales and daydreams as Gloria held Cyrus's gaze. Even in her most romantic imaginings, no man had ever said such a thing to her.

Gloria opened her mouth, hoping this was the first of many sweet memories she would make with the handsome young man beside her.

* * *

Two weeks later, Jonathan was on his knees before the entire congregation—which included his parents and a few other family members who'd made the trip from Ohio to see him and Cyrus baptized. Why was he so nervous, so sweaty? Bishop Monroe and Preacher Marlin were officiating, and they'd encouraged him, his brother, and Allen all during their instruction period. He truly believed that joining the Old Order was the right thing for him to do—and generations of his family and friends had gone through the baptismal ceremony and taken the same vows.

And besides, if you don't commit to the church, Laura won't take you seriously and you can't ever marry her.

Yet he was trembling. He and his two friends had been given a chance to back out during their final instructional session the previous week, and again before the church service that morning, but they were all in. Making a public profession of his faith was the most serious event in his life so far, and the vow he took was irrevocable. Not only was he promising to follow the *Ordnung* and the ways of the Old Order, he was also agreeing that should God call him by the falling of the lot, he would serve the church as a deacon, a preacher—or even a bishop—someday.

It was a lot to get his head around. Jonathan wanted to be right with God, yet he was so scared of messing up that he could barely speak.

"Can you renounce the devil, the world, and your own flesh and blood?" Bishop Monroe asked solemnly. They had discussed this question and its ramifications during their sessions, so it came as no surprise.

"*Jah*, I will," Jonathan replied. His words were almost a whimper, and his voice sounded embarrassingly adolescent. It was comforting that neither his bold younger brother nor Allen sounded any more confident than he did.

"Can you commit yourself to Christ and His church,

and to abide by it and therein to live and die?" the bishop asked them next.

It was another question they'd talked about, yet Jonathan's heart was pounding so frantically it seemed he might die before he could answer. But somehow he got the words out. He was swallowing so hard that the final question about obeying and submitting to the Old Order and the word of the Lord went past him in a blur. Not wanting to be the one who stalled the ceremony, Jonathan managed to nod and reply when he heard his companions answering. His eyes remained tightly shut.

He heard water being poured beside him. It splattered to the floor as the bishop baptized Cyrus, on his left.

Jonathan felt Monroe standing before him as Preacher Marlin poured water from a pitcher into the bishop's hands. As the cool liquid trickled over his scalp and onto the floor, Jonathan let out the breath he'd been holding.

It was done. He was officially a member of the Amish church—and within moments, Allen had been baptized, too. Bishop Monroe helped them stand up with a stalwart handshake and the brief holy kiss on the cheek that officially welcomed them into the Old Order. After the bishop spoke a few words to the congregation, the ceremony was over.

Jonathan sucked in air as Troyer and his brother pumped his hand. Bishop Monroe and the preachers led the three of them to the doorway to form a reception line so folks could greet them on the way to the common meal. He was shaking hands and being hugged by the same people he'd known since he'd arrived at Promise Lodge—along with his proud parents and a couple of older brothers and their wives—yet they looked at him differently now.

Was he supposed to *feel* different? Radically changed inside? Jonathan didn't have a chance to assess exactly how he felt—except that when Laura hugged him tight, beaming at him, his world started spinning so fast it gave off sparks. He watched Cyrus return Gloria's hug when she threw her arms around his neck.

Does taking the baptismal vow mean that Cyrus is sincere about courting Gloria? Or is he only dating her to win our Thanksgiving bet?

It was a question that gave Jonathan pause, because his feelings for Laura had nothing to do with the five hundred dollars that were riding on the line. She was a delightful young woman who didn't seem to notice that he was a tongue-tied klutz, usually clueless about saying and doing things that would make her feel special. And when he saw Phoebe grasping Allen's hand, so deeply in love with him, Jonathan wanted that same sort of devotion to develop between him and Laura.

Is it realistic to believe such a love can bloom in the next few weeks? Is it fair to push Laura toward an engagement, just to avoid paying off Cyrus's bet?

Not for the first time, Jonathan regretted getting caught up in his younger brother's bravado. All thoughts of romance vanished, however, when Bishop Clayton reached the reception line.

"*Gut* to have you men in the fold," he declared as he shook their hands.

Monroe's smile was wide. "As of this morning, one hundred percent of our eligible young people have joined the Old Order, Bishop Clayton," he said as they pumped hands. "Can you say the same for your district back east?"

Bishop Clayton blinked. "Well, no—but we have a lot more young people, and some of them are still teenagers," he quickly pointed out. "You've got a *gut* track record on that account—and I understand we're soon to celebrate a wedding?" Bishop Clayton asked as he smiled at Allen.

"*Jah*, Phoebe and I will tie the knot this coming Friday," Troyer replied.

"Congratulations," King said with a nod. "And what a *blessing* that you can move right into a new house on a plot of land with a lake on it! Most young couples start out in a room at their parents' place, the way I did."

As King headed for the dining room, Jonathan realized that their guest had just gotten in another jab at the prosperity he'd criticized in his sermon the previous Sunday. Jonathan was also aware that if he and Laura got engaged, he'd have to plan for where they would live—because he didn't have parents who would donate land and the labor to build a house, the way Troyer did.

When Jonathan looked at the crowd gathering in the dining room, Laura was gazing at him. She beckoned him with wide blue eyes, as though to ask *will you sit by me?*

He started toward her. Would Laura be content to live in one of the cabins until he could afford to build them a house? Or would they take up residence with Bishop Monroe and Laura's *mamm*? Suddenly, it seemed he had a lot of major decisions to make.

Don't put the cart before the horse. First you have to work up the nerve to introduce Laura to your parents and older brothers.

What would his family think when he—and Cyrus— both came to the table with girlfriends?

They'll be amazed—and very happy, wondering if they might have two weddings in the future . . . unless they get wind of the wager you and Cyrus have made. They won't be one bit proud of that.

Jonathan sighed as he approached Laura and reached for her hand. If she ever learned what he and Cyrus were up to, she'd be heartbroken. What girl wouldn't feel cheapened—betrayed—if she found out her guy was dating her because of money rather than love?

He really needed to talk his kid brother out of their daredevil arrangement.

"By the way, Bishop Clayton—" Preacher Marlin spoke above the chatter that filled the dining room. "We're all wondering what you've heard from the Council of Bishops. It's been two weeks since you preached about all the ways we've fallen short of their expectations."

The crowd immediately fell quiet. Plenty of folks had been discussing the points of King's sermon among themselves, but they hadn't asked him point-blank for a progress report.

Bishop Clayton cleared his throat ceremonially. "As you can imagine, such a council oversees the well-being of Amish communities in a large region," he replied. "Promise Lodge is only one of the communities about which they're concerned. You'll be the first to know when I hear back from them."

Was it his imagination, or did the three preachers and Bishop Monroe share a meaningful glance? Jonathan could understand why these hardworking men of the church wanted the council's verdict as soon as possible—and he could tell that other folks, too, were eager for information that would affect the life they'd come to love.

"We preachers have our weekly meeting on Tuesday morning, and we'd like you to join us," Bishop Monroe said. "Ten o'clock at my kitchen table."

Bishop Clayton's dark eyebrows rose. "I don't know that it's my place to interfere with your day-to-day—"

"Interfere?" Preacher Amos repeated. "You've kept us hanging long enough. Even if you have nothing to report

from the council, it's time to discuss *our* side of the issues you've raised."

As many folks in the room murmured their agreement, Bishop Clayton held up his hand for silence. "Patience is a virtue," he reminded them.

"*Jah*, it is," Preacher Eli chimed in from near the serving line, "but if your council's going to demand that we make a lot of major changes, we need to know about them."

"We're hoping you'll take a couple hours from your busy schedule to consider our response to your sermon," Preacher Marlin stated. "After all, you've been here for three weeks now, and we're no closer to settling the issues you've raised than we were when you first arrived."

All eyes were on King. Some folks appeared speculative, and some began to whisper again—until Bishop Monroe addressed them. "Shall we bow for a word of silent thanks before our meal gets cold?"

As Jonathan bowed his head, the tension in the room intensified. Several folks wondered how Bishop Clayton spent his time—what he did to earn a living and how he remained engaged in his livelihood while he was so far from home. It wasn't unusual to see King's buggy and beautiful horse heading off for parts unknown during the week, which only made the folks of Promise Lodge more curious about what he might be doing.

Just before Jonathan opened his eyes, he felt a small, warm hand slipping into his.

When Laura smiled at him, he forgot all about Bishop Clayton. Had he ever seen blue eyes as beautiful as Laura's?

"I made a pan of brownies to celebrate your baptism,"

she murmured. "For when we might slip away from the crowd later today."

Jonathan's heart beat wildly. Suddenly the nervousness and fear he'd endured during the ceremony seemed worth his while, if Laura wanted to be with him.

Chapter Twelve

Monroe wasn't surprised that Marlin, Amos, and Eli showed up for Tuesday's weekly meeting about half an hour earlier than usual. Christine filled a carafe with hot coffee and set out trays of cookies and cinnamon rolls before excusing herself to join Rosetta and Mattie in one of the produce plots.

"I understand you're cleaning out some of the garden today," Amos said as he took his usual seat beside Monroe. "I suspect you three sisters will be clucking over a lot more topics than the end of the season for the roadside stand."

Christine laughed. "We'll expect a full report from you fellows after you've quizzed Bishop Clayton," she shot back. "Too many of us—men and women alike—have a lot riding on what he says. But we're also awaiting news about Deborah and Noah's baby," she added with a smile for Eli.

The preacher grinned. "*Jah*, it's due any minute now."

Christine glanced out the kitchen window. "Clayton's on his way, so I'll give him a big smile when I meet him on the road. I hope your meeting goes well—and that every-one realizes we're all trying to carry out God's will."

"It's a matter of agreeing on exactly what His will *is*," Eli said as he took a cookie.

After Christine closed the door behind her, Monroe looked at his three friends. "Are we ready for this?" he asked softly, tapping on the sheet of paper in front of him. "We've written down the issues King raised during his sermon, and we have a few other things to ask him about, as well."

"A lot depends on whether Clayton gives us answers or redirects the conversation where he wants it to go," Amos replied.

The four of them looked toward the doorway as their guest came inside. King paused when he saw them all gathered around the table with cookies and coffee.

"Am I late?" he demanded, glancing at the wall clock. "You said we were to start at ten, and it's five till—"

"You haven't missed a thing." Monroe gestured toward the empty seat at the opposite end of the table. "Help yourself to refreshments, and we'll begin with prayer."

He gave King a moment to settle in before bowing his head. "Lord, we invite Your presence and Your discernment as we determine what You'd have us all do in Your name. We thank You for this opportunity for discussion and growth. Amen."

"As we begin," Amos said before King could get a word in, "I believe we should address your assertion that from its very beginning, Promise Lodge has been 'following the devil's own lead'—because three of our women started this new community, and because you feel that I was wrong to join them." He paused, looking their guest in the eye. "Please understand that only after much prayer for God's guidance did we pursue the purchase of this property.

We firmly believe that had our Lord not been leading us, we would never have *found* this piece of land—"

"But who's to say it wasn't Satan whispering in your ears?" Clayton countered. "We most often follow the voices that tell us what we want to hear."

"From the very beginning of the Amish faith in this country, in Lancaster County in the seventeen and eighteen hundreds," Eli put in earnestly, "groups have split away to begin new communities, either because they ran out of land, or they had disagreements with their leadership. What we did was nothing new, Clayton. Indeed, it's been the only practical way for the Plain faith to grow and prosper."

"True enough," King said with a dismissive shrug. "But it was the *men* who made those decisions. You've been far too permissive with your women. Amish society will deteriorate and fail completely if we disregard the Bible's insistence that our women are to submit to their men and obey them."

"I disagree," Monroe stated firmly. "I wasn't here at the formation of this community—the Lord led me to Missouri a bit later—but I immediately realized that the three women you're condemning were also following God's will as they knew it. Their leadership has breathed fresh perceptions into our faith."

"I disagree, as well, about men always making the best leaders," Eli insisted. "Our family followed the Bender sisters and Amos out of Coldstream because the bishop there looked the other way when his son Isaac was burning down barns—and after Isaac nearly molested my daughter, as well," he added vehemently. "God might've chosen Obadiah Chupp as our bishop, but Chupp's taken a wrong turn, using his position to get his own way instead of God's.

We had to call in the sheriff to arrest Isaac, to keep my daughter safe. I thank God that Deborah knew enough to come here, and that we followed her."

"And along with that," Amos chimed in, "one of the bedrock concepts of our *Ordnung* states that we tolerate no spousal abuse—a major step in the right direction, considering the broken nose and battering my Mattie endured at the hands of her first husband. The God we worship—and Jesus, His beloved son—never intended for wives to suffer physical or emotional cruelty. Nor does He condone husbands' violence as a means of keeping their wives in line."

"Amen," Marlin murmured. "And we fully support Annabelle Beachey's presence in a lodge apartment after Phineas abandoned her. We four have prayed over the matter and we're awaiting God's response about how best to resolve that couple's situation."

King sipped his coffee, never dropping his gaze. "See there? You're redesigning the Old Order's basic tenets to suit yourselves," he countered. "You're being too liberal with Phineas! Those who forsake their vows are to be cast out—and they've understood that since before the day they were baptized."

Monroe set his mug on the table, choosing his words carefully. What King said was right, as far as it went. "But where's the chance for forgiveness and reconciliation in that?" he challenged the man at the other end of the table. "Adam and Eve were allowed back into the Garden after they'd defied God's command—and the wayward Israelites were time and again restored to God's *gut* graces after they'd turned away from Him to worship other gods. Jesus was all about forgiving sins to allow people—"

"If you don't wish to follow the rules of the Old Order, perhaps you should defect to the Mennonite church," King interrupted brusquely. "That's the very mistake the council sent me here to warn you about, considering that you've already allowed one of your members to marry a Mennonite. You're either Amish or you're not. You're in—or you're out. Banished from the true faith with no hope of God's salvation."

Monroe swallowed hard. Clayton was declaring the doctrine he'd heard from Amish leaders all his life, but it rubbed him wrong these days. Monroe—and the other folks at Promise Lodge—believed they'd evolved away from condemnation and shunning toward a faith that more closely reflected the values Jesus taught. Was that grounds for banishing their entire community from the faith they'd followed for generations?

"While you men chew on that, there's another matter I'd like to clarify," King said. He took his time choosing his words, just as he was deliberating over which treat to take from the cookie tray. "The way I understand it, after the Bender sisters—and you, Amos—pooled your money to buy this property, you then sold plots of ground to new residents as they arrived. Considering that you've got ten fine houses, you must have built up quite a cash reserve in the year and a half you've been here."

Monroe blinked. Where was King going with this new topic of conversation? Why was he asking about their finances? "We had to have homes to live in, after all—and we've been blessed by the abilities of several carpenters, as well as by Bishop Floyd and Lester Lehman's siding and window business," he pointed out. "I assume you've gotten your information from Lester, while you've been staying at his place?"

"Lester's been very informative. Nice fellow, and happy to have my company," Clayton replied with a nod. He cleared his throat, resuming his autocratic attitude. "To me, all these fancy houses are a sign that your prosperity has overshadowed the humility our Old Order requires—"

"But let's correct the assumption you've just made," Amos interrupted tersely. He appeared as surprised—and irritated—by King's conversational tactics as Monroe was quickly becoming. "*Jah*, it's true that several of our new residents paid us for their property—"

"Five of them, by my count," Eli put in as he quickly counted on his fingers.

"—but when we moved here," Amos continued, "the sisters and I agreed that our kids would be allowed to choose plots of land as they married and set up house-keeping. Which means that the other five plots—and the homes we've built on them—were gifts that involved no exchange of money."

"It's our way of providing for our children and keeping them close, to grow our community and ensure that our families can stay together," Marlin explained. "Lester probably told you that when I married his sister-in-law, Frances, I gave my house farther up the hill to my son, Harley, and his wife. When Frances's daughter, Gloria, is ready to marry, we intend to provide her with an acreage and a house, as well."

"And you're the deacon of the Promise Lodge district, I understand," Clayton put in without missing a beat. "I hope you're keeping a tight rein and an accurate account of all this money folks have entrusted to you—all of these extremely generous *gifts* you've been talking about."

The kitchen fell silent as Monroe and his three friends considered their responses. Marlin appeared genuinely puz-zled about the direction King's questions were heading—although, again, their guest was speaking about the duties of a district's deacon, which were deeply ingrained in the Old Order faith.

Amos cocked an eyebrow as he looked at King. "Long before Marlin arrived, we deposited our funds in the bank in Forest Grove," he explained. "When we learned Bishop Obadiah's business accounts in Coldstream were being compromised by his son, we suspected the church's funds could've been misappropriated just as easily—so we solved that problem before it happened to us. Sort of falls into the category of 'lead us not into temptation.'"

Monroe had observed a number of expressions on Bishop Clayton's face as Amos recounted their financial story. When King spoke again, he appeared genuinely appalled.

"You've entrusted your money to an English *bank*?" he demanded in a whisper. His brownie dropped to his napkin. "Here's yet another irregularity I'll need to report to the council—another way in which you've gone against Old Order traditions and values—"

Monroe's patience snapped like a dry twig and he was suddenly ready to be finished with the meeting. "On the topic of temptation," he blurted, "I may have to report to this *council* of yours about the way you cornered Annabelle Beachey in the lodge kitchen—"

"I was *counseling* her about the dangers of associating with a husband who's committed the unforgivable sin," King shot back. "As a bishop, I have that responsibility. And mark my words," he went on in an ominous tone, "you won't make any points with the Council of Bishops if you play tit for tat. I'm appalled that you've even considered it, Burkholder."

Monroe inhaled deeply to calm himself, holding the gaze King challenged him with from the other end of the table . . . *his* table. It *was* beneath him to make petty threats, and his hasty retort warned Monroe that he was sinking to King's level. When he glanced at his three preachers, he could tell they'd also had enough of a conversation that seemed more unproductive with each passing moment.

Monroe slowly stood up, considering his words very carefully. The last thing he wanted was to jeopardize the future of Promise Lodge as they knew it, because the families in his care were depending upon him to do the right thing. But he had to be sure that King and his council fully understood that this Old Order congregation had been carrying out God's will as He'd revealed it to them.

"I apologize if I misspoke," Monroe said softly. "But when Annabelle came to me and said that from here on out, she was making sure she was surrounded by her friends—in case you approached her again—I agreed that she was being prudent. I think we all need to pray about what we've discussed today—"

"I get the feeling that you and your council surely must worship a different God than we do—a harsh, judgmental, unforgiving God," Amos stated as he stood up beside Monroe. "We've tried to explain that we have earnestly sought God's responses, His will for us, about all these matters you claim will separate us from Him and the Old Order."

"And as far as I can tell," Eli put in as he, too, rose from his chair, "you haven't listened to a thing we've said. Every one of us was elected by the falling of God's lot to serve other church districts before we heard His call to bring our families to Promise Lodge. We were elected with the same holy process by which *you* were chosen, Bishop Clayton. That doesn't make us any better than you, but it levels the playing field, ain't so?"

King slid his chair back from the table. "I can see it's time for us to think carefully—*jah*, to pray—about what we've discussed this morning, and to reconvene after our tempers and tongues have cooled. *Gut* day, gentlemen."

After plucking three more cookies from the tray, Bishop Clayton strode across the kitchen. The door slammed behind him as he left.

A puzzled silence filled the room as Monroe went to the window to watch King head down the hill. He shook his head as he turned toward his friends again. "What did you fellows make of that conversation?"

Amos let out an exasperated sigh. "He came in with a chip on his shoulder, and when he left he was carrying an entire *tree*."

"We need to find out more about this Council of Bishops," Marlin muttered. "Do any of you know folks from Lancaster County who could fill us in on who they are—"

"Along with their telephone numbers," Eli put in with a humorless laugh. "Have you ever heard tell of such a group reaching out halfway across the country—like the long arm of the law—to clamp down on a church district, just because of what they read in *The Budget*?"

"I'm as puzzled and frustrated as you are," Monroe replied. "But I think I got my point across regarding Anna-belle. At least King knows our women aren't afraid to speak up when they don't like men putting the moves on them."

A smile lit Eli's face. "We've done all we can for now, so I'm heading home to see if Noah needs somebody to help him pace," he said.

"Your Alma's there with Deborah, of course—and Minerva, too, I hope?" Marlin asked, helping himself to another cookie.

"*Jah*, and we're blessed to have your daughter-in-law's

midwifing skills at Promise Lodge," Eli replied as he started for the door. "With any luck, I'll get there after the baby's born. Bless her heart, Deborah was hollering like a calf caught in the fence when I peeked in on them this morning."

Monroe found a silver lining to the cloud of doubt and dismay hanging over them. "No matter what sort of trouble King's cooking up, life goes on and God continues to bless us with children and grandchildren," he remarked softly. "We have to keep believing He holds the future for us, and that we're safe in His loving hands."

Chapter Thirteen

Annabelle was so happy while helping with preparations for Allen and Phoebe's wedding meal that she sang along when Beulah and Ruby burst into a chorus of "Oh, Susanna." It felt good to feed people, to work with her friends on the big dinner for Friday, just two days away—and it was a special treat to have Mattie, Christine, and Rosetta cooking with them. Because Irene took Wednesdays off from baking pies for the Promise Lodge Pie Shop, she'd taken charge of the wedding pies. The entire lodge smelled like cinnamon, fruit, and sugar, and Annabelle was peeling apples to fill the crusts Irene was making.

"Nothing like a wedding to lift our spirits," Christine remarked after the song ended. "Monroe's really in a pickle, figuring out how to deal with the things Bishop Clayton's been saying."

"And a new baby—another grandbaby! We can be happy about that," Mattie put in as she cut chicken meat away from the bones. "Deborah's doing well, Noah looks ready to pop with pride, and little Sarah is just perfect. We have a lot to be thankful for no matter what kind of trouble that other bishop's kicking up."

"And after this wedding meal's behind us, the crochet club has *gut* reason to take up our hooks again," Beulah said.

She stopped kneading bread dough to check the sausage and bean casserole she'd put in the oven for the day's noon meal. "What with so much going on lately, we haven't crocheted many blankets or booties for Deborah. Last time we were in town, we got that birdseye cotton to make her some diapers, too."

"Oh, I'll get right on those!" Annabelle put in quickly. "They'll be a *gut* project for when I need to get off my feet this evening."

"I bet the rest of us could join you—make it a sewing and crocheting frolic in your apartment," Irene said. She smiled at Annabelle after fitting another circle of dough into a pie pan. "Unless you end up spending your evening with Phineas—or Clayton," she teased.

Annabelle waved her off. "What with those two circling each other like snarling dogs, I have to watch every little thing I say to either one of them," she said with a sigh. "I really appreciate the way you gals are sticking with me."

She picked another apple from her pile. "When I was a schoolgirl, I thought it would be so romantic to have two fellows vying for my attention—but now, not so much," she added pensively. "All I want is a life where I can be happy with one *gut* man. It won't be Bishop Clayton, for sure and for certain—but who knows how things will work out with Phineas?"

"*Jah*, it can't be easy, with things left unsettled," Rosetta said softly.

"I sense that Monroe's inclined to let your husband confess and have a shot at reconciling with you and the Old Order, if Phineas is willing to do that," Christine put in. "What would *you* like, Annabelle?"

What *would* she like? It was a question Annabelle had pondered often of late, even though she figured the church might have more to say about it than she did. "I recall being the happiest girl in the world when Phineas wanted to court me," she replied in a faraway voice. "He was so handsome, and such a dependable worker that he'd already built up enough money to—"

At the sound of the lodge's front screen door opening, the women froze in their places, listening.

"Smells mighty fine in here!" Jonathan called out.

"*Jah*, we came to the right place for lunch," Cyrus chimed in with his usual good humor. "I don't suppose you'll let us sample any of the wedding goodies you've been making. I'm pretty sure I smell rhubarb pie."

Everyone in the kitchen relaxed, but the time for girl talk had ended. Beulah removed the big casserole from the oven. "We'll be right there with lunch, fellows," she called out. "Make yourselves at home."

"Sounds like a fine idea."

Annabelle's body stilled at the sound of Phineas's voice—and then the front screen door squeaked again.

"Put another plate on the tables, ladies," said Bishop Clayton in a thundering voice. "The aromas of your cooking have drifted through your windows all morning, and I can't stay away any longer!"

Annabelle's eyes widened. "This might get interesting," she whispered.

Mattie's smile was catlike as she placed cut corn bread in a basket. "*Jah*, and who knows what might get said or done if we stir the pot a little, girls?" she replied softly. "We've got them outnumbered, after all."

"And they're on my turf," Rosetta pointed out as she removed the dome from the cake stand. "I don't care *who's* here—we expect a certain level of civility from the folks gathered around our table. Meanwhile, let's keep planning for happiness," she added with a lilt in her voice. "We shouldn't allow quibbling men to interfere with making a satisfying life for ourselves."

With that, Christine put on oven mitts and took hold of Beulah's steaming casserole. "Onward and upward, friends. We're doing exactly what we're supposed to, after all—cooking and serving the men."

"Puh! This is our dinner, too!" Beulah said as she and Ruby fell into line with a bowl of fresh slaw and a lime and pineapple gelatin salad. "Don't think for a minute that I'm going to stay in the kitchen like a meek little mouse while those men gobble it all down!"

Irene took out a plate, a glass, and a setting of silverware, smiling at Annabelle. "We'd be missing all this excitement if we hadn't come here to live, ain't so, dearie?" she teased softly. "Our best bet is to jump in feet first, because somebody's bound to step in it anyway. Better to make our own mess than to clean up somebody else's, *jah*?"

Annabelle had to chuckle. Who, indeed, could be a meek little kitchen mouse even if two men who despised each other had shown up for the noon meal? Her friends wouldn't let her hide—nor would they let her down if she needed them. As she entered the dining room after the other women, Annabelle couldn't miss the uneasy expressions Clayton and Phineas wore as they took their seats on opposite sides and opposite ends of the table. She caught the wry smiles that Cyrus and Jonathan flashed, too.

"What've we got here?" Cyrus asked as Christine set the bubbling casserole on the trivet in front of his place. "Looks like meat and beans—"

"And it smells scrumptious-*gut*," Jonathan put in.

"The recipe was my *mamm*'s, and she called it Posse Stew," Beulah replied as she set down her bowl of slaw. "When she served it, she reminded us that law and order were to be maintained at her table, or she'd call in the sheriff," she added in a purposeful tone.

Annabelle bit back a smile. Leave it to Beulah to state her case so Bishop Clayton and Phineas couldn't possibly miss her meaning. The two older men kept their remarks to themselves, although Clayton rolled his eyes.

"And corn bread! My favorite," Jonathan piped up. "Let's hope there'll be some left for the rest of you folks after I help myself."

"I'll fetch a big jar of honey," Ruby put in, patting the young man's shoulder. "My little bees love working for folks who enjoy it the way you do."

By the time Irene had handed Clayton his place setting—rather than putting it in front of him, Annabelle noted—she felt more positive about the way the visiting bishop had come in unannounced. Phineas, after all, was paying for his meals, but he apparently thought better of reminding Clayton about that.

After the women had taken the chairs interspersed among the men, silence filled the dining room during their prayer. Annabelle was grateful to her friends for sitting beside Phineas and Clayton, leaving her a spot between young Cyrus and Christine.

Help us remember, Lord, that we're all Your beloved children, she prayed with her eyes squeezed shut. *If we start acting out, remind us that You're in charge here. And* denki *for these fine ladies who love You—and me—with all their hearts.*

When Annabelle opened her eyes, Clayton was gazing at her like a cat perched beside the canary cage. Phineas smiled at her—that same casual, knowing smile that had always signaled his awareness of her as a woman. She busied herself with filling her plate as the side dishes came around, and then passed it to Beulah, who was dishing up the sausage and bean stew for everyone.

Bishop Clayton cleared his throat as though the silence in the room needed to be filled. "How's the wedding meal coming along, ladies?" he asked cheerfully. "I'm looking forward to chicken and stuffing roast, and creamed celery, and mashed potatoes, and all those other wonderful-*gut* foods with which we celebrate a happy couple."

Mattie and Beulah exchanged smiles. "Well then, Bishop, you're going to be disappointed," Mattie replied, "because Allen, our groom, has asked for venison roast— always a favorite of his and his *dat*'s—"

"And my Phoebe's been partial to chicken spaghetti since she was a wee girl," Christine chimed in. "So we've been baking the chickens and making the cheesy sauce for that dish today. None of that chicken and stuffing for these two."

"We'll also have a nice assortment of veggies that Mattie's grown in her produce plots," Ruby said, "such as mashed yams, zucchini and yellow squash casserole, and fresh green beans cooked with onions. Phoebe has never cared for celery, so there you have it."

"Chocolate wedding cake, too, instead of white," Beulah added with a chuckle, "because everyone here loves Ruby's chocolate cake with mocha frosting. And Irene's pies, of course. At least those are traditional."

The expression on Bishop Clayton's face was priceless, even if it signaled an oncoming lecture. "Have you people held on to *nothing* that is sacred?" he asked in a terse whisper. "Am I to assume you're holding the wedding here in the lodge, too, instead of in the bride's parents' home? You might as well be Mennonites, if you hold your worship services in a designated place such as the meeting room!"

Mattie set down her forkful of casserole to focus on Bishop Clayton. "Keep in mind that when we first came here, we had no homes to meet in—so we congregated in the lodge," she pointed out in a deceptively calm voice.

"And for the life of me, Bishop, I can't see how a menu of the bride and groom's favorite foods would displease God or reflect in any way on our faith in Him. Are you suggesting that every way we differ from tradition makes us more heathen and even farther from attaining salvation than you already believe we are?"

Annabelle's eyes widened. She understood Mattie's frustration, but she also thought her friend might have overstepped the bounds—especially because Mattie was a preacher's wife. Indeed, Clayton was glaring across the table at Mattie as though he might bore holes through her head with the intensity of his gaze.

"Our faith is no laughing matter—not a topic to make light of," the bishop began in a coiled voice. "If you can show no better respect than—"

The shrill ringing of the telephone interrupted Clayton's diatribe, and Annabelle was happy to head for the kitchen to answer it. She hadn't even made it to the door before the bishop was demanding, "Why do you have a telephone in here? Of all the—why do you women think you're above going to a phone shanty like your neighbors do?"

"Our first bishop, Floyd Lehman, asked the same question when he arrived," Rosetta quickly pointed out. "But he allowed us to keep it because all of the apartment and cabin residents use it as a group phone, and several of us run businesses with it."

"And how did you convince him to let you keep the electrical outlets? Is this place still wired?" Clayton came back at her.

Annabelle reached for the receiver and stepped into the mudroom with it, hoping the caller couldn't overhear the escalating conversation in the dining room. "*Jah*, hello?" she asked breathlessly. "You've reached Promise Lodge and this is Annabelle—"

"Oh, but it's *gut* to hear your voice, Annabelle! It's Edna

Schlabaugh," the caller interrupted. "I would've called back sooner but we've been up to our ears with canning tomatoes and we've had folks coming down right and left with an early run of the flu and—"

"Edna!" Annabelle said, turning her back toward the dining room. It was just like old times, with her neighbor flapping on and on like a chicken in a dither. "I'm sure sorry to hear about folks getting sick with the flu already. How are *you*?"

Heart pounding with anticipation, she listened to an answer that required several minutes. Annabelle hoped Edna would soon remember why she was calling. . . .

"—and you know we're gearing up for the fall festival, collecting consignment items to sell," she rambled on, "and everywhere we went around the county, we asked about Bishop Clayton King. It's the oddest thing, Annabelle. Nobody's ever heard of him—not even at the grocery warehouses where we stopped. And don't you think *Clayton* is an odd name for an Old Order Amish man? Sounds more Mennonite—and of the younger generation— if you ask me!"

Annabelle couldn't breathe. She gripped the receiver, staring at the deep freeze and the laundry sink and the back door—anything to keep herself focused on what her neighbor from Lancaster County had just said.

Nobody's ever heard of him.

"Annabelle? You still there?"

"*Jah*, I'm here," she murmured into the phone. *But who's that man sitting at our table?*

"Tell you what, Edna, you've caught me in the middle of things," Annabelle continued. "You've been a tremendous help, and *denki* so much for asking around for me. I'll call you back soon, okay?"

When Annabelle returned the receiver to the phone

cradle, her hand was shaking. At the sound of footsteps, she turned nervously.

"Annabelle, you're as white as a sheet," Christine said as she hurried over. "I came in for more corn bread—but also to see about you. Is everything all right? Bad news?"

"Well . . . *odd* news," Annabelle murmured, quickly making a decision. "The sort of thing I can't tell just anybody. Is Monroe home today?"

"*Jah*, if he's not at the house he's working with his horses." Christine frowned, leaning closer. "Annabelle, what is it? You can tell *me*—"

"I—I really think Bishop Monroe needs to be the judge of that," she said. "If anybody asks, just say I—I took him a slice of his favorite pie while it's still warm," she stammered. "Please don't ask me to say more, and please don't let on to anybody at the table that I've had a bit of a fright. Make it sound as though Monroe called to tease one of us into bringing him some pie, and I'm the one who picked up the phone."

Christine nodded doubtfully, but she didn't ask any more questions. By the time she'd loaded her basket with more golden squares of corn bread, Annabelle was hurrying up the road with an entire peach pie. She figured that was the least Monroe deserved, considering the news she was about to drop on him.

Monroe sat down hard on a kitchen chair, gesturing for Annabelle to do the same. "Now tell me this again to be sure I heard you right," he said. "Your friend from Lancaster County called you back—"

"And she said that she and her husband—who's a preacher in our district—couldn't find a single soul who knew of anybody by the name of Clayton King," Annabelle repeated slowly. "I called her a few weeks ago, because neither Phineas nor I had heard of him, either, and I was just *curious*, you know?"

Monroe rubbed his hand over his eyes. He felt a headache coming on, and aspirin wasn't going to touch it. "So who *is* he?" he whispered. "And why is he here pestering us?"

Annabelle grasped the bishop's hand in sympathy. "I wish I knew," she replied gently. "I'm still waiting for letters from a couple of friends back home, so maybe they'll have different answers—or more details that'll help us figure him out. Phineas and I haven't mentioned to him that we used to live just down the road from Paradise—"

"That shouldn't matter, if he's telling the truth." Monroe shook his head, totally baffled. "So why does King think he can fool us? What's in it for him?" he muttered with a sigh. The peach pie Annabelle had set on the table was still warm and it smelled like absolute heaven, yet he'd lost his appetite. One thing seemed prudent, however. "Annabelle, I'm asking you not to breathe a word of this to *anybody*— do you understand why?"

"Oh, *jah*, I figured you'd say that," she replied solemnly. "I won't tell Phineas for sure and for certain, because he'll just use this information as bait and wave it in front of Clayton's nose. Or whoever he really is," she added with a shake of her head.

"I'm not even going to mention this to the three preachers yet," he continued, "because the more folks who know, the more chance this information will slip out. Something's telling me to keep this tidbit under our hats until the time comes when we can best use it."

Annabelle nodded. "I couldn't go back into that dining room with him sitting at the table," she murmured. "Your wife thought I looked mighty upset, and if Clayton had started quizzing me about that phone call, I don't know if I could've kept this information to myself." She scowled.

"He was on his high horse again anyway, about what we're serving at the wedding meal and the fact that the ceremony's being held in the lodge instead of here at your place."

Monroe sighed, rubbing his temples. "I suspect he'll use the occasion to preach at us again about how we've fallen short. We need to be ready for whatever he says—because Allen and Phoebe's wedding is *not* the proper place for him to pontificate, or to hold the loss of our salvation over our heads."

"I'll let you know what those other friends write to me," Annabelle assured him. Then she let out a short laugh. "When I made my way to Promise Lodge, I thought I was escaping a confrontational situation—but here I am, smack in the middle of another one!"

Monroe focused on the woman sitting beside him. Annabelle was blond and attractive—in her early forties, but didn't look it—and she'd picked up on the spirit the other women in the lodge exuded. She deserved the life of peace and healing she'd come here for, and he intended for her to find it no matter what Phineas and King might do.

"By now you've had a chance to consider the ins and outs about this, so what are your thoughts about Phineas coming back for you?" he asked softly. "Do you want him to stay, or to go on back to his English way of life without you?"

"What are *your* thoughts, Bishop?" she countered quickly. "The Old Order spells out what's supposed to happen when somebody forsakes his vows to the church. Clayton King may be showering us with more fire and brimstone than we'd like, but most of what he's said about Phineas's situation is true. In most Amish communities, anyway."

Monroe's heart softened. Annabelle knew she was in a

tough spot, and she wasn't trying to wheedle her way out of it. "All of us at Promise Lodge came because we wanted a fresh start—a second chance at happiness," he murmured. "I believe that with God, all things are possible—just as the Bible tells us—and to me that now means there's no such thing as an unforgivable sin. If Phineas sincerely wants to make amends and reconcile with you and the church, I'm inclined to give him that chance. But I'm placing your welfare—your wishes—ahead of his."

Annabelle's mouth dropped open. "You'd do that for *me*?" she whispered.

"I would." Monroe considered the consequences of his decision, and decided to clarify it. "If you want Phineas to go, you'll still be married to him—and you can't marry anybody else until he passes, because we don't allow divorce," he said. "But you'll have a home here as long as you want one, so you won't be alone. At this point, I can't think any of us wants you to leave, Annabelle."

Her hand fluttered to her heart. "Oh my, that's—that's such a blessing you've just granted me, Bishop Monroe," she whispered. "It's so comforting to hear."

He smiled. "You're a blessing, too, to all of us here. I appreciate you coming to me with your information—and this fine pie! It was probably baked for the wedding, but I intend to enjoy every bite of it over the next couple of days while I figure out this situation we're in. The mystery of Clayton King."

Chapter Fourteen

As Gloria sat on the front pew bench of the women's side of the congregation, she thrummed with excitement. The regular church service had just ended and it was time for the wedding. Phoebe stepped up in front of Bishop Monroe, and Allen joined her. The bride blushed with eager happiness in her wedding dress of royal blue with a white organdy apron that shimmered in the morning sunlight. Allen's black church pants, matching vest, and white shirt appeared stiff with newness because Annabelle had just sewn his clothing this past week. He, too, appeared ready to promise himself to his mate forever.

An expectant hush fell over the crowd. Everyone knew the ancient wedding vows by heart, yet each bride and groom brought fresh energy to the ceremony.

Not a word had been spoken, but to Gloria, this wedding felt vastly different from the previous one, when her mother had married Preacher Marlin. Her heart stilled when Phoebe and Allen exchanged a nervous smile. They were set for life, with everything to look forward to: a lovely new house situated on a double-sized plot of ground that surrounded Rainbow Lake, not to mention Allen's burgeoning tiny home business and Phoebe's productive pie shop.

Or will Bishop Clayton change all that? What if he tells them they're too well-off and forces Phoebe to close her business?

Glancing around the roomful of folks in their Sunday clothes, Gloria knew that many of them had the same questions. Their smiles seemed tight for such a joyous occasion. Some folks glanced toward the burly man who sat on the preachers' bench amid Amos, Eli, and Marlin as though wondering if he'd nudge Bishop Monroe aside—or even take over the ceremony, the way he tended to disrupt any conversation he joined.

"Phoebe and Allen," Bishop Monroe began with a lilt in his rich voice, "you're ready to take the second most important vow of your lives, and I must ask you one final time if you're doing the right thing. If you have doubts, or if you have secrets or intentions that will compromise your life together, now's the time to back away from the lifelong commitment you're about to make."

Bishop Monroe glanced at the crowd, speaking a little louder. "If anyone else in this gathering knows of a reason these two should not become husband and wife, speak now or forever hold your peace."

Absolute silence rang in the big room.

Bishop Monroe flashed his boyish smile. "Very well, then. We stand before God with open, loving hearts and minds attuned to His will for us."

Laura grabbed Gloria's hand, her face alight with excitement. Gloria squeezed back, delighted that Phoebe had asked the two of them to be her side-sitters—and that Allen had invited his best buddies Cyrus and Jonathan to serve in that capacity.

When Gloria looked across the small center space where Phoebe and Allen stood, Cyrus was waiting to hold her gaze. A smile eased across his handsome face. With his hands in his lap, he subtly pointed first at her, then at himself, and then toward the place where the happy couple gazed raptly at the bishop who was conducting their wedding.

Gloria stopped breathing. Was Cyrus hinting that he wanted to be the next groom at Promise Lodge, and that he wanted her to be his bride? She'd dreamed about that happening sometime in the future, yet surely—well, if Cyrus wasn't giving her a sign, what could he possibly be doing?

Cyrus repeated the motions, pointing at her, then at himself, then at the bride and groom. And then he raised his eyebrows in a question.

Oh my word, is he asking me to—

Jonathan elbowed his brother. He probably considered Cyrus's gestures inappropriate—especially because the women's side of the congregation, along with the preachers, could see him if they weren't focused on the bishop as he led Allen in his vows.

For Gloria, the rest of the ceremony was a blur. During dinner, she and Cyrus would be seated together up on the raised *eck* table in the corner. Would he dare whisper his proposal there, in front of everyone? Or would he wait until they could be alone? Cyrus had a knack for finding places around Promise Lodge where they could spend time together away from prying eyes—over the past couple of weeks they'd gone on several evening walks. And each time he'd kissed her—

Oh, but his kisses hold promises that I so want him to keep!

Gloria's cheeks got so hot that Laura might think she had a high fever, so she again focused on the ceremony. She needed to pay attention, so her own wedding would go just right when she and Cyrus stood before the bishop.

What color would her dress be? Where would she shop for the high-topped black shoes brides traditionally wore, and for the special white fabric for her apron?

Has Cyrus saved enough to build us a house? We won't be able to live in my apartment after we marry, so—

"It's my pleasure to introduce Mr. and Mrs. Allen Troyer," Bishop Monroe announced in a booming voice. "Let's spend the rest of the day celebrating the start of their life together!"

Applause filled the meeting room and folks began to stand up—but before Allen and Phoebe could make their way to the dining room door to accept congratulations, another voice rose above the commotion.

"Before the ladies begin setting out the meal," Bishop Clayton called out, "I need a few moments to make an important announcement. Please be seated!"

The bride and groom looked perplexed, but they sat down on the front pew of the men's side. Bishop Monroe turned toward Bishop Clayton with a frown. "Surely you can find another time to—"

"What I have to say affects every man, woman, and child in this room," the visiting Bishop insisted. He gazed purposefully at Bishop Monroe, until he, too, took a seat on the other side of Cyrus and Jonathan.

"I know you're eager to hear what the Council of Bishops has decided," Bishop Clayton continued after complete silence filled the room. He took a folded sheet of paper from his inside vest pocket and opened it with a flourish.

"October thirtieth, Lancaster County, Pennsylvania," he read in a ceremonial voice. "After much deliberation and prayer, we members of the Council of Bishops are installing Bishop Clayton King as the new leader of the Promise Lodge community, to correct inappropriate leanings toward a more worldly way of life than is allowed by the Old Order Amish faith."

Everyone gaped or sucked in their breath. Across the room from Gloria, Bishop Monroe's eyes widened, but he made no comment because Bishop Clayton immediately continued reading.

"Furthermore, we recommend that a monetary offering—"

"This is uncalled for!" Preacher Amos said as he rose abruptly from the preachers' bench. "The most *inappropriate* behavior I see is that you've jumped on your bandwagon at my son's wedding rather than breaking this news to us preachers and Monroe first."

"This is outrageous!" Preacher Eli called out as he, too, stood up. "In all my years as a leader of the church, I've never heard tell of a Council of Bishops out east horning in on what other church districts do—much less displacing the bishop that God Himself selected for a community."

When other men protested, as well, Bishop Clayton raised his hand for silence. "I'm only the messenger here," he reminded them as he held up the letter. "There's one more point the council wants me to make, and then you'll have plenty of time to discuss their decisions among yourselves. As I was saying—"

Again Bishop Clayton focused on the page before him. "We recommend that a monetary donation in the form of a tithe be collected from each family of Promise Lodge as a sign of the community's willingness to comply with Old Order ways," he continued earnestly. "Ten percent of their earnings for the current calendar year, as well as from the funds Promise Lodge has banked—the biblically recommended amount since Old Testament times—will surely not be a burden to anyone in this prosperous settlement. It will ensure that the families we've placed in Bishop

Clayton King's care are serious about following the path to salvation in Jesus Christ our Lord. The council will continue to monitor the community's progress under Bishop Clayton's guidance."

Everyone was so stunned that Bishop Clayton's refolding of the letter seemed to crackle in the silence.

Gloria tried to grasp exactly what the council's letter meant. If every family was to donate 10 percent, would *she* have to tally what Rosetta had paid her so far? She wondered if this was the council's first step toward convincing women to give up their businesses and to be supported by—

"Where will this money go?" Preacher Marlin demanded. "And for what purpose? I find it highly irregular—"

"Of course you do, Deacon Marlin," Bishop Clayton said as he turned toward the preachers' bench. "You've helped create a community where married women run businesses and where Mennonites and Amish are allowed to marry, so the Old Order ways have come to seem *irregular* to you," he pointed out. "As your new bishop, I'll be sending the Promise Lodge tithe to the council as soon as possible—hopefully within the next week—to prove that you're sincerely invested in being right with God, making your way toward everlasting life instead of sliding down the slippery slope to damnation."

Bishop Clayton pivoted to face the congregation. "If you have questions, feel free to visit with me anytime," he said in a less strident, more compassionate tone. "We're all in this together, folks. Let's spend the rest of the day celebrating Allen and Phoebe's marriage, and the fact that they've chosen to remain in the Old Order faith to enrich this community with their presence."

Gloria glanced at Laura, who appeared as shocked and confused as everyone around them did. They didn't dare speculate about what Bishop Clayton had just announced, because he was standing close enough to hear them.

A few moments later, Allen took Phoebe's hand and they headed toward the dining room doorway. With dazed expressions, the women behind Gloria stood up and made their way to the kitchen. As members of the wedding party, she and Laura were excused from helping with the food, yet it didn't seem right to leave all the work to the older women with such a momentous announcement hanging over everyone's heads.

"Let's go help," Gloria whispered. "If we're in the kitchen or carrying food to the buffet line, we'll have something to *do*—and Bishop Clayton won't be as likely to strike up a conversation with us."

"*Jah, gut* idea," Laura murmured. "I feel as if Ruby's bees are all swarming inside my head. What will happen to Monroe now? I feel really bad for him, finding out in front of all these people that Bishop Clayton is taking over."

When Gloria looked at the tall, handsome man who'd recently become Laura's stepfather, she paused. He had the oddest expression on his face, as though he was about to make an announcement of his own—but then he looked at the three preachers and nodded toward the front door. Amos, Eli, and Marlin followed Monroe out of the meeting room as Bishop Clayton watched—and then Clayton left, too, as though he intended to be in on their meeting.

"Oh, things might get nasty," Gloria said under her breath.

The moment the church leaders were gone, the room rang with speculative conversations. Gloria glanced over at Cyrus, thinking he'd have something to say to her about the situation, but Jonathan was steering him out the back way. She couldn't read Cyrus's expression, but his older brother appeared clearly displeased about the turn things had taken in the past few minutes.

These changes will affect us all just as Bishop Clayton said, Gloria thought with a sigh. The only thing that seemed certain was that it was time to serve Allen and Phoebe's wedding meal, so she and Laura headed for the kitchen.

When Monroe stepped outside, Daisy rose eagerly from beneath the porch swing to greet him.

"We've got a rogue ram for you to herd, girl—but not right now," he said under his breath. "Go lie down, Daisy."

The border collie obediently returned to her post as Monroe descended the lodge steps, followed by the three preachers. He was bursting to tell them what he'd learned about King from Annabelle a couple days ago, but he kept his mouth shut and his expression carefully composed. He wasn't surprised to hear another set of footsteps behind them.

"Let's go to the far end of the building by the cabins, so folks won't wander out and overhear us," he suggested to his friends before turning around. "Except for *you* of course, King. How did I know you wouldn't allow the rightful leaders of this community to meet without your interference?"

King's smile turned saccharin. "That's not a very charitable attitude, considering I've been appointed to keep you from descending into hell on Judgment Day, Burkholder."

Amos was having none of it. "Let's see that letter," he said, holding out his hand. "Why on God's *gut* earth would I believe a word you said to us this morning? You were just putting on a show—"

"*Jah*, talk about a lack of humility," Eli butted in angrily.

"The Council of Bishops is going to hear about how you strutted around like a peacock, reading a letter I suspect you made up yourself!"

King stared at each of them in turn, appearing disappointed, hurt—and appalled—as he reached into his vest pocket.

"You're off to a questionable start already, accusing me of pride and telling lies," he muttered as he held out the letter. "After all, the council will rely upon *my* reports—my judgment—as to when this place will pass muster."

Amos plucked the page from King's fingers and held it open so they could all stand around him and read it. Monroe stepped behind Amos, as he was tall enough to read over his shoulder. He clenched his teeth to keep his face from showing any emotion as he studied the handwritten page. The penmanship wasn't the best, but the letters were all clearly formed, tall and angular. Apparently a fellow named Joe Mast had written it, as the handwriting matched his signature, which was followed by five others.

Monroe wasn't surprised that every name on the list was so common that it probably belonged to a dozen men in the Lancaster area. But because Annabelle's friends hadn't found anyone who knew of a Bishop Clayton King, Monroe suspected that every signature was as phony as the letter itself.

He didn't say that, of course. He didn't want to tip his hand that this whole situation felt as bogus as a bull with an udder.

"I find it odd that these bishops didn't name the church districts they represent," Eli remarked. "Matter of fact, King, we don't have any idea which community *you* come from, because you always change the subject and ignore our questions about your personal life!"

Taken aback by the preacher's remark, King drew himself

up to his full height. "Once again your lack of faith in the man God sent to redirect you *wounds* me, gentlemen," he said in a theatrical whisper. "What must the Lord be thinking, each time you make such accusations? Today alone you've committed enough new sins to require a full kneeling confession the next time we meet for church. You won't be getting off your knees for a month of Sundays, the way you're going."

"What I've noticed," Marlin put in earnestly, "is that this Council of Bishops has given us no way to contact them or to respond to the case they have against us. If these men are so concerned about our souls, why did none of them come out here with you, Clayton—and especially, why are none of them present today to discuss the two issues in this letter?"

Monroe bit back a smile at this perceptive question. Marlin was clearly as doubtful about King as the rest of them were.

"*Jah!* If any of us—especially Monroe—was on a council that was displacing a community's bishop," Amos put in tersely, "we'd show up in person!"

"And where's all that money going?" Eli demanded. "If we're to donate as a token of our *gut* will, why can't the money stay in Missouri, where plenty of Plain folks in a pinch could make use of it? Lancaster County's got some of the richest farmland—and the richest Amish folks—I've ever heard of, so why should our money go there?"

"Suffice it to say that although we appreciate your efforts to save us from ourselves, Bishop Clayton," Monroe put in smoothly, "we require more documentation—more proof—before we'll give ourselves or our money over to you."

Monroe held the gaze of each of his preachers, to be

sure they understood that he had a strategy. "We could stay out here pointing fingers all day and waste this special occasion that should be about Amos's son and his new bride—but we won't," he continued before King could butt in. "Before we submit to a single one of your new rules as our bishop, and before we contribute one dime to this tithe you're asking for, we need to see the addresses and phone numbers of all these bishops on the council."

King's eyes widened dramatically. "Are you accusing me, a man appointed by God, of misrepresenting myself or the council—or of trying to cheat you out of your money?"

"That pretty much sums it up, *jah*," Amos replied without missing a beat. "I've heard enough. My only son has joined the Amish church and married a fine young woman—two events I thought I might never witness. I'll be *dogged* if I let you take this day away from me!"

"*Jah*, you give us that list of addresses and phone numbers," Eli put in. "Then we'll have something to talk about."

"I totally agree," Marlin added as the three of them headed toward the lodge's front porch.

Monroe clasped his hands behind him, waiting for King to leave next—because *he* refused to walk away from the biggest test his community had ever faced.

King took his time refolding the letter, shaking his head as he recreased the folds between his fingers. "This obstinate attitude—your blatant refusal to cooperate—will only make things harder on you," he warned. "What am I supposed to say when the other council members ask why you've refused to listen—or to obey their recommendations?"

Monroe shrugged. The more King blustered, the more Monroe smelled a hoax, and the more confident he felt that they would eventually find the proof they needed to send Clayton King—or whoever he was—packing. "If you provide the information we've asked for, and if we all speak only the truth before our God, we have nothing to worry about. Nothing to hide. Right?"

Chapter Fifteen

As Gloria made a final check of the steam tables, her stomach rumbled. Emotionally, her morning had resembled a roller-coaster ride, and now that Allen and Phoebe were ready to fill their plates, she was, too. She looked around the crowded dining room. "Have you seen Cyrus and Jonathan?" she asked Laura, who'd been helping at the pie table.

"I haven't," her friend replied as she, too, gazed around the crowd. "And since the wedding party's supposed to eat before the other guests, we should round them up. You'd think they wouldn't be late for *this* part of the day!"

"They went outside. I'll go find them." Gloria hurried through the kitchen, where Ruby and Beulah were arranging big metal pans of food in the ovens, to be ready for refilling the steam table. "Dinner looks amazing, ladies! I'll be back in a few with a couple of our side-sitters!"

When Gloria stepped out through the mudroom door, she looked around the lodge's lawn. Black buggies belonging to the guests from Coldstream were parked along the road, and orange-tipped leaves were drifting slowly from the big maple trees. She saw no one until she spotted Daisy lying in the leaves, looking toward the cabins. Jonathan and Cyrus stood behind their place, and she nearly called out to them—but their harsh expressions stopped her.

Curiosity prodded her to approach them, however, staying in the shadow of the lodge. What topic could possibly be so important to keep dozens of guests waiting for their dinner? And why was Jonathan scowling at his younger brother, who stood with his fists on his hips?

"—got to call off this stupid bet!" Jonathan insisted vehemently. "It's just *wrong* to manipulate the girls' feelings by pushing toward—"

"You're falling behind with Laura and you don't want to pay up!" Cyrus jeered. "There's nothing wrong with a little wager to keep things interesting—"

"But I really *like* Laura, and she deserves better than—and those hand signals you were sending Gloria during the wedding were way out of line!"

"You just wish *you* had thought of them!" Cyrus shot back. "She was eating it up! So when I'm engaged by Thanksgiving and you're not, you'll just have to hand over that five hundred bucks, *jah*?"

Gloria fell back against the lodge building, feeling as though the air had been sucked from her lungs. *Five hundred dollars? For a bet that Laura and I will say yes before Thanksgiving? That's only three weeks away.*

Tears sprang to her eyes. Cyrus had obviously been the instigator of the wager, and Jonathan was mature enough, sincere enough, to call him on it—but their conversation changed *everything.* For once, a handsome young man had been asking her out and she hadn't been pursuing a relationship that only she was interested in. But it was only a game to him, a total sham, to prove that he was better at sweet-talking and making eyes and suggestive comments than his introverted brother.

Gloria covered her mouth so the two young men wouldn't hear her sob. As she turned away from their escalating argument, it occurred to her that the wedding guests—and even the newlyweds—might still be waiting for the side-sitters before they started through the buffet line. She had to go inside no matter how humiliated she felt. And she had to let Laura know what she'd heard.

As Gloria entered the mudroom, she desperately tried to compose herself, but folks would know she'd been crying. In the kitchen, Laura's *mamm* was placing more slices of bread in baskets, so Gloria approached her as she mopped her face with her apron.

"Gloria! What's wrong, sweetie?" Christine asked gently.

Gloria swallowed hard so she could get words out. "I— I can't talk about it," she whispered miserably, "but could you let folks know that they should go ahead and fill their plates—"

"Oh, Allen and Phoebe jumped in a while ago, and the guests are in line now," Christine said with a concerned nod. "I suspect everybody's so antsy about what Bishop Clayton announced that we're not so concerned about who goes in what order today."

Gloria sighed. The last thing on her mind was food, now that she knew how Cyrus really felt about her. "Could you—well, I really need to talk to Laura, but I don't want to go out there and have everybody quiz me about why I'm such a mess."

Christine wrapped her arm around Gloria's shoulders. "*Jah*, I can do that. And I'll tell Phoebe and Allen something's detained you side-sitters," she murmured reassuringly. "Whatever it is, honey, I'm sure you'll work it out. I'm sorry you're upset when we all need to eat together and shore ourselves up for whatever happens next with Bishop Clayton. Maybe you girls should fix your plates here in the kitchen and take them up to your apartment—"

"I couldn't eat a thing, but *jah*, tell Laura I'll be up-stairs," Gloria said. "*Denki* for understanding."

With a glance at all the covered pans of food waiting to go out to the steam table, Gloria started up the back stairs empty-handed. When she reached her apartment, she glanced out the window. Cyrus and Jonathan were no longer behind their cabin.

Maybe they're looking for Laura and me. It'll serve them right to sit at the eck *and have folks ask them where we are.*

There was a tapping at the door.

"Gloria? What happened when you went outside?" Laura asked as she came in. "Mamm said you needed to talk to me, and—oh my, you're crying. Where are Cyrus and Jonathan?"

Gloria turned, grateful for Laura's hug. "Right now, I—I don't really *care* where they are," she replied tearfully. "I hate to spoil Phoebe's big day for you but—"

Laura waved her off. "What could possibly upset the apple cart any more than Bishop Clayton's announce-ment?"

Gloria sighed loudly and wiped her face again. "I overheard Cyrus and Jonathan talking," she replied sadly. "They have a bet going about being engaged to us by Thanksgiving, and if one of them isn't, he owes the other one five hundred dollars."

Laura's jaw dropped. "Five hundred dollars? That's outrageous," she whispered. "And Thanksgiving's less than a month off! Too soon to say we'll marry them, don't you think?"

"*Jah*, but haven't you at least daydreamed about that?" Gloria asked glumly. "When I saw Cyrus signaling me during the wedding, I thought . . . but now that I know it's just a game to them, I'm hurt. And furious."

Laura looked away, frowning as the details sank in. "I can't believe Jonathan would make such a crazy bet— especially when our feelings and our—our *futures* are involved!"

"To be fair, he was the one telling Cyrus to cancel the bet because it's not right, and because he sincerely likes you and knows you deserve better treatment."

Laura crossed her arms, frowning. "Even so, I *really* don't like knowing that this started as a—a *game* to them! I don't like being toyed with, Gloria."

Gloria appreciated this sentiment, even though at eighteen, blond, blue-eyed Laura hadn't been rejected by two other young men the way she had. The situation would be easier if they had other fellows to choose from at Promise Lodge . . . and if Gloria wasn't twenty-three with no apparent alternatives to becoming a *maidel*. Even though she enjoyed her job managing Rosetta's apartments, the prospect of doing it for the rest of her long, lonely life seemed very bleak.

"Well, I'm not desperate enough to pretend I don't know what they're up to!" Laura stated firmly. "I'm going downstairs to inform them that I want no part of it! Are you coming with me?"

"I'm a mess from crying," Gloria protested. "I wish I could just get in their faces as though my feelings weren't hurt—"

"I'll do that part. Come on, girl," Laura said as she

grabbed Gloria's hand. "Unless we state our case, folks might think the guys called it off. I want everyone to know that we refuse to play their game!"

The idea of making a scene in the dining room mortified Gloria, but there was no backing off when Laura started for the door. *Kapp* strings flying behind them, they hurried down the back stairway and through the kitchen, not stopping to answer the questions in the eyes of the women who were loading more food onto the rolling carts. At least the *eck* table was in the corner closest to the kitchen door so the two of them didn't have to cross the dining room.

Gloria winced when Laura approached Cyrus and Jonathan, who were sitting together to the left of the newlyweds with their full plates of food. She wanted to disappear into a crack between the floorboards when Laura leaned over the table and smacked it with her hand.

"We know about your little bet, *boys*," her friend whispered vehemently. "Don't think for a minute that we'll go along with your engagement plan—or that we'll ever go out with you again! Right, Gloria?"

When Cyrus dropped his fork and stared at her, speechless, Gloria felt a tiny glimmer of gratification—but all she could do was nod at Laura's remark. She was red-faced with humiliation, knowing that Phoebe and Allen could hear what Laura had said—and because she'd foolishly believed that the Helmuth brothers were sincerely interested in Laura and her.

Jonathan appeared mortified as he grabbed Laura's hand. "Wait! It's not that way for me—I tried to—"

"Trying doesn't cut it!" Laura retorted as she pulled her hand free. "You went along with Cyrus's bet, and you're both old enough to know better! We're out of here. Come on, Gloria."

Once again Laura grabbed her hand, and Gloria followed her into the kitchen before the brothers or the bride and groom could ask any questions. She wondered if other folks had overheard their confrontation, but there was no going back—and truth be told, they'd done the right thing. What if she hadn't overheard Cyrus and Jonathan bickering? What if she and Laura had believed the Helmuth brothers were proposing for all the right reasons?

"What was *that* about, girls?" Ruby asked gently. "We couldn't hear what you said, but it must've been mighty important if it's kept you from filling your plates."

The Kuhn sisters, Rosetta, Mattie, and Christine—and her mother—had all stopped what they were doing to listen to the answer. Even though Laura was getting upset enough to cry, she slung her arm around Gloria's shoulder.

"Gloria overheard that Cyrus and his brother had a five-hundred-dollar bet going about being engaged to us by—by Thanksgiving," she stammered. "So I told them exactly what we thought of that obnoxious idea, and that we're not going to see them anymore."

"Oh, but I'm sorry to hear that," Beulah said softly. "It was so nice to think you girls and the Helmuth brothers were together—"

"But I can understand why you're upset," Rosetta put in. "Maybe it's not much comfort to you right now, but I've never been sorry I called off my engagement with Truman when I thought he was getting too cozy with Maria Zehr."

"And that situation turned out the way it was supposed to," Ruby pointed out with a nod.

Gloria nodded glumly as her mother slipped an arm around her waist.

"It's best to be honest about such things rather than acting as though you don't know about them," Mamm murmured. "But I'm sure you're disappointed, sweetie. I'm sorry this has happened to you."

"*Jah*, I'm disappointed, too," Christine said as she came to stand beside her daughter. "I was pleased when Cyrus and Jonathan showed an interest in you girls—but now they know they can't get away with such immature behavior, even if they made that bet in fun."

"We're on your side, girls," Mattie put in gently. "In your place, I'd make those boys do some *tall* explaining before I spent any more time with them."

Gloria pressed her lips together to keep from bursting into tears again. Although it felt good to have the support of these women, their kindness didn't mean that she'd ever go out on another date, did it? "Guess I'll head back upstairs," she murmured. "I'm not hungry, and I don't want to be a wet blanket on Phoebe and Allen's wedding day."

"*Jah*, maybe I'll get something later," Laura said with a glance at the pans of food.

As the two of them trudged up the back stairs, Gloria's heart felt heavy. In the close-knit community of Promise Lodge, there was no way to avoid contact with Cyrus in the days to come. If he tried to sweet-talk his way back into her life, what would she say to him?

As they closed the door of her apartment behind them, the only answer Gloria could think of was a long, sad sigh.

Chapter Sixteen

As Annabelle took the last bite of her apple pie, her thoughts circled like dry leaves in a whirlwind. The folks from Promise Lodge were suppressing their true feelings as they ate, because Bishop Clayton was circulating between the tables making conversation—and the friends who'd come from Coldstream surely must be wondering about the outspoken man who'd announced he was taking over as the community's new bishop. She was thinking of an excuse to head for the kitchen as Clayton approached her table, but then Phineas, seated beside her, clasped her hand.

"Let's go for a walk," he said, scooting back his chair. "I have nothing to say to King, and everything to discuss with you, Annabelle."

Little red flags shot up in her mind, but she couldn't deny that all through the meal her husband had been attentive and pleasant. They'd been sitting across from Preacher Marlin and Frances, talking with Marlin about his barrel-making business.

"Excuse us, folks," Phineas said. "I'd rather spend my time with Annabelle than say something I'll regret when King gets here."

Marlin and Frances nodded, and Annabelle followed

Phineas sideways down the aisle between the closely arranged tables. When they reached the lobby, he slipped his arm around her and opened the front door, leaning so close that she caught the familiar masculine scent that was uniquely Phineas Beachey. She'd missed the day-to-day contact with him and the little things like the sound of his voice and the feel of his work-roughened hand on hers, yet she felt wary of whatever topic was pressing him to take her off so they could be alone.

Once outside, Annabelle inhaled deeply. "What a day," she remarked with a shake of her head. "You can just *feel* the way folks are holding in their reactions to Clayton King—"

"Let's find a more gratifying topic of conversation, shall we?" Phineas asked with a wink. "It won't be difficult."

A nervous laugh escaped Annabelle as they descended the porch steps together. In light of the announcement Bishop Clayton had made, she was even more curious about his true identity, but she hadn't shared her secret with anyone since she'd talked to Bishop Monroe—and Phineas had just given her the perfect reason not to tell him, either. "*Jah*, he dropped a couple of bombs today, for sure and for certain," she said.

Phineas held her gaze. "Will it be all right if we talk in my cabin? I know you've been . . . reluctant to be alone with me, but what I have to say is rather private."

Annabelle swallowed hard. The expression on his lean face made her wonder what Phineas planned to reveal—as though *anything* could be quite as unexpected as what Clayton had announced after the wedding.

But what did she have to fear? In all their years of marriage he'd never become violent, even when he'd spoken gruffly or complained about something she'd done. "All right. Sure."

"I think it's time we settled things between us," Phineas murmured. "I've been here a month now, so we've both had time to consider our feelings."

Annabelle allowed him to steer her past the cabins, his hand warm on the curve of her lower back. As surely as the colored leaves on the maple trees signaled the onset of winter, the next couple of hours might be the most important ones she'd spent with Phineas in many years. As he opened the door of the last cabin, he seemed almost hesitant—and what a difference that was from his usual confident swagger.

The main room of the cabin was neatly kept, and she saw a small bathroom in the back with its door ajar. The bed was made up with a quilt of dark blues; the only other furniture consisted of a small kitchen table with two chairs and an armchair with a battery lamp on a table beside it. As Phineas gestured for her to sit in the armchair, Annabelle realized that he'd been leading a very simple life since he'd arrived, with few of the comforts they'd known at home.

Phineas brought over one of the chairs from the table so he could sit facing her. He looked lean and elegant in his black trousers and white shirt, and with his English haircut and close-trimmed beard, Annabelle wondered if any other women had noticed how attractive he was in the weeks they'd been apart.

"I'd like to explain why I left the church, Annabelle."

She clasped her hands in her lap to keep from fidgeting. "All right. I'm listening."

Phineas sighed, leaning his elbows on his knees. "Did you ever wonder why God gave us the intellect to discover and harness electricity, yet the church won't allow us to use it for running power tools—or even kitchen appliances?" he began softly. "What does electricity have to do with our faith in Him? Do you think it's all right with God that we can't sleep because we're too hot at night, when a simple air conditioner would keep us from being tired and grouchy all summer long?"

Annabelle blinked. This kind of talk wasn't what she'd been expecting. "I—I don't know those answers," she admitted. "I guess I've always figured we weren't supposed to ask the questions."

Phineas nodded. "Same goes for using zippers and belts rather than fastening our clothes with pins or holding up our pants with suspenders," he continued earnestly, "and for mandating that married men grow a beard yet we're forbidden to have mustaches—and for forbidding you women to cut your hair at all. Do you believe God will condemn me on Judgment Day because I've been to a barber shop a couple of times instead of coming home so you could cut my hair?"

His sincere confusion took her aback. He wasn't railing about perceived injustices or defying Old Order ways so much as he was daring to consider. Annabelle sensed he didn't expect answers, so she merely held his gaze, waiting for him to go on.

Phineas sighed, shrugging. "It's stuff like that I got really tired of—along with our bishop's inflexible attitude about me working on his projects rather than my own— that drove me to try the English way. I wanted to see if I felt any different about God, or if God sent a bolt of lightning through the roof to warn me that I really was putting my soul's salvation at risk."

"And what did you decide?" Annabelle asked carefully.

A boyish grin relieved the tension on Phineas's handsome face. "So far so *gut*, as far as the lightning bolt goes," he replied. "But truth be told, reestablishing my remodeling business—using electric tools and living English—didn't give me the satisfaction I thought it might."

Was he going to elaborate? Again Annabelle remained quiet, waiting to see what else he felt compelled to say. She wasn't accustomed to watching Phineas shift nervously in his seat—and his gentle, confessional tone of voice was a welcome change from what she'd become accustomed to during their marriage, as well.

"Although I got upset when I returned home to find that you'd moved on," he continued, "it was partly because I'd been ready to admit how much I missed you, Annabelle, and you weren't there to talk to. The past month of being here at Promise Lodge has given me a new perspective— a new way of looking at the religion that's felt like a burr on my backside . . . and a new way of looking at *you*."

Annabelle's heart stilled. "Promise Lodge is a very special place," she murmured.

"It is," he agreed without a moment's pause. "I appreciate the way Bishop Monroe and the preachers here are open to change even as they don't criticize the Old Order ways. They seem like such practical men, who genuinely care for the folks in their congregation—and I think King is dead wrong to declare himself the bishop here. Who's ever heard of such a thing? Why does he think he can get away with that?"

Annabelle's eyebrows rose. Somewhere there had to be an answer to Clayton King's actions. Although she believed they would eventually ferret out the truth about him, she could only hope that somebody proved him an impostor before he made sweeping changes at Promise Lodge. "I suppose Bishop Monroe and our preachers want some concrete proof before they send him packing," she suggested. "Out of respect, most folks won't point a finger at a bishop—and who would dream that a God-appointed leader of the church would deceive them? It's unheard of."

"*Jah*, well—enough about King. I want to confess to something else before he takes it upon himself to barge in on us."

As he rose from his chair, Annabelle wondered what her husband of more than twenty years could possibly reveal to her. Phineas Beachey wasn't a man to confess to *anything* unless there was no way out of it. Had he changed? Or was he afraid Clayton King was wooing her away from him? He raked his fingers through his silvery hair until she wanted to reach out and smooth it down for him. When he began to pace, she knew something was weighing heavily upon him.

"Annabelle, I'm sorry I couldn't give you children—"

Her hand fluttered to her chest.

"—and I'm sorry I let this inability come between us over the years we've been together," Phineas continued in a nervous rush. "There, I've said it."

Tears sprang to Annabelle's eyes, yet she'd never felt more confused. "Phineas, I don't understand," she whispered as he walked to the window. "As time went by and God didn't bless us with children, I assumed it was me who couldn't conceive—"

"And I—I allowed you to think that," he interrupted in a halting voice, "because I was too proud to tell you my suspicions, or to get tested by a doctor. What man wants to find out he's more a hen than a rooster when he's spent most of his life acting as though he's the cock of the walk?"

Annabelle stared at him. He was as serious as she'd ever seen him—not that a good-looking, physically robust man like Phineas would joke about such a deeply private matter. When he glanced at her and then turned away in embarrassment, Annabelle went to him and clasped his hand between hers.

"How do you know you can't have children?" she whispered. "Did you see a doctor before you came to that conclusion?"

He shook his head miserably. "I caught a program on TV about how some childhood diseases like mumps can affect a man's ability to—to procreate." Phineas sighed. "I had a very dangerous case of mumps when I was about twelve; in fact I almost died. By the time my parents took me to the hospital, the damage to my body could easily have messed up my hormones."

Phineas swiped his hand over his face, clearly humiliated by this sort of talk. "I vaguely recall the doctor telling my parents that I might not be able to have children when I got older, but my *dat* dismissed that possibility because he didn't want to hear it. He got me into the habit of talking up my—my manliness, mostly to override my shyness around girls because I was shorter than a lot of them," he went on in a rush. "As I got older, he had me convinced that I would be a real bull in the bedroom like he was, fathering ten kids—"

Annabelle nipped her lip. Indeed, Phineas had always been eager to have his way with her . . . perhaps he'd been trying to prove he *could* bed her. But as an innocent bride, she hadn't suspected anything might be wrong with her husband. She'd been flattered by his constant attentions, and the fact that she was a few inches taller than he was had never mattered to her.

"—and he went so far as to tell me I shouldn't discuss such a thing with the woman I took as my wife," Phineas continued in a tight voice. "He had me so buffaloed, I let my pride get in the way, Annabelle. I wanted you for my wife from the first time we met at my cousin's wedding and—and I couldn't let any hint of *failure* on my part give you a reason not to marry me."

With a wry smile Annabelle recalled the wedding where they'd met. "I wasn't much impressed with you that day, Phineas," she recounted softly. "I thought I was in love with Edwin Plank, except you repeatedly refused to take no for an answer when you asked me for dates."

Phineas shook his head. "See how bullheaded I was? Totally unconcerned about your feelings," he admitted. He gazed sadly at her with his pale green eyes—eyes that had always mesmerized her and seen through her defenses. "I'm sorry, Annabelle. I knew you dreamed of having a family—knew you'd make a wonderful mother—and because I didn't tell you I might be unable to give you kids, you didn't have the chance to marry a man who could have made those dreams come true. Can you forgive me, dear wife?"

Annabelle trembled as her husband's confession sank in. Very few Amish men would admit to the physical disability Phineas had just discussed. Truth be told, he could've remained silent for the rest of their lives—

And I'd have been none the wiser, her inner voice pointed out. She couldn't help thinking about Edwin, and how he'd married another girl after Phineas had wooed Annabelle away. He'd had six children, a very happy family from all appearances.

Those six kids could've been yours, Annabelle thought with a pang of longing. It was the first time she'd dared to imagine that, because she'd assumed she was the barren one.

But they're not yours, and you've made the most of the life God gave you with Phineas—until he left you last spring. Are you going to leave him hanging, now that he's apologized?

Annabelle glanced at their clasped hands as she stood so close to Phineas that she could feel the warmth radiating from his body. She cleared her throat. "Why are you telling me this?" she whispered.

Phineas let out a humorless laugh. "Now that I've been away from the narrowness of our church district in Lancaster, and I've talked with so many folks here about the new lives they've made for themselves, maybe I want to start fresh, too—and I had to come clean to you," he said softly. "And maybe it's time to stop covering my disappointment about my disability by lashing out at you. Time to stop being angry because God ignored my prayers about having a family with you."

Annabelle's eyes widened. She was ready to assure him that he'd always seemed intensely masculine to her, but the flicker of his smile made her wait him out.

"Or it could be that the way King looks at you makes me realize what I stand to lose if you fall for him."

"What?" she blurted. "Even if I believed the lines he's been casting my way, I couldn't marry him."

"Ah, but there's a difference between not *wanting* to be with him and being forbidden by the church to pursue such a relationship." Phineas held her gaze, and she found she couldn't look away.

"King's a smooth one," he continued softly. "If anybody could create a biblical loophole to justify a secret romance, he's the one."

Annabelle suspected Phineas was right, just as she realized that jealousy was part of her husband's motivation for talking to her so frankly. To her befuddled, abandoned heart, however, Phineas's revelation was liberating. He was admitting that she had the power to choose—to prefer—another man over him.

"I still want you for my wife, Annabelle, if you'll have me

back," he pleaded in a voice she could barely hear. "Bishop Monroe would allow me to confess, to go through whatever discipline this church district deems appropriate—no matter what King claims about jumping the fence being the one unforgivable sin. I think it's refreshing—a lot more *Christian*—to believe that God can forgive every sin, no matter how large or small. Don't you?"

Annabelle inhaled slowly, considering her words before she spoke. She didn't want a discussion about doctrine to derail their conversation about the personal issues that really mattered to her. "Does . . . does this mean you're willing to live Amish again, Phineas?"

"*Jah*, I will," he said without hesitation. "At Promise Lodge, I believe I could abide within the rules of the Old Order—if you'll stand by me."

And if I don't?

The question popped into Annabelle's mind, yet she sensed it should remain unspoken. As the moments passed and his pale green eyes took on a shadow of worry, she knew she'd regret it forever if she didn't give Phineas another chance. With a little sob she stepped into his embrace and he held her close. His breathing slipped into the same rhythm as hers. His heartbeat settled into a steady thrum as he rested his head against the curve of her neck, as he always had.

"When I first came here, I poked around in some of the buildings and businesses—trying to find things *wrong* with this place," Phineas said softly. "I came on like a prickly cactus, determined not to like Gloria and the Kuhns because the way they enjoyed life seemed too *gut* to be true. I—I hope your friends will believe I've changed my attitude."

When she looked at him, Phineas gently kissed away her tears until his lips settled on hers. Annabelle closed her eyes, awash in a sweetness—a rightness—that eased the pain of his abandonment. He'd seen the error of his ways—he'd *missed* her—and now that Phineas had found her again, he'd opened his heart to starting afresh in Promise Lodge! Even the dark cloud of Bishop Clayton's intentions couldn't overshadow the joy and the hope Annabelle felt because her husband had seen the light.

"Oh, Annabelle," Phineas murmured when he finally eased away from their kiss. "Seeing how you've reestablished yourself so comfortably here without me, I was afraid you'd tell me to leave when I admitted why we couldn't have kids. But here you are, in my arms again."

"*Jah*, I am," she said as tears dribbled down her cheeks. After all the times she'd cried her eyes out after Phineas had left her to live English, it felt wonderful to well up with tears of joy. "And I'm willing to try again—"

"We could do it differently this time," he interrupted urgently. "We're still young enough to handle a family, so if you want to adopt children—"

Annabelle gently laid a finger across his lips—something she would never have dared to do to the outspoken Phineas Beachey she'd known before. "Let's take this one step at a time," she murmured as she gazed into his beautiful eyes. "For right now, my heart's so full it can't hold another thing."

Chapter Seventeen

Monroe clucked at the horse as he steered the buggy onto the road that would take them into Forest Grove on Saturday morning. "We'll go to the bank before we get our roofing supplies at the lumberyard," he told Amos and Marlin, who'd come along with him. "I got an . . . unusual phone message, and we need to check it out."

Amos's bushy eyebrows rose. "How do you mean, *unusual*?"

Monroe considered his answer. All morning he'd been debating with himself about revealing the secret he'd kept concerning Clayton King's identity, and if he guessed correctly, this visit to the bank would add another twist to the tale of their mysterious visitor. "Let's see how it plays out," he murmured. "I hope I'm wrong."

From the backseat, Marlin let out a short laugh. "Does this message have anything to do with the way you've been chewing your lower lip ever since we started for town?" he teased. "Confession's *gut* for the soul, you know."

Monroe laughed out loud, not surprised that his friend was so perceptive. "*I* have nothing out of the ordinary to confess," he replied quickly. "But after all the goings-on at the wedding yesterday, I'm wondering what the Helmuth boys did that upset Laura and Gloria. And I'm definitely curious about what went on in cabin number ten while Annabelle and Phineas were in there for a long while."

"Puh! Small potatoes," Amos said as they approached the main street of Forest Grove. "I'm wondering what King's up to—and I'll be hanging by my fingernails until he gives us those addresses and phone numbers we demanded of him. Wouldn't you think he'd know most of those without having to think about them?"

"*Jah*, I think it's odd that he's been stalling us on that," Marlin put in.

"The ball's in his court," Monroe pointed out. He pulled the buggy up alongside the bank building, where a hitching rail was provided for Plain customers. "Come inside with me. You might find this interesting."

"Better than the fresh chocolate chip cookies and coffee in their lobby?" Amos teased.

Monroe laughed as they got out of the buggy. "Maybe we'd better fortify ourselves with cookies before I talk to the gal who called me. Might not have much of an appetite afterward."

As he opened the bank's front door, the wind nearly blew it out of his hand, a sure sign that November had arrived and that winter was on the way. Once inside, he studied the faces of the women and men who sat behind the desks. As usual, because Monroe and his companions were the only men wearing black coats, full beards, and broad-brimmed black hats, they stood out from the English customers and staff.

"How can I help you gentlemen?" a young woman at the reception desk asked.

Monroe smiled, recognizing her voice. "I believe you're the gal—Michaela Sloan—who left me a message about a possible irregularity concerning our Promise Lodge accounts," he replied. "I'm Monroe Burkholder, and this is Amos Troyer and Marlin Kurtz. We're the account trustees."

Her pretty face lit up and she rose from her chair. Monroe couldn't help noticing that her skirt was snug enough to follow the flair of her hip, and short enough to leave nothing to his imagination. "You've got me pegged, Mr. Burkholder. Shall we talk in this room over here?"

As they followed Michaela into the nearby room, Monroe wondered how serious the situation was, that they couldn't speak about it in the lobby. But then, English folks and banking institutions were probably more concerned about privacy and security than folks were at Promise Lodge. After she gestured toward the padded leather chairs in front of the room's desk, she shut the door behind them.

"Do you recognize this man's name—his signature?" she asked as she pulled a rectangular card from the top drawer and laid it in front of him. "He was asking about your accounts, wanting to make a withdrawal, until the teller realized that he's not listed on any of your records."

Monroe got a sick feeling in his stomach, yet his suspicions were confirmed.

"Well, I'll be jiggered," Amos whispered tersely.

"You didn't give him any money, did you?" Marlin asked.

"Absolutely not," Michaela replied. "And that's why we immediately called to notify you about this attempted transaction."

"We appreciate it more than you know," Monroe said, shaking his head. "And if he comes in again, maybe giving you one of our names, will you notify us, please?"

"Oh, yes, sir. We've recorded a snapshot of him from the security film of his visit to the teller window—and we have your security snapshots, as well," Michaela replied.

Monroe glanced at Amos, who appeared uncharacteristically pale. "We Amish don't allow our photos to be taken as a rule, but in this case I'm glad you folks have our identities covered. Anything else we need to know?"

Michaela smiled ruefully. "I suspect you've already learned more than you bargained for. Thanks for stopping in to verify your records—and be sure to help yourself to cookies and coffee before you head out into this cold morning. It feels like winter out there all of a sudden!"

He appreciated her offer of hospitality, but on their way out of the bank, Monroe had no appetite for the large, freshly baked cookies on a tray beside the coffee urn. They were barely out the door before Amos began to rant.

"What on God's *gut* earth—that *shyster*!" he exclaimed in a strained whisper. "What was King doing, trying to withdraw money from our account?"

"Couldn't he wait until folks handed over that tithe he was preaching about yesterday?" Marlin asked in disbelief. "Why did he think he could get away with this?"

"I don't have any more answers than you do," Monroe muttered. He unhitched the horse and gestured for his friends to get into the buggy. "I'm going to tell you something Annabelle found out the other day—but it has to remain amongst us preachers, understand?"

Amos slammed the buggy door, staring incredulously at Monroe. "You're not heading back to Promise Lodge to call him out on this?" he demanded. "King must've been here earlier in the week, before he read us that letter yesterday, and—and folks need to know what we're dealing with—"

"We'll have our answers in *gut* time," Monroe interrupted, grasping Amos's shoulder to settle him down. "Meanwhile, I think it's best if King doesn't know we're on to him. We have to have enough rope to hang him with before we corner him. And first off, we need to find out his real name."

Marlin frowned. "What do you mean, his real name?"

Monroe cleared his throat. "Remember how he told us he's from Paradise, in Lancaster County? Well, Annabelle and Phineas lived just down the road from there, and they couldn't place him, so she wrote and asked some of her friends to check him out. Turns out no such bishop as Clayton King exists anywhere around there."

"What?" Amos's scowl deepened the wrinkles around his eyes. "Then who is he?"

"And why's he here, thinking he can take over Promise Lodge?" Marlin demanded.

"You've just summed up the mystery of Clayton King," Monroe replied with a shake of his head. "Do you understand why we can't let this out yet? And why we have to watch this fellow like a hawk without seeming to be suspicious of him?"

Amos fell back against the buggy seat, appearing stunned. As the men considered the details they'd just learned, Monroe backed the horse out of their parking spot.

"Jah, I suppose you've got that right," Marlin said after a few moments. "If the women get wind of this, they'll want his head on a platter and we might not get our answers. King—or whoever he is—will probably turn tail and run in the night."

"That's the way I've got it figured, too," Monroe agreed. "At least now we've confirmed our suspicions about his intentions—and we know he's not quite as smart as he thinks he is."

"This is an outrage," Amos muttered as the buggy headed on down the main street of town. "I'd be inclined to say he's not even Amish, the way he's been carrying on—except he preaches with too much authority."

"And he knows his Scriptures and the ins and outs of traditional Old Order behavior," Marlin pointed out. "Truth be told, if he hadn't gone so far as to say we should all contribute a tithe, I'd believe he was sincere about reforming us away from our progressive tendencies."

"*Jah*, that money talk was what made me doubt him, too," Amos muttered. "That, and the fact that I've never heard of a Council of Bishops from out east having any say-so about settlements this far away from them. It's probably all a pack of lies. But *why*?"

Monroe steered the horse alongside the mercantile and parked the buggy. "Got our list of supplies and dimensions?" he asked Amos. "Let's load up our plywood, shingles, and nails, and ask Eli to join us on the lodge roof when we get back. I'm ready to *pound* on something."

Annabelle winced as she and the other ladies who'd gathered in her apartment looked up at the ceiling.

Zap, zap, zap . . . zap, zap, zap.

"Sure is a shame the men are putting on the lodge's new roof *today*," Beulah remarked as she maneuvered her hook along the baby blanket she was crocheting. "My word, but they're kicking up a racket with those nail guns."

"*Jah*, we've needed a new roof since we bought the place," Rosetta said as she focused on the diaper she was cutting out. "Amos originally told me they'd work on it next week."

Zap, zap, zap . . . zap, zap, zap.

Christine let out a short laugh. "When Monroe returned from Forest Grove this morning, he was like a man on fire," she put in. "I asked if the roof couldn't wait until after our frolic, but he insisted that most of the other men could help today—and it's gotten colder, so he wants to be sure they finish before the first snowfall. If you ask me, however, he's got a different bee under his bonnet."

Annabelle wondered if that *bee* might be named Clayton King. She was hemming the diapers on the sewing machine after Rosetta, Christine, and Mattie cut them out of birdseye cotton, and when her machine wasn't whirring, they could hear the loud hum of the men's generators on the ground below.

Whummmmm . . . Zap, zap, zap . . . zap, zap, zap, zap.

"Marlin was so distracted he nearly left the house without his work gloves and stocking cap," Frances said softly. "Whatever those men did in town, he's in a dither about it."

Laura opened her mouth to say something, but the whine of a saw cut her short.

"We could move down to the first floor and work in the meeting room," Gloria suggested. She appeared tired and a little gloomy as she and her mother stuffed cotton batting into some dolls they were making. "I know we came up here so Clayton wouldn't interrupt us, but we could lock the doors if you want to."

"But then the men on the roof wouldn't have access to the bathroom," Mattie pointed out.

A loud *whump* made them all jump in their chairs. Frances sighed loudly as she tried for the second time to thread her needle. "Must've dropped a bundle of shingles right over our heads," she said. "I thought they were working on the other end of the building."

"Every able-bodied male we know, except the four Helmuths working at the nursery—and Clayton—are working up there, so they've probably divided into groups," Rosetta said. "Once Alma and Deborah get here with little Sarah, we might want to move the party to somebody's house. This racket will upset the baby."

"I'd thought of that," Beulah put in, "but we already have our refreshments set out across the hall—"

"If we were nice, *thoughtful* wives," Christine interrupted, "we'd make extra hot chocolate and another pot of coffee and offer some goodies to the men. It's raw outside, the way the wind's blowing."

"*Jah*, that's the least we can do," Rosetta agreed. "For whatever inconvenient reason, they're working awfully hard this afternoon. If they don't come down for a break now and then, somebody might fall or hit his hand with a hammer."

"Amen to that," Mattie said. "Amos was as cranked up as I've ever seen him when he was gathering his tools to come over here. He took his turn falling off a roof last year, and we don't need to go through *that* again."

Zap, zap, zap . . . zap, zap, zap. Whummmm.

Annabelle clipped the threads from the diaper she'd just finished. With four women working on them, the top of the nearby card table was nearly covered with finished diapers. She stood up to stretch and check the weather outside. After a gust of wind hurled a torrent of gold and orange leaves past her window, she gazed more intently.

"There goes Clayton in his buggy—off to do whatever he does when he leaves," Annabelle remarked. "Let's shift the refreshments for the party downstairs into the dining room. It's not as noisy there, and it'll make our serving easier when the Peterscheim gals get here with the baby, and when the men take a break."

"Truth be told, I don't like the idea of going into hiding to avoid Clayton anyway," Beulah declared as she rose from her rocking chair. "If he comes into the lodge and starts up on his big-idea preaching, all of us together can find a way to shut him down. This is our home, after all."

"And besides, it's not Sunday!" Annabelle blurted out.

"After the way he threw water on Phoebe and Allen's wedding reception, we need to show that man that we can socialize without listening to any more of his big announcements. That was uncalled for."

"It was totally inappropriate," Mattie agreed staunchly. She set the diaper she'd just cut beside Annabelle's sewing machine. "The more I think about that council telling us Clayton's to be our new bishop, the angrier I get! Let's take our party downstairs, girls. It'll be nicer anyway, with tablecloths and better chairs."

"I'll keep sewing for a while," Annabelle said as she looked at the wall clock. "We've got another half an hour before the guests of honor arrive."

With a flurry of new purpose, all the other ladies carried the party cake and dishes downstairs. When her apartment had cleared out, Annabelle smiled. She'd felt happy with everyone gathered in her main room, as though she was one of the longtime residents of Promise Lodge, and when she recalled Phineas's wish to live here permanently, her heart thrummed. They'd agreed to keep their plans to themselves for now, but considering the ruckus Bishop Clayton was kicking up, it was wonderful to have something so positive to look forward to—

Unless Clayton really does take over as our bishop, she thought with a pang. *If he refuses to let Phineas back into the fold, our plans for staying here are for nothing. Phineas is a changed man, and I'm so looking forward to starting fresh with him, having a new house among these friendly folks. . . .*

When Annabelle went downstairs, she glanced at the countertop to see if the mail had arrived—and made a beeline for the envelopes there. A few of them were addressed to the Kuhn sisters, Gloria, and Irene, but when she saw the familiar handwriting on a small envelope addressed to her, Annabelle snatched it up. *Weeks* she'd been waiting for word from her neighbor, Orva Shank, and as she stepped into the mudroom she lost all track of the ladies who were making extra coffee and trays of treats for the men.

Annabelle skimmed the words Orva had written from one edge of the lined paper to the other without leaving any spaces. She rapidly passed over everyday details about the home place and who'd taken sick and how the Overholts' sale had gone—

"And what's this about a Council of Bishops? Nobody here's ever heard tell of such a thing, and when Bishop Ephraim asked the leaders from nearby districts about it, they all shook their heads. The area bishops get together now and again, but there's no such thing as a Council of Bishops with any say-so over us—or over you folks in Missouri."

Annabelle sucked in her breath. The sentences had jumped off the page at her, and to be sure she'd understood them correctly, she read them again—and again. Her head spun as she continued to the end of Orva's letter.

"Is that bishop fellow you wrote about still there? Sounds to me like he's up to no good, and I'd send him on his way. Maybe you'd better come back to PA, Annabelle! We miss you and Phineas. Maybe if you come back, Phineas will, too."

Annabelle leaned against the deep freeze to steady herself. Surely this was all the proof they needed to keep Clayton King—or whoever he was—from displacing Bishop Monroe and further disrupting their lives at Promise Lodge.

But it's not your place to say that. You need to show this letter to Monroe right away.

"You all right, Annabelle?" Ruby asked from the mudroom doorway. "Bad news from your hometown?"

Annabelle folded the letter back into its envelope. "A bit of a shock," she replied in the steadiest voice she could muster. "But not bad news so much as . . . *interesting* news."

As she slipped the letter into her apron pocket, Annabelle wanted to blurt out what she'd just learned, so her friends could rejoice with her. But instead, she would give the letter to the bishop as soon as she could, confident he'd do the right thing.

"The truth shall set you free," the Bible said. And as always, God's word had it right.

Chapter Eighteen

Gloria's mind was only partly focused on the fun as she and Laura and the other ladies watched Deborah open a second box of cloth diapers.

"My word," the new mother said as she held up the stack, "you must be thinking little Sarah is full of you-know-what."

Friendly laughter filled the dining room. "There's no such thing as too many diapers," her *mamm*, Alma Peterscheim, remarked. "When a baby has tummy troubles, you can go through a drawerful of them long before you have a chance to do laundry."

Once again Gloria slipped her hand into her apron pocket, touching the letter that called out to be opened immediately. It had no stamp or return address, so she suspected Cyrus had written it—and now that she'd recovered from the initial shock of discovering his bet with his brother, her curiosity smoldered. Whatever he had to say seemed much more relevant than watching Deborah *ooh* and *ah* over crocheted booties and caps, even if Gloria had vowed not to fall for Cyrus's sweet talk.

When Laura approached the refreshment table, Gloria

joined her. "Did you get a note from Jonathan?" she whispered.

Laura's eyes widened. "No—or at least I haven't seen one. I've been here at the lodge most of the day—"

"Let's walk up and check your mail," Gloria suggested as the ladies' laughter rang out once again. "We need to keep track of those guys so they don't pull another whammy on us."

Laura downed her punch and led the way into the kitchen. "So you got a letter from Cyrus? What'd he say?"

"We'll find out while we're walking. Considering I'll probably never get married, a baby shower seems like a waste of my time right now." Gloria grabbed her coat from its peg in the mudroom and tied her *kapp* strings before stepping outside.

When they saw that Bishop Monroe and the other men were starting down the ladders from the roof, Gloria jogged toward the road before any of them could call out to her. She snatched the envelope from her pocket and ripped it open.

Cyrus's handwriting was so crisp and neat that he'd surely copied this version of his letter from an earlier draft. Gloria cleared her throat and began to read aloud.

"'Dear Gloria, I've been a total jerk and I hope you can forgive me.'"

She blinked as she and Laura reached the curve in the road that led toward the Burkholder home. "Maybe he's taking his vows to the church seriously, confessing his transgressions."

"Maybe there's hope for him yet," Laura remarked as they kept walking. "Now you've *really* got me wondering if Jonathan's written me an apology, as well."

Gloria focused on Cyrus's precise penmanship again.

"'You must've overheard the talking-to Jonathan gave me after the wedding, about that stupid bet I put him up to. And for once, he was right,'" she continued reading. "'It was probably the worst idea I've ever had in my life, and I'm sorry I hurt your feelings. You are worth so much more than money to me, Gloria. I hope you can believe I sincerely mean that.'"

Gloria blinked rapidly. Cyrus's words were making the big white house on the hill appear blurry around the edges. "What do you think, Laura?" she whispered. "Does he mean it? Or is he just buttering me up because he doesn't have any other girls to choose from at Promise Lodge?"

"Ask *him* that," Laura replied without missing a beat. Then she sucked in her breath. "Look at that big blue pot on the porch! It wasn't there when I left this morning—"

"And look at the *four* different colors of mums in it!" Gloria put in. "Do you suppose Jonathan—"

"Well, it's certainly not from Mamm or Monroe," Laura remarked as she jogged up to the porch. She plucked a small envelope from the profusion of orange, gold, magenta, and pale yellow blooms. "Jonathan doesn't always say a lot, but he can be very thoughtful. And generous."

Gloria was tempted to be envious of the eye-popping gift Laura had received, yet she held her emotions in check. The Helmuth brothers were as different as night and day, so it was only natural that each of them had his own way of expressing what he felt. She'd always been glad that it was Cyrus who'd taken a fancy to her, because he was bolder and more fun to be around, even if his antics sometimes got out of hand.

Laura beamed as she read the note. "He wants to talk things over," she murmured as she skimmed the message. "He's sorry about the bet, and he wants me to know that it was Cyrus's idea, and that he's nothing like his younger brother—which is so true."

"*Jah*, it is," Gloria agreed as she admired the mums and the planter. "So what do you think? Shall we give them another chance? I don't want to give Cyrus the idea that I'll fall for any more pranks just because he's my last chance at—"

"He is *not* your last chance, Gloria," Laura said firmly. "Other families will move to Promise Lodge. Or maybe that special fellow God intends for you might come for a wedding, or to one of our shops, and you'll be here waiting for him."

Gloria sighed. It was easy for Laura, at eighteen, to entertain such romantic notions—especially since she stood a good chance of making up with Jonathan. "Maybe, maybe not," she said softly. "It's fun to be in this with the four of us together, but maybe we shouldn't act as though we girls—or the Helmuth brothers—are a package deal. Maybe we should each see how this plays out."

Laura nodded as she read Jonathan's note once more. "They've asked for our forgiveness," she pointed out. "We can grant them that without agreeing to go out with them again. We should make them prove their intentions—work harder to convince us that they're sincere."

"That sounds like something our *mamms* would say," Gloria teased. And as she finished reading the note in her hand, she had to smile. He had ended the letter with: "Can we please talk this over, Gloria? I'd do anything for you, if you'd give me another chance."

A few months ago, Cyrus would never have written her such a note, much less begged her forgiveness. Maybe he was capable of change, of mending his ways.

And maybe you don't want him to change completely. Cyrus wouldn't be Cyrus if he always toed the line.

"That's a *gut* plan, Laura," Gloria said. "I'll keep Cyrus hanging, at least until I've had some goodies at Deborah's party—or maybe until tomorrow after dinner, because there's no church service."

"Phoebe always recommended playing hard to get," Laura remarked as they started back down the hill. "Not that she ever made Allen wait, that I can recall."

As Gloria thought back to Phoebe and Allen's wedding, when Cyrus was signaling her with his hands, she brightened. Cyrus wouldn't have hinted at standing with her in front of Bishop Monroe unless making such a commitment was on his mind. He was better at gestures and jokes than he was at putting his serious feelings into words—so his heartfelt note had convinced Gloria to give him another chance.

But it would be on her terms.

As Monroe pulled off his stocking cap and work gloves, he was deeply grateful that the women were bringing a big urn of coffee and trays of sweets into the meeting room for him and the other men. They all needed a break after working in the wind for the past few hours.

"Bless you, Beulah," he said when she brought a pan of fresh caramel rolls into the room as the men removed their wraps. "I have a feeling you baked these for your Sunday breakfast—"

"And what if we did?" Ruby teased as she placed a tray of coffee mugs by the urn. "It's the least we can do when you fellows are keeping a roof over our heads on such a blustery day."

"We probably could've waited for warmer weather," Amos remarked as he filled a cup with the steaming coffee, "but work is *gut* therapy when you've got problems to solve."

"We're thinking of it as a roof frolic," Marlin teased, placing one of the warm, gooey rolls on a plate. "You ladies have your hen parties and sewing frolics, and we men gathered in a higher place today. But I was getting so cold I could barely wrap my fingers around the hammer and saw anymore."

Annabelle sidled up to Monroe with a tray of utensils, as well as a big carafe of hot chocolate. "This should warm you up, Bishop," she murmured as she slipped him an envelope. "But you'll want to read it in private."

Monroe's eyebrows rose. "All right, *denki* for the heads-up. I need to use the bathroom anyway."

He could feel the other men's curious gazes following him out of the meeting room, but Monroe sensed he should take Annabelle at her word. After he'd entered the bathroom off the lobby, he skimmed the page, which was completely covered with tiny, irregular handwriting—

"And what's this about a Council of Bishops? Nobody here's ever heard tell of such a thing, and when Bishop Ephraim asked the leaders from nearby districts about it, they all shook their heads. The area bishops get together now and again, but there's no such thing as a Council of Bishops with any say-so over us—or over you folks in Missouri."

"Gotcha!" Monroe whispered as he read the paragraph again. On the roof, the men had aired their frustrations and speculations about the eloquent man who'd declared himself the new bishop of Promise Lodge, but Monroe and the three preachers—and Annabelle—were still the only ones who knew that their visitor was an impostor with a fake name who'd tried to access their bank account. No one else realized that King still hadn't produced the list of addresses they'd asked him for, either, so time was on their side.

But how long would it take to figure out who this guy was, so they could nail him?

Chapter Nineteen

At dinner on Sunday, Gloria stayed busy helping her *mamm*, Mary Kate, and Minerva set their simple meal on the table—hoping no one would notice that she was distracted by her thoughts of Cyrus. Marlin's younger kids, Fannie and Lowell, were in charge of entertaining baby David, who would be a year old in a few weeks—and who insisted on playing with pots and pans whenever anyone was working in the kitchen. His shrieks of laughter came from the front room as Gloria carried a big bowl of peas and carrots—David's favorite vegetables—to the table.

"It's a blessing to have such a happy baby in the family," Mamm remarked wistfully. "Last year about this time, we were all so worried about Floyd after Amos fell off the shed roof and landed on him—"

"And I was huge, and so ready to have that baby," Mary Kate put in with a chuckle. "So much has happened in the last year. I married Roman, and we lost Dat, and now you've remarried, Mamm."

"I was happy to help you with David's delivery, too. It's been a big year for our combined family—and for everyone at Promise Lodge," Minerva agreed as she cut up two baked chickens. "And just amongst us hens, I have to say

Marlin's as happy as I've ever seen him—even if Bishop Clayton has really stirred the pot."

"God is *gut*," Mamm put in firmly. "He stands by us in sunshine and shadow, and He'll shine light on this situation with Clayton King when the time's right. I hope it'll be soon, so Marlin and Bishop Monroe and our other leaders can get back to doing the Lord's work amongst us."

Minerva's eyebrows rose. "You don't think Bishop Clayton is doing the Lord's work?"

An edge to Minerva's voice made Gloria focus more closely on the conversation. The local midwife was as puzzled—and skeptical—about Clayton as most folks were.

"Let's just say I was relieved when he declined my invitation to dinner today," Mamm replied with a shake of her head. "It was only right to ask him, since Lester was coming over, but he said something about going to Coldstream because they have church this morning."

"Really?" Mary Kate put a basket of dinner rolls at each end of the table. "Do you suppose he met some of the Troyers' friends at Allen and Phoebe's wedding and he's checking out their church district—to see if their bishop needs as much guidance as ours supposedly does?"

The ladies laughed as they finished setting out the food. When the men came in from the front room, David was riding on Roman's shoulders and crowing like a rooster. When they got the little boy seated in his highchair, Mary Kate reminded him to fold his hands and bow his head—and to be quiet during the silent prayer. As everyone at the table gave thanks, Gloria opened one eye.

Eleven of us around this table. Considering how many meals Mamm and I ate alone after Dat passed, this is such an improvement . . . and if it's Your will, Lord, maybe

*Cyrus will join us someday. Should I invite him to dinner
in two weeks, for our next visiting Sunday?*

Marlin said a quiet "amen" and the men reached for the
bowls and platters in front of them. Harley was a hefty
fellow and speared two pieces of chicken, while Roman
spooned peas and carrots onto David's small plate before
putting some on his own. As Gloria took a soft, warm roll
and passed the basket to Lester, she was pleased to see that
he was in good spirits—and he was hungry enough to take
two rolls.

"It's been a while since I've seen you, Uncle Lester,"
she remarked. "Have you been busy installing the windows and siding at that new subdivision where Truman's
working?"

"I have," he replied with a nod, "and as winter blows
in, I'm glad we're nearly finished with that project. But
the money's been *gut*, and Truman's a first-rate man to
work for."

"And how're you getting along with your housemate?"
Harley asked as he cut into his baked potato. "Does he
preach at you of an evening the way he lights into the rest
of us every chance he gets?"

Lester's knife paused on the roll he'd been slathering
with butter. His expression grew pensive. "Clayton and I
have more in common than you might expect," he replied
softly. "He lost his wife, too, you know. It's done me a
world of good to share stories about Delores with him, and
to have him pray with me about it."

Unexpected tears sprang to Gloria's eyes. Her uncle had
been devastated after his son and his wife had been killed
in a buggy accident back east—he'd built the home next
door for Delores to move into when she joined him at
Promise Lodge. Gloria would never have guessed that
Bishop Clayton would spend time comforting Lester.

"I'm glad to hear that," she whispered, patting his arm. "Knowing how lonely this house felt with just Mamm and me here after Dat passed, I can only imagine how quiet your place gets."

"I tried to remedy that, remember?" Lester teased with a glance at her mother. "But truth be told, Frances is better off with Marlin. Even if he *is* a preacher."

Gentle laughter filled the room. Gloria couldn't miss the way Marlin squeezed her mother's hand under the table.

Mamm placed a piece of chicken on her plate. "I'm glad you and Clayton have had some meaningful conversations," she said softly. "Unfortunately, after the way he's come on like a house afire and announced that he's taking over as our bishop, most folks don't have much *gut* to say about him. Nor do they seem to trust him."

"Has he talked about his family? Or about his bulk grocery warehouse in Lancaster?" Marlin asked. "When we preachers ask about his personal life—or ordinary, everyday matters about his business and his church district—he changes the subject."

Lester shrugged. "Some evenings I get back from work pretty late, and he's already had his supper," he replied. "Clayton spends a lot of time in his room, and I don't tap on his door for fear of interrupting—in case he's praying or reading his Bible."

Gloria considered this, wondering why Bishop Clayton would close his door while his housemate wasn't at home—but then, hadn't she sometimes done that when she'd lived with her parents? Uncle Lester seemed relaxed and ready to chat, so rather than asking his opinion about closed doors, she let him continue.

"Some days Clayton drives out to the various bulk stores in the area, which are serviced by his warehouse out east," her uncle said with a lift in his voice. "More often than not he brings back groceries for us, too, which is generous of him."

"*Jah*, I've seen containers from the stores in Forest Grove and Cloverdale when we've been there to clean," Minerva remarked. "I just wish he'd stop harping at us about how being so progressive will lead to—"

"King cooked his goose with me when he suggested that paying a tithe to that Council of Bishops might earn us some brownie points," Harley blurted. "When he puts it that way, it's like we can pay our way to salvation. And I don't believe God holds it against Bishop Monroe because he married Truman and Rosetta, either, or because he raises Clydesdales, or any of those other issues King's been yammering at us about. Why is that any of *his* business?"

The kitchen got very quiet in the wake of Harley's outburst. Gloria wasn't sure how much a tithe would come to for him and Minerva, based on the income from his sheep and his share in his *dat*'s barrel factory—but a lot of trucks had been hauling Kurtz barrel products away from Promise Lodge over the past months, so Marlin and his older son must be doing well.

Uncle Lester cleared his throat. "I understand why Bishop Clayton rubs folks the wrong way," he murmured in a voice that thrummed with emotion. "But what if he's *right*? What if we've been like those sheep in the Bible that have gone astray—or what if, on Judgment Day when God separates the sheep from the goats, *we* are the goats and He sends us away to the flames?"

Forks stopped halfway between plates and mouth as everyone focused on Lester. Color had risen into his cheeks, as though he'd been thinking a lot about this topic and had some deep convictions about it.

"I mean, what if we really *are* veering too far off the

Old Order path, and we've become so used to doing it that we don't see the error of our ways?" Uncle Lester continued softly. He swallowed so hard that his Adam's apple bobbed in his thin neck. "The more I talk with Bishop Clayton, the more he reminds me of Floyd. And we all know that if my brother were still alive, life at Promise Lodge would be a *lot* different."

Gloria blinked back sudden tears. Uncle Lester sounded genuinely concerned—and he was mourning his brother and the life they'd shared with him. The emotional catch in his voice caught Gloria off guard and made her miss her *dat* terribly. Mary Kate swiped at a tear. Mamm looked at her lap, bunching her apron in her fist as she, too, struggled with a moment of grief.

After a moment, Marlin leaned forward. "Lester, do you believe Monroe's been leading us astray?" he asked gently. "And have we preachers gone along with him because . . . well, because we—and certainly our wives—have felt happier?"

The kitchen got uncomfortably quiet again. Lester looked away, uneasy about being asked such a question.

Gloria shifted in her chair, too agitated to eat. What if Bishop Clayton *was* right? What if her *dat* had been right, as well? While she'd been growing up, she'd never doubted that Bishop Floyd's authority had come directly from God as he'd raised her and led his congregation.

But we also believed God sent Monroe Burkholder to us when Dat's health was failing. Monroe was here to shepherd our church when Dat died—and he often came to comfort Mamm and me, too.

Gloria's head throbbed. She didn't usually delve into matters of religion, because she'd been taught to believe without question what her *dat* and the preachers told everyone. She'd been more concerned about remaining a *maidel* forever than she'd been about what might happen to her on Judgment Day.

"I don't know the answer to your question, Marlin," Uncle Lester murmured. "It would be presumptuous of me to say I could discern the will of God better than you preachers He chose as our leaders."

"Amen to that," Roman whispered with a shake of his head. "It seems we can do the best we know how and still not be living right, the way Bishop Clayton sees it. After his announcement at Allen and Phoebe's wedding, I'm surprised he hasn't already taken over and forced Monroe out."

Marlin's expression suggested that he knew more than he was saying about that matter. "*Jah*, we preachers are, too," he murmured. "We've been waiting for Clayton to tell us how things are going to be. But he seems to be avoiding us lately."

"Who are we supposed to believe, Dat?" Lowell asked plaintively. "Bishop Monroe's a *gut* man. He's teaching Lavern and me that it's important not just to work well with his Clydesdales, but to be honest with their owners about the progress they've made in their training. How can that be wrong?"

Gloria smiled at her new half brother. Lowell and his best friend, Lavern Peterscheim, had been delighted when Bishop Monroe had hired them to help with his magnificent Clydesdales. Both boys had matured emotionally, and they'd also put on some muscle from doing the physical labor of working with the bishop's huge horses.

Marlin smiled at his younger son. "This situation is affecting every one of us, Lowell," he replied softly. "I don't have answers to any of the questions we've asked, so I suggest we pray over them. As we go through the remainder of our sabbath, we should continue to ask God for His *gut* and perfect guidance. When the time's right, He'll reveal the answers we need."

As the others around the table bowed their heads, Gloria joined them. Her thoughts were jumbled with her emotions, however, and she felt anything but prayerful. Was she even worthy to approach God about an issue so complex that Preacher Marlin and Bishop Monroe didn't know how to deal with it?

Dat, I miss you so much—and we could really use your help. If you know what we should do about Bishop Clayton, could you send us a big, unmistakable sign? It's scary to think that God might be displeased with the way we're living. I don't want to make Him angry by asking Him my clueless, helpless questions.

For the remainder of the meal, the family was more subdued than usual. When everyone had eaten dessert, they seemed eager to be up and away from the table. The men went into the front room, taking baby David with them. When Mary Kate and Minerva began scraping the plates, Gloria and Fannie carried the bowls and platters of leftover food to the counter.

"Are you okay, Gloria?" Fannie asked softly. "You look pale."

Mamm turned from the sink, where she was running dishwater. "I was thinking the same thing, sweetie," she said. "You're not coming down with something, are you?"

Gloria blinked. Were her emotions written so plainly on her face that everyone could see her distress? "I do have a pounding headache," she admitted. "I—I was thinking some fresh air and a walk might help, after we're finished here."

"Go now," Mamm insisted, waving Gloria off. "We've got plenty of help, and plenty to think about. Your *dat* always said a walk worked wonders when he needed to clear his head."

Nodding, Gloria passed through the mudroom to get her jacket. Why should she work in the kitchen when Mamm had just affirmed that one of Dat's habits might be good for her, too? The afternoon was breezy but warmer than the past few days had been, and as Gloria strode across the back lawn, she lifted her face to catch the sunlight.

Should she go find Cyrus? He and Jonathan would probably be eating their dinner over at the big Helmuth house on this visiting Sunday. Or should she walk off the anxious energy that Uncle Lester had stirred inside her? As Gloria's thoughts went in one direction and then another, she kept walking without any destination in mind, just to keep moving.

When she realized she was approaching the back of Uncle Lester's house next door, Gloria felt as though an invisible hand was steering her in that direction. If Bishop Clayton had gone to Coldstream for the day, what would it hurt to step inside and look around? It would be no different from the times she'd helped with cleaning the house or had gone over to visit with Uncle Lester, would it? *He* wouldn't mind that she'd gone into his home.

Seeing no one who'd wonder what she was up to, Gloria made a beeline for the back door. She stepped inside Lester's big house and held her breath, listening, to be sure Bishop Clayton hadn't returned early from Coldstream.

The house was absolutely still.

She had no idea what she was looking for, but she felt compelled to snoop, to see if she could find even the tiniest hint about the personal side of Clayton King that he seemed so reluctant to reveal. It wasn't as though she'd see anything that she and the other ladies hadn't already dusted or straightened, after all.

Gloria removed her shoes and hurried through the kitchen and front room with them. Her mind was racing a mile a minute, knowing she shouldn't sneak around. If she ran into Bishop Clayton, she had no idea what explanation she could give him for being there. Up the wooden staircase she went, peering through the window at the landing to be sure his buggy wasn't rolling toward the house. She passed Uncle Lester's bedroom and continued toward the room at the end of the hall. The door was closed—

And why is that? What's in there that he doesn't want anyone to see?

As Gloria reached for the knob, it occurred to her that when she'd been there with Mamm to clean, Bishop Clayton had remained in his armchair reading the paper, chatting with them a bit—

But he insisted that you only change his sheets and dust, and that nothing in his closet needed attention.

Was it her imagination, or had Bishop Clayton been urging them along so they didn't spend much time in his room? As Gloria grasped the doorknob, she knew she shouldn't be prying into his private affairs. Yet something was goading her to go inside for a quick, secret peek. Was she being too nosy—or was Dat guiding her to look around, as the answer to her prayer?

The door swung open on silent hinges. Gloria sensed she shouldn't dawdle—she secretly feared that Bishop Clayton had been lurking in the house all along, and that he'd catch her and force her to confess at church for invading his privacy. A messy stack of magazines beside the chair didn't seem of interest, nor did his unmade bed. She went straight to the closet and eased open the door, half expecting the bishop to spring out at her.

But all she saw were a few dark shirts and pairs of broadfall trousers on hangers, along with a black straw hat perched on the shelf above them. Nothing different from what she would see in Uncle Lester's closet, or in Dat's when he'd been alive. The closet extended sideways beyond the doorway for a few feet, and Gloria noticed a couple of quilts stacked on the floor back there. Nothing out of the ordinary—

But why would those quilts be on the floor? Gloria wondered as she shut the door. *Why wouldn't they be on the bed now that the weather's cooler—or up on the shelf, where they wouldn't get dirty?*

She opened the closet again to gaze at the quilts. The closet had no light, so she knelt on the floor beneath the hanging clothes for a closer look. When she lifted the top quilt, her eyes widened. The quilt beneath it had been arranged so it covered a large wooden crate and a fancy suitcase with wheels on it.

Gloria's heart began to pound. Should she open the box or the suitcase? It was wrong to snoop in the bishop's belongings—

As her eyes grew accustomed to the dimness of the unlit closet, Gloria noticed a suit hanging against the back wall, above the crate. It was gray with thin white stripes. When she stood up for a closer look, she saw that a collared white shirt was hung behind it, with a plaid necktie draped around its hanger.

Her mouth dropped open and her thoughts raced faster. Why would an Amish bishop have English clothing in his closet?

Gloria's pulse hammered so loudly that she wouldn't hear Bishop Clayton come into the house or up the stairs, yet curiosity drove her on. She set the quilts out of the way and unzipped the suitcase. Once again Gloria gaped— and she knew better than to meddle with a slender metal rectangle that had the silver logo of an apple with a bite out of it. Why did Bishop Clayton have a laptop computer?

Driven faster by the fear of discovery, Gloria zipped the suitcase and felt for a latch on the wooden crate. Her heart sank when her fingers found a small padlock—but it swiveled open! Her hands shook as she opened the crate and found scads of papers, which—messy as they were—had apparently been tossed into the box in a hurry. Gloria could tell that some of them were printed forms but she couldn't make out the words.

Instinct—or was it Dat's spirit?—told her to get out of the bishop's room very quickly. Gloria had no idea what she'd discovered in the crate, but Bishop Clayton had clearly intended for no one else to see those papers. Her heart hammered as she snatched a couple of them from near the bottom of the pile and stuffed them into her jacket pocket. After she closed the crate, she replaced the padlock the way she'd found it and rapidly arranged the crate and the suitcase with the quilts carefully covering them again.

Gloria stood up, listening carefully as she closed the closet door. Hoping she'd left everything as it had been—praying Bishop Clayton wouldn't sense that an intruder had been present—she hurried out of the bedroom and closed the door behind her. Down the stairs she went, holding her breath, slipping back into her shoes at the back door. As she burst outside, she sucked in air to settle her nerves.

God surely must be watching over you, Gloria thought as she loped across the back of Uncle Lester's lot. *Otherwise, you'd have been caught in that closet, or someone would've seen you entering Uncle Lester's house or—*

It occurred to her that if she appeared frantic, anyone who spotted her would assume she'd been up to no good. Gloria rested against the back wall of Mamm and Marlin's house, considering her best strategy. Her fingers itched to pull the papers from her pocket, yet whatever she discovered would show all over her face when she went inside. She'd already seen too many inexplicable items in Bishop Clayton's closet to keep quiet about them. What should she do?

Take a leisurely stroll down the hill into the trees, and then amble toward the lodge. That way, if someone in the house spots you, Mamm and Fannie can say you've been taking a walk to clear your head.

Taking another deep breath to settle her nerves, Gloria followed her plan. It was difficult to take her time, and to leave the papers in her pocket—except she still had to make it past the Kuhn sisters and Irene when she entered the lodge. She crossed the grassy lawn, admiring the pumpkins, mums, and Indian corn the ladies had arranged on the porch steps, and strolled around to the back. Gloria eased open the door and stepped inside the mudroom, listening carefully.

Laughter broke out in the dining room. "I can play all seven of my letters! Watch this!" Beulah crowed.

Gloria slipped off her shoes and climbed quietly up the kitchen stairway. The ladies' Sunday afternoon Scrabble game was yet another answered prayer. When she'd closed her apartment door behind her, Gloria walked carefully to her sofa so her footsteps wouldn't alert anyone downstairs to her presence.

She perched on the sofa and took the two papers from her jacket pocket. The pages rustled slightly as she held them in her trembling hands.

The first page appeared to be a receipt for three clocks consigned to a shop called Simple Gifts in Willow Ridge, Missouri. Nora Hooley, apparently the owner, had signed it at the bottom. It was dated October twentieth of the previous year.

Gloria frowned. Why would Bishop Clayton from Lancaster County, Pennsylvania, have such a receipt for clocks among his papers?

The second form was even more puzzling. The printed line across the top said "Riehl Clocks—Riehl Service, Riehl Timely." It was a handwritten estimate of repairs needed on two antique clocks, along with the charges for the labor and a list of parts required. The penmanship was slightly slanted, unusual because the *L*'s, *F*'s, *P*'s and *Y*'s had straight lines instead of the loops most folks wrote them with. The total, $657.00, was followed by the words "I will begin work when I receive your payment in full. Cornelius Riehl."

Why would such a paper concerning clocks be in Bishop Clayton's crate? Gloria desperately wanted to share her newfound discoveries with someone who could explain them—but who would that be? And of course if she talked to anyone, she'd have to admit that she'd been snooping in the bishop's closet.

As she rose from the sofa, her headache returned with a vengeance. Gloria's stomach felt like a ringer washing machine agitating a load of clothes as she gazed out the window—just in time to see Bishop Clayton's buggy rolling up the road to Lester's house. She stepped away from the window, imagining that if he spotted her he'd immediately know she was guilty of a heinous invasion of his privacy.

"Dat, what should I do?" Gloria whispered. "I thought it was *you* steering me to Uncle Lester's house, but you would never want me to rifle through somebody else's stuff . . . *would* you?"

Her *dat* didn't answer. The three ladies' laughter downstairs was the only sound in the house, except for the relentless hammering of Gloria's heart.

She swallowed hard. Deep down, she knew her father would've expected her to confess her wrongdoing—preferably to Bishop Clayton, face to face.

The thought of walking back to Uncle Lester's house and owning up to her misadventure made her stomach churn even harder. And the longer she stood in the middle of the room, imagining Bishop Clayton's wrath—the way his face would turn red, and the torrent of Old Testament judgment he would quote as he condemned her to confess at church next Sunday—the more ill Gloria felt.

"Sin is a sickness and guilt erodes the soul," her father had often preached in his sermons.

For the first time in her life, Gloria believed him.

Chapter Twenty

As Monroe stretched out in his recliner after Sunday dinner for a rare nap, he sensed sleep would evade him. He was trying to keep his concerns about Clayton King to himself, but lately Christine had been quizzing him about the visiting bishop—and about what he planned to do if King took over as the new leader of Promise Lodge.

"What's going on with him?" Christine had asked over their dinner of vegetable beef soup and corn bread. "The way he spouted off at the wedding, I thought he'd be making his big changes by now. Why's he keeping us in suspense?"

Monroe had replied, truthfully, that he didn't know—and that he and the three preachers were waiting for King to make the first move. "King will probably preach about his plans for Promise Lodge at church next Sunday," he'd replied. "God moves in mysterious ways, and so does the man from Lancaster County."

Christine's expression had told Monroe she wasn't buying his answer. Other neighbors had expressed similar doubts about King's silence, and as days went by the situation would only become more problematic. But what could he do? Amos, Marlin, and Eli agreed that if they confronted Clayton with the information Annabelle had shared, he would bolt before they figured out who he really was. Monroe had prayed daily over the situation, but God seemed as unresponsive as King.

God is not unresponsive, Monroe reminded himself as he settled into his recliner. *God knows exactly what's going on, and He has a reason for waiting this out.*

Or, the more contentious voice in his head chimed in, *God's given you plenty of clues and you're missing His point. King's a clever man. He'll make his next move in his own gut time.*

Monroe sighed as he closed his eyes. A thousand thoughts about what he'd do if King closed down his Clydesdale business—or told him he could no longer live at Promise Lodge—had plagued him over the past week. The new home and the new wife God had provided him had changed him so completely that Monroe dreaded anything that threatened his wonderful life, even if a bogus bishop had no real power.

It was the *waiting* that kept him up nights.

As his thoughts circled like suspicious dogs, Monroe heard a knock at the front door. "Stay right there, Monroe, I've got it," Laura said as she came from the kitchen.

He settled deeper into his chair. Christine's daughters were yet another blessing God had granted him since he'd come to Missouri.

"Gloria!" Laura called out moments later. "Come in! It's *gut* to see you."

"I, um, had to get out," Gloria whimpered. "It's *gut* to see you, too, Laura, but I came to speak with Bishop Monroe. Something awfully . . . *important* has come up."

The tremor in the young woman's voice alerted Monroe to her distress, so he immediately lowered his recliner. "Come on in, Gloria," he called across the room.

She shook her head as she watched him sit up and find his slippers with his feet. "I—I didn't mean to interrupt your nap, Bishop—"

"I wasn't asleep," he assured her kindly. He'd often seen Gloria's brown eyes widen with flirtation when she'd been pursuing Roman Schwartz and Allen Troyer, but she appeared deeply troubled as she stood in the doorway. "What can I do for you, dear? Has something gone wrong at home, or with your *mamm*, or—"

She quickly shook her head. "I—I need to talk to you. Only you, Bishop," she added with an apologetic glance at Laura. "I've gotten myself into a bit of a . . . pickle."

Monroe's insides tightened. After hearing Laura's account of the Helmuth brothers' bet, the last thing he wanted to hear was that Cyrus had gotten Gloria in the family way. She was impulsively desperate about being twenty-three and still unmarried—and Monroe hoped that for her mother's sake, Gloria wouldn't go through an unwed pregnancy the way her younger sister had done.

"Let's talk in my office," Monroe suggested, gesturing toward a short hallway. "Would you like some tea or coffee? Something to munch on?"

Gloria shook her head. She walked quickly ahead of him into the room where he kept his Clydesdale accounts, and perched on the chair facing his big desk. As Monroe closed the door, he prayed for guidance.

Without any preamble, Gloria yanked two folded sheets of paper from her jacket pocket and tossed them onto his desk as though they were burning her fingers. "I have a confession, Bishop Monroe," she whispered. "Something—I thought it was Dat's spirit, but maybe I was just hoping for his help, you know?—made me go into Uncle Lester's house and upstairs into Bishop Clayton's room and into his closet, and that's where I found these," she continued in a breathless rush. "I—it was wrong of me to do that, but these papers aren't all I found in there."

Monroe's eyebrows went up as he reached for the papers. "How'd you know Bishop Clayton wasn't at home?"

"Uncle Lester said he'd gone to the church service in Coldstream today. He went on and on about how much Bishop Clayton had helped him, because they've both lost their wives." Gloria paused, her expression tightening. "Then he said, 'What if Bishop Clayton has it right? What if we *have* gotten too progressive at Promise Lodge?' He compared Bishop Clayton to my *dat*, saying we're doing things that Dat would never have allowed if he was still the bishop."

Monroe's eyes widened. This was the first time he'd heard that Bishop Clayton had befriended anyone—or convinced any of the Promise Lodge residents that his preaching might be on target. "And Lester wasn't teasing?" he asked gingerly.

"Oh no, he was dead serious."

Monroe paused, watching Gloria closely. "So what happened then? I can tell your uncle's words affected you deeply."

"*Jah*, they did," Gloria agreed. "We'd been talking to Marlin about when Bishop Clayton would take over, and it didn't sit right with me. *Everyone*—except Uncle Lester—has their doubts about him, so I sneaked into the house and went into Clayton's room," she admitted as she looked away. "When Mamm and I go there to clean, Bishop Clayton always stays right there with us and insists that *nothing* needs to be done in the closet. And—and now I know why."

Again Monroe's insides tightened, but for a different reason. When he glanced at the first page she'd given him, which had come from a shop in a town called Willow Ridge, nothing rang any bells. He'd seen signs for Willow Ridge when he'd first come to live in Missouri, but he'd traveled quite a ways north of that town to reach Promise Lodge, so the name of the Simple Gifts shop meant nothing to him. The moment he set eyes on the second page, however, he recognized the distinctive handwriting on the letter King had shown him, supposedly from the Council of Bishops.

"'Riehl Clocks,'" he read softly. "'Riehl Service, Riehl Timely'" . . . because Cornelius Riehl, who'd signed this estimate for repairs, was the owner of the clock business.

Monroe felt dizzy. The missing piece of the puzzle he'd been praying for was in his hands—and all because Gloria had sneaked into King's closet.

"I found the papers in a crate—grabbed a couple of sheets willy-nilly because I was afraid he'd come home and catch me," Gloria continued in a nervous whisper. "He also had an English man's suit with a shirt and necktie hanging in the back of his closet. And in a suitcase, he had a laptop computer."

Monroe gaped at Gloria. The more he heard, the more he wondered if Clayton King—who also went by Cornelius Riehl—was even Amish. Along with being a phony bishop, was he also a clockmaker with a reason to pass himself off as Plain? Monroe couldn't imagine that many English men were named Cornelius these days—and Riehl was a common Amish surname—but what if this was another fake identity? And Monroe still had no idea *why* this man had come to Promise Lodge.

"What does this mean, Bishop Monroe?" Gloria asked in a childlike voice. "Dat would've made me go straight over to Bishop Clayton and confess that I'd sneaked into his closet—"

"Don't say a word about this, Gloria!" Monroe blurted. He caught himself, hoping his voice hadn't carried through the walls. "What I mean is, I've been keeping some other information about Bishop Clayton under my hat until I knew what to do about it. And now that I've seen these papers, I know what I need to know, but I still don't know what to do. Does that make sense?"

Gloria's face relaxed into a smile. "I know just how *ferhoodled* you feel, Bishop," she murmured. "It was wrong of me to go into that closet—and if you want me to confess at church, I will, but—"

"Far as I'm concerned, you've just confessed to *me*, Gloria—and we're going to leave it at that for now," Monroe interrupted. He held her gaze somberly. "You realize that you can't say anything about this to *anybody else*, right? If Clayton King—who is also Cornelius Riehl—gets wind that we're on to him, he'll be off like a shot before we can learn the whole truth. There's something terribly *wrong* going on here. Do you understand that, Gloria?"

She nodded solemnly.

"Everything this guy's told us is a pack of lies—*serious* lies," Monroe continued cautiously. "We'll only get the real story if we ask somebody else about him—"

"Like Nora Hooley in Willow Ridge?" Gloria whispered.

Monroe suddenly had a whole new appreciation for the way Gloria Lehman's mind worked. She'd always come across as a boy-crazy, impulsive young woman, sometimes without the sense God gave a goose, but she'd just handed him the answer he'd been looking for.

"We can start with her, *jah*," he murmured as his mind raced. "Trouble is, if the preachers and I take off for Willow Ridge and King gets wind of it—"

"What if *I* go?" Gloria piped up. "What if Laura goes

with me? We could say we wanted to shop in Nora's store and—"

"You're not telling anybody anything, remember?" Monroe reminded her quickly. "It takes a couple hours to drive there, if I recall correctly. If something really crooked is going on, however, I can't risk letting you girls go—"

"So what if Cyrus and Jonathan drive us?" Gloria blurted triumphantly. "They owe us *that* much for the way they played games with our feelings, *jah*? They've been asking for a chance to make it up to us—"

"And when folks see the four of you leaving, they'll assume it's a date," Monroe murmured as he mulled over the possibility. After conducting several sessions of church instruction for Cyrus and Jonathan, he trusted them—believed they were responsible young men who'd made one crazy mistake in the way they'd treated Gloria and Laura.

And what guy hasn't messed up with women? Monroe's thoughts teased.

"I'd also feel better about you young people going because who knows what King might do if all of us church leaders are gone at the same time?" he mused aloud. "I don't want anybody starting rumors about why I might've left Promise Lodge with our preachers, either—or what I might be doing if I go alone."

Monroe gazed at the pretty brunette sitting across the desk from him. Not long ago the thought of sending Gloria on a fact-finding mission would've been out of the question, yet it seemed she'd provided the answer to his most urgent prayers.

"It's true that your *dat* would've been running things differently if he were still our bishop," he said softly. "But maybe it *was* his spirit guiding you, Gloria. Maybe Bishop Floyd realizes we need some heaven-sent help to deal with

Cornelius Riehl. *Jah*, sneaking into that closet was wrong, but sometimes desperate situations call for desperate measures."

The shine in Gloria's eyes made Monroe glad he'd said that. He was also pleased about entrusting this mission to her and her friends. A lot of people would be happy if the Helmuth brothers became engaged to Gloria and Laura, because it meant two more young couples would be staying at Promise Lodge to start their families.

He took a pen and paper from his desk drawer. "I'm going to write a note for you to take along to the bishop of Willow Ridge. Once you locate Nora Hooley and her shop, she can direct you to him—so you can ask him to call me," Monroe said as he thought through the details. "I'll ask Sam and Simon to give their cousins the day off tomorrow, so you four can leave first thing. After all, we're talking about the future of our *home* here, and we need to move quickly on this."

Gloria nodded, wide-eyed. "I—I'll be happy to go, Bishop Monroe," she whispered. "I really do like Cyrus. . . ."

Monroe gently clasped her wrist. "He really likes you, too, Gloria," he said, feeling happier than he had in days. "I'm glad you're giving him another chance. We guys mean well, but sometimes we get crazy around girls who make us want to behave like adults and take life more seriously—but you didn't hear *me* repeat what Cyrus said about you, okay?"

Chapter Twenty-One

"Off we go!" Cyrus crowed from the backseat of the buggy his brother was driving. "We've got directions to Willow Ridge, we've got the day off—and best of all, we've got two cute girls willing to spend time with us again."

He turned to Gloria, waggling his eyebrows. "I told Jonathan it was his turn to drive because I wanted to focus on *you* instead of on the road. What a great way to spend a sunny Monday, ain't so?"

Gloria's smile was demure and hinted at secrets. "It was a nice surprise when Bishop Monroe decided we four were perfect for the . . . adventure that's presented itself," she agreed. "And *denki* to you fellows for coming along. He wasn't going to let Laura and me go by ourselves."

After Jonathan guided the horse onto the shoulder of the state highway, he glanced over his shoulder. "What sort of adventure are we talking about? Bishop Monroe didn't say much about it, except to tell Sam and Simon our help was important for securing the future of Promise Lodge. *That* got everyone's attention!"

Gloria gazed out the small window in the back of the buggy. "I, um, can't reveal all the deep, dark details just yet," she replied, "but they'll come out eventually. Let's just say that there's a lady we need to see, and she owns a consignment shop in Willow Ridge—"

"And I for one plan to spend time there looking around," Laura put in quickly. "Mamm's never been to Willow Ridge, but she's heard that this Simple Gifts shop sells unique things crafted by Plain folks—and she's heard the restaurant in town is top-notch, too. Sounds promising for lunch, ain't so?"

Cyrus was too caught up in slipping his hand over Gloria's to think as far ahead as lunch. "I seem to recall that Willow Ridge had a rogue bishop at one time—but all I know is what I read in *The Budget*."

"*Jah*, he got caught driving a car and got himself excommunicated, among other things," Jonathan commented. "The column in the paper didn't give all the details, but he set the restaurant on fire during the Willow Ridge Christmas Eve program, when hundreds of people could've been hurt."

"Oh my," Gloria murmured. "I hope the restaurant's open again."

"It is," Cyrus reassured her. "The town pulled together and put everything to rights pretty fast, as I recall. Sometimes troublemakers bring out the best in *gut*-hearted people . . . and I'm hoping it'll be the same for me, after the trouble I've caused you girls. I—I'm really sorry about putting Jonathan up to that stupid bet."

Gloria's brown eyes widened as she focused on him. "You're on the right track, Cyrus," she said softly. "If Bishop Monroe didn't believe you deserved another chance, he wouldn't have let you two escort Laura and me today."

Cyrus's heart thudded steadily. It was a good sign that

Gloria hadn't withdrawn her hand from his, and that she was talking so calmly about the conversation she'd overheard on the day of Troyer's wedding. "*Denki* for believing in me, girl," he murmured. "I owe Bishop Monroe a lot for coaching me during our instruction sessions, and for pointing out that it's not always smart to go for the big finish or the dangerous dare—especially when other people's feelings are at stake. I should've taken his advice to heart."

"And when he hinted to Sam and Simon that our trip to Willow Ridge is connected to the problems Bishop Clayton has caused, Cyrus and I were all in," Jonathan added as he stopped the horse at an intersection to check for traffic. "Made me sick—and really suspicious—when King announced he was taking over Promise Lodge and putting Bishop Monroe out. Yet after that initial hoo-hah at Allen's wedding, he hasn't done a thing. What's with *that*?"

Cyrus had watched Gloria's face closely as his brother mentioned the bishop from Lancaster County. Without saying a word, she was expressing her own disdain for King. It was clear she knew things she wasn't telling. "I'm not sure what we'll find out today," she said hesitantly, "because Bishop Monroe wants to have all the details in place before he lets a big cat out of the bag. *Denki* to all of you for helping with this, even though I can't say anything more about it."

Intrigued by what might lie ahead of them, Cyrus relaxed in the backseat of the buggy. He felt good knowing that Bishop Monroe had given him a vote of confidence—and he felt even better that Gloria had included him in the day's mission. Even though her black bonnet and coat covered everything except her face, her cheeks glowed with enthusiasm—and her eyes sparkled when she looked at him.

"I'm looking forward to having you buy us lunch," she teased softly. "It's a treat to go to a restaurant for a meal."

"It's a treat to treat you," Cyrus replied quickly. "I guess I'm surprised—but gratified—that Bishop Monroe isn't the one who's going to Willow Ridge. If he's concerned about Bishop Clayton—"

"He's learned things that convinced him not to leave Promise Lodge for any length of time," Gloria put in. Her brown eyes widened as she squeezed Cyrus's hand.

In the front seat, Jonathan was shaking his head again. "Why do I get the feeling Bishop Monroe doesn't trust King? And that maybe Clayton King's not who he says he is—maybe not even a real bishop?"

Gloria's quick intake of breath told Cyrus his brother had hit upon a vital clue.

"That's it, *jah*?" he murmured. "When Preacher Amos and Preacher Marlin quizzed King about his accusations early on, they were doubting his authority even then. And now we're finding out that he's pulled the wool over our eyes . . . that he's a fake. A wolf in bishop's clothing."

"Which means that when King told us the Council of Bishops wanted a big bunch of money, he probably intended to take it for himself," Jonathan added vehemently.

When Gloria released the breath she'd been holding, she sounded like a balloon losing its air. Cyrus was sorry they'd spoiled her secret, yet he was also impressed that she'd been involved in discovering proof that Jonathan's suggestions were true. "Have we got it right?" he asked as he squeezed her hand. "You might as well tell us, sweetie. If Bishop Monroe's sending us to Willow Ridge to check on King, we're going to find out about him sooner or later, ain't so?"

Gloria smiled sheepishly. "Okay, so I'm not so *gut* at keeping secrets," she admitted. "But I suppose Bishop Monroe realizes that by the time we return from Willow Ridge, you three will know some of what's been going on—"

"What are you saying?" Laura demanded as she turned to gaze at Gloria. "If Bishop Clayton's not a bishop, who is he? And how do *you* know he's not?"

Gloria's cheeks took on some color. "I'm not sure what Bishop Monroe had already found out, but when I showed him a couple of papers that mentioned a fellow in Willow Ridge who consigned clocks to the gift shop we're visiting today," she replied in a low voice, "he acted like he'd just found the missing piece of the puzzle he and the preachers have been working on."

Laura scowled. "Clocks? Why would a guy who runs a Lancaster County bulk food warehouse be involved with *clocks*?"

"Because he lied about all that stuff," Jonathan said softly. "Because he doesn't want us to know who he really is. Wow, this is huge."

"But—but where did you get those papers?" Laura persisted. "What if we're making a lot of *wrong* assumptions—"

"They, um, were in his closet," Gloria admitted as she looked out the buggy window. "I found a bunch of papers in a wooden crate underneath an English-style man's suit and necktie, alongside a fancy wheeled suitcase with a laptop computer in it. Which, *jah*, means I was sticking my nosy nose where it didn't belong. And I've already confessed that to Bishop Monroe."

Cyrus's mouth fell open. "Get out!" he whispered. "You sneaked into King's—what if he'd caught you, Gloria?"

"He was in Coldstream for church." Gloria licked her lips nervously. "I know it was an awful, deceitful thing to do—and maybe now that you know I did it, you won't want to go out with me anymore."

Cyrus was touched by her fearful expression, even as he clutched her hand between his. "Are you kidding me? I wish I had thought of it!" he replied in an admiring whisper. "All this time we've been wondering about King—or whoever he is—and *you* stopped speculating and took action."

Gloria gazed at him gratefully. Cyrus sensed he'd just gotten into her good graces again, simply because he'd taken her seriously. Who would've guessed that the flighty, flirty girl who'd chased after Allen Troyer so relentlessly with her bad brownies would be the one to outfox an impostor out to take advantage of all the folks at Promise Lodge?

The more Cyrus thought about this, the more impressed he was with Gloria. She'd taken action—improper as it was—and she'd reported her findings to Bishop Monroe so he could move in on Clayton King from the position of utmost authority in Promise Lodge. She could've gone running out of Lester's place waving her evidence around, babbling about that English suit and laptop computer, but she'd known better. She'd shown maturity and discretion . . . and maybe he could take a few lessons from her on those topics.

"So *that's* why he always sat in his room while Mamm and I were cleaning at Lester's place," Laura said disgustedly. "He didn't want us finding his—his *disguise*."

"He didn't want us women to discover the truth," Gloria

agreed. "What galls *me* is that he's been wrangling a free stay out of us—meals and laundry and a room at Lester's—while he's been lying to us. And meanwhile he's been pointing the finger at Phineas for committing an unforgivable sin!"

"Well, our trip has already taken an interesting turn, and we're still an hour away from Willow Ridge," Jonathan remarked as he steered the horse onto another county highway. "Who knows what else we might learn when we get there?"

Chapter Twenty-Two

As they passed through the bustling town of Morning Star, Gloria gazed out the buggy window. "Do you suppose Willow Ridge is anything like this place?"

"According to Bishop Monroe's directions, we'll find out in about ten minutes," Laura replied. "It's fun to see all these new places—and I'm glad we didn't come by ourselves, Gloria. I suspect we'd have gotten lost, trying to find so many different roads!"

"Probably so," Gloria agreed. She smiled at Cyrus. "Guys can come in handy sometimes."

Cyrus's wink sent little tremors up her spine. During the entire ride he'd held her hand without making her feel he was holding her to any further commitment. "As we were hitching up the horse this morning, Jonathan and I agreed that today's trip was truly a gift because you girls were willing to spend the day with us," he said softly.

"And we might be able to get more help for Bishop Monroe just because we're guys," Jonathan pointed out. "As King has reminded us so often, you ladies have gotten used to having more say-so than Amish women who live in more conservative church districts."

Gloria nodded and took the two sheets of paper from her coat pocket. What did she have to gain by keeping them to herself? "We'll be looking for Nora Hooley at the Simple Gifts shop," she remarked as she handed the papers to Cyrus. "She accepted three clocks from a man named Cornelius Riehl—and I have another sheet about some clock repairs this Cornelius was going to do for a customer. Somehow, when Bishop Monroe saw the estimate for the repairs, he knew we'd painted Clayton King into a corner he wasn't going to get out of."

Cyrus glanced at the page from the shop and then studied the handwritten estimate. "I have no idea how this Riehl clock fellow can be Clayton King," he said after a few moments. "But there must be a connection, if you found the papers in the closet of the room King's staying in. Why else would he have these papers stashed away?"

"And why else would he be *hiding* them?" Laura pointed out.

Jonathan let out a short laugh. "King's going to wish he hadn't carted such documents along with him," he remarked. "What other kinds of papers did you see, Gloria?"

She shook her head. "I was sure Bishop Clayton was going to catch me rifling through his crate—and the light wasn't *gut* enough to read by," she added. "So I stuffed these two sheets in my pocket and hightailed it out of there. Maybe God and Dat's spirit were telling me to move along, or maybe it was just my guilty conscience."

"*Jah*, guilt's a powerful motivator," Cyrus murmured as he gave the papers back to Gloria. He pointed out the window. "The sign says we're only two miles from Willow Ridge. Won't be long until these mysteries are solved—and by then I'll be ready to chow down in that restaurant you were telling us about. Playing detective is hungry work."

Gloria nodded, gazing eagerly at the passing scenery. Soon the road made a big curve around a pasture where sheep were grazing. As they saw the sign for the Willow Ridge town limits, they spotted a farm with red barns where a herd of black-and-white Holsteins looked up from the hay bales they were munching on.

"Dairy cows and sheep so far—just like at Promise Lodge," Gloria remarked as her pulse quickened.

"*Jah*, and over in that orchard I see some white beehives like Ruby's," Laura said.

Cyrus moved closer to Gloria so he could gaze out the window on her side. "And they've got a vineyard here, just getting started by the looks of it."

Gloria's breathing quickened as Cyrus remained so close to her that his breath tickled her neck like a feather. "It's a nice town," she whispered.

"And you're a nice girl, patient and kind," he murmured. "Am I doing okay so far? I really don't want to mess up this time."

As he eased away from her, Gloria smiled shyly at him. What a difference in his behavior, compared to the swaggering bravado he'd always shown before. "I won't be pushing you out of the buggy any time soon," she teased softly. "I—I'm glad you came along, Cyrus. Now that we're getting close to the store, I'm feeling antsy."

"The instructions say to turn left at this intersection, onto the state highway," Laura said. She leaned forward in the front seat to help Jonathan watch for traffic. "Oh, look! There's a quilt shop and a place called the Grill N Skillet. Is that the café you've heard about, Gloria?"

"I can already smell the meat they're cooking—and look at those big metal grills behind the building," Cyrus said, inhaling deeply. "Yessirree, that's where we're heading for lunch—and I'll be happy to pick up the tab!"

"And up the hill from there's a big red barn with a

sign that says 'Simple Gifts,'" Laura put in excitedly. "We're here!"

"That's it!" Gloria's stomach tightened. "I sure hope Nora's at her store today. What if it's closed on Mondays? Or what if she's not working—"

"We can ask the folks at the café where to find her," Jonathan reassured her as he turned the buggy onto the state highway. "You know how it is in Plain towns. Everybody knows everybody. Willow Ridge looks like a great place."

As the buggy pulled into the parking lot of the Simple Gifts store a few moments later, Gloria wondered if she'd be able to talk once she got inside. It was one thing to snoop in Uncle Lester's house, but it was another thing altogether to show the papers she'd brought to a complete stranger. "Oh, but I hope this goes all right," she murmured. "What if—"

"What if we pray about it before we go inside?" Cyrus asked quietly. "Who knows how folks might react when we tell them why we're here?"

Gloria gazed at Cyrus with a sense of grateful wonder. "That's a fine idea," she replied as he wrapped his hand around hers again.

After the four of them bowed their heads, Cyrus began. "God, we're here to learn the truth about a fellow calling himself Clayton King, who came to Promise Lodge supposedly to do Your work," he said in a low, clear voice. "We need all the help we can get, so *denki* for being with us. Amen."

The simple, direct prayer made Gloria feel more confident about what they were about to do. Once again she was pleasantly surprised at Cyrus's quiet, take-charge demeanor—and she'd never anticipated that he would invoke God's presence.

"All right, here we go," she murmured. "We're all in this together."

"How can we go wrong if we do our best and let God do the rest?" Jonathan asked with a gentle smile.

After they got out of the buggy, Gloria admired the colorful bunches of Indian corn tied on either side of the shop's door, as well as wreaths made with silk fall foliage, acorns, and small bunches of bittersweet. After Jonathan had hitched the horse to the rail on the side of the building, she took a deep breath and opened the shop door.

Scents of warm vanilla and cinnamon enveloped her as they stepped inside the most fascinating store she'd ever seen. Displays of beautiful Amish-made furniture, sets of pottery dishes, and colorful handmade baskets caught her eye first. Beyond that she saw a couple of ornately tooled saddles and a garden gate that reminded her of the decorative welded metalwork Noah Schwartz was so good at. When Gloria glanced toward the upper level, her eyes widened.

"Laura, would you look at those banners?" she whispered loudly, grabbing her friend's arm. "Am I seeing things, or are that little girl and boy on a swing wearing a real *kapp* and straw hat?"

A woman in the next aisle looked up from the kitchen linens she was straightening. Her red hair was tucked up into a bun beneath a round black *kapp*, and her calf-length calico dress suggested that she was Mennonite. "You've got it right," she said as she approached the four of them with a freckle-faced smile. "Feel free to go upstairs for a closer look—or to ask me about anything you see here. Everything in my store has been crafted by Plain folks from around mid Missouri, and what with the upcoming holidays, we've got quite a nice selection right now."

Gloria's heart thudded hard in her chest. "Are—are you

Nora Hooley, by chance?" she asked as her hand closed around the two folded papers in her coat pocket.

"I am! How can I help you folks?" she replied pleasantly.

Glancing around, Gloria was relieved that the only other people in the store were at the opposite end of the room. She looked at Cyrus, Laura, and Jonathan to bolster her courage. "We—we're hoping you can tell us something about a man who's come to Promise Lodge, where we live," she began in a rush. "We think he's up to something underhanded—"

Hoping the papers in her pocket would express her meaning better than her uncertain words, Gloria thrust them at Nora.

One look made Nora's jaw drop. She glanced at the page from her shop and then at the handwritten estimate, her eyes widening. "You know where this man is?" she whispered.

Gloria nodded, sensing the urgency of Nora's question. Her body trembled as though she'd plugged it into an electrical socket.

Nora glanced toward the people at the store's other end. "Let's talk in my office," she murmured, walking toward the checkout counter.

Eyes wide, Gloria fell into step behind Nora. When the five of them had entered the small room behind the cash registers, the shopkeeper closed the door and looked at them gravely. "Are you saying Cornelius Riehl has come to your settlement? The young woman who's working for me this morning is his daughter, Rosalyn, so I don't want her to get wind of this just yet," she explained quickly. "When you say *underhanded*, exactly what do you mean?"

Gloria wondered where she should begin. "Well, he

showed up out of the blue saying he was from Lancaster County, and that his name was Bishop Clayton King—"

"And he claimed to be from some Council of Bishops who sent him to set us straight because we've become too progressive," Cyrus continued.

"Last Friday he announced that the council had told him he was to take over as our new bishop," Laura put in quickly. "Needless to say, our current bishop—my step-*dat*—is wondering if a bunch of men out east even has any say over us."

"And when King suggested that each family in Promise Lodge should donate a percentage of their year's income as a sign of their intention to walk the straight and narrow again," Jonathan put in, "we started getting suspicious."

"As well you should!" Nora blurted out. She shook the papers angrily, lowering her voice. "This man is no more a bishop than I am! After we caught him going to a casino to gamble, he claimed he would stop—but we discovered he was still gambling on a computer, and—"

Nora crossed her arms hard, so upset that she pivoted to look away from them. "Cornelius left this town—and his poor family—reeling from the extent of his thievery," she explained in a terse whisper. "I hope you've caught on to him before he pulled the same evil tricks as—oh, but we need to tell Bishop Tom about this!"

Gloria nodded, touched by Nora's reactions. "*Jah*, that's why we came," she said softly. "Our Bishop Monroe wants the bishop here to give him some advice about what to do, to make sure he's got his facts straight before he confronts Bishop Clayton—er, Cornelius Riehl, if it's really him."

Nora turned, inhaling to settle herself. "Does he have dark hair that's going gray? About as tall as these fellows, but heftier?" she asked, gesturing toward Cyrus and Jonathan. "Big booming voice, when he reads the Bible or—"

"Preaches," Cyrus put in with a roll of his eyes. "This guy can really work a crowd. Doesn't bat an eye when he says we're all damned if we keep to our progressive ways. He says we give our women way too much freedom, and claims he's come to put us back on the path to salvation."

"That's him," Nora confirmed with a sigh. "Full of himself. And in general, if his mouth's open, he's lying." She glanced out her office window, toward where a few customers were entering the store. "How about if you wait for me beside the black van parked out back? I'll let Rosalyn know I'm leaving for a bit, and we'll go visit Bishop Tom."

Once they'd exited through the office door, Gloria gazed at her friends in disbelief. "Did you hear what Nora said about this man?"

"Evil tricks and thievery—and *gambling*," Laura whispered.

"It's a *gut* thing Gloria found those papers when she did," Cyrus said, smiling at her. "And now that we're going to talk to the bishop here, Bishop Monroe won't have to take Clayton—or Cornelius's—word for anything again."

The shop door opened and Nora stepped outside with keys in her hand. She gripped the handle of the black van's door. "My reaction to your news about Cornelius probably seemed over the top or extremely judgmental—hardly an example of Plain forgiveness," she said apologetically. "But after the way he took off without warning or any sign of remorse—almost a year ago, it's been—I'm surprised to hear that he's shown up in central Missouri again. I have to wonder what he's been up to all this time, even though I don't really want to know."

Gloria's thoughts whirled as everyone got into Nora's van. Why would an Amish man turn to gambling, to such an extent that he'd devastated his family and his community? As they rode past Zook's Market, the Grill N Skillet, and the quilt shop again, everything in town appeared to be prospering, however. The homes they passed weren't as new as the ones in Promise Lodge but they were well maintained—and the animals grazing in the pastures were healthy and sleek. From all outward appearances, Willow Ridge was a picture-postcard rural town where Plain families were thriving and running successful businesses.

"This is the home where Cornelius lived, and where Rosalyn and her new husband, Marcus Hooley, have remained," Nora said as she pointed to a tidy white house on their right. "His daughter Edith and her family live across the road. The other Riehl sister, Loretta, lives in that new home farther back, beyond the vineyard. She and her husband are expecting their first child any day now, so she no longer works in the store."

Nora shook her head sadly. "Although I'm a firm believer in families staying together, I certainly hope Cornelius doesn't come back to cause more trouble for his girls," she said sadly. "After enduring their *dat*'s hateful behavior—and the humiliation when folks learned he'd stolen the district's money—they're doing their best to move on."

Gloria recalled the times Bishop Clayton had pointed his accusing finger at Phineas Beachey for committing what was considered the one unforgivable sin. And yet, it seemed that Cornelius Riehl was intimately acquainted with wrongdoing for which he hadn't even tried to seek forgiveness. She was wondering about other details of his tangled story when Nora turned down a long gravel lane that led to the farm where they'd seen the Holsteins grazing.

"It's not yet milking time, so hopefully we'll catch Bishop Tom in the house," Nora said as she parked near the front door. "In his *spare* time—when he's not shepherding his Amish flock or tending his cows," she said with a chuckle, "he carves the most fabulous Nativity sets, which the customers in my store snap up as soon as I display them. He's such a wise, patient bishop—but this news about Cornelius will take him by surprise."

"*Jah*, King has that effect on people," Jonathan remarked as they all got out of the van.

Nora preceded them up to the small porch and knocked on the door. As they waited, Gloria prayed that their mission would once again reach a person who'd be willing to help Promise Lodge. The more she'd heard, the more she wondered if the bishop of Willow Ridge would want to recall the harm Cornelius Riehl had done.

When the door opened, a slender man with graying brown hair and a kindly smile greeted them. "Nora, *gut* afternoon!" he said as he gestured for them to come inside. "My Nazareth has gone to Schrocks' quilt shop, so you and your friends'll have to deal with the likes of me, I'm afraid. I'd offer you coffee, but it's gotten cold—"

"Well, Bishop Tom, the news we have will be enough to heat it up, I'm afraid," Nora said with a reluctant chuckle. She turned to the four of them as they filed into the bishop's simple front room. "It seems I was so stunned by what these young people had to say, I didn't even get their names!"

Gloria laughed in spite of how nervous she felt. "I'm Gloria Lehman, and this is Laura Hershberger," she began, gesturing to everyone in turn. "Cyrus Helmuth and his brother Jonathan have been kind enough to drive us today, and to help us deal with a—a *mystery* that has *ferhoodled* us in Promise Lodge for the past month or so."

"I'm Tom Hostetler," the bishop said, offering his hand. "If I recall from what I've read in *The Budget*, Promise Lodge is the settlement that started up when three sisters bought an abandoned church camp, *jah*? North and west of here, near the Iowa line. Sounds like you folks are growing and doing quite well."

"That's us," Cyrus confirmed. "It amazes me how quickly new homes and businesses have sprung up there in the past year and a half—"

"And maybe *that's* why Cornelius Riehl made himself out to be a bishop and declared himself our new leader," Jonathan muttered. "He already *knew* how prosperous we were, and he was all set to tap into our success. Who knows how long he'd been checking us out before he showed up?"

Bishop Tom's face, swarthy from spending time outside, had gone pale. "Did you say *Cornelius Riehl* has come to Promise Lodge?"

With a sigh, Nora handed Bishop Tom the two sheets of paper Gloria had given her. "The man these kids have described has to be him," she said softly. "Apparently he's devised a new con game."

"We'd better sit down." Bishop Tom raked his fingers through his hair and gestured toward a sofa and some armchairs. "After the way Deacon Cornelius pulled the wool over my eyes—and lied to and cheated everyone else in town, including his own family—I never figured to hear of him again after he took off."

"May I take your coats?" Nora asked quietly. "We might be here awhile."

"Oh my *gut*ness, where are my manners?" the bishop said as he took their wraps. "*Jah*, if we'll be talking about Cornelius, it might take a while to unravel what-all he's gotten himself into. I believe in the will of Almighty God and the power of His grace and forgiveness, but that doesn't mean I'll forget how that remorseless swindler deceived us."

Gloria blinked. Bishop Tom was a soft-spoken man yet

his words rang with bitterness—a rancor her *dat* had often warned his congregations to pray over before it consumed them from the inside out. After the bishop had laid their coats on a loveseat across the room, he returned to where they'd taken their seats.

"Forgive me," he said as he sat between Cyrus and Jonathan on the long sofa. "If you've come to me for guidance, I shouldn't allow my prejudice to color the way I speak. Shall we pray for some attitude adjustment?"

As they bowed their heads, Gloria was struck by Bishop Tom's earnest desire to help them despite the harm Cornelius Riehl—*Deacon* Cornelius—had done in his church district. What a blow it must've been for the leaders of Willow Ridge to discover that one of their own—the man entrusted with the district's finances—had deceived them.

"God and Father of us all, we bow before You," Bishop Tom said reverently, "and we ask for Your guidance as we rise above our misgivings about one of Your children and continue to move beyond the past, closer to our forever with You. Amen."

The bishop appeared calmer and more in control of his emotions when he looked up. "So tell me how Cornelius came to be at Promise Lodge—under a fake name, misrepresenting his mission," he added with a sigh.

Cyrus, sitting to Bishop Tom's right, spoke first. "He showed up out of the blue one afternoon, announcing that he'd come from Lancaster County, where a Council of Bishops feared that Promise Lodge was on the path to perdition because we've become too progressive."

"And the council had drawn this conclusion from reading our columns in *The Budget*," Jonathan added. "Our bishop, Monroe Burkholder, was his main target, partly because he and our preachers had recently allowed one of our Old Order members to marry a Mennonite."

"*Jah*, I recall reading the column about that event," Bishop Tom remarked with a nod. "I was surprised, but I have a hunch intermarriage will become more common in the future. Amish folks get along better in today's world with the help of their Mennonite neighbors, so the dividing lines between our faiths is beginning to blur."

"Bishop Monroe's also been taking some heat from Bishop Clayton—er, Cornelius—about his business, which is training Clydesdales for English clients who show them," Gloria continued. "And the husband of one of our newest residents has come back to her after leaving the Old Order. He wants to reconcile with her and our faith, but Cornelius claims that Phineas has committed the one unforgivable sin—and that he's already damned himself forever."

Bishop Tom's lips curved. "Let the man who's never sinned cast the first stone," he paraphrased softly. "*Jah*, many conservative Old Order settlements would refuse to allow Phineas a chance to come back. For other bishops, however, that rule goes against the very nature of forgiveness and redemption that Jesus preached—depending on the circumstances, of course."

When he smiled at the four of them, Bishop Tom's face took on a boyish humility that further convinced Gloria they'd come to exactly the right place.

"I've gotten the impression that Promise Lodge has pushed several of the Old Order boundaries since Monroe Burkholder arrived there, but you know, that's not always detrimental," he murmured. "It's one thing to give in to the worldly habits and desires of the English—to sell out the ancient ways of the Old Order for the sake of convenience. But it's another thing altogether to examine those ancient ways when they no longer seem to serve the common *gut*.

"Especially when it comes to the welfare of our women,"

the bishop added in a thoughtful tone. "I believe our faith would improve if we respected wives and mothers as pillars of their families with valid opinions, and if we allowed them to contribute their abilities to the community rather than forcing them into whatever roles their men allow them to fill."

Gloria's eyes widened. She hadn't expected a bishop of her father's generation to express such progressive ideas.

Nora laughed and clapped her hands together. "Bishop Tom, had *you* been in charge when I was growing up Amish, I might've returned to the faith when I came back to Willow Ridge," she crowed. She gazed at Gloria and her friends. "Do you understand now why Willow Ridge has rebounded quickly from the damage Cornelius Riehl did to our town? Bishop Tom thinks outside the box—and he believes the box has transparent walls where no one can hide. Including Cornelius."

Gloria considered this. She sensed Nora had lived her life outside that proverbial box, yet she'd returned to this town to run her business—and folks had accepted her even though she'd turned Mennonite. Rather than derail the conversation about Cornelius, however, Gloria kept her curiosity about Nora to herself.

"So . . . what exactly did Cornelius do here?" Cyrus asked after a few moments of silence. "If you don't want to talk about it—"

"Oh, but we *must* discuss it if we're to keep him from deceiving other trusting souls," Bishop Tom insisted. "Riehl is *counting* on me and the preachers remaining quiet about all the money he stole from us—hundreds of thousands of dollars our members had contributed over the years. He knew we wouldn't call in the English police or an attorney, and he believed we'd be too ashamed to admit to other church districts that we'd been hoodwinked by the man we'd entrusted our money to. But if we keep silent about our mistake, we're playing into his hands."

It took Gloria a few moments to wrap her mind around what Bishop Tom had said. Not only had he admitted to an *astounding* amount of money that Cornelius had stolen, but he'd plumbed the dark depths of a devious mind that worked in ways she didn't understand. It was a scary thought, to realize that such a man as Cornelius Riehl had been living among them at Promise Lodge, pretending he was there to save their souls.

"To answer your question, son," Bishop Tom said to Cyrus, "Cornelius was taking money from the church vault to a casino and gambling it away. And when we—well, when Nora and one of our young men—caught him red-handed, he claimed he'd been so grief-stricken after his wife's passing that he'd succumbed to the thrill of gambling. He vowed to attend grief counseling; promised us he had his habit under control, so we gave him another chance," Bishop Tom added ruefully.

"He stopped going to the casino, but another of our young men discovered that Cornelius had found a way to gamble with a *computer*," the bishop continued with a shake of his head. "I don't understand technology, but by the time we caught him, he'd all but bankrupted us. Preacher Ben and I believed we'd been doing the right thing, giving him the opportunity to repent and come clean, but we were wrong. Naïve, and very, very wrong."

"And rather than serve out his punishment after his kneeling confession at church," Nora put in softly, "Cornelius skipped town. He'd bullied his daughters into keeping their noses out of his business—they had no idea why bills were arriving marked 'Past Due,' or why their *dat* would no longer allow them to shop for groceries. He left them in debt, after making a lot of nasty remarks and threats they'll never forget."

Gloria's eyes widened as she met Laura's troubled gaze. "Oh my," she whispered. "I can't imagine finding out that my *dat* had been doing all those horrible things—not to mention stealing money from folks who'd trusted him."

"Bishop Monroe would *never* do that, and neither would Amos or Marlin or Eli," Laura put in. She looked at Bishop Tom, who sat between the Helmuth brothers. "We're hoping you can help us," she entreated. "Bishop Monroe, my new step-*dat*, has been keeping quiet about some things concerning Cornelius, so maybe if you talked to him—"

"I'll do everything I can to help you folks," Bishop Tom said earnestly. "We've got to prevent Cornelius from getting his hands on Promise Lodge's money. If you've got Monroe's phone number, I'll call him today."

Feeling greatly relieved, Gloria pulled a piece of paper from her apron pocket. "*Denki* so much, Bishop Tom," she said as she handed it to him. "Bishop Monroe's so wary of Cornelius, he didn't want to leave Willow Ridge to visit with you."

Bishop Tom stood up, flashing them a smile. "You young folks have done your community a great service," he said as he shook hands all around. "I see this as a chance to right some of the wrongs Cornelius did us, even though we're not supposed to seek revenge or payback."

"But we're to be the hands and feet of Jesus here on earth," Nora countered brightly. "So maybe we can be the long arm of God's law, while we're at it."

Gloria chuckled. As she and her friends said their good-byes to the bishop, she had a good feeling about the direction their mission was taking. When they stepped out onto Bishop Tom's front porch, Cyrus inhaled deeply.

"I think our next stop ought to be the Grill N Skillet," he said.

"You can't go wrong eating there," Nora said with a nod. "The Witmers have a lunchtime buffet or you can order from the menu—"

"Will you join us, Nora?" Gloria asked as they got into her van. "You've been so helpful, the least we can do is buy your lunch."

"I appreciate your offer, but I should get back to the shop," Nora replied as she started the engine. "We're putting out a lot of new items for the holidays—and I'm hosting a big in-store reception for my customers the day after Thanksgiving—so I need to be stocking my shelves."

A few minutes later Nora pulled the van into the parking lot at the side of the Grill N Skillet. "Enjoy your lunch!" she said. "It's been such a pleasure to meet you today."

"Even though we brought along our problems with Cornelius Riehl?" Jonathan asked as they exited the van.

Nora smiled pensively. "It'll work out the way it's supposed to," she assured them softly. "With God—and Bishop Tom—all things are possible."

Chapter Twenty-Three

Cyrus closed his eyes over the first bite of his country-style ribs. "I've died and gone to heaven," he murmured. "This pork is awesome—"

"Ditto for my steak," Jonathan said. "I hardly need my knife to cut it."

"Really *gut* grilled chicken, too," Gloria put in with her mouth full. "And what a selection of side dishes they have on their buffet."

"Wish we had a restaurant like this closer to Promise Lodge," Laura remarked. "This place puts the Skylark Café in Forest Grove to shame."

Cyrus forced himself to eat more slowly, because all four of them had taken an unbelievable amount of food. He fought the urge to kiss off a smudge of barbeque sauce on Gloria's cheek. It was satisfaction enough to be seated beside her in a booth while they enjoyed a fabulous meal that was very reasonably priced. The restaurant was noisy, crowded with Amish, Mennonite, and English alike, and he enjoyed watching folks chat and laugh as though they were good friends.

When he'd taken the edge off his hunger with some of his ribs, scalloped potatoes, turnip greens, and homemade applesauce, Cyrus wiped his hands on his napkin. "What'd you think of what Bishop Tom told us?" he asked. "I'll never understand how deceitful Cornelius has been—how he had the nerve to fleece his friends."

"Crooked as a dog's hind leg," Jonathan muttered. "And *meaner* than any dog, by the sound of it. We don't want to get crossways with him."

Gloria wiped her mouth, shaking her head. "I was sorry to hear that any human being—much less an Amish deacon and a father—was capable of such thievery. It makes me wonder what he's been up to in the months since he left Willow Ridge."

"Do you suppose he's been pulling the same bishop act in other places?" Laura asked. "If he's given up his clock shop, he has to be bringing in money somehow."

"I don't even want to know." Jonathan buttered a square of corn bread. "I have no idea how Bishop Monroe's going to handle this situation, but I want to be there when Cornelius gets what's coming to him—when all his lies come out, so folks see him for who he really is."

"Thanks to you, Gloria, light will shine on Cornelius's scandals," Cyrus said gently. When roses of humility bloomed in her cheeks, he reached for her hand under the table. "I mean that, sweetie. We couldn't have gotten Bishop Tom's help if you hadn't found those papers—"

"But it was still wrong to sneak around in Cornelius's closet," Gloria pointed out. "When folks find out *how* I found those papers, they'll probably want me to make a kneeling confession."

"I doubt that," Laura said, reaching across the table to squeeze Gloria's wrist. "What you did is *nothing* compared to all the ways Cornelius has cheated so many people."

"I admire you one-hundred percent, Gloria, and I'll stand by you," Cyrus murmured. "It was a brave, necessary action you took, in light of how much our friends would've lost had they shelled out the money Cornelius was asking for."

When her eyes widened, shining like hot coffee as she returned his gaze, Cyrus's insides got tight. Had he told her he loved her, in so many words? And was she saying, without any words at all, that she wanted to be with him for the long haul, too? For a few moments the people around them disappeared and it was just the two of them, gazing into one another's eyes.

"*Denki*, Cyrus," Gloria whispered. "I appreciate your help today, and your support. We're in this mission together—all of us," she added as she smiled at Laura and Jonathan. "We love Promise Lodge, and we don't want a fake bishop tearing down what our families have worked so hard to establish."

"Hear, hear," Jonathan said as he raised his water glass. "My brother and I are beholden to you girls for giving us another chance. We'd do just about anything for you two, you know."

Laura's eyebrows rose playfully. "Well, in that case," she teased, "we should find something in Nora's store—right, Gloria? We'd be supporting Plain crafters, after all—"

"And we'd be showing our appreciation to Nora, too," Gloria agreed. "She could've washed her hands of us when she realized why we'd come to Willow Ridge. She's Mennonite, so Cornelius didn't steal any of her money."

"But he lied to his daughters and left them to pay his bills," Cyrus pointed out. "Nora impresses me as a woman who wants the best for those young women because she cares about them—but also because loyalty and trust are important to her."

He looked around the crowded café again, delighted that his mission with Gloria was turning out as well as their trip to Willow Ridge. Cyrus thought about the special gift he'd stashed behind the seat of the buggy, yet he wanted to do *more* to show Gloria how he felt about her.

"I want to shop in Nora's store, too," he added. "Right after we answer the call of that dessert counter."

When Laura entered Nora's Simple Gifts store half an hour later, she felt she was walking into a magical place where fairy tales and dreams could come true. Soft music was playing. Subtle scents of vanilla and cinnamon filled the air. Several customers were in the store, yet the spacious barn and its loft allowed them plenty of room to stroll between the aisles admiring the wonderful items on the shelves and display tables.

Nora wiggled her fingers at them from the checkout counter. "Welcome back, friends," she called out. "Let me know if you have questions about anything."

Cyrus pointed toward the store's front corner. "I've got to check out those fancy saddles," he told his brother. "It's nice that Nora carries some *guy* stuff."

When Jonathan gazed at Laura, her heart stilled. "You fellows look at whatever you want. I want to see those three-dimensional banners on the loft level."

"Me, too—and those quilts," Gloria chimed in as the two of them started toward the stairway. "Look at these colorful pottery dishes! And that gorgeous set of walnut bedroom furniture—and all the embroidered linens. Wouldn't it be awesome to shop here and buy everything you needed for a new home?"

Laura's eyes lit up. "Do you suppose this is the shop

where Truman bought the furniture for Rosetta when they got engaged?"

"I think you're right. They're such a romantic couple," Gloria added with a dreamlike sigh. After they'd reached the loft level, she lowered her voice. "Do we dare to think in that direction with Cyrus and Jonathan again? We're having a wonderful-*gut* day with them, even though we've had to conduct some difficult business."

"What would we have done without them?" Laura whispered with a glance toward the lower level. "Truth be told, Jonathan and I have cleared the air about Cyrus's bet. I don't see us getting engaged in any big hurry, but we've, um, definitely kissed and made up."

"*Gut* for you," Gloria murmured. "I think Cyrus is headed in that *kissing* direction again, but he's keeping me on pins and needles."

Laura started toward the wall where several of the extraordinary banners were hanging. "Jonathan has suggested that we go some places without you and Cyrus—not that we don't like you," she put in quickly. "But he and his brother operate on different wavelengths—"

"And when Cyrus gets excited, he tends to lasso Jonathan into going along with him," Gloria put in with a chuckle. "That's fine by me, Laura. You and I aren't joined at the hip, after all, and neither are they."

Laura stopped in front of the banner that had caught her eye earlier in the day. She fingered it lovingly, amazed that the little Amish boy and girl on the swing were indeed wearing a real straw hat and *kapp*—which the crafter had cut in half and carefully attached to the banner. When she looked more closely, she realized that the children were also wearing pieces of actual clothing that had been cut and lightly stuffed to make the two figures appear even more lifelike.

"This is just amazing!" she declared. "The colors are so cheerful, and the kids look like they ought to start talking to us. I can practically feel the breeze, even though their swing isn't really moving."

"*Denki*, Laura," Nora said as she topped the stairway behind them. "I started making these banners years ago as a way to pay my bills. They also gave me the idea for opening a store that featured handmade items."

"And it's a fabulous store, too!" Gloria put in. "I could spend *hours* here—but I suspect we'll have to start home soon. I'm going to look at your quilts before we go, though."

Nora stepped over to a nearby shelf to arrange a stack of embroidered placemats she'd carried upstairs. "Take your time, girls," she said with a secretive smile. "I was sent up here to eavesdrop, so I could make suggestions about items you like—but you didn't hear that from me!"

Laura sucked in her breath. She had no trouble believing that Jonathan had asked Nora to help him shop, because he enjoyed choosing thoughtful gifts for her. "Well, you already know what I'd love to have," she whispered as her heart raced.

"I haven't seen a thing I don't like," Gloria murmured as she gazed around the loft. She pointed toward a quilt hanging on a rack that extended from the wall. "Wouldn't that coverlet brighten up an entire room? But maybe the bright red flowers are too showy for a Plain bedroom and— and maybe it's an awfully expensive piece—"

"Don't look a gift horse in the mouth!" Nora quipped as she went over to take the quilt from the rack. "If you like something, you *like* it. Let's spread it on this display bed so you can see the full design."

Laura couldn't miss the way Gloria nipped her lip as she helped Nora unfold the quilt. Shades of red, fuchsia, and deep orange were skillfully arranged to form the three large amaryllis blooms in the quilt's center, with stems and leaves of deep greens to fill out the design. The border was formed by blocks of those same colors in a log cabin pattern, around a rich cream-colored center.

"I've never seen anything like this," Gloria murmured as she walked around the bed to admire the quilt.

"It's a one-of-a-kind piece made by the gal who co-owns the quilt shop down the road," Nora said. "She's Amish, but she loves bold colors—and her unique quilts sell better here than they would in her own shop, where the customers are mostly Plain ladies. It's her way of being an artist without going against the rules of the church," she added with a smile.

Gloria sighed wistfully. "Oh, but I could never expect Cyrus to—"

"Never say never," Nora interrupted playfully, slipping her arm around Gloria's shoulders. "What does it hurt to express your preferences? Maybe you won't get this quilt as a gift, but if you don't ask you won't receive," she pointed out. "If nothing else, you've had the pleasure of seeing a beautiful quilt that pushes the boundaries of what most Old Order quilters consider acceptable."

"And it's not as though you're buying it for yourself," Laura said, taking up the thread of Nora's pep talk. "If you receive it as a *gift*, Gloria, what can you do but put it on your bed and feel delighted every time you look at it? Especially when you consider who might buy it for you."

"That's the spirit!" Nora said happily. "If you see other

items you like, come and find me before you leave. Me, I'll just mosey back downstairs as though I only came here to set out those new placemats."

Laura couldn't help smiling as she glanced at the other three-dimensional banners displayed around them. "Nora's a lot of fun—and if Jonathan actually buys that banner, I'll enjoy knowing that she made it," she said. "It'll be a nice souvenir of our trip to Willow Ridge, ain't so?"

"I'm not looking at the price tags on either of those pieces we like," Gloria said as she fingered a few other colorful quilts. "And I'll tell myself not to be disappointed if Cyrus doesn't buy that quilt, because I'm sure it costs hundreds of dollars.

"But *jah*," she added wistfully. "Even though we learned some scary things about the fake bishop of Promise Lodge, I've enjoyed our trip. It's been nice to see places we've not been before—and to spend time with you and Cyrus and Jonathan."

When the four of them left the store, Laura noticed that neither of the Helmuth brothers had loaded any parcels into the buggy. She didn't feel bad about it, however. The furtive smiles on Cyrus's and Jonathan's faces—the way they chatted happily all the way home—told her all she needed to know.

After Monroe hung up the phone, he sat in the phone shanty for several minutes thinking about what he'd just learned. The stories about Cornelius Riehl were so farfetched as to be unbelievable—except Tom Hostetler's voice had resonated with credibility as a sincere, down-to-earth Amish bishop whose district had been swindled too easily out of too much money for him to lie about such things.

And there but for Your grace, God, Promise Lodge would've gone, too. You've led us this far, so don't abandon us before we bring this matter to a conclusion, all right? A lot's riding on Your presence with everyone involved in holding Cornelius accountable.

As Monroe went into the house, he was greeted by the rich aroma of soup bubbling on the stove—beef vegetable, his favorite. The sight of Christine kneading bread dough at the kitchen counter gratified him immensely, and he was deeply aware of how much he would've missed this home, this community, if Cornelius Riehl had banished him. When he walked behind his beautiful wife to take her in his arms, her smile made him fall in love all over again.

"Something tells me you had a *gut* conversation," Christine said before turning to initiate the kiss Monroe had been yearning for.

"I did," Monroe murmured after their lips parted. "Laura and her friends did us proud today, and I have a plan in place."

"Where'd they go? And what's this big plan?" she asked lightly.

Monroe rested his forehead against hers. "All in *gut* time, dear," he replied. "I trust you totally, but the future of Promise Lodge is riding on what happens next, and I can't tell you what I know. You won't be able to keep it from your sisters, and before long the whole hen house will be squawking so loudly that our fox will know we've set a trap. End of story."

"Ah." Christine sounded mildly disappointed, but she smiled. "The story has a happy ending, though?"

"God's the author of all our stories," Monroe said as he gently stroked her cheek. "He creates each of us as characters in a tale that's sometimes a tragedy and sometimes a triumph, but He always intends the best for the children who love and follow Him. Tie your *kapp* on tight, Christine," he added as he tweaked her nose. "Come Sunday, we might be in for quite a ride."

Chapter Twenty-Four

"Bye now, Laura!" Gloria called out from the backseat of the buggy. "*Denki* for coming along today!"

"I wouldn't have missed it for anything," Laura said as she waved from the lane in front of her home. Beside her, standing close enough that their bodies were touching, Jonathan wore a radiant smile. The two of them made a fetching picture as the breeze riffled their coats.

They'll be engaged soon, Gloria thought as she withheld a sigh. *Laura claims they're in no hurry, but the expression on Jonathan's face says it all. He's head over heels for her.*

"How about if I walk you home, Gloria?" Cyrus asked. "After riding for so much of the day, I really need to stretch my legs."

She nodded as she stepped out of the buggy. "*Jah*, I'm tired of being cooped up, too. It was a great trip, though."

"Wait a sec. I've got something in the back."

Gloria fought her feelings of eager anticipation, even though neither of the brothers had been carrying a package when they'd left Willow Ridge. Her pulse sped up when Cyrus lifted a paper sack from behind the backseat by its handles. Had it been riding right behind her all day, while he'd given her no hint about it?

Don't jump to conclusions. Maybe Cyrus took along some stuff in case things went wrong in Willow Ridge—

"I've been waiting for the right time to give this to you, Gloria," he said in a tight voice. "But we've spent every moment with Laura and my brother, and I'm not supposed to go up to your apartment, so maybe you should take it now."

Gloria's eyes widened. Was this the same Cyrus who'd bet his brother five hundred dollars that he'd be engaged to her by Thanksgiving? He sounded shy, and maybe afraid of how she might react to whatever was in his sack.

As she accepted the gift, she swallowed hard. "Shall I look at it now, or wait until I get home?"

"Um—" Cyrus gazed ahead of them and pointed toward the wooded area at the bottom of Allen and Phoebe's hill. "How about if we go over there, where somebody looking out their window won't see us?"

Like Uncle Lester or Cornelius—or Marlin or my mamm?

Gloria walked faster as they followed the curve of the road, however. When they stepped between the trees near the road, leaves crunched and crackled beneath their feet. A vee of migrating geese honked overhead. When Gloria stopped in the shelter of a few fat old cedar trees, silence fell around them—except for the rapid thumping of her heart.

She glanced at Cyrus and he nodded. When she reached into the sack, she grasped a small wooden crate that felt slightly larger than a cheese box. As she lifted it out, she saw that it contained two bulbous objects covered in colorful coatings.

Cyrus plucked one of the bulbs out of the case, unable to suppress his smile any longer. "The nursery got these in from Holland just yesterday," he said excitedly. "They're the newest thing in amaryllis bulbs, because this thick wax coating means you don't have to plant them and you don't even have to water them! You just set them in a sunny spot—in the box or freestanding—and pretty soon the shoots will come out. Sometime around Christmas you'll have flowers."

Gloria's heart beat faster. Was it a coincidence—or a sign—that Cyrus had brought her amaryllis bulbs, and that she'd chosen the quilt with those same blooms on them in Nora's shop? "I love amaryllis," she whispered. "I don't have much of a green thumb, but I can get amaryllis to bloom every winter. So this is wax?" she asked, fingering the thick maroon coating on one bulb and the cream-colored coating on the other.

"Yup. I've only seen the pictures in the catalogs," he continued eagerly, "but most of them had three or four big blooms. No need for dirt or water," he repeated as he gazed into her eyes. "All you add is love. And—and maybe by the time these flowers are in full bloom, we'll know that our love is in bloom, too, Gloria."

Her breath caught in her throat. He'd used the *L* word. And he'd been looking at her straight-on. "Oh, Cyrus," she murmured. "What a beautiful idea—and a wonderful-*gut* gift, too."

"I didn't know whether you'd rather have red flowers or white, so I got you one of each," he continued. "I—I'm glad we're spending time together again, Gloria. It's only been a few days since you found out about that dumb bet, but the time has made me aware of what I stood to lose if you didn't give me another chance."

Gloria set the little crate on the ground so she could hug Cyrus hard. He pulled her close, cradling her head in his hand as he kissed her, slowly and thoroughly. By the time she came up for air she felt light-headed. Her imagination was spinning with pretty daydreams, yet Cyrus felt like the solid anchor she needed in her life.

"We all take our turns at doing stupid things," she whispered. "*Gut*ness knows I acted like a fool while I was chasing after Roman and Allen. I'm amazed you'd even want to take me out after the way I acted then."

"You've changed," Cyrus insisted. "Once you took on the management of the lodge apartments and started writing our column for *The Budget*, I realized you were more than just a pretty face, Gloria. And you've shown me that I needed to upgrade my behavior if you're to seriously consider me as . . . husband material."

Gloria almost couldn't believe what she was hearing. There was no denying Cyrus's sincerity as he gazed at her with such hopeful tenderness, however. "Well, now!" she whispered breathlessly. "We've given ourselves quite a lot to talk about in the coming days. But after what we've learned in Willow Ridge, it's *gut* to have such a happy subject we can discuss—because we four have to keep this business about Cornelius Riehl totally quiet, you know. It's in Bishop Monroe's hands now."

"It is," Cyrus confirmed. "And you're in *my* hands. I like the sound—and the feel—of that."

As he kissed her again, Gloria felt a welling up of joy and hope. Cyrus thought she was pretty—and capable! He believed she'd grown out of her silliness and was ready for a serious relationship. The words *I love you so much, Cyrus* were on the tip of her tongue, yet she realized they could wait. At this moment, her heart was already so full she just wanted to savor the images and words of a day unlike any other in her life.

Cyrus took her hand and picked up the little crate with the bulbs in it. As she folded the paper sack and tucked it under her arm, Gloria felt bubbly and alive—ready to watch her amaryllis plants send up shoots and burst into bloom, along with her feelings for the handsome young man who was walking beside her.

Full of eager anticipation, Gloria focused on the lodge building down the hill and on the future.

So this is what it feels like when a dream comes true.

Later that night, Gloria felt like one of Ruby's bees, buzzing with so much hope and excitement that she couldn't sleep. What a day they'd had in Willow Ridge, learning the truth about Cornelius—but they'd also met Nora Hooley and Bishop Tom, and they'd eaten a wonderful lunch, and she'd seen a beautiful amaryllis quilt . . . and she'd fallen in love with Cyrus.

This time, she was sure.

The full moon shone brightly through her window, lighting up half her apartment, yet it wasn't enough. She felt compelled to slip outside and experience its light full-on, despite the chill in the air. Wrapping her cream-colored shawl over her shoulders, Gloria padded down the back stairs barefoot—not that she would waken anyone. At one-thirty in the morning, Irene and the Kuhn sisters were deeply asleep, as were most of the folks who lived at Promise Lodge.

As Gloria stepped out onto the front porch, she held her breath in awe. The moon shone like a golden coin, regal and serene. The night sky was deep blue, cloudless and breathtaking, spangled with stars that sparkled like tiny diamonds. The white homes and buildings along the road took on a special glow, steeped in peaceful silence.

Was it silly to imagine that God had made this night especially beautiful just for her? Was He celebrating the fact that she'd found a man to marry despite her previous fears?

The white porch posts glowed as she leaned against one to turn her face up to the moon and bask in its cool, placid light. Folks often claimed the full moon made people and animals act a little crazier than usual—and she'd done her share of crazy things. Yet this moon was different.

As she gazed up toward heaven, Gloria felt worthy and mature, filled with love come straight down from God into her soul. Mesmerized, she continued to focus on the moon until she attained a still, silent joy.

Is this a gift from You, God—or are you here, too, Dat? Stick around, as we're not nearly finished with this business concerning Cornelius. And stay with me, too . . . because you both know I need all the light I can get to see my way with Cyrus.

Gloria inhaled the cool night air and let it out slowly, filled with wonder. Then she went upstairs to bed, knowing without a doubt that God Himself had touched her with His love.

Chapter Twenty-Five

Annabelle's heart was hammering as Phineas knocked on the Burkholders' front door. It was one of those moments of truth that would determine her future, and she prayed that this unscheduled meeting would go smoothly. As light footsteps approached the door from inside the house, Phineas clasped her hand, appearing almost as anxious as she felt. In his purple shirt, broadfall trousers, and suspenders he looked almost Amish again—except for growing out his hair.

"It's the right thing we're doing," he whispered. "It'll all work out, Annabelle."

When the door swung open, Christine greeted them with a bright smile. "What a nice surprise! Come in, come in—don't mind my mess," she warned as she waved them into the front room. "I'm rearranging my pantry, figuring out how to store more jars of canned fruits and vegetables in it, so I've carried all the contents out here. What brings you folks over on this fine Friday afternoon?"

Sidestepping the bins of flour, quart jars of tomatoes, and stacked cooking pots, Annabelle glanced around. "Well, we'd like to speak with Bishop Monroe—"

"To settle my status with the Old Order, once and for all," Phineas added firmly.

"Ah. He's in the stable working with his Clydesdales," Christine said apologetically. "One of his clients is coming with a trailer to take four horses that are trained and ready."

Annabelle sighed, disappointed. "I don't suppose he wants to be bothered, then," she murmured. "Maybe we should come back later, when—"

"Considering how important your situation is, I bet he'd be happy to talk with you," Christine insisted. "This business with Bishop Clayton claiming Phineas can't come back into the fold has a lot of folks upset, and Monroe would like to see your status resolved the way he—and the rest of us—believe it should go. Head down through the upper gate, across the pasture, and holler into one of the barns. You'll find him."

"*Denki* so much," Annabelle said. "Truth be told, I've always wanted to see what Bishop Monroe's big barns look like inside."

Phineas smiled at Christine. "And how about if I take a look at your pantry? Maybe I could design some more efficient shelving—unless Monroe's already got plans for that project, of course."

"He's been so busy getting the horses ready for this pickup date—and so preoccupied with other things—my pantry project's the last thing on his mind," Christine admitted. "I'm trying to save myself so many trips to the basement for our canned goods. Nothing earth shattering—"

"But it's the sort of redesigning project I do all the time," Phineas put in. "You're under no obligation to have me do the work after I show you some sketches."

Christine's face lit up and she gestured for them to follow her into a large, sunny kitchen. The white cabinets and counters appeared fresh and new. The room seemed more spacious than many Amish kitchens—and Annabelle realized that because the Burkholders had no children to raise, they got by with a much smaller table, the way she and Phineas always had.

It touched her, that Christine and Monroe's second marriage had so much in common with the relationship she and her husband shared. As Phineas stepped into the pantry and chatted with Christine, Annabelle walked slowly around the kitchen, allowing herself to imagine what her new kitchen might look like when they built their home at Promise Lodge. Their Bird-in-Hand farmhouse had been nearly eighty years old, and the kitchen had only one small window, cracked plaster walls, and cramped cabinet space.

But Annabelle knew better than to set her heart on a new home before Phineas had been readmitted into the Amish church.

"I can think of a couple different directions to go with this project," her husband was saying as he and Christine emerged from the pantry. "I'll sketch them out and you can tell me what you think."

"That would be wonderful, Phineas," the bishop's wife said. "Monroe will appreciate your help with this effort as much as I will. Come back for coffee and goodies after your chat, if you'd like. I haven't seen nearly enough of you folks lately."

Once again Annabelle set out with Phineas to find the bishop, being careful to close the white plank gate behind them before crossing a lush green pasture where colorful autumn leaves had caught in pockets of tall grass. A few Clydesdales looked up from their grazing to watch her and her husband—such majestic creatures with their muscular necks, thick manes, and shaggy, cream-colored legs that ended in huge hooves. What a picture they made with the two large red barns in the background.

And what will happen to this property—these horses—

if our fake bishop bamboozles folks and banishes Bishop Monroe?

Annabelle tried not to let such frightening thoughts overwhelm her. Surely the evidence in her friends' letters would be enough to prevent Clayton King from taking over, yet Bishop Monroe seemed to be waiting for more proof before he pounced. As this past week had ticked by, Annabelle wondered if Monroe had made any progress.

"I say we try the barn on the left," Phineas suggested, interrupting her gloomy thoughts. "We need to be careful about spooking these huge horses when we peek inside, though."

"*Jah*, we wouldn't survive if one of them reared up and came down on our heads," Annabelle agreed as they approached the barn door. "And yet, I've seen Bishop Monroe hop on and ride them bareback, without a bridle, so he surely must've trained them so they're accustomed to meeting strangers."

The walk-in barn door swung open on silent, well-oiled hinges. When they peered inside, they were greeted by the scents of leather tack, fresh hay, and the muted pungency of manure. On the wall to their right hung numerous harnesses. The main floor of the barn was divided by a wide pathway between stalls, which were formed by thick wooden support poles. A couple of young horses looked up from their feed bins and nickered, tossing their heads as they eyed Annabelle and Phineas curiously.

"This is the cleanest barn I've ever seen," Annabelle murmured. The thudding of heavy hooves and jingling bells near the back made her look up. "You in here, Bishop Monroe?" she called out.

"It's Phineas and Annabelle," her husband added loudly. "Hope we're not disturbing you!"

The bishop's familiar laughter rang high in the rafters. "You're just in time for a show, folks!" he replied. "Open both of those main doors, wide as they'll go—and then stand back!"

Annabelle and Phineas hurried to do as Monroe had instructed, unbolting the tall metal doors and shoving them in opposite directions on their tracks. By the time they scrambled outside, the concrete floor was vibrating with the weight of massive hooves stepping in cadence. The jingle of bells filled the air as four full-grown Clydesdales thundered out of the barn in black parade regalia, their silver harness and bridle ornaments glistening in the sunlight as they trotted outside.

Perched on the seat of a glossy black wagon, Monroe was grinning like a kid. He allowed the horses to pull the wagon completely out of the barn before he called out, "Whoa, boys! We're gonna give these folks a ride."

Annabelle's eyes widened. She'd watched state fair and holiday parades that featured horses in such ornate bridles and harnesses, but never had she imagined getting to ride behind a team like this one.

"Use those metal steps on the side and grab my hand," the bishop instructed as he leaned down over the side of the wagon. "This team's owner will be here in about an hour, and I want him to put these boys through their paces before he takes them home. It's not often I get to use my parade equipment, so your timing's perfect."

Grasping Monroe's broad hand, Annabelle scrambled up the rungs on the side of the wagon. Phineas followed close behind her, and soon they were seated on the driver's bench on either side of the bishop.

"Before you ask—I own this fancy gear with all the flashy silver and jingling bells because these Clydesdales have to be trained with such paraphernalia so they'll be accustomed to it when their owners take them to exhibitions," Bishop Monroe explained. "These boys are also *gut* at pulling extraordinary amounts of weight—not just in fancy draft horse competitions but, say, if a loaded eighteen-wheeler needed to be hauled up out of a farmer's ditch. So they're not just pretty faces, trained for shows. They're workers."

Annabelle gazed at the four huge horses standing perfectly still in front of them. Their brown coats glistened in the sunshine, and their manes had been braided with black ribbons. Their heads were proudly erect, and their ears were up, waiting for Monroe's next command.

"Easy, boys. Stand and wait," he said quietly, allowing the lines to relax. He turned to Annabelle and Phineas. "Let's chat until my assistants meet us at the gate. I'm guessing Christine sent you to find me because you're ready to declare yourself, Phineas," Monroe said.

"*Jah*, Bishop, we've come for your blessing," Phineas confirmed. "I'm ready to make a kneeling confession this Sunday so Annabelle and I can be together again. If you preachers and the members put me on the usual six-week probationary *bann*, I'll do whatever's asked of me."

"Phineas wants us to start fresh at Promise Lodge," Annabelle put in eagerly, "and I do, too! We've talked things out, like you suggested, and we've settled our differences."

"I've fetched the first load of my tools and equipment from Ohio, too, so I can operate my remodeling business in this area now," Phineas put in.

"Glad to hear it!" Bishop Monroe said as he shook Phineas's hand, and then Annabelle's. "We'll make it happen this Sunday, and I have no doubt your new friends here will want nothing but the best for both of you. It promises to be an . . . *unusual* church service, however, so if things get a little out of hand, hang on and keep the faith."

Phineas frowned. "Do you expect King to raise such a ruckus that he won't allow—"

"Keep the faith—and welcome back to it, Phineas," Bishop Monroe repeated firmly. "That's all I can say."

Annabelle blinked. What did bishop mean by *a little out of hand*? She'd grown suspicious of the way Clayton King had skulked about lately, as though he planned a big set down when he preached on Sunday. She had full faith in God, however—and as far as she was concerned, Monroe Burkholder was next in line behind Jesus and Phineas when it came to ranking the men she believed in.

"And there they are," the bishop said, gesturing toward the gate. "Lavern and Lowell worked hard helping me train this team, so I told them they could ride along for this final road trial. Shall we go?"

As the wagon rolled forward behind the Clydesdales, Annabelle's heart thumped like a happy drum. When they reached the top of the pasture, Lavern Peterscheim and Lowell Kurtz opened the white slatted gate. Their eager faces glowed with excitement and true devotion to the horses—and the bishop—they'd been working with for several months.

"Lookin' real *gut*!" Lavern called out as the team and wagon passed through the opening. "Nice to see we have honored guests coming along, too."

"It's a big day," Lowell said as he closed the gate behind them. "I've been looking forward to this ride forever!"

When the team stopped, the boys scrambled up over

the wagon's sides. Bishop Monroe smiled over his shoulder at them. "Here we go, boys—slow and steady now."

With a jingle of harness bells, the four Clydesdales eased forward. Yipping once, Daisy raced over from Preacher Marlin's barrel factory to lope alongside the wagon, as though she was their special escort. When Harley and Minerva waved from their front yard, Annabelle returned their greeting—and then saw that Christine was waving from her porch, as well.

Was it Annabelle's imagination, or was the sun shining brighter, making the orange, red, and gold leaves glisten on the trees? Could there be anything more glorious than riding in this wagon with the bishop, spotting all the neighbors who came outside as the thunder of hooves and the ringing of bells alerted them to the momentous occasion?

Lester Lehman jogged out into his yard for a closer look, grinning like a young boy, and down the hill from him, Preacher Marlin and Frances stood waving with awestruck expressions on their faces. Preacher Amos and Mattie came out of their house, too. When Annabelle saw the Kuhn sisters step out of their cheese factory—and then Irene and Phoebe emerge from the little white bakery building—her heart was so filled with joy she could barely breathe. Farther along they passed Roman Schwartz with little David on his shoulders, alongside Mary Kate and Gloria—and the younger Peterscheim kids were calling out to them as they waved wildly, as well. Even Deborah and Noah Schwartz, with their new baby, had come to witness the excitement.

When they passed under the white metal Promise Lodge sign at the entry to the property, Bishop Monroe slowed the horses to check for traffic. "All right, boys, carry on!" he called to his horses. "Gee!"

When they made a right turn onto the pavement, the rhythmic clatter of the Clydesdales' hooves got louder and a bit faster. Annabelle held the strings of her *kapp* to keep it from blowing off, gazing ahead to the Helmuths' nursery at the intersection of the state highway. Several cars filled the parking lot in front of the greenhouse buildings, and when she spotted redheaded Sam and Simon helping customers load colorful mums into their vehicles, she returned their smiles. Their wives, Barbara and Bernice, turned from picking pumpkins in the garden behind their double house to wave, as well.

Annabelle grinned blissfully as the bishop urged the horses into a fast trot on the highway. Could there be any place more wonderful, more welcoming than Promise Lodge? The thought of building a home here and starting fresh with Phineas filled her with such happiness that tears trickled down her cheeks.

When she felt Phineas gazing at her from the other side of Bishop Monroe, Annabelle leaned forward to look at him. His pale green eyes glowed with hope as he blew her a kiss.

Between them, the bishop let out a long, contented sigh as he held the lines easily in his big, capable hands. "Life doesn't get any better than this, friends," he murmured.

Chapter Twenty-Six

When Bishop Clayton stood up to preach the first sermon on Sunday morning, everyone in the meeting room tightened at the sight of his scowl. The opening hymns and prayers had sounded subdued, as though folks expected to be lectured and disciplined like wayward children at the hands of a harsh father.

From her place beside Laura in the center of the women's side, Gloria saw the man they knew as Cornelius, the suave impostor, more clearly through a lens wiped clean by the truth. She didn't know what to expect as the service progressed, but she was determined not to let her friends fall for any new lies he might use to ensnare them. Sensing that important matters might come to a head, the Kuhn sisters and the three Wickeys were attending this service instead of their Mennonite church in Cloverdale.

Bishop Monroe and the three preachers appeared wary as they sat on the preachers' bench, waiting. Did they have a plan? How did they figure to handle Cornelius, especially if he refused to cooperate with them?

Help us discern Your will, Lord, Gloria prayed. *And stand with our leaders as they reveal Cornelius for the thief he is.*

"When I came here about a month ago, sent from the

Council of Bishops—and God," Cornelius began in an ominous tone, "I had high hopes for Promise Lodge and the ability of its leaders to reform, to lead you folks back toward the light of God's salvation. But instead of listening to my wisdom, these four men have *challenged* me at every turn, as contrary as Missouri mules and refusing to return to Old Order standards. So I stand before you a *sorely* disappointed man."

Cornelius's scowl deepened as he raked the congregation with his gaze. "Unless we make drastic changes—right here, right now—your souls will be forever damned," he continued, dramatically pointing downward. "I'm determined, however, that such a catastrophe won't happen during *my* watch, because—as we touched upon earlier—I *am* the newly appointed bishop of this district. And I'm taking the necessary action *now*."

The room suddenly felt airless. Folks stared in confusion between the man standing before them and their four leaders on the preachers' bench. Gloria swallowed hard. She and Laura exchanged a fearful glance, but it wasn't her place to rise up and speak out.

"When Jesus prepared His disciples for the ministry they were to begin after His death, He granted them the power to cast out demons," Cornelius reminded them with a flourish of his hand. "As His devout disciple, I must therefore assume the same responsibility, to rid Promise Lodge of a cancerous growth that threatens the life of this community.

"*You*, Phineas Beachey," he whispered, as though the words felt like poison on his tongue, "be gone from here! You plan to come before this congregation today begging for reinstatement into the Old Order, and I cannot allow that to happen! You've committed the one unforgivable sin, and unless I cast you out, your presence will continue to contaminate the community."

The room's silence rang like a siren. Phineas stood up slowly, his jaw clenched. "Begging your pardon," he began, barely controlling his temper, "but you have no power to—"

"It's too late to beg for pardon!" Cornelius blurted, pointing toward the doorway. "I've repeatedly beseeched Burkholder and the preachers to do the right thing by sending you away, but in the face of their weakness—their blindness to God's will and the Old Order—I must banish you this minute. Get thee behind us, Satan!"

"You can't do this!" Annabelle cried out as she sprang up from the pew bench a couple of rows in front of Gloria. "We're going to build a new home here! Bishop Monroe has assured us—"

"Silence, woman!" Cornelius commanded, glaring at her. "Had Burkholder kept you and the other women here in your rightful places—had you paid attention when I warned you of the dangers of associating with Phineas— we wouldn't be separating the wheat from the chaff and casting the chaff into the fire right now. *Sit*."

Aghast, Annabelle dropped back onto the pew bench. As she and Phineas looked to Bishop Monroe for guidance, Gloria caught his subtle motions. Behind Cornelius's back, Monroe was shaking his head at Phineas. Just as Cornelius turned, Monroe pointed toward the door—and then quickly gripped the bench and put a blank expression on his face.

"Enough of your signals, Burkholder!" Cornelius spat. His face grew ruddier as the pitch of his voice rose. "Matter of fact, *you* might as well leave the room, too, because I'll be calling for a congregational vote concerning your shunning before this service concludes!"

As folks sucked in their collective breath, Cornelius pivoted to face them. "Might I remind you of how far gone, how worldly, your deposed bishop has become—and how blindly you've followed him? Every single one of you rushed outside on Friday to watch as he paraded his exorbitant horses in their finery down the road—and you waved and cheered him on! Did it not occur to you that Burkholder's extreme *pride* and *vanity* have become so deeply engrained that he's practically *English*?"

Bishop Monroe rose slowly from the preachers' bench. Gloria sensed he was putting on a calm façade, but his glances toward the doorway betrayed his anxiety. Across the room, Cyrus and Jonathan were looking at one another as though they couldn't believe what they were witnessing.

"And who was riding high along with him, shameless and gleefully unaware of their own guilt by association?" Cornelius demanded without even pausing for breath. "The Beacheys! You saw them for yourselves!"

Annabelle's whimper made Gloria feel so sorry for the poor woman that she nearly began to cry. Never had she witnessed such an upsetting tirade, as though their self-proclaimed bishop wasn't going to stop until he'd chastised every last member of the congregation.

"Out, all three of you!" Cornelius commanded. "Pack up and leave, Phineas, and don't come back! We'll see if your sadly deluded wife and Burkholder have backbone enough to accept the disciplinary action we'll be voting on at the close of the service. Meanwhile, you Mennonites need to leave, too," he added as he glared at them. "Your permissive, progressive attitudes are the root of this evil, after all."

Gloria gripped the pew bench with both hands. Cornelius had enjoyed countless meals in the lodge dining room, apparently unconcerned about Irene and the Kuhns' beliefs, yet he was banishing them with an imperious wave of his hand. Beulah wasted no time getting up, steering Ruby ahead of her with a disgusted frown. Rosetta appeared more defiant, perhaps ready to argue with Cornelius, but when Truman and his *mamm* rose to go, she reluctantly left the room with them.

Without a word, Bishop Monroe started for the aisle between the men's and women's sides of the meeting room. His head was bent low, as though he were a sheep being led to the slaughter. He paused to allow Phineas out of his row to precede him.

Annabelle, too, made her way to the aisle, her fist pressed to her mouth and her face wet with tears. Her heart-shaped *kapp* quivered with her suppressed sobs.

A pang of deep fear shot through Gloria's soul. Cyrus and Jonathan were gaping at her, looking ready to jump up and protest—yet worried that their outburst would make the situation worse. Outside, Daisy's distant barking seemed to express the same note of desperate concern.

"If you're sending Bishop Monroe away, *I'm* certainly not sticking around," Preacher Amos announced as he stood up and started walking.

"Same here," Preacher Eli said sourly. "This is no way to conduct a worship service—and if you were any sort of bishop, you'd know that, King."

"Count me out, too," Preacher Marlin muttered as he followed the others. "If God's calling the likes of *you* to lead this community, I want no part of it."

Gloria's body vibrated with the need to stand up and shout at the impostor before them. "Laura, this is *wrong*," she whispered frantically. "If all of our real preachers are leaving, *somebody* has to stop Cornelius before he—"

As Bishop Monroe passed by the end of her pew bench, he caught Gloria's eye. He was shaking his head, pressing his hand downward, telling her to keep her seat and keep silent. She stared at him, dumbfounded by the way he was abandoning his friends—the faithful members of his congregation who were depending on him and the three somber men behind him to restore order to a morning that had gone desperately awry.

Didn't it mean *anything* to Bishop Monroe that Gloria had shown him those incriminating papers from Riehl's closet? Had her trip to Willow Ridge—the evidence she and her friends had gathered against Cornelius—been for nothing? She couldn't bear to look at the despicable man who was standing before them with his arms crossed, chuckling triumphantly.

"This is a sight for sore eyes," Cornelius said. "We're getting rid of the chaff faster than I'd anticipated—which is clearly the Lord's way of saying that I'm doing exactly as He wants me to do. We must totally annihilate the disease in this community if we wish to be healed and emptied, ready to receive the Lord's new direction for our lives. But there's one more wayward soul to ferret out before we proceed."

The congregation shrank in upon itself as Bishop Monroe, the Beacheys, and the three preachers disappeared through the doorway. Folks gazed fearfully at one another, too afraid to ask the question on everyone's mind. *Is it I?*

"Last Sunday when I was attending church in Coldstream," Cornelius said, eyeing the people around him suspiciously, "*someone* entered my room, obviously without my permission. And that *someone* also rifled through the contents of my closet."

Gloria's throat got so tight she couldn't swallow. The blood drained from her head and she looked down at her lap, praying she wouldn't pass out—praying Cornelius wouldn't notice how guilty she appeared. Laura clasped Gloria's hand, but she released it quickly before Riehl could see her gesture of support.

"Every last soul in this congregation knows it's wrong to enter someone's private space. That's *trespassing* in its most odious form," Cornelius continued relentlessly. "I'm asking the intruder to rise and confess his—or her—sin. If this person doesn't respond voluntarily, I'll be coming to stand before every last one of you to question you. I'll be able to spot the guilt on your face immediately, *won't* I?"

Gloria couldn't breathe. The direction of his voice told her that Cornelius was looking at the women's side— possibly staring straight at her. The room began to spin, and she was vaguely aware of the rustling of women's dresses and aprons as they shifted nervously on the wooden benches. Did this mean Cornelius was starting on the front row, with the older women, and working his way back—to *her*? Did he intend to make her sweat until then, so she'd be a nervous wreck by the time he called her name?

"Bishop Clayton, as a fine upstanding man of God, you surely have nothing to hide," one of the men called out. "So what was in your closet that you didn't want anyone else to see?"

Gloria's heartbeat went wild. Cyrus had dared to speak up—to divert Cornelius's attention away from *her*—and his impertinent question brought the congregation out of its stunned stupor. Folks began whispering, incensed by the way this interrogation—this witch hunt—was being conducted.

"You're way out of line, King," Harley Kurtz muttered.

"*Jah*, this isn't the time or the place for these goings-on. Not during a church service!" Gloria's *mamm* chimed in.

"Silence!" Cornelius thundered, raising his clenched

fist. "As your new bishop, I've come to shine light on Promise Lodge—to chase away the black clouds of unforgiven sin that stand between you and our God."

A tense stillness again filled the meeting room. Gloria had detected a note of rising anxiety in Riehl's voice, and she wondered if other folks were becoming as concerned about his mental state—and their safety—as she was. When had anyone ever witnessed an Amish man shouting during church, with his fist raised?

"Well, Cornelius, it's *gut* to hear you speaking on a topic you're very familiar with," a man behind the congregation said calmly. "Shall we tell these folks about the black clouds of unforgiven sin in *your* life?"

At the sound of Bishop Tom Hostetler's words, relief rushed through Gloria's soul. She grabbed Laura's hand and turned, as everyone else was doing, to get a look at the man who was starting down the aisle. In his black suit and white shirt, Bishop Tom looked like a tried-and-true Amish bishop, but it was the serenity radiating from his weathered, bearded face that brought a sense of God's presence into the room with him. A younger man was walking alongside him, watching Cornelius intently as he, too, conveyed the reverence befitting a Plain man of God.

As Bishop Monroe and the others who'd left came to stand at the back of the room, Gloria turned toward the front again. Cornelius's face had turned the color of paste. As he raked his fingers through his dark hair, he scowled.

"What are you doing here?" he demanded, taking a step backward. "How did you know I was at Promise Lodge?"

"What are *you* doing here?" the man beside Bishop Tom countered calmly. "It appears you've changed your name and promoted yourself to being a bishop. But you're up to your same old tricks, Cornelius, and we've come to shine light on them."

"*Jah*, you can run from your past lies and deception, but you can't hide from God," Bishop Tom said as he reached the front. He turned to face the curious crowd. "*Gut* morning, folks. I'm Bishop Tom Hostetler from Willow Ridge and I've brought along Preacher Ben Hooley to assist with this difficult situation you're facing. Let's ask God for His guidance in a moment of prayer."

As Gloria and everyone around her bowed their heads, Preacher Ben took a seat on the bench and insisted that a very defensive Cornelius sit beside him.

"Lord, we ask for Your wisdom and Your discernment as we address the wayward tendencies that dwell in our human hearts," the bishop said in a hushed voice. "Help us to understand what this morning's confrontation is truly about. And help us to forgive Cornelius in the same way You forgive us, so we might move forward on the path to Your everlasting salvation. Amen."

When Gloria opened her eyes, she felt a worshipful serenity returning to the room even though folks were wide-eyed, wondering what Bishop Tom would say next. Cornelius had recovered from his initial shock and appeared annoyed enough to walk out. Would he have his horse and buggy hitched up before the men from Willow Ridge had finished talking about him? Or would he stay to defy them and defend himself?

"Where shall I begin?" Bishop Tom said with a shake of his head. "The man you've known as Clayton King, supposedly from a Council of Bishops in Lancaster County, has been leading you astray, folks. First of all, there's no such thing as a Council of Bishops," he clarified matter-of-factly. "And this man's real name is Cornelius Riehl. He was our church's deacon—until he skipped town after gambling away nearly all of our money."

All around Gloria, mouths dropped open. Folks gaped at one another in disbelief.

"When Preacher Ben and I got word that our deacon had been visiting a casino, we called him on it—asked him to confess in church," the slender bishop continued. "But Cornelius pleaded for our forgiveness and vowed he'd never set foot in a casino again, so Ben and I gave him a second chance. Didn't make him face the humiliation of admitting his gambling habit to his friends."

"And that was the wrong thing to do," Preacher Ben put in ruefully. "As you know, Cornelius can be very persuasive—and we were too trusting. Next thing we knew, he was gambling online with a laptop computer after secretly depositing our money in a bank account."

"Hundreds of thousands of dollars we lost," Bishop Tom continued somberly. "It was the money our members had been entrusting to the church's aid fund for *generations*, and by the time we caught him, it was almost gone."

Several folks glared at Cornelius, and Roman Schwartz stood up. "How much have you stolen from *us*?" he demanded. "That's why you wanted us all to pledge a tithe, ain't so? You had no intention of sending it to the council—because there *is* no council!"

"It's this stranger's word against mine, isn't it?" Cornelius blurted, pointing at Bishop Tom. "Who're you going to believe?"

"For starters, we're going to believe what the bank in Forest Grove told us," Bishop Monroe put in from the back of the room. "When a teller informed me that you'd tried to access our money, we preachers knew we'd better keep an eye on you. All of our funds are intact, by the way," he added to reassure everyone.

"Around that same time, I got word from our friends in Lancaster County, where Phineas and I used to live," Annabelle chimed in smugly. "Nobody there had ever heard of a Bishop Clayton King, so a few of us have known for a while that your story had holes in it! We just didn't know who you really were!"

"And we kept this information to ourselves so you wouldn't run out on us before we could hold you accountable," Bishop Monroe added quickly. "You can quit playing games with us now, Cornelius."

"It was *you* who was nosing around in my closet! Trespasser!" Cornelius whispered angrily. "Is that any way for a bishop to behave?"

Gloria swallowed hard. Folks around her were growing more appalled with each bit of information they heard, and her stomach knotted with the realization that her snooping would soon be revealed. Part of her yearned to stand up and declare that *yes*, she'd found the incriminating evidence that had led to contacting Bishop Tom—but she was afraid that Cornelius might somehow, someday take revenge.

"No, I was never in your room," Bishop Monroe replied. "Rather than naming names, let's just say that the person in question confessed this trespassing to me—and told me about the laptop and the English suit in your closet. The papers this person found suggested that folks in Willow Ridge might know about you."

Cornelius appeared ready to spit nails. "*Someone* invaded my privacy and betrayed my trust—"

"Hold on just a minute!" Lester blurted, springing to his feet. "All this time you've been staying at my place rent free, eating meals the ladies have brought in and letting them do your laundry—counseling me in my grief—but it was all a *lie*!" he continued in a rush. "You said you were saving our souls even as you intended to steal us blind—and I was fool enough to fall for it."

"Not just you, Lester," Mattie put in from the front row. "We didn't want to believe what this man said about our being too progressive—or too independent and opinionated, *Cornelius*," she added bitterly, "but we all know other bishops who would say the same things. You were weaving a web of deception with just enough truth in it to blind us to your lies. Now *that's* a betrayal of trust!"

Cornelius stood up, scowling. "I don't have to listen to this—"

"But wait—before you run off again," Preacher Ben said as he, too, rose from the preachers' bench. "We don't have to leave this situation unresolved. Your soul doesn't have to remain in the same tarnished state it was in when you left Willow Ridge with your debts unpaid."

"It's like you were saying when Ben and I walked in," Bishop Tom continued earnestly as he faced Cornelius. "A huge black cloud of unforgiven sin still hangs between you and God—and it's not all about money. These *gut* Amish Christians would be willing to hear your confession and help you wipe your slate clean, Cornelius. You could apologize right here, right now, and start the process of reconciliation—with them, and with God."

"God's grace and love are greater than our sin," Preacher Ben put in eloquently. "You don't have to keep running. You can start fresh right this minute, if you say the word."

Cornelius's face morphed into a mask of such vile hatred that everyone gasped. "Claptrap," he spat. "That's my word for it—*claptrap*. Don't hold your breath until I repent—and don't try to stand in my way while I leave."

Chapter Twenty-Seven

As Cornelius strode out of the meeting room, the congregation sat in stunned silence. Even Bishop Tom and Preacher Ben appeared taken aback by the vehemence of his words and the blackness of his attitude.

After a few moments, Bishop Monroe walked up beside Tom and Ben, placing his hands on their shoulders. "You men gave him every chance—and *jah*, we would've listened to his confession and given him our best effort at a fresh start, because that's what we do here at Promise Lodge," he said with a sigh. "Meanwhile, we're grateful that you came to help us with this unfortunate reckoning."

"*Jah*, you got here in the nick of time!" Lester remarked.

"Well, I was starting to sweat a little," Bishop Monroe admitted with a chuckle. "You see, folks, after Tom contacted me and told me the whole story behind Cornelius Riehl, we scripted a scenario for this morning's service so Cornelius would have no room to wiggle out of what he's been doing—"

"And part of the plan was to go along with whatever he said until Bishop Tom got here," Preacher Marlin added. "Don't think for a minute that any of us preachers—or Monroe—were leaving you at Riehl's mercy."

"We're sorry about what he said to you Kuhns and

Wickeys, too," Preacher Amos put in as he and the other preachers came forward to their bench. "I hope you know that your Mennonite faith has never been an issue to us."

"Puh! This mess is all *his* doing, not yours," Ruby replied. She took a seat on the end of a row when the women scooted over to make room. "We've always known God led us to Promise Lodge, just as we believed you folks would accept us."

"I smelled something foul about Clayton King the moment he walked in," Beulah said as she, too, sat down. "He's like a manure pie. The crust might look golden and perfect, but the filling's nasty. And there's no fixing it."

After Beulah's remark sank in, soft laughter filled the meeting room. Bishop Tom's eyes crinkled with humor even as he nodded sadly. "We don't like to admit that some souls are beyond our help," he said, "but *jah*, there are things that only God can make right. If Cornelius won't submit to Him, the Lord will hold him accountable in the end."

"We did our best to help him—twice," Preacher Ben added.

As Bishop Monroe gazed around the roomful of people, he nodded. "Again, we're grateful to you fellows for helping us restore order before Cornelius wreaked total havoc on what we've worked so hard to establish here. We'd be honored if you'd help us lead the rest of our church service."

Bishop Tom smiled. "I'd be pleased to worship with you folks."

"And stay for our common meal, so we can get better acquainted," Beulah piped up. "I can assure you our pies will be much tastier than the kind I mentioned earlier!"

Preacher Ben laughed out loud. "We've never been known to turn down food and fellowship. Count us in."

A collective sigh of contentment filled the room. Folks settled themselves on the pew benches with expectant expressions—until Lester raised his hand.

"Before we get back to our worship," he said earnestly, "I'd like to know who snuck into Clayton—er, Cornelius's—closet. We owe that person our thanks for finding the stuff that nailed him as a fraud."

Lester looked around the meeting room, hoping to spot the one responsible. "I—I'm appalled that he was living under my roof, looking me in the eye every single day," Gloria's uncle continued ruefully. "I had *no idea* that he was lying, intending to bilk us out of our money. He seemed so sincere."

"*Jah*, I want to know who discovered Clayton King's real identity, too," Gloria's mother chimed in. "A lot of us had our doubts about that man—especially after he asked us to donate a tithe to a council we'd never heard of. But nobody else had the presence of mind—or the gumption—to check into his personal belongings."

"Now we know why he sat in his chair watching us women like a hawk when we changed his sheets," Christine put in with a humorless laugh. "Wouldn't let us *near* his closet."

Once again Gloria's stomach got tight. Even though it was her uncle, her *mamm,* and the bishop's wife asking, she still had reservations about admitting that she'd sneaked into Cornelius's closet.

Bishop Monroe clasped his hands behind him. "I assured this person that their confession would remain confidential," he said softly. "So unless he or she wants to be recognized, we'll just have to let it remain a mystery."

"That's the way I see it, too," Bishop Tom remarked as he fought a smile.

Gloria felt very grateful, yet the longer folks looked

around in anticipatory silence, the more anxious she got. Should she admit what she'd done? How would she explain her actions, if anyone asked what had led her to the closet in her uncle's upstairs guest room?

When she glanced across the room, however, Cyrus was flashing her a thumbs-up, his dark eyes alight with love. Beside him, Jonathan motioned for her to rise and be recognized. Laura elbowed her lightly, her blue eyes wide with encouragement.

And suddenly, as though lifted by unseen arms, Gloria stood up. "It—it was me," she admitted. "I've always been a busybody, you know."

A few folks chuckled good-naturedly—and then everyone beamed at her, applauding with such appreciative expressions on their faces that Gloria almost couldn't stand to look at them. After all, wasn't she the boy-crazy girl who'd tried to win Roman Schwartz away from her sister with overbaked brownies? And hadn't she dumped a fruit pie on Allen Troyer's plans for a tiny house—and then tattled on him and Phoebe when she'd caught them kissing? And hadn't she tossed her shawl on the stairway in a snit, and then Mamm had fallen on it and been laid up for weeks?

Everyone in the room had shaken their heads over the many foolish things she'd done . . . so the love and admiration on their faces left her speechless.

"Gloria!" Uncle Lester crowed. "It's hardly a crime for my own niece to come into my house. You and your *mamm* have been cleaning every nook and cranny of it since I moved here, after all. What possessed you to look in King's closet?"

Mamm appeared astonished. "Is that where you went last Sunday on your walk, sweetie? We'd been talking about your *dat*, as I recall, and we were all a little teary-eyed."

Gloria let out the breath she'd been holding. Bless them, her family was making this explanation easier than she'd feared it would be. "I did," she admitted. "Do you recall how Uncle Lester told us that Clayton King reminded him of Dat? And how Bishop Clayton was saying things to us that Dat would've said, about being too progressive and such?"

"*Jah*, and what was I thinking?" Uncle Lester muttered as he gazed up at the ceiling. "Floyd, I was *so* wrong to compare that con artist to you. I hope you can forgive me, brother."

Gloria blinked. Her uncle had just spoken to Dat as though he were here—and in front of other people, too. Yet the folks around Uncle Lester were smiling and nodding as though he'd done the most natural thing in the world.

"Well, when I found myself headed to your house last Sunday, Uncle Lester," she continued softly, "I could feel Dat guiding me. It was so *real*—and even though I knew it was wrong to rifle through that closet, and I knew Dat would *never* have condoned my snooping—I felt I had to do it."

Gloria inhaled deeply, grateful for a chance to get this matter off her chest. "After I found that computer, and a man's English suit, and a wooden crate full of papers about some man named Cornelius who was a clock maker in Willow Ridge," she went on, "I knew they were the key to who Clayton King really was."

"Then she brought those papers to me," Bishop Monroe explained further. "I didn't want to arouse Cornelius's suspicions by going to Willow Ridge—and I didn't feel *gut* about leaving Promise Lodge while he was here, either— so the Helmuth brothers drove Gloria and Laura to Willow Ridge to confirm our suspicions with the bishop there."

"And here we are," Bishop Tom put in with a nod

toward Preacher Ben. "No doubt in my mind that it was the hand of God guiding us all—along with a nudge from your *dat*, Gloria," he added with a smile. "We must believe in things seen and unseen, and be grateful for God's bringing us the light of the world in Jesus Christ—a light that the darkness will never overcome."

Several folks nodded and murmured "amen" as they faced forward to resume the church service. Rosetta stood up, however, dabbing at her eyes. "We should also be grateful for the light our young people bring to Promise Lodge," she said with a special smile for Gloria. "I don't even want to *think* about all the unpleasant things that would've happened had Cornelius Riehl actually taken over. Everything my sisters and Amos and I worked so hard for would've been wiped out within days," she added with a hitch in her voice. "*Denki* from the bottom of my heart, Gloria. And *denki* to you, as well, Jonathan, Cyrus, and Laura."

Gloria was so overcome by the love in the room that she had to sit down. Who could've foreseen such a welling up of gratitude and appreciation?

Laura hugged her. "We did good," she whispered.

Gloria blinked back the tears that were filling her eyes. "*Jah*, I guess we did."

Outside, Queenie's barking and the rapid clatter of hoofbeats announced Cornelius Riehl's departure. Folks sat quietly until the noise died away.

"Close call," Preacher Amos remarked from the bench up front.

"*Jah*, but we came through it," Preacher Marlin put in. "Thanks be to God."

Bishop Monroe stepped forward to resume the worship service. "I feel compelled to preach about the many ways and times through the centuries when God has led His people away from ruin, toward the righteous life He would have us live," he said as he clasped his hands before him. "First, however, I suggest we place an ad in *The Budget*— some sort of warning about Cornelius Riehl, so he can't take advantage of other Amish districts with his smooth talking and deceitful ways. Will you help me compose something after the meal today, Bishop Tom?"

"I'd be happy to," the bishop from Willow Ridge replied. "I see it as our Christian responsibility to share what we know about Cornelius with friends of the faith."

Gloria nodded, noting that the folks around her appeared pleased with Bishop Monroe's idea. As he led them in prayer and began to preach in his resonant, comforting voice, she felt enveloped by a deep sense of peace and gratitude.

Order had been restored. God had truly rescued Promise Lodge from a ruthless impostor.

And I thank You, Lord, for allowing me to play a part in Your plan.

Chapter Twenty-Eight

As the church service drew to a close with Bishop Tom's benediction, everyone sighed gratefully. Even though it was well past noon, no one was in a hurry to leave the meeting room for dinner because as Bishop Monroe rose to address them, they knew what came next.

Annabelle was on pins and needles. The moment that would determine her future at Promise Lodge had arrived.

"As our Mennonite friends and our unbaptized children leave the room, please, let's call our members' meeting to order," Bishop Monroe said. "Phineas Beachey has lived amongst us for more than a month, and he has expressed his sincere desire to reunite with the Old Order, and with his wife. As Clayton King reminded us, many Amish settlements consider Phineas's abandonment of our faith the one unforgivable sin, and today we must decide where we as a community stand on that important issue."

Bishop Monroe gazed around the room, where folks were nodding in accord. Annabelle prayed that the goodwill generated by Cornelius's departure would hold sway—because what would she and Phineas do if these folks shut them out?

"We must hear Phineas's confession, and then vote on whether to readmit him," Bishop Monroe reminded them.

"If we accept him back into the Old Order, we're to decide whether he'll undergo the usual shunning for six weeks, or another form of penitence we deem more appropriate. Phineas, if you'll come forward, we'll listen to what you have to say."

Annabelle clasped her hands tightly in her lap. When Phineas glanced at her before he knelt in front of the bishop, she hoped her smile appeared encouraging and supportive. Her husband had changed since he'd returned. Their relationship felt much stronger than when he'd abandoned her in Pennsylvania, and she believed that her future with this kinder, gentler—*happier*—man would be blessed if they could settle at Promise Lodge.

Please let it be so, Lord. Help these folks to open their hearts and decide in favor of Phineas's reinstatement.

She was so focused on her prayers that she didn't really hear her husband's confession. She was barely aware when Bishop Monroe asked Phineas to step outside while the congregation voted.

"Folks, our *jahs* and *nos* will be cast not only for Phineas's request, but to determine where Promise Lodge stands on the issue of reinstatement," the bishop reminded them. "This is an important decision, requiring a unanimous vote. If anyone has questions or reservations, now's the time to speak up."

The meeting room was silent.

Annabelle swallowed hard. The voting began with the front row of the men's side, going from oldest to youngest.

"Jah . . . jah . . ."

The vote proceeded quickly to the back row of men and then took up with the front row of the women's side.

"Jah . . . jah . . ."

Annabelle's heart was beating so hard she could barely speak. *"Jah,"* she put in, grateful when Rosetta, Christine, and Mattie squeezed her shoulders and smiled brightly at her. Moments later she heard Gloria's *jah*, and Mary Kate's and Laura's—and then an expectant hush.

"Well done, friends," Bishop Monroe said. "I'd hoped we would decide in favor of Phineas's reinstatement, because it signifies our belief that *every* sin is forgivable. It rids us of the notion that a soul who calls on the Lord in humility and sincerity would be refused His mercy—or ours—and be forever condemned to remain an outsider."

"I like the way you folks do things," Bishop Tom said from the preachers' bench. "Makes me think it might be time for our congregation to reconsider some of the old beliefs that put a limit on love. Because in the end, this life is *nothing* without our love for God and for one another."

Bishop Monroe nodded as he smiled at Annabelle. "Fetch Phineas and let us share our *gut* news," he said. "Then we'll consider whether to impose the usual six-week *bann* or—"

"While we're doing things a new way, I propose we readmit Phineas without the lengthy separation a shunning calls for," Preacher Amos put in. "He's been forthright with all of us preachers about his intentions. I feel his confession today and his behavior this past month speak to his change of heart."

"To me, the real testimony to Phineas's transformation is the radiant smile Annabelle's worn these past several days," Frances said boldly. "Her happiness tells me that she and her husband have reconciled and she's fallen back in love with him. That was *not* the case when Phineas first showed up on Marlin's and my wedding day."

"*Jah*, we women were all worried that Annabelle would have to go back to Phineas against her will," Mattie pointed out. "And that's not the case anymore."

"I say we plan for their happiness starting this very

minute!" Rosetta blurted out. "Why not congratulate Phineas and Annabelle and welcome them to Promise Lodge as our newest neighbors? They're wonderful-*gut* people and we're pleased to have them here."

Annabelle could only gape at the folks who were nodding enthusiastically, especially when someone began a round of applause.

"Hear, hear!" one of the men put in above the happy ruckus.

"Don't keep him out there waiting, Annabelle!"

"*Jah*, you two are the guests of honor—along with Gloria and Tom and Ben!—for our dinner together," Lester proclaimed as he and the others continued clapping wildly. "It's a big day for Promise Lodge!"

Reeling with joy, her head spinning with her neighbors' enthusiasm, Annabelle rushed toward the lobby. She flung open the front door and found Phineas on the porch, gazing out toward Christine's dairy barn and Rainbow Lake in the distance.

"Do you hear all that noise in the meeting room?" she asked as she rushed toward him. "These folks are so glad we're here—so happy about the way we've turned ourselves around—that they've reinstated you without any shunning or discipline whatsoever! Why, back in Lancaster County—"

"Ah, but we're not in Pennsylvania anymore," Phineas reminded her. His pale green eyes danced with love light as he grabbed her waist and spun her around. "We're at Promise Lodge, Annabelle. We're *home*."

"And we're together again," Annabelle said before he kissed her excitedly. "That's all that matters to me, Phineas. The two of us, together again."

Chapter Twenty-Nine

Around six that evening, everyone drifted back to the lodge to continue celebrating. After enjoying Bishop Tom and Preacher Ben's company for the common meal and giving them an appreciative send-off, folks had decided to return after the men did the evening's livestock chores.

"After all," Rosetta pointed out, "we were on the verge of losing everything we held dear—including Bishop Monroe, and the right to run our businesses, and the Beacheys!"

"Not to mention a bunch of money!" Preacher Amos put in with a laugh. "I'm grateful to God that our Promise Lodge family has remained intact and in *gut* spirits. The day could've ended a lot differently."

Gloria's heart remained light as folks entered the dining room at dusk, because they thanked her repeatedly for ferreting out the truth about Clayton King. Phoebe and Allen brought the last section of their wedding cake from their freezer, other women carried loaves of fresh bread, and Uncle Lester showed up with several packages of freshly sliced deli meats.

"That housemate of mine was always bringing food back from his visits to the bulk stores hereabouts," he said as he laid the packages on the kitchen counter. "Now I'm wondering if he even paid for it. Do you suppose he had those store owners buffaloed into giving him groceries because he said he was their supplier from back east?"

Gloria's *mamm* shook her head as she got out a platter. "We'll never know," she replied. "He had a knack for convincing people to go along with whatever he wanted. But it's not as though you could return this meat, so we might as well enjoy it."

"We'll put these bars out, too," Beulah said as she took the lid from a freezer container. "Ruby and I made them a while back to use up some dibs and dabs of chocolate chips and coconut, along with overripe bananas."

"I got some sausage and cheddar biscuits out of the freezer, too," Irene said as she turned on an oven. "By the time everyone gets here, they'll be warmed through."

"*Jah*, it pays to have food stashed away just in case a party springs up!" Ruby put in cheerfully. "Mattie said she'd bring some jars of her pickled beets, and Christine's got quarts of the applesauce she put up earlier this fall. It'll be quite a feast, and nobody had to go to any trouble."

As their remaining neighbors arrived, Gloria helped set out their food contributions on one of the long dining room tables while other women got out dishes and utensils. It was wonderful to hear the noise level rising with everyone's excitement, because these families had arrived for church several hours earlier in a much more somber mood. When Bishop Monroe stepped into the dining room to gaze at the crowd, a lighthearted yet grateful smile lit his handsome face.

"Shall we give our silent thanks before the meal, friends?" he asked above the noise. "We have a lot to be thankful for, and I'm feeling particularly blessed because God has preserved us as a community—a family. We stand as an amazing testament to the power of His love and the love we share with each other."

"You got that right, Bishop," Harley put in. "Had Clayton King become our leader, I suspect a bunch of us would've been moving elsewhere before long."

When the bishop bowed his head, a reverent silence settled over the crowd. The roomful of people seemed to breathe and pray of one accord, and as Gloria sensed the serenity that filled the room she felt deeply happy in a whole new way.

These people love me, Lord, and they accept me for who I am—and isn't that as much a miracle as the way Cyrus and I have found each other? Where would any of us be without You?

"Amen," Bishop Monroe said—and as though they hadn't eaten in days, folks thronged toward the table covered with food and formed a line to fill their plates.

Cyrus broke away from the crowd to stand beside Gloria. "It's been a day I won't forget," he remarked, holding her gaze.

"It has, for many different reasons," she agreed. "Bishop Tom was a sight for sore eyes when he showed up unannounced—and then there was the expression on Cornelius's face a few moments later."

Cyrus smiled secretively as he grabbed her hand. "I'm hoping tomorrow will be another memorable day, Gloria. And that's all I'm going to say about that."

A tingle of anticipation made her squeeze his hand. "What do you mean, *memorable*?" she teased as she picked up a plate.

"Never mind," Cyrus replied breezily. "Don't ask me any more questions, because I won't give you any more clues."

"Teaser," she taunted under her breath.

"*Jah*, I am—because I like to watch the sparks come out to play in your big brown eyes," he murmured. "Now pay attention to what you're doing, sweetie. What'll folks think if they see that you're putting applesauce on your sandwich?"

What could she do but laugh at herself? With Cyrus standing so close, tormenting her with the hint of something *big* happening tomorrow, was it any wonder that she felt *ferhoodled*? When she looked for seats, she noticed that Laura was sitting with Jonathan and his redheaded cousins, Sam and Simon, cooing over Corene and Carol in their carriers as Barbara and Bernice beamed at them. It made her wonder if her friend might become the mother of twins someday, as well, because she already appeared to be part of the Helmuth family.

Cyrus placed his warm hand on the small of her back and steered her in a different direction. When Gloria spotted two places to sit near Uncle Lester, Phoebe and Allen, and the Beacheys, she knew her smile gave away the fact that she was head over heels in love—

And isn't that the best feeling in the world? Maybe it's okay to be boy crazy and do silly things when you know your fairy tale's headed toward a happy ending that is just the beginning.

"Gloria! Sit by me, sweetie," Uncle Lester said as he pulled out a chair. "You won't believe the conversation your old uncle's just had—and I want you to be the first to hear my news!"

Gloria's eyebrows rose as she sat down. Across the table, Annabelle and Phineas were smiling just as brightly as her uncle, while Allen and his new bride were holding a quick, whispered conversation. "What are you up to now, Uncle Lester?" she asked. "You look ready to *pop*."

"I'm gonna sell my place to the Beacheys!" he exclaimed. "And I've asked Allen if he'll build me a tiny home."

Gloria's eyes widened. Her uncle hadn't said a word about wanting to move out of his house. "*Really?* What brought this on?"

Uncle Lester's expression mellowed as he slipped an arm around Gloria's shoulders. "I intended to live in that place with Delores, you know, and it's never going to happen," he said softly. "Those empty rooms are a constant reminder of that—and I can't think of anybody nicer than Annabelle and Phineas, who need a place to start over—"

"He caught us *completely* by surprise with his suggestion!" Annabelle put in excitedly.

"And we'd be delighted to live there," Phineas added. "I don't even have to look at the house to know it's as well-built as every other place here. And with winter coming on, who wants to be starting construction—or waiting for spring to do that?"

"This is the most wonderful thing since—well, since Phineas came back!" Annabelle blurted as she smiled at her husband. "And as we were saying, Lester, you can use a room until you have another place of your own. It's the least we can do for you, for making us feel so welcome."

Allen eased away from his new wife, his face alight with a smile. "What if you lived in *my* tiny home, Lester? Now that Phoebe and I have a house—"

"Your place on Rainbow Lake? *Really?*" Lester cried out.

Phoebe laughed gently. "Why not? Try it out for a while to see if living small is really your cup of tea—"

"And if it is, we'll work out the finances later," Allen put in. "If it's not—no harm done. You can figure out where you'd rather live and move forward from there."

Noting how the dining room had grown quiet around

them, Gloria waved her hand to get everyone's attention. "We have more *gut* news to celebrate today!" she announced. "Phineas and Annabelle will be moving into Uncle Lester's place—"

"And I get to upgrade to lakefront property and Allen's tiny home!" Lester crowed. "I don't know who's happier—the Beacheys or me!"

"Congratulations!" Rosetta called out. "That makes us *all* happy, Lester."

As applause filled the dining room, Mattie and Christine went into the kitchen and came out quickly with a tall gift sack. They paused at the end of the table by the Beacheys until folks got quiet again. Everyone shifted, watching them with anticipation.

"Annabelle and Phineas, we have a little gift for you, and this seems like a *gut* time to present it," Mattie said as she placed the sack on the table.

"Because we're delighted that you're our newest neighbors," Christine added with a lilt in her voice.

After a moment's hesitation, Annabelle lowered the sack enough to peek into it—and then flushed happily. "Pleated *kapps* like the ones you gals wear here—and a new black hat for Phineas!"

"Welcome back to the Old Order, Phineas," Bishop Monroe said from across the room. "We thought a new winter-weight Stetson might come in handy."

Gloria thought Phineas might cry as he ran his finger reverently along the wide brim of the black hat. When he put it on, his face took on an inexplicable expression—a combination of serenity and joy and gratitude.

"*Denki*, friends," he said quietly. "It . . . it's a perfect fit for me now. Seems God's love and forgiveness—and yours—are just the right size."

"I second that emotion," Cyrus whispered as he took Gloria's hand under the table. "Where would we be without love and forgiveness?"

Folks nodded, savoring the meaning of the moment. Gloria couldn't look away from Cyrus's gaze, his dark eyes so full of feelings that he wouldn't have expressed a few weeks ago. Was this how it felt to get beyond the boy-crazy stage and think of Cyrus as a *man* . . . because she'd become a woman?

A girlish giggle across the table made them both glance at Annabelle as Mattie helped her adjust one of the new pleated *kapps* over her blond hair.

"Well, now!" Annabelle said. "I don't know how it looks, but it has more *substance* to it than a prayer covering made of organdy. These *kapps* are made to last!"

Phineas smiled gently as he gazed at her. "We can say that about a lot of things at Promise Lodge," he murmured. "You look beautiful, Annabelle."

Cyrus squeezed Gloria's hand again. "Phineas is stealing all my *gut* lines," he whispered. "You're the best, Gloria—*and* you're beautiful. I hope to prove I mean that every day from here on out."

Chapter Thirty

Early Monday morning, Gloria went downstairs filled with a sense of great anticipation. True to his word, Cyrus hadn't given her a clue about what was to happen—but she couldn't stop smiling. During the remainder of the party, he'd made his long-term intentions clear.

"Somebody's looking mighty happy," Ruby remarked as she arranged strips of bacon in a skillet.

"*Jah*, mark my words, a couple of young ladies we know will soon be making big announcements." Beulah looked up from the biscuits she was cutting. "And we're tickled pink, Gloria. Makes us curious about who'll manage the apartments after you and Cyrus get hitched—but it'll work out. Always does."

Gloria recalled that she'd once referred to the Kuhn sisters as *biddy hens* and had refused to live at the lodge with them. They'd become like a pair of favorite *maidel* aunts since then, however, and Gloria realized just how much she had changed over the past months.

"It'll work out," she agreed. "Cyrus knows I'm a total failure in the kitchen, yet he still wants to be with me—so we have to believe that anything's possible!"

Beulah chuckled patiently. "Ruby and I could help you learn to cook, if you'd like."

"You're probably more motivated than you were before," Ruby pointed out as she placed her skillet on the stove. "And you're so used to thinking of yourself as a failure, it's become a self-fulfilling prophecy—but we can *change* that. You *are* what you believe you are."

Gloria blinked. She'd never thought about it that way—but the Kuhn sisters wouldn't lie to her. "Maybe we could give it a shot. What could it hurt?"

When the mudroom door opened, Laura stepped inside. Her blue eyes twinkled in a face made pink by the chilly morning air. "Jonathan told me I'd want to be here for breakfast," she said as she hung up her coat. "Any idea what's going on?"

Beulah and Ruby shrugged, but Gloria suspected they knew more than they were saying.

"Annabelle and Phineas have gone over to eat with Lester, so they can discuss the details about buying his house," Ruby said.

"And of course, Irene's been baking pies with Phoebe for an hour already, so she won't be here, either." Beulah placed the biscuits on a baking pan and slipped them into the oven. "Seems to me we could let the young folks have the meal to themselves, don't you think, Ruby?"

"Fine idea! I hear the Skylark Café calling my name for breakfast in town, because I wanted to shop this morning, anyway," Ruby replied with a laugh. "Let's go, Beulah!"

"But—" Gloria looked at the stove and the oven, panic rising inside her. "You said you'd teach me to cook, not that you'd run out on me!"

"Experience is the best teacher," Beulah quipped as she and her sister put on their coats. "You'll do just fine, girls. Cyrus and Jonathan will be here any minute, so—"

"They put you up to this!" Gloria blurted. "What if I burn the bacon, or—"

"Just pay attention to the skillet," Ruby suggested. "Give those biscuits about ten more minutes. See you later!"

As the back door closed, Laura peered through the oven window. "We've got this, Gloria. Let's scramble some eggs in a bowl, and set out plates—but you *do* have to watch that skillet in the meantime."

"Ah. I got so rattled, I forgot that you've been cooking for years," Gloria murmured. "We're in *gut* hands."

When Cyrus and Jonathan arrived a few minutes later, Gloria was removing perfectly cooked bacon from the skillet and Laura was taking the biscuits from the oven. Rather than waiting at the table, the brothers came into the kitchen as though they felt right at home there.

"Smells really *gut* in here," Jonathan remarked. "I'll set out the butter and honey—"

"And how about if I take charge of these eggs?" Cyrus asked as he turned on the gas burner. "Looks like you ladies have them mixed with milk and ready to go."

Puzzled, Gloria watched Cyrus pour the mixture into the skillet she'd used for the bacon. "You know how to cook?"

He winked at her as he stirred the eggs with a spatula. "I can handle basics like eggs and roasts and baking potatoes—but Jonathan's the pastry chef. Makes a mean pan of cinnamon rolls."

"We were born into a family of all boys, and our older brothers were already working with Dat at the nursery," Jonathan explained as he returned to the kitchen. "When Cyrus was about eight, our *mamm* had twins, and then another set of them came along a couple years later. She gave us a choice of either minding the babies or manning the kitchen."

A smile eased over Laura's face as she put the biscuits

in a basket. "Isn't *that* interesting?" she teased. "I had no idea you two were such happy homemakers!"

Gloria laughed. "*Jah*, the girls who marry you fellows will be really lucky," she blurted. And then she had a second, less presumptuous thought. "Then again, maybe you'll get promoted at Sam and Simon's nursery. Maybe you'll be like most men and turn over all the kitchen work to your wives."

Cyrus shook salt and pepper over the eggs as they cooked, considering his response. "Do you think I'm like most men, Gloria?" he asked softly.

Had she hurt his feelings? Offended him? Gloria stood closer to him, impressed with the way his eggs were looking. "Well, no. Not at all," she admitted.

"Cyrus and I have talked a lot this week," Jonathan said, slipping his arm around Laura's shoulders. "We've decided that because each partner in a relationship contributes abilities that the other one doesn't, we shouldn't limit ourselves to the concept of *men's* work and *women's* work."

"For example," Cyrus continued, stirring shredded cheese into the eggs, "my brother and I work hard and we're putting money away, but we're not yet able to provide you girls with homes. When we went to declare our intentions—and our predicament—to your parents, figuring to get on their *gut* sides because we'd be living with them for a while—"

"We were gratified to receive their blessings right off," Jonathan put in. "And after Christine said she was providing Laura with a plot of land, and Bishop Monroe offered us a house as a wedding gift—"

"Preacher Marlin and Frances made the same offer for you, Gloria—whenever the time's right," Cyrus said as he took the skillet from the burner. His grin shone like the sun.

"They *like* us! And they want us to stay at Promise Lodge and make their daughters happy. So—when the time's right—maybe we guys can take on some of the cooking and household chores, *jah*? Seems like a small trade-off, considering that you can provide us with homes."

Gloria was stunned. "I—I had no idea—"

"I figured it might work that way, after Mamm gave Phoebe a plot of land," Laura admitted. "But I didn't want to hold property over your head as an obligation, Jonathan—and I did *not* want you to marry me because of my land!"

"I loved you long before I knew about that, sweet Laura."

Gloria sighed, in awe of the eloquent simplicity—the sincerity—of Jonathan's declaration. Cyrus might've been the bolder of the Helmuth brothers, but he wasn't ahead in everything. He'd come to love her by a different path, stumbling and falling over a five-hundred-dollar bet before picking himself up to move forward again. He'd made his share of dumb mistakes, just as she had.

"How about we eat our breakfast before it gets cold?" Cyrus suggested. "You ladies need to fortify yourselves before your next surprises arrive."

All during their meal, Gloria wondered what could possibly be more surprising than learning that Mamm and Marlin would give her a plot of land and a house when she was ready to marry. As founders of Promise Lodge, the Bender sisters and Amos had given such gifts to their children, but she hadn't expected that trend to continue with newer residents' kids.

"Don't the eggs suit you, sweetie?" Cyrus murmured beside her. "You've hardly eaten a bite of your breakfast, after I slaved over a hot stove cooking for you."

His teasing tone brought Gloria out of her thoughts—

and she saw that her friends had cleaned their plates. "You've given me a lot to think about," she admitted.

"*Gut*," he said. "I don't want you to ever assume you've got me all figured out."

"Hah—*gut* luck with that!" Jonathan teased from across the table. "I've known you for twenty years and I'm still at a loss."

Cyrus sat up straighter, as though rising to a dare his brother had thrown at him. "Actions speak louder than words, brother—and who challenged you to find a girlfriend in the first place?" he asked as he stood up. "Let me show you how this is done."

Why's he going toward the storage closet? Gloria wondered as Cyrus crossed the room. After he opened the double doors where the Kuhns stored dishes used for weddings and other large gatherings, he lifted a large, wrapped bundle from the floor. Where had *that* come from?

Cyrus's smile dazzled her as he approached the table with the bundle. It was large, shaped like a tube, so he stood it on end beside her. "For you, Gloria," he said softly. "If I'm lucky—if I ask the right question when you're ready to answer it—you'll share this with me someday."

Her heart pounded as she slipped a finger beneath the tape that held the wrapping paper in place. The gift was cushy and tightly rolled, and when an edge of deep red and green fabric was revealed—

"It's your quilt, Gloria!" Laura cried out. "Oh, I was hoping you'd get it!"

Tears suddenly filled her eyes and Gloria stood up to throw her arms around Cyrus. "I—I don't know what to—how to thank you," she murmured in a rush.

His arms tightened around her. "Will you marry me, after we court for a while?" he whispered. "By the time your other amaryllis blooms, maybe you'll be ready to commit to an answer—"

"*Yes*, Cyrus!" Gloria sang out. Her heart had known the answer ever since the full moon had illuminated her feelings, so she felt no hesitation whatsoever. "We'll be engaged, we'll figure out where to live, and we'll plan for happiness! Rosetta's got that right, you know."

"She does," Cyrus murmured before his lips moved over hers. "Her strategy's already working, too, because I've never been happier, Gloria. I—I love you so much!"

As she gazed into Cyrus's shining eyes, Gloria savored the words she'd longed to hear from just the right man. And they sounded every bit as sweet and romantic as she'd imagined. "I love you, too, Cyrus," she murmured.

"So, Jonathan," Cyrus teased, "now that I've shown you how it's done—ah. Guess they figured it out for themselves."

Gloria giggled. Laura had already opened the three-dimensional banner she'd chosen in Nora's shop, and she and Jonathan were too lost in a deep kiss to realize they were being watched.

"Let's look at this gorgeous quilt," she whispered, grasping the bundle in her arms. "We can spread it out on the table over there."

"*Jah*, I'd like to see what you chose," Cyrus remarked. He quickly pushed two tables together so the quilt wouldn't drag on the floor. "I trusted Nora not to steer me wrong, but I didn't get a chance to look at it when we were in her shop."

Gloria stopped unrolling the soft, bulky quilt. "You—you bought it sight unseen?" she whispered. "You must've spent a fortune on this piece."

"It's what you wanted," Cyrus replied with a shrug. "When I called Nora and asked her to send it, she assured me it was well made—said it would last a lifetime. That's a worthwhile investment in our future, the way I see it."

He smiled as she unrolled the rest of the quilt so the red, fuchsia, and orange flowers in the center were fully visible. "Wow, I've never seen a quilt like this," he said. "It reminds me of *you*, Gloria. Bold and bright, and unlike anyone else. I can't wait to see it on our bed, in our home."

On our bed, in our home. What a picture his words created in her mind!

As Gloria hugged Cyrus again, brilliant rays of the sunrise beamed through the window and bathed them in glorious light. It was God's blessing upon them, and she knew His light would shine on them and their life at Promise Lodge forever.

From the Promise Lodge Kitchen

The ladies of Promise Lodge are always whipping up good things to eat, and here are the recipes from most of the dishes they concocted in this story! These are down-home foods Amish women feed their families, along with some dishes that I've concocted in my own kitchen—because you know what? Amish cooking isn't elaborate. Plain cooks make an astounding number of suppers from whatever's in their pantry and their freezers. They also use convenience foods like Velveeta cheese, cake mixes, and canned soups to feed their large families for less money and investment of their time.

These recipes are also posted on my website,
www.CharlotteHubbard.com.
If you don't find a recipe you want,
please email me via my website to request it—
and to let me know how you liked it!

~Charlotte

Amish Pumpkin Crunch

Here's a wonderful fall dish that bakes up like a pumpkin pie on the bottom with a layer of streusel-like cake on the top—and your house smells fabulous while it's baking! Serve it warm as a dessert or even as a brunch dish, or serve it chilled.

    1 15-oz. can solid-pack pumpkin
    1 12-oz. can evaporated milk
    3 eggs
    1 cup sugar
    2 tsp. cinnamon
    1 tsp. ground ginger
    ¼ tsp. ground cloves
    ½ tsp. salt
    1 box yellow cake mix
    1 cup chopped pecans
    1 cup butter, melted

Preheat oven to 350° and spray a 9x13-inch baking pan. In a large bowl, combine the pumpkin, milk, eggs, sugar, and spices. Pour this mixture into the pan, then spread the dry cake mix evenly over the top of it. Sprinkle the pecans over the top of the cake mix, and drizzle the melted butter evenly over everything. Bake 55-60 minutes or until top is golden brown and the center is set. Serves 12. To serve warm, allow the crunch to set about 20 minutes. Refrigerate leftovers.

Annabelle's Homemade Barbeque Sauce

Here's a tangy sauce made from simple ingredients—and without the high-fructose corn syrup found in commercially bottled BBQ sauce. I especially like to use this sauce with pulled pork or chicken I've cooked in the slow cooker, or in place of taco sauce for nachos. It adds a whole new dimension of zing as a pizza sauce, as well!

    1 cup ketchup
    ¾ cup water
    ¼ cup cider vinegar
    1 T. maple syrup
    1 T. Worcestershire sauce
    1 tsp. each celery seed and salt
    1 T. each garlic powder and dried onion

Place all ingredients in a small saucepan and bring to a boil. Reduce heat and simmer for 30 minutes, or a little longer to make a thicker sauce. Stir occasionally. Makes about 2 cups. Store in the refrigerator—keeps for several days.

Date-Raisin Spice Bars

Nothing's easier than a bar recipe that you stir up in a pan and bake! This recipe is from my mother-in-law's collection, and I doubled the spices to make these moist, fruity bars a truly memorable treat!

    ½ cup shortening
    1 cup sugar
    1 cup water
    1 cup raisins

1 8-oz. pkg. chopped dates
½ tsp. salt
1 T. cinnamon
1 tsp. ground cloves
2 cups flour
¾ cup chopped walnuts
1 tsp. each vanilla and baking powder
½ tsp. baking soda

Preheat oven to 350°. Spray/grease a 10x15-inch pan. In a 2-quart saucepan on the stove, combine shortening, sugar, water, raisins, dates, and the spices. Simmer gently for 3 minutes and remove from heat. Stir in remaining ingredients until mixture is well blended. Spread batter in pan and bake about 15 minutes, or until center is set. While bars bake, make the frosting. Place bars on a rack to cool, and frost the bars while still hot. Cool completely before cutting.

Frosting

2½ - 3 cups powdered sugar
2 T. softened butter
¼ cup milk
Dash of salt
1 tsp. vanilla
1 tsp. of rum or almond flavoring

Posse Stew

Maybe this recipe was first created over a campfire out West? No matter what you call it, this stew goes together quickly from staples in your kitchen and provides a filling meal for all the folks around your table! Great with cornbread or biscuits!

1 lb. ground beef
1 large onion, diced
Salt, pepper, garlic powder to taste
1 15-oz. can diced tomatoes, undrained
1 15-oz. can chili beans in sauce, undrained
1 15-oz. can hominy, drained
1 15-oz. can corn, drained
1 T. cornstarch
¼ cup water

In a large skillet, cook the beef and onion until all the pink is gone. Drain and return meat mixture to the skillet. Add the vegetables and beans and heat through, then stir the cornstarch into the water and add this to the skillet to thicken the stew. Adjust seasonings and serve. About 4-6 servings.

Kitchen Hint: *For more kick, add a 4-oz. can of undrained jalapeños or a packet of dry fajita seasoning. You can also replace the cornstarch/water mix with a small can of tomato paste and add a dash of chili powder or more garlic powder.*

Brown Sugar–Cinnamon Bars

Love cinnamon? Here's another bar recipe that goes from a saucepan to the oven in minutes! Don't let their plain, unfrosted appearance fool you—these bars are moist and chewy and indescribably delicious!

2 cups flour
2 T. ground cinnamon
1 tsp. baking powder

¼ tsp. baking soda
2 cups brown sugar, packed
⅔ cup butter
2 eggs
2 tsp. vanilla
2 T. sugar
1 tsp. cinnamon
1 T. melted butter

Preheat oven to 350°. Line a 9-inch baking pan with foil so that a flap extends on 2 sides, and spray/grease the foil. Combine the flour, 2 T. cinnamon, baking powder, and soda in a small bowl and set aside. In a 2-quart saucepan on the stove, cook and stir the brown sugar and butter until butter is melted. Cool slightly. Stir in eggs and vanilla, then stir in the flour mixture. Spread the batter in the pan and bake 30-35 minutes, until a pick in the center comes out clean. (Bars will still seem a bit doughy, but don't overbake!) While bars are still warm, brush with the melted butter and sprinkle with the remaining cinnamon-sugar mixture. Cool completely. Lift out of the pan with the foil to cut. 24 small bars.

Kitchen Hint: Double this recipe to make in a 9x13-inch pan.

Read on for an excerpt from Charlotte Hubbard's
newest Amish romance,
coming soon!

The Maidels of Morning Star
Book 1

Morning Star
by
Charlotte Hubbard

Spring had painted the Missouri countryside with a palette of vibrant greens and gentle pastels only God Himself could create. The pastures were lush with new grass, and the dogwood and redbud trees added splashes of pink, cream, and fuchsia to the untamed landscape. Jo Fussner and her four *maidel* friends were on their usual afternoon walk on a visiting Sunday, soaking up the midday sunshine. An occasional car passed as they strolled alongside the county highway, but otherwise, Morning Star seemed to be nodding off for its Sunday nap.

As they reached the edge of town, Jo gazed at a dilapidated white stable that sat back from the road, surrounded by a few acres of land. The plank fence around it was also in a sorry state of disrepair. She couldn't recall the last time she'd seen horses in the pasture, or any sign of the English folks who owned it. The harsh winter hadn't done the stable any favors, and Jo thought the place looked sadder than usual as the April breeze riffled some of its loose shingles.

The wooden sign posted on the fence alongside the gate startled her. "Did you know this place was for sale?" Jo blurted. "I haven't seen this sign before."

"Me neither," Molly Helfing replied. She glanced at her rail-thin twin sister, Marietta, who was recovering from chemo treatments. "Last I knew, that Clementi fellow who owned this property died in the nursing home—"

"And his kids have been squabbling over the estate," Marietta put in. Despite the spring day's warmth, she pulled her black cloak more closely around her. "I still haven't figured out how the English can bear to put their parents in places like the Senior Center. It seems so cruel, separating older folks from their families."

"*Jah*, Mamm exasperates me, but I could never shut her away in a care facility," Jo agreed. An idea was spinning in her head—an adventurous, totally impractical idea—as she gazed at the long white stable with its peeling paint and missing boards. Her longtime friends would think she was *ferhoodled*, yet her imagination was running wild with possibilities.

"The kids must've decided to sell the place rather than keep it in the family," redheaded Regina Miller remarked. "I can't think it'll bring much, though, run-down as it is."

"Anybody who bought it would have to invest a lot of money to make it usable as a stable again. And replacing the slat fence would cost another small fortune," Lydianne Christner said with a shake of her head. "Folks around town have been hoping the family will just tear this eyesore down—"

"But wouldn't it make a great place for some shops?" Jo blurted out. "You Helfings could sell your homemade noodles, and Mamm and I would have more space to display our bakery stuff and our summer produce—and we could get other local folks to rent spaces, and—and it's on the main highway! Think of how much more business we'd attract here than we do at the roadside stands in our yards."

Her friends stared at her as though she'd sprouted a second head.

Molly's brow puckered. "How could we run a store on this side of town—"

"—while we were making our noodles in our shop at home?" Marietta finished doubtfully.

Regina appeared more positive, yet she shook her head. "Would Bishop Jeremiah allow that? He's always preaching about how we should keep our businesses to a manageable size. When some of our men have talked of expanding their shops, he's reminded them that bigger isn't better."

"Are you talking about *us* running such a place?" Lydianne asked with a frown. "How would we pay for the property, much less the repairs it needs?"

"And what makes you think a handful of *maidels* could manage a bunch of shops?" Marietta chimed in again.

Jo planted her fists on her hips, grinning despite her friends' very reasonable objections. "What makes you think we couldn't?" she challenged. "We manage quite well without husbands, ain't so? We've been supporting ourselves for years, so we certainly have the smarts to keep a joint business afloat—especially since Lydianne's a bookkeeper. I think it would be great fun to run a marketplace!"

"Puh! Your *mamm* would never go along with that!" Regina teased.

"*Jah,* I can already see Drusilla shaking a finger at you," Molly agreed as she shook her own finger. "And I can just hear her saying 'No *gut* will ever come of such an outrageous idea, Josephine Fussner! Who ever heard of unhitched women doing such a thing?'"

Jo laughed along with her friends at Molly's imitation of her mother. "You've got her pegged," she said, even as she gazed wistfully at the stable. The weathervane on the center cupola had lost its rooster, and enough boards were missing that she could see daylight on the structure's other side. Even so, she could imagine the building glowing with fresh paint. She could hear the voices of shoppers who'd be delighted to discover the products Plain folks from the Morning Star area would display in their tidy open booths.

"We've got our homes and our work—not to mention the *Gut* Lord and our church family to sustain us—and we get by just fine," she continued in a voice that tightened with unanticipated emotion. "But haven't you ever wanted to do something just for the *fun* of it? Something *new*? Whatever happened to sayings like 'where there's a will there's a way'—and Bible verses like 'with God, all things are possible,' and 'I can do all things through Christ, who strengthens me'?"

Her friends got quiet. The four of them stood beside her in a line along the fence, gazing at the forlorn stable and the pasture covered with clumps of green weeds, yellow dandelions, and the occasional pile of dried horse manure.

Regina finally broke the silence. "You're really serious about this."

After a few more moments of contemplation, Lydianne squeezed Jo's shoulder. "I can see how opening shops might be fun, but—"

"It sounds crazy and impossibly expensive," Jo admitted, "and it would take an incredible amount of carpentry work and elbow grease and commitment and organization, but I just thought—"

As her voice trailed off into a frustrated sigh, Jo gazed at the long barn with the three cupolas along the top of its roof. "Without a house on the property, I can't think many folks will want to buy this place. It would be such a shame to tear the stable down—"

"We know plenty of men who could fix it up," Regina said, "but why would they want to?"

"—and maybe it's just *me*," Jo continued softly, "but come springtime, when Mother Nature puts on her pretty fresh colors, I wish I could take on a whole new appearance, too—like the rebirth Bishop Jeremiah preached about on Easter Sunday. I long ago accepted that I'll never have a husband or kids, but some days I long for something different. Something *more*. You know?"

Her four closest friends *did* know. For one reason or another, each woman believed marriage wasn't an option for her. Jo didn't regret her unwed state, yet the way Marietta sighed when Molly hugged her angular shoulders, and Regina gazed into the distance, and Lydianne pressed her lips together told Jo that sometimes they, too, grew weary of their solitary state . . . and a future that held little opportunity for change.

Even though Plain *maidels* enjoyed a few more freedoms than their married friends, their faith placed limitations on them. They weren't allowed to train for careers or travel to faraway places or break out of the mold of conformity. Amish women who'd been baptized into the Old Order knew their place—and they were expected to stay there.

Jo turned to continue on their walk. "Well, it was an interesting thought, anyway."

* * *

For the next few days, however, Jo couldn't let go of the idea of a marketplace. She was so engrossed in her vision—even thinking up possible names for the new shopping area—that she planted rows of onion sets where Mamm had intended to put the hills for the zucchini and summer squash.

"Josephine Fussner, what's gotten into you?" her mother demanded in exasperation. "You might as well be living on another planet, for all the response I've gotten from you lately!"

After she endured a talking-to about the garden chart Mamm had drawn, Jo headed into town to do the week's shopping—and to pay a visit to Bishop Jeremiah Shetler. If the leader of their church district refused to go along with her idea about refurbishing the old stable, she would put it out of her mind and move on. It was a big stretch, thinking the property could ever be brought up to the glowing images she'd seen in her daydreams.

And yet, as they sat in wicker chairs on his front porch, Bishop Jeremiah listened patiently as Jo described her ideas for shops—and about how she and her four friends would manage the place. She hadn't exactly gotten full agreement from Lydianne, the Helfings, or Regina, but she felt the bishop would be quicker to approve if she presented an organized business plan, which she'd devised over the past few days.

"Wouldn't it be *something* if we transformed the Clementi stable into shops where local folks could sell what they make?" Jo began excitedly. "It would take a lot of work, but can't you imagine Amish stores along three of the walls, with an open central area where shoppers could gather at tables and enjoy homemade refreshments? With some fixing up and a fresh coat of paint—maybe some colorful shutters and flower boxes at the windows—it could become a big attraction for Morning Star, don't you think? If we rented out the shop stalls, we could make money for our church district."

The bishop sat forward, as though Jo's last sentence had snagged his attention. "*Jah*, I saw that the Clementi place was up for sale," he said, "and I can tell you've given your idea a lot of thought, Jo. Who do you suppose might want to rent space in this new marketplace?"

Jo blinked. Instead of waving off her dream as something only a silly, impractical *maidel* would come up with, Bishop Jeremiah was nodding as he listened to her. He was a patient, forward-thinking leader—younger than most bishops, with dark brown hair, expressive brows, and a matching beard. His deep cocoa eyes seemed to search the soul of whomever he was talking to.

Jeremiah's steady gaze made Jo answer carefully. "The Helfing twins could sell their homemade noodles. Mamm and I could expand our baking and produce business—and sell those refreshments I mentioned—"

"And what does your mother say about this?"

Jo laughed when she caught the twitch of the bishop's lips. "Well, Mamm doesn't know about it yet. I figured if you wouldn't go along with our idea, there was no reason to mention it to her.

"But think about it!" she continued brightly. "We have a lot of local folks who make toys and furniture and such! Maybe Martha Maude and Anne Hartzler would want to sell their quilts, and maybe the Flauds would put some of their furniture in a booth—and we could advertise for more Plain crafters from this area! We could have the marketplace open only on Saturdays, so nobody has to mind a store all during the week. That would really cut into a family's daily life."

Bishop Jeremiah stroked his closely trimmed beard. "What about the land? There's about five acres with the stable, and we'd have to maintain it somehow."

Jo hadn't thought about the pasture, but she hated to admit that when the bishop seemed sincerely interested in her idea. "What if we used it for our annual mud sale—or even for big produce auctions in the summer, like other Amish districts have?"

This was an all-or-nothing proposal, so Jo gathered her courage as she presented the idea that would make it or break it. "Truth be told, I'm hoping our church district will use the land somehow, because while we *maidels* could organize the shops, we have no way to pay for the property or for rebuilding the stable. Maybe the church would help with that part, too."

After giving the bishop a few moments to contemplate her proposal, Jo held his gaze. "I'm asking for a lot, ain't so? And maybe nobody but me will see any benefit to this marketplace. But I had to ask."

Bishop Jeremiah's smile brought out the laugh lines around his eyes. "If you don't ask, you probably won't receive," he pointed out. "If you don't knock, who will know to open the door for you?"

When the bishop rose from his chair, Jo took this as her cue to leave—yet she felt greatly encouraged. "*Denki* for listening," she said as she stood up. "I appreciate the way you've heard me out, because some men wouldn't have given my idea even a minute's consideration."

Jo immediately wondered if she'd sounded too critical, too much like a *maidel* with a habit of complaining.

The bishop chuckled, however. "Some folks—men and women alike—pass over new ideas because they'll have to put out extra effort or change their habits to make their dreams a reality," he remarked. "I'll pray over what you've told me today, Jo, and we'll see what happens. When you skip a little stone across a lake, you never know how far the ripples might travel."

Connect with

Us

Visit us online at
KensingtonBooks.com
to read more from your favorite authors, see books
by series, view reading group guides, and more.

for sneak peeks, chances to win books and prize packs,
and to share your thoughts with other readers.

facebook.com/kensingtonpublishing
twitter.com/kensingtonbooks

Tell us what you think!

To share your thoughts, submit a review,
or sign up for our eNewsletters, please visit:
KensingtonBooks.com/TellUs.

Books by Bestselling Author
Fern Michaels